Pra...
of R...

"Rob Thurm...
I've come to...
tagonist, fas...
and a surpri...

—*New York Times* bestselling author
Charlaine Harris

Madhouse

"Thurman continues to deliver strong tales of dark urban fantasy. . . . Fans of street-level urban fantasy will enjoy this new novel greatly." —SFRevu

"I think if you love the Winchester boys of *Supernatural*, there's a good chance you will love the Leandros brothers of Thurman's books. . . . One of *Madhouse*'s strengths is Cal's narrative voice, which is never anything less than sardonic. Another strength is the dialogue, which is just as sharp and, depending on your sense of humor, hysterical." —Dear Author . . .

"A fast-paced and exciting novel . . . fans of urban fantasy will love this series." —*Affaire de Coeur*

"If you enjoyed the first two wisecracking urban adventures, you won't be disappointed with this one; it has just enough action, angst, sarcasm, mystery, mayhem, and murder to keep you turning the pages to the very end." —BookSpot Central

continued . . .

Moonshine

"[Cal and Niko] are back and better than ever . . . a fast-paced story full of action." —SFRevu

"A strong second volume . . . Cal continues to be a wonderful narrator, and his perspective on the world is one of the highlights of this book. . . . The plotting is tight and fast-paced, and the world building is top-notch." —*Romantic Times*

Nightlife

"A roaring roller coaster of a read . . . [it'll] take your breath away. Supernatural highs and lows, and a hell of a lean over at the corners. Sharp and sardonic, mischievous and mysterious. . . . The truth is Out There, and it's not very pretty." —Simon R. Green

"A strong first novel." —SFRevu

TRICK OF THE LIGHT

A TRICKSTER NOVEL

ROB THURMAN

A ROC BOOK

ROC
Published by New American Library, a division of
Penguin Group (USA) Inc., 375 Hudson Street,
New York, New York 10014, USA
Penguin Group (Canada), 90 Eglinton Avenue East, Suite 700, Toronto,
Ontario M4P 2Y3, Canada (a division of Pearson Penguin Canada Inc.)
Penguin Books Ltd., 80 Strand, London WC2R 0RL, England
Penguin Ireland, 25 St. Stephen's Green, Dublin 2,
Ireland (a division of Penguin Books Ltd.)
Penguin Group (Australia), 250 Camberwell Road, Camberwell, Victoria 3124,
Australia (a division of Pearson Australia Group Pty. Ltd.)
Penguin Books India Pvt. Ltd., 11 Community Centre, Panchsheel Park,
New Delhi - 110 017, India
Penguin Group (NZ), 67 Apollo Drive, Rosedale, North Shore 0632,
New Zealand (a division of Pearson New Zealand Ltd.)
Penguin Books (South Africa) (Pty.) Ltd., 24 Sturdee Avenue,
Rosebank, Johannesburg 2196, South Africa

Penguin Books Ltd., Registered Offices:
80 Strand, London WC2R 0RL, England

First published by Roc, an imprint of New American Library,
a division of Penguin Group (USA) Inc.

First printing, September 2009
10 9 8 7 6 5 4 3 2 1

To the real Leo.
Thanks for letting me borrow your name.
You will never be forgotten.

Acknowledgments

I would like to thank my mom—an ass-kicking woman in her own right. No demon would dare cross her path. I would also like to thank my evil twin, Shannon (your ability to not strangle me on a daily basis continues to amaze me); my patient editor, Anne Sowards; my infallible link to the publishing world, Cam Dufty; Brian McKay (the Once and Future King of copy writing); kind and wonderful author Charlaine Harris; Agent Jeff Thurman of the FBI for the usual weapons advice; the incomparable art and design team of Chris McGrath (an art *god*) and Ray Lundgren; Jennifer Jackson; Tony Lopes for his weak negotiation skills in the matter of one Slimer; great and lasting friends Michael and Sarah-of-the-red-shoes; Mara—keep those books coming; and last but never least, my fans—all of you are what makes this worthwhile. And a special thanks to Marjorie Liu for her inspired assistance with the photo situation.

Chapter 1

To every thing there is a season, and a time to every purpose under the heaven. I'd read that in a book once, a fairly famous one. Right now I was going with the time of reaping. Fire had been sown and fire would be reaped. Now. By me, personally. Why?

One: Fire burns. Fire destroys. Fire cleanses.

Two: Fire drives up your insurance rates like crazy.

Three: It was deserved. Oh yes, it was very much deserved.

And how do I know this? A lot of ways, but mainly because I know there are demons in the world. Monsters. Creatures that would steal and eat your soul. Devils that would . . .

Wait. You've heard this before, right? Seen the movies. Read the books. You might hide under your covers at night or avoid the deepest shadows of the darkest alleys and pretend all's right with the world, but you know. I don't need to tell you. I don't need to show you the light . . . or the dark.

You know.

Like me, you know. Even if you don't want to admit it.

Chickenshit.

But that's okay. Since I knew, I could personally

pitch a Molotov cocktail at a nightclub that sat halfway between the university and the Strip, an area otherwise and ironically called Paradise. No hiding under the covers for me. I knew about what hid in the dark all right, and there was nothing I enjoyed more, at least tonight, than watching some son of a bitch demon's club burn to the ground. Demons in Paradise. Could they be any more smug?

It was six a.m. and the club was empty. The last drunk had staggered out twenty minutes ago into the dark November morning. Frying patrons wasn't on the agenda and a fire wouldn't do the demon or his demon employees much harm even if they were standing in the middle of it, not if they changed from human form back to the genuine article fast enough, but I still enjoyed it. You get your kicks where you can.

And this was a kick. I inhaled the fragrance of burning gasoline, felt the hot wind lift my hair, and the thud of the ground under my sneakers—my normal high-heeled boots were out for this one. I also felt the adrenaline squeeze my heart, pumping my blood faster and faster. Damn, I loved that feeling. I looked up at the sky, faintly orange because Vegas was never dark, fire or not. The neon made us a sun all our own. It was exhilarating: the smell of smoke and alcohol, the sound of shattering glass as the bottles smashed through windows, and the glorious red and yellow of leaping flames.

"Beautiful," I murmured, feeling the sear of heat against my face. It didn't touch the heat of satisfaction inside me.

"Not without its charm," Griffin commented dryly next to me before turning and following me. "You and your hobbies, Trixa."

"Yeah, great. I'm hungry. Let's go." That would be Zeke. Griffin Reese and Zeke Hawkins, quite the pair. I wouldn't say Zeke had a short attention span; he didn't. But when a task was done, it was done, and what was the point of hanging around? Zeke was a born soldier at heart. I came. I saw. I kicked ass. What's next? But it was a little more than that. Zeke was special, in more ways than one, which was why there was a Griffin. The Universe saw a need and filled it. Saw an imbalance and stabilized it. The Universe was good at that. Unless you wanted to get laid . . . then you were on your own. It was the downside of putting business before pleasure.

But this was a pleasure too, and I was cheered as I stood at the side of two boys I'd watched grow to men and we watched the smoke billow. Family came in all shapes and sizes. It even sometimes showed up Dumpster diving outside your bar. Family also shared hobbies, but this little excursion was close to being over. Time to go. I turned and ran, vaulting over the low chain-link fence that surrounded the dirt and gravel vacant lot next to the club. Running across the street, I hopped over the door to Griffin's car and into the backseat. He had an old convertible. I'd no idea what make. It was old, big as a tank, and with an engine that would've been better suited in a jet. It was great for fast getaways and even better for mowing down whatever unholy thing playing crossing guard might stand in the way of your escape.

As the sirens began far away, I turned and pillowed my arms on the back of the seat, ignored the dig of a slight rip in the upholstery under my skin, and watched the fire recede into the distance. I didn't ask them to put the top up in the fifty-degree weather. I loved the bite of chill air against my skin. And I didn't need to look up front to know Griffin was driving. Zeke didn't take to driving too well. If he wanted to go, he went. Red light? Stop sign? What did that have to do with anything when you were following a demon? Hellspawn trumped traffic codes. Between his absolute attention on his goal and his black and white judgment, things—such as driving into a bus with painted strippers cavorting on the side—tended not to work out so well.

Especially when the bus was full of German tourists in shorts so short that they required a Brazilian wax for the men as well as the women. There had been thighs as bountiful as baking bread, as wobbly as Jell-O, and as pitted as the surface of the moon. I still had flashbacks over that one, and all thanks to one of Zeke's few attempts at taking the wheel.

Zeke with his dark copper hair pulled back into a short, three-inch braid; eyes that were the green of the first leaf to bloom in the Garden of Eden; a scar on his neck that looked like someone had tried to cut his throat and half succeeded . . . No, Zeke wasn't right. Not that he was wrong . . . just different. It wasn't his fault. No damn way it was his fault. Whoever had borne Zeke had done him serious damage. I think he knew right from wrong, but sometimes in doing right he went so far that wrong was just a kiss away. "Don't do the crime if you can't do the time" was more than Zeke's philosophy. It was his very reason for being. And if the punishment far outweighed the cause, well, that was Zeke. He saw individuals and their actions in black and white only; gray didn't exist for him. He simply couldn't feel it, and he certainly didn't see a point to it.

And if he did slip into doing wrong while trying to do the opposite, he was sorry. Extremely sorry. Unlike most, he didn't count himself exempt from his own code. So far Griffin had kept him from doing anything that would make him so sorry that he'd throw himself off a building. Then again, I didn't know the story behind the scar on Zeke's throat.

Maybe I didn't want to know. Maybe that was why I'd never asked.

Griffin. Griffin was a good guy, much better than I was sure he knew. He wasn't so much modest as . . . well, he simply didn't know. The patience he had with Zeke, it would've put Mother Teresa to shame.

He had thick, straight pale blond hair that fell just past the bottoms of his ears. He kept it parted in the middle and when he bowed his head, it hung like a curtain hiding blue eyes. Pacific blue, calm without a single wave to disturb the surface. He looked like a trashy romance novel's version of an angel. Funny, considering the arson we'd just committed. Funny, considering a lot of things.

Griffin the angel. I smiled to myself. Griffin the angel was Zeke's guide dog, so to speak. Where Zeke was blind, Griffin could see just fine. You want to do this, but should you? And Zeke listened—and Zeke rarely ever listened to anyone. Griffin, always. Me . . . mostly. Leo . . . sometimes.

Zeke listened to Griffin because they'd grown up in the same foster home. I doubted there were any picket fences or puppies or cupcakes. I doubted they had anyone but themselves and when that's the case, you bond. Sometimes forever. They'd needed each other and they'd gotten each other. Things do work out for the best.

Sometimes.

I turned around and wrapped my arms around them as we passed stucco buildings with red roofs, my left arm along Griff's shoulder and my right along Zeke's. "You owe the Universe big."

Both snorted, but it was Griffin who asked why. I ignored the question and added, "You also owe me lots and lots of money for all those empty bottles you filled with gasoline."

He sputtered, "They were empty. You were just going to throw them away anyway."

"Not so." I smiled, the flash of my teeth bright in the rearview mirror. "I recycle."

We went back to my tiny bar, Trixsta, located on Boulder Highway along with a few older rickety casinos and car lots. The FSE, the Fremont Street Experience—Vegas's way of redoing the ailing and progressively sleazier and sleazier casinos, strip clubs, and trademark-Vegas neon signs of "Glitter Gulch" into a high-end pedestrian mall with light and sound shows, concerts, the works—that was all still far down the highway. It hadn't made it close to my place. That was fine by me. I loved my little neck of the woods, so to speak. It was a tad run-down and tight with the locals, but it kept overhead to a minimum and random, lost tourists accidentally exposed to exploding demons to only one or two a year. My regulars were either passed out, had gotten on meds, or found a new bar when that sort of thing happened. They were happy. I was happy. What more could you want?

Privacy in the bathroom, maybe.

As I checked the mirror for smoke smudges on my face, a big hand opened the ladies' room door—a bit rickety, but it still worked—and its owner took in my reflection. Dark gold skin, hair that fell in an outrageous mass of uncontrollable curls just past my shoulders. It was nowhere near elegant or perfectly styled. It was wild and untamed, and who was I to tell it to behave? It was also black with the occasional streak of dark bronze and rusty red. My eyes, with their Asian tilt, were an amber that was a shade lighter than the streaks in my hair. My nose, a little long, was pierced with a small ruby. I liked red. It tended to be the theme in my life. Neon was Vegas's trademark and red was mine.

With my hair, my eyes, my skin, I'd seen people squint in confusion as they tried to slap a label on me. People, my mama had once said, will be idiots. Not *can* be or *might* be, but *will* be. Sooner or later, every person alive will be an idiot about one thing or another. Trying to take the mystery out of something for sheer "had to know" obsession was one of those things.

Let them be confused. I was everything. No one could pin me down, name me, or put me in a box, and I liked that too, even more than I liked red.

"Iktomi, stop your primping and get out here."

"Problem, Leo?" I tucked a curl behind my ear. It promptly fought its way to freedom.

There was a problem, I knew; otherwise Leo wouldn't have stuck his nose—a nice hawklike nose it was too—into the bathroom.

"Your demon is here," he said gruffly.

"Already?" I fished my lipstick, red with just a hint of copper, from the pocket of my black pants and applied it. It'd barely been twenty minutes. His place still had to be on fire. Couldn't he stand around and make nice with the firemen? That was not to mention the arson inspector, whom I felt rather bad for. We were giving him some long working days, the poor guy. We'd burned the place down four times now. Maybe I'd send him a fruit basket and a nice card: *Sorry for the overtime*.

"Okay, okay. I'll be out in a sec." As the door shut, I touched the pendant around my neck. It was a teardrop of polished black stone on a gold chain. It cried when I couldn't. "A long time, little brother. A long time gone. I miss you." I raised it, kissed it lightly, then let it fall back into place and went back into the main bar. What there was of it.

I was in the bar business, but I wasn't *into* the bar business. It was temporary, like most things in my life. There's always someplace else to go if you have to. Always something else to do. Although, this particular temporary had gone on for ten years now. I think that was an all-time record for me.

It was small, with a few pool tables, a couple of dartboards, some tables and chairs, old paneled walls, one TV above the bar—definitely not big-screen—and alcohol. That's all I wanted or needed. I had this place, my apartment above, and I had purpose. What else would I need?

Solomon stood at the bar. I'd always thought it was pretty ballsy of him to choose the name Solomon. There were rumors floating around in ye olden times that King Solomon had imprisoned demons to build his temple. How'd I know that? It wasn't from Bible school—not that I didn't know the Bible, several versions in fact, including the books a cranky pope had decided not worthy to be included. But it didn't matter where I picked up the information; in this business it paid to pick up little scraps of factoids here and there, most in the nonbiblical realm. It kept a roof over my head, selling information just as I sold alcohol. And to keep myself busy while I wasn't doing the first two, I dabbled in my hobby. I might not officially be in the demon-destroying business, but I dipped in a toe now and again. A toe, a shotgun—whatever it took. I liked to help my boys out.

Zeke and Griffin stood motionless on either side of Solomon. Griffin's face was blank; Zeke's was not. It would've been better had it been. They did know not to cause trouble in my place if they could help it. They were welcome, always, but fights and cops and ambulances weren't. Besides, the general public was standing around. You couldn't kill a demon right here in front of You-know-who and everyone . . . not unless you absolutely had to.

My boys—and they were my boys since I'd given them their first jobs at fifteen and seventeen, sweeping up the place and taking out the trash—knew the rules and stepped back as I walked up. They were twenty-five and twenty-seven now, all grown-up and a demon's worst nightmare. Me? I'd come to Las Vegas ten years ago when I was twenty-one. Griff and Zeke had wondered back when I'd hired them how I'd been able to afford to buy a bar at that age. I could've told them I inherited it from my father or mother or great-uncle Joe, but I told them the truth.

Lying and cheating.

I wasn't ashamed. Far from it. I deceived only those who deserved it, and you'd be amazed how many did. Then again, if you were smart and kept your eyes open, you might not be so surprised after all. And that held true for everywhere, not just in Sin City. Bad guys were fair game and the one in front of me was rumored to be the worst in town. A bit of an occupational hazard when you're a demon, being bad. Like a steering wheel on a car, you didn't have to pay extra for it—it was part of the package.

"Trixa Iktomi," Solomon said with the warmest of smiles. Solomon, whom I'd made it my business to know, had been in Vegas as long as, if not longer than, I, and knew how to sling the bullshit or to turn on the charm, if you preferred the more elegant term. Whichever you called it, it had the same result—a woman hanging on his every word. "My sweet Trixa. Do I detect the faintest smell of smoke? A new scented shampoo, perhaps?"

I could've said something like, "Yes, it's a new perfume. Everyone's dying for it."

Please.

I'm not that woman and I never will be. I wasn't that trite, and I wasn't playing his games. Any I played would be my own. "Actually, it's the smell of an asshole's burning nightclub," I remarked pleasantly. "Thanks for noticing." I didn't have the cleanest mouth, but I blamed it on Zeke. I was working on it though. Self-improvement was one of my many goals. One day I planned on getting around to a few of them. I motioned to Leo to pour me and the asshole two shots of tequila with beer backs.

Solomon, as I'd made very clear, was an asshole, but a sexy one. Short black hair with a faint widow's peak, a slightly cleft chin, broad shoulders, good height, and full, Latin lips that got me every time. He was dressed in a simple gray shirt, black slacks, and a black leather jacket.

Demons, in human form, are almost always good-looking—*too* good-looking really—and why wouldn't they be? They're hot, loaded with charisma, deeply fascinated by you and everything you say or do, and are everything nature designed to make you want to jump their bones. It's how it works. They want your soul. They have to make you want to give them your soul. Looking like a plumber with a gut and a bit of tasteful butt-crack showing isn't going to get the job done. You have to want them . . . enough to give them anything—and the soul is pretty up there in the anything department.

But if that's all it was—smart demons getting stupid humans to hand over their souls—I couldn't care less. If you're stupid enough to sell it, then that's your vacation pit of agony and despair to worry about, not mine. But that's not all there is. That would be too easy. No, demons like to kill too—all demons—no matter what Solomon said about himself. If there's a serial killer uncaught, or a random massacre with no clues as to why, or someone who just disappears, drops off the face of the earth—chances are there's a demon behind it. They tortured their victims, mutilated them, and killed them. Why?

As one dying demon had once said to me as black blood gushed out of his grinning mouth, "It beats reruns."

"Why, Trixa?" Solomon said, interrupting my thoughts. He examined the shot glass for fingerprints, and then looked down at the tequila as if the pedestrian drink were so far beneath him that he could barely see the pale gold glitter. Sighing, he tossed it back and then rolled the beer bottle between his two palms. "You know I don't kill. I'm not a murderer. I take souls, but only those freely given." His temper turned immediately and drastically. "So why, Trixa, loving bitch of my life, do you keep burning down my goddamn nightclub?"

There was a dangerous glitter in his eyes, velvet gray, as his dark, thick eyebrows slashed downward in an anger that almost shimmered in the air. The slightly olive skin even whitened over his jaw. It was well-done—I had to give him that.

"Bravo." I tossed back my own tequila, then clapped politely. "Anger, domination, an almost sexual rage. Give props to the gentleman, please, for one hell of a show."

The warm smile reappeared, rueful and just the tiniest bit sheepish. "Too much? Too little? Where was I off?"

I touched the red of my long-sleeved silk sweater. "This is what I see when a demon really gets pissed. Red. Blood. Then there might be some pinkish gray of lungs and intestines." Horrific, but true. "And when things get really interesting, really in-depth, there will be—"

He held up a hand. "Enough. I get your point. You should've met Shakespeare. He said I was a magnificent actor."

The smile never changed. Sexy, warm, and sheepish. I'm a bad boy and you've caught me. But under every bad boy is a good one waiting to be redeemed, right? Wrong. Which was how so many naïve high school girls got pregnant before they could drive. Redemption doesn't come from without. It comes from within. Leo, my bartender, could give a lecture series on the subject.

As for the situation at hand, Solomon was a bad boy, no matter how attractive or charming. I wasn't about to forget that for a moment, no matter the smile, the lips, the eyes, or the challenging give-and-take between us.

Demons are liars by nature, killers by choice, and forgetting that was a mistake I couldn't afford to make.

"Pay for the drinks and get the hell out of here, Solomon. Go tell some other girl how you only take souls and what a great guy that makes you. What an honest *monster*, because, frankly, I'm tired of hearing it. And," I added with emphasis, "I'm insulted you think I'm that gullible."

"No. You're not gullible. You're cynical, in fact, and that blinds you. You can't see the truth when it's right before you. And caveat emptor doesn't even apply here, you know," he said softly, his hand once again reaching out for mine. "They pay and I deliver. Whatever they ask for, they get. Without fail. How can you hold me in contempt for being an honest tradesman?"

I shook him off . . . not instantly, but I did shake him off and tried not to count the seconds that it took me to make my hand move beneath his. His touch was warm, the same exact warmth of human flesh. The same give. The same electric touch of life. I looked away from him as I said flatly, "Never even touched the hair of an innocent. Never so much as scratched a child, woman, man. Never cut a driver off on the interstate. Go tell it to someone who doesn't know demons like I do."

"What if I could prove it?" he challenged.

"You can't," I replied, dismissing him, but I did look back, surprised he'd even pretend that he could. Demons were all about pretense, but Solomon usually knew better than to try that with me.

"Maybe not," he admitted with a shrug and a slow, serious curve of his lips. "But what if I could? Think about that, Trixa. What if I could?"

"No demon can because all demons are killers." I pointed at the door. "No exceptions."

"Maybe, just maybe, you don't know them at all," he whispered in my ear. "Or maybe it's just that you don't know this one."

Then he was gone. Paid for the beer and tequila and left. To give him credit, he paid for his and mine. The gentleman demon.

"Why the hell do you screw around with him?" Zeke came up after Solomon disappeared out the front door and hissed at my elbow.

I raised my eyebrows sharply. Griffin grabbed Zeke's wrist and squeezed lightly. It was his guiding signal. Think. What do we say, this or that? What do we do, this or that? What are the consequences of each choice? *Think.*

Zeke blinked at me, considered for a second, then said, "Shit . . . I meant, why the hell do you put up with him? Messing with you?"

I smiled and leaned over to kiss his jaw, a whisper of copper stubble against my lips. I wanted to say he'd done well, very well, but he would've hated that . . . attention brought to his problem. He was proud, stubborn, and temperamental—add that to the all-or-nothing hardwiring of his brain and he was a handful. More of a hell-raiser than any demon.

"Because Solomon is big or he wouldn't stick around Vegas." But they knew that already. The minor demons never stay in one place too long and they definitely don't own and operate nightclubs . . . those that aren't burned to the ground. "You know that. Your organization knows that. Everyone who knows demons exist knows that. Solomon has useful information. And you know how I like information." As I'd said, it kept the roof over my head just as much as the bar did. I sold information. It didn't have to be demon related, especially since ninety-nine point nine percent of the people out there refused to believe in them, but it didn't necessarily mean it couldn't be demon related either. Lucky horse? High-stakes illegal poker game? Jewelry store robbery? Who stole your gorgeous gold Cadillac? You heard a lot of things in a bar and I'd tell any one of them for a price. As long as no one was hurt . . . no one who didn't have it coming, anyway.

Leo interrupted, disgruntled—no more a fan of demons than the rest of us—and jerked a thumb toward the back exit. "There's another one in the alley trying to eat a homeless guy. This is one bitch of a night."

Zeke grinned, and when Zeke grinned that was never a good thing, at least for the person or nonperson that grin was meant for. It was the grin of a hungry wolf in midleap on something tasty and slow—damn happy and utterly without remorse. He headed immediately for the back door. Griffin looked at me. "Yeah, yeah," I sighed. "I'll get the shotgun out of your car. Go." Right now Zeke had his objective in sight: Kill the demon. The homeless guy—let's hope he was out of the way when Zeke went into action. That was why Griffin was going with him and I was going after the shotgun. Zeke was white, the demon was black, and the homeless guy was that shade of gray Zeke had so much difficulty seeing.

Being saved from a demon didn't do you much good if you were accidentally between the shotgun and your attacker when rescue came.

God had supposedly given man free will—so it was debated anyway—but without a good deal of practice or an inborn instruction manual, free will . . . well, it could be more a nightmare than a blessing. We all saw it and we all knew it, but Griffin knew it most of all.

Their current employers had apparently tried psycho-therapy and every medication known to the field, but nothing had improved Zeke's condition; nothing had worked. Only Griffin worked ... to a certain degree. "How many damn drugs did his bitch of a mother take while she was pregnant to make him this way?" he'd asked once over a drink after a particular mission had gone sideways because of Zeke and his inability to stop, once in motion, to exercise that will. "How could someone do that? To their own baby?"

How indeed?

But that had been last year that Griffin had spilled his frustration over whiskey—last year, and this was now. And now required a shotgun, so let's concentrate on that. I had it out of the car and in the alley in seconds. A dirty, disheveled man went tearing past me, so it was safe to say Zeke hadn't trampled over the top of him to get to the demon—or shot through him. Either that or it was one tough homeless guy, and he was gone so fast, I didn't have a chance to look for footprints on his back or a hole in the middle of him.

Zeke was still grinning in the gloom of the ill-lit alley. He was never happier than when he had a job to do, a task to perform, a demon to kill. A strand of hair had fallen free from his short braid as he wrestled the demon to keep him on the ground. He had one arm and Griffin had the other, and both had buried knives in the man's chest.

The *man's* chest because the demon looked like a man now. Actually, he looked like Elvis ... the very best Elvis impersonator in the city, thanks to a demon's chameleon abilities. If you didn't know better, you would've thought the King himself was spitting foul curses at us. Zeke did know better because, like several other local demon chasers, he was telepathic. He could sense a demon's surface thoughts if he was close enough. I once asked if he'd ever rummaged around in my thoughts. He'd said no and with Zeke-honesty, admitting that it was only because he hadn't thought of it. "Good," I'd said, pointing the knife I was using to cut lemons at the bar. "If you do, I'll *rummage* around inside you with this." Zeke definitely comprehended that consequence. Whether he could only sense surface thoughts or not, my thoughts, no matter how shallow or deep, were my own. I made sure of that.

Griffin, because he was an empath, knew the man was a demon, and this was why Eden House had recruited Zeke and Griffin both. They had the abilities Eden House prized above all, a mirror of the Above and Below.

Angels had telepathy, which was useful for impressing long-ago shepherds by pushing God's word directly into their minds, and demons had empathy—very good for feeling out what a human would trade for his soul. A human empath could feel a demon's emotions, which were similar to a human's emotions—if he was one helluva bad human—only multiplied ten times over. And a telepath could hear a demon's recruitment plan forming in its head or its murdering intent—unless you were a high-level angel or demon, in which case it all went out the window. No one could tell what you were up to. It was a peculiar balance the Universe had come up with—if the angels and demons had those powers, then so did the humans.

It gave Eden House and its demon hunters an extra edge. To destroy demons and bring Eden back to Earth . . . as if demons were the only thing keeping that from happening. But men were men. Try telling them

anything, especially as the occasional angel reinforced
the belief by showing up and giving an order or two.
Free labor—not even angels would turn that down.

Now, when it came to me, how did I know a demon
in human form? Griffin and Zeke had asked me that
when they became aware that what they'd found out
regarding the world around them when they were recruited by Eden House wasn't precisely news to me.
Demons were real. They were here. For once, movies
and TV hadn't lied.

I told them the truth. My family had been gypsies and
travelers since—since before anyone could remember.
We'd seen a lot in our travels and we passed on our
stories to relatives when the reunions came around.
And then I told them a lie, but a small one. I also told
them that my family, my ancestors, had been pagans
before a druid had ever danced naked under the moon.
I said we'd worshipped the gods of nature when they
were the only gods known to man. Honestly, I wasn't
into worship myself. Respect and reverence, yes, but
not worship.

But regardless, hear about and see enough demons
over the years and you knew one when you saw it. You
didn't need any fancy, psychic empath abilities. You
just knew. The blinding good looks, the waves of un-
natural charm they put off, the sly glint in their eyes . . .
the scales and tail tended to tip you off as well, when
they were caught.

Like now.

Suddenly the human form under their hands flickered. It was trying to go back to Hell, but it couldn't.
When a demon was physically anchored to this world,
it was stuck and it couldn't take you to Hell with it unless you'd consented, sold your soul. At least Heaven

had given humans that one advantage when it had tossed the rebels to the pit. That and an age limit on selling what God gave you. More of a maturity level really. One didn't want little Billy selling his soul to go to Disney World.

When escaping didn't work, the demon shifted to its true form. Serpentine with thrashing wings and tail, it was patterned like a rattlesnake, but in swamp green and dull black. It opened its mouth and hissed, showing jagged teeth of dirty glass, but nowhere as brittle. "Pathetic, motherfucking humans," it snarled. "Death is what—"

I stuck the single-barreled shotgun, a Remington and a beauty, under its pointed jaw and pulled the trigger. The slug changed a snake skull into something a little more avant-garde. Black blood flew, splattering Zeke and Griffin on their faces, necks, and chests. *"Trixa."* Griffin groaned. I had ruined his gray-blue silk shirt and fawn-colored ostrich skin jacket. When Eden House had hired him away from sweeping my floors, there'd been a definite increase in salary. And it showed. The man liked his clothes.

"Sorry," I said with utter insincerity as I pumped another slug into place. You never knew. Demons were tough, but they could be killed in their physical form, human or demon, if you used the proper tools and aimed at the vulnerable area, the head—or the brain or whatever passed for it in a demon. You could rip the rest of them to pieces, but they'd keep coming. "But that's my mama he was talking about. And that I will not put up with." Not that my mother wouldn't laugh at the thought of me protecting her "good" name. "And you know Elvis wouldn't talk about his mama that way either," I finished.

"That was too quick. Let's go find another," Zeke said as the body by his knees melted away to the next best thing to an oil slick. It spread across the cracked gray asphalt, staining it a permanent black.

"Think again, workaholic. Time to go home." Griffin stood, spread his arms to take in the mess, and frowned. "Safety on." It was Griffin's way of telling Zeke he was serious. Zeke could go literally forever once he started something—at least until he keeled over from exhaustion or dehydration. And if he started on a demon hunt in an unsatisfied state of mind, he would do it. He was a gun that would fire until the ammunition ran out. Unless . . .

"Safety on," Zeke echoed with a sigh, dissatisfied but cooperative. Then he took in Griffin, who looked as if a bucket of black paint had been tossed on him. This grin was different from the one for the demon. This one was genuine. It softened the too-lean face, lightened the green of his eyes, and relaxed the scowl of dark red-brown brows. "That's gonna cost you."

Griffin gave a scowl of his own, but it wasn't a serious one. Zeke's smiles were rare. It had taken him so long to actually learn how that not I, not Leo, and especially not Griffin could give him hell for it. Simply couldn't.

Griffin turned to look at me, and I tossed him his shotgun and waved my fingers. "Better get out of here in case someone actually calls the cops this time."

"You're not paying for this, I take it," he said, resigned.

"Sugar, you're so cute when you joke around like that." I patted his cheek.

The night was more or less over anyway. I let Leo close up and went to my apartment above the bar. It was basic as they came: one room—a bedroom and a bathroom combined with a big bed and a huge claw-foot tub. But basic is good. I don't cook. And I don't mean I don't like to cook. I flat out do not cook, so I didn't need a kitchen. Food was meant to be bought already prepared. Takeout was the single highest accomplishment of modern civilization.

My bed was waiting. On its headboard, carved in Mexico, animals prowled back and forth: leopards, foxes, wolves, coyotes, birds—all painted as bright and bold as you could get. In the sink by the tub, I brushed my teeth, stripped off my makeup, then touched the teardrop around my neck, and finally I cried. I cried every day for my brother. My overall family wasn't that big, and the immediate family was even smaller. With my brother gone, a third of my family went with him. When he had been killed and left in the bloody sand, he'd taken a third of my world with him.

I gave it only a few minutes: There was mourning and there was wallowing. And wallowing wasn't going to help do what had to be done, was it?

Dressed in my Rugby shirt and panties (it didn't feel like a silk night), I climbed under the red bedspread and turned off the bedside light. I'd only dozed off when I had a feeling, smelled spice, and then the springs of the mattress gave under a warm weight that straddled my hips. I heard the soft, dark words, "I want to touch you so badly. Your bare skin, the silk of your hair . . . ," as I reached down, pulled my shotgun from beneath the mattress, and had it jammed under Solomon's jaw in less than three seconds. I could see his shadowed eyes in the light from the street that seeped through the blinds.

This was why I'd kept my favored silk sleepwear in

the drawer tonight: Solomon and his games. I'd suspected he wasn't done when he'd left the bar.

"I don't know what chick flick you stole that from, but you deserve your money back," I said as I pulled back the hammer.

"Not a good time, then, I take it?" he asked with amused gravity.

The steel of the trigger was as cool against my finger as the sheets were against my skin. "An absolutely perfect time," I disagreed with dark cheer. He was shirtless, but at least he was wearing pants. If he hadn't been, I think he knew I would've blown his head off right then and there.

"So stubborn. Pity." The corner of his mouth quirked up and although he didn't move, the weight of him seemed even heavier and far more intimate. Then he shimmered out of existence.

His chest had been as lightly furred as I thought it'd be, and broad. Did demons have some sort of hot-male-body catalogue to choose from? Snorting at myself, I replaced the gun after easing the hammer back down and turned over on my stomach. Solomon could put on any face or body he wanted—I'd never forget what was on the inside. I wouldn't let myself. This time I went instantly to sleep. And I had dreams. . . .

Not the kind you'd think.

I dreamed of blue-green water, black sand, and blood.

So much blood.

More than anyone could hope to live without.

Chapter 2

Morning was slow. I liked it that way. I could run errands if I wanted or go back upstairs and sleep in late . . . if Leo didn't bitch too much. Right now he was too busy with two tourists from the pasty East. How they'd wandered into this part of town, I hadn't a clue. This was definitely off the tourists' beaten track.

"I've never met an American Indian before," the first chirped. She was a chirpy kind. Wavy red hair, freckles, round blue eyes, and skin whiter than snow. "What's your Native American name?"

Leo's dark eyes looked down the bar at me, literally pleading for help. I propped my chin in my hand, winked, and watched the show. Exhaling, he said with perfect seriousness, "Leo Thrusting Moose Phallus."

That was a new one. I liked it. *You wish*, I mouthed, but held up nine fingers out of ten for scoring. In the past there had been Leo Constipated Elk, Leo Maker of Warm Yellow Water, Leo Mounter of Unwilling Dogs, and whatever idiots actually remained after one of those were treated courteously with the name of his tribe when they asked: the Tribe of None of Your Fucking Business.

These two weren't that stupid. They were already headed for the door. Despite his hawk nose, lightly copper skin, and black hair that hung to his waist, all of which made Leo one fine-looking man, he'd tired a long time ago of the tourists' American Indian fascination. Shaking his head in disgust, he tossed a towel over his shoulder and disappeared into the kitchen. A minute or two later Lenore came flapping about and posted on his roost anchored to the bar.

"I've never figured out how you get away with him when the health inspector's around." Griffin, my usual late-breakfast crowd, moved up and sat on a stool in a blue shirt, some horrifically expensive brand naturally, and artfully faded jeans.

"Ah. Then watch this." I looked at Lenore. "Health inspector, Lenore."

Immediately the raven froze, dark eyes glassy, chest unmoving. Then he slowly pitched forward until he hung upside down from the perch, possibly the deadest stuffed bird ever seen.

Griffin gave a low whistle. "I'm impressed. He never did that when we worked here."

"Yes, he did. Lenore's special. He's been around a long, long time." And then some. Doing tricks was the very least of his repertoire. "He's an old fart."

I tapped him on his back and he sprang back up, pecking me on the hand in outrage, and cawing, "Nevermore, ass-wipe. Nevermore."

"You just didn't stick around long enough to see his little trick then," I went on, stepping back out of beak range. "You and Zeke were still not precisely seeing eye to eye with the local authorities yourself. You'd be hiding in the back. And watch the language, Lenore." If I could give it a shot, so could he.

I'd known what Griffin and Zeke were the minute I caught them loitering in my alley, ready to scour the

Dumpster for food. They were homeless when I hired them, and just . . . lost—lost as you can get. I'd given them the job of keeping the storage rooms cleaned up and pretended I didn't know they slept there—two kids with two changes of clothes and literally nothing else. We didn't serve real food at Trixsta, but we served bar food—anything fried with cheese—and I let them eat free and take what was left over at the end of the night. And I'd run them over to the diner to fetch supper for Leo and me every night. Four meals instead of just two—Zeke simply ate his and didn't wonder why I did this. Griffin wondered, wanted me to take it out of the money I paid them, but gave up when I scowled and threatened him with bathroom puke duty every night. After that he just worked harder and mooned after me like a puppy for a few months. It was cute and at least he didn't piddle on the floor.

"You never asked back then." He picked up a glossy black feather that had fallen to the bar. No more the teenager with a crush. He was a man now and a good one. I liked to think I had something to do with that. "What we were running from."

"At first it wasn't my business." Or rather, they didn't want it to be my business. I started scooping the ice into the bins. "And later I figured it out. Zeke."

The blue eyes darkened. "The social workers told those goddamn foster parents to watch him. Told them to never leave him alone. I should've known better than to think they actually listened. I should've been there." He shook away the guilt, at least the visible kind. "They never cared about us and they especially never cared about what Zeke needed." He dropped the feather. It twisted once in the air before drifting down. "And don't ask me what happened, all right? Don't."

"I won't." I'd just wait until the time came. I picked the feather back up and handed it to him. "Keep the feather. Raven feathers are good luck."

"Like that?" He reached forward and lightly touched the teardrop around my neck. "Is that good luck?"

"No." The roughness of Griffin's combat-worn skin was an interesting sensation on my neck and his serious expression almost irresistible. Almost. Nothing had yet been able to let me forget they were anything but boys I'd all but raised for a few years, no matter what their ages now. Four or five years can be nothing, or it can be all the difference in the world.

Plus . . . well . . . I smiled to myself, then moved his hand away.

"Not luck," I continued, giving the ice a break as Lenore sidled over to sit on my shoulder. "It's a Pele's tear from Hawaii. Lava that solidifies into the shape of a drop or tear, named for the Hawaiian goddess of fire and volcanoes."

"So you've been to Hawaii?" he asked curiously.

"Once or twice. I wear it for my brother." Lenore moved back to his roost and tucked his head under his wing. He picked up the emotion in my voice easily enough. So did Griffin.

"A brother," he said slowly. What he meant was, "You had a brother," *had* not *have*, but he didn't want to come out and say that, did he?

I said it for him. "That's right. I had a brother." End of topic as I closed my lips tightly and went back to shoveling ice with a vengeance.

Griffin turned the feather in his fingers, looking for a painless way out. Painless for me. "So you've been to Hawaii, but you never lived there? You're not part Hawaiian, Trixa?"

That did make me laugh. "Look at me, Griff. I'm part everything." I untied the apron around my waist. "Watch the bar for me, would you? Just until Leo gets back."

Good-naturedly, especially for a demon killer, he moved behind the bar. "You really are going to give that bird a complex calling him a girl's name."

I shrugged and smiled. "What else are you going to call a raven? Edgar Allan Poe? It's a little long. But you can call him Lenny if it has your testosterone in an uproar."

He snorted, "I've noticed Leo and *Lenny* are never around at the same time. What are they? Superman and Clark Kent?"

I shoved some money into my jeans pocket and figured my light sweater would do for a sunny November day; it was probably in the high sixties. "There was an incident. Bird crap, vacuum cleaner retaliation. It wasn't a pretty sight. They tend to avoid each other now, which is probably for the best." I gave him a quick wave and was gone. I had errands to do and it was a perfect blue-sky morning to do them. I took my car, blazing red as I liked most things in my life—red my favorite color and blazing my favorite philosophy—and drove slowly past the still-smoldering nightclub. I lowered the window to catch a whiff of smoke. A floating memory in the air. Talk about warming your heart.

I did the rest of my chores in a few hours and was back at the bar with four grocery bags of frozen minipizzas, potato skins, and fried cheese of varied colors. Lenore was gone, and Leo and Griffin were watching the small TV mounted over the bar. The rest of the bar was empty except for one guy dozing at a corner table.

"What's up? Did they vote another demon into office?" I demanded, putting the bags down with a loud thunk that said, *Thanks so much for the help.* "Not that they do much worse than humans sometimes."

"No, someone was eaten at the zoo," Griffin said absently, still watching. "At least, the vast majority of him was eaten."

I wasn't a fan of the zoo. I didn't like to see animals locked up, but I'd been on occasion. The TV was showing a security tape of a little girl, maybe four, sitting on a bench by herself. She had long, light brown hair, melancholy dark brown eyes that could break your heart, and was dressed in a yellow top, pants, and matching tennies, with a red balloon in her hand. Now, wasn't that a coincidence. She liked red too, and she watched the balloon float in the air with those wide, wistful eyes. If her parents were around, they didn't show up. The only immediate adult was a man with a leash and empty collar in his hands. He had a friendly smile, light jacket, and oh . . . how sad . . . you didn't have to hear the words to know what he was saying. *I've lost my puppy, sweetie. I'll bet she's so scared. Could you help me find her?*

Never mind he couldn't smuggle a puppy into a zoo and not be seen at some point. But a leash and empty collar fit right in your pocket.

The little girl looked around and static started to fuzz the video. She bit her thumb, smiled back shyly, and held out her hand. Then it was nothing but static.

"Wait until you see this." Zeke had joined us at some point. He must have shown up after I left and he didn't look too unhappy. In fact he looked pretty cheerful. Zeke's sense of humor—such as he had—tended to tilt toward the dark end of the spectrum. "I saw it earlier. It's good stuff."

When the static cleared, the video had switched to another part of the zoo. You could hear screaming—throat-rending screaming—see running zoo personnel, and hear the howls of wolves looking for who had invaded their pen.

It seemed a man had been looking for his puppy and now a whole pack of puppies was looking for him. Apparently they found him too. When the zoo personnel were able to recover his remains, what few there were, he was identified as one Richard Charles Hubbins Jr.—a multiply convicted pedophile. No one was going to be shedding tears over him.

I tucked a wild strand of hair behind my ear and started unpacking the bags with a warm sense of satisfaction. "I have to say I love it when a pervert gets what's coming to him. And the puppies got a nice treat too. It's a win-win."

There was one last security shot of the empty bench with the red balloon tied to the armrest. Bright and shiny in the sun, it swayed lightly as if waving at the camera. The police never found the girl or her parents but were asking that they step forward to give statements.

"What kind of statement do they need?" Zeke snorted. "He made a good chew toy?" Zeke wasn't into clothes like his partner. Black on black was good enough for him, but today he was wearing jeans and a gray T-shirt. A completely no-name brand; the jeans probably came from the thrift store. Zeke didn't care much about all the money Eden House paid. He didn't care much about material things period. Just killing demons, drinking beer, and beating Griff at pool. Well . . . and guns. He did like guns.

"They're probably curious to know who tossed the son of a bitch into the wolf pen." Griffin's eyes narrowed. "You weren't just at the zoo, were you?"

Zeke, copper hair hanging loose to his shoulders, shrugged and reached for the bowl of pretzels. "No. I'd have just shot him. I wouldn't have thought of anything that fun." He looked up at the TV again, hoping for another repeat. "Anyone tape it?"

"Fun?" Griffin responded with disapproval, ignoring the tape remark. "Don't you mean ironic? Poetic justice? His just deserts? Hoisted on his own petard?"

Shaking his head, his partner scooped up a handful of pretzels. "Nope, fun."

Griffin gave in and took some pretzels himself. I could tell he wanted to ask how Zeke had gotten here . . . what with the entire no-driving thing occasionally slipping Zeke's mind. If he needed to be somewhere, he could be five miles down the road before he remembered he didn't have a license. Griffin definitely had his reasons for wanting to know. Bus accidents aside, purposely cutting Zeke off in traffic was grounds for punishment. And our boy? He did not do little punishments.

But Griffin didn't ask how Zeke had arrived; he wouldn't do that in front of Leo and me. As tight as the four of us were, Griffin and Zeke were two halves of a whole. Tight didn't begin to describe their partnership.

But Zeke knew Griffin every bit as well as Griffin knew him. "Jackie dropped me off. We have a job up in Red Rock today. Demon. Maybe." This meant demon or someone had turned loose their pet iguana.

Jackie meant Jackson "Stick up his Ass" Goodman, as Zeke labeled him. As much as I disapproved of labeling, it was a good one. Very accurate. The FDA would completely approve. Goodman was second in command of Eden House in Las Vegas. There was an Eden House in Los Angeles, Chicago, Miami, Dallas, Washington DC . . . fat lot of good it did us there . . . and a few other places I'd forgotten offhand. And that was just in the continental United States. Eden House was worldwide and had been around since, hell, nobody really knew, but long enough to have seen the pyramids built, Griffin had once said.

"Goodman brought you?"

Zeke snorted at Griffin's surprise. Jackson Goodman as second at Eden House was far too important, in his own opinion, for ferrying around people. "Everyone else is out on a job. I offered to take a taxi, but . . ." He shrugged again.

I could see Goodman's point of view, considering that the last time Zeke had taken a taxi, the driver had tried to overcharge Zeke, and Zeke had quite righteously, from his point of view, put him through the windshield, resulting in shattered safety glass, screaming people, a mildly confused Zeke who explained reasonably to the yelling, howling cab driver that stealing was a crime. In Zeke's mind, assault with a windshield was apparently not, and only deserved retribution. As for the Jackie thing . . . Zeke, who mostly did as he was told as long as he was told in the line of duty or outside the line by someone he trusted, refused to call Jackson anything but Jackie. I was sure Jackie had made it clear a thousand times that it was Mr. Goodman or Goodman, not Jackson, not Jack, and definitely not Jackie. Zeke's green eyes would blink and out would come Jackie, smooth as hundred-year-old scotch.

So, on the rare occasion when I saw the anal-retentive stiff waltz in here looking for the guys, which wasn't often, I called him Jackie to give Zeke moral support. Not that he needed the latter, and the former were so out of the ordinary, extraordinary in fact, that most people wouldn't understand them. Griffin would glare at my encouraged disrespect of management, Lenore would caw, "Nevermore, Jackie. Nevermore," and a good time was had by all.

"Going hiking?" I tilted my head at Griffin to take in his expensive casual wear. "That's not an activity that matches your look today."

On demon-hunting occasions Griffin did dress down for the hunt. Not for burning-down-club occasions, but scheduled hunts. He did black on black like Zeke, cheap and disposable. Demon blood? It takes more than a little detergent to take that out. Zeke kicked a duffel bag at his feet. "I brought you some hiking clothes, but I didn't know you were already wearing jeans."

"These jeans? Hell, no," Griffin refused instantly. "These aren't hiking jeans. These cost two hundred damn dollars."

"That's sexy, Griff," I said with mock sincerity. "A demon chaser in two-hundred-dollar jeans. Manly. Very manly."

He glared a smoldering response, but since I was in the right with the jeans, he went with the other. "Demon *catcher*, not demon *chaser*."

"Very nice. I like how your voice got deeper there. *Muy* macho," I said, then asked Zeke, "How are you going to haul the kind of firepower you need without being spotted by a ranger? A shotgun stands out."

Holy water, crosses, none of that worked on demons; it was all myth . . . maybe because the demons once were angels. Maybe they were already inoculated, so to speak, by their time in Heaven; maybe not. Who knew? They were resistant to the paraphernalia of all religions: Hinduism, Islam, Judaism . . . any of them. So leave your crucifix at home and don't even get me started on *The Exorcist*. Diapers and a pea soup–free diet and that girl would've been fine. For a demon, however, you did need heavy firepower or an angel with a flaming sword, and as angels hadn't been too enthusiastic about getting their hands dirty for quite some time now, heavy firepower it was.

Shotguns were the usual weapon of choice for the coup de grace, slugs the ammunition. Even demons needed their brains. Knives, smaller guns—smaller than a shotgun anyway—were good for slowing them down, but for taking them out, a shotgun was the best. Unless you were into axes or swords for whacking off the head. My boys used them all, but the shotgun was their favorite.

"Hand grenades," Zeke said complacently. "They fit in the bag with the knives, guns, etcetera."

"Hand grenades." Griffin said it as calmly as he would've said, *Watch out for that gum on the sidewalk*. "The ones we keep locked up in the weapons arsenal and have to have Mr. Trinity's permission to use. Those grenades?"

Mr. Trinity was head of Vegas Eden House. He did not have a nickname. He might not even have had a first or middle name. Mr. Trinity could make Jackie boy pee his pants with the rise of one iron gray eyebrow.

"Yep." Zeke waved for a beer, the pretzels apparently having made him thirsty, before wiping the salt on his jeans with combat-scarred hands just like Griff's.

"Did you get permission?"

The green eyes slid uncertainly toward Griffin. "No."

"Did you break the lock or kick down the door?" Griffin was now pinching the bridge of his nose before slipping on his sunglasses and threading an agitated hand through his hair.

"Kicked down the door. Maybe that wasn't the right thing to do?" From Zeke's tone he'd figured out just now that, no, it wasn't the right thing to do. It was the expedient thing to do, the black and white thing, but perhaps not the correct thing.

"Never mind. They needed a metal door anyway." Griffin dropped his hand and dismissed it as if it were nothing, just that quickly, and slung an arm over Zeke's shoulder. "Let's go kill ourselves a demon, assuming it's not just a pissed-off gecko." Zeke looked mildly relieved and they sauntered out with their duffel bag.

Zeke was going to be in big shit and Griffin was going to get him out of it. Bottom line, Eden House couldn't afford to lose a telepath. They might only be able to sense surface thoughts, but it was enough to spot a demon—or a robber, but that's something we found out later.

Regardless, the House knew if they tossed Zeke, Griffin, their empath, was gone too. They couldn't afford to lose two of their best. They did have a few more telepaths and empaths, but humans with talents were few and far between, at least until evolution picked up a little speed, and Griffin and Zeke were their strongest by far.

Griffin looked back at me, his expression both desperate and fierce. I put a finger to my lips. Their bosses would hear nothing from me. If he thought he could hide the fact that Zeke had done it, more power to him. I wouldn't give him away.

"Those two," Leo grunted as he refilled the pretzel bowl with a rustle of a bag a few weeks past expiration.

"They have a long way to go," I admitted as I watched them pass the window to turn the corner that led to the alley where Griffin parked his car—the same alley where we'd destroyed the demon last night, "but I think they just might get there. As long as they learn Eden House isn't the be-all and end-all of existence."

"So it's not the shit?" he said solemnly, and shoved the pretzels my way—already knowing the answer.

"No, not nearly the shit it thinks it is," I said absently as I crunched some stale bread and salt, but he already knew that. "Has Robin called back yet?" He'd called last night when I was out. He said he'd call back today. Robin Goodfellow was one of the many contacts I'd made throughout my life. If I didn't know something, which was rare, he was likely to.

"No, but he's not exactly punctual. The orgies tend to slow him down," Leo said dryly. True. Robin did like his extracurricular activities. I finished up with the ice, ran a cold, tousling hand through my unruly mass of hair, and had just started working on the glasses when the phone call came. Robin's impatient, snarky voice was on the other end. It was his usual smooth tone, a tone that always seemed to carry the message *Let me fly down to Vegas and show you, or you and Leo, or you, Leo, and anyone else you might have in mind, a good time*. "The Light of Life, that's what you said you were interested in, right?" he asked. "Instead of my naked and amazingly sculpted body? Your loss. Your horrifically catastrophic loss."

I ignored the usual bragging . . . truthfully, it wasn't all bragging . . . and focused on the Light. I was "interested" in it and had been for years. I'd spent the past few of them waiting for news of it to surface, a whisper of a dying demon two months ago to finally echo the rumors, and then set to tracking Robin down via the network of people like me. People in the business of knowing things.

The demon hadn't known the location of the Light and very probably didn't genuinely *know* anything at all—demons like the little sin of gossip as much as humans do, but Robin . . . Robin definitely knew his shit, which made finding him worth my while. He didn't stick in one place too often, but if there was anything worth knowing that I didn't, then he would.

"Yes, the Light of Life. I'm looking for it just like I said the last time I called and the time before that and the time before that. Have you found anything?" I demanded. I'd noticed Eden House had been looking for it as well and looking hard. Whether they'd known about it as long as I had was a different story. Griffin and Zeke couldn't tell me. They weren't high enough to be in the real loop. They were strictly demon chasers, nowhere near management level. They didn't know what their bosses did. And in some cases, such as this one, they didn't know what I did either.

"I've heard something, but I'm in New York and I'm in no position to leave. I have friends in trouble. *I'm* in trouble. It's like the bad old days when we chased the demons and Eden House out of the city all in one night. I never was able to get the scales and feathers out of my best cashmere coat. I billed the Vatican and the Church of Satan, but did I get my money? No, not a damn penny. Of course, the party afterward almost made up for it. You've never seen so many drunk vampires and werewolves in your life. Even Wahanket showed up, and you know what it takes to pry his dusty, mummified ass out of the museum basement. I remember . . ."

It was honestly awe-inspiring, who and what you could see if you traveled every corner of the world and kept your eyes open. What you could hear as well, but I didn't have time for Robin's trip down memory lane, as entertaining as it usually was. I cut him off impatiently, only verbally, although if he'd been talking to me in person . . . It's so difficult to be good sometimes. "Robin, I thought you were in a hurry. I know *I* am."

"Fine. Fine. Deny me a little stress relief. The best I can do is give you a name." He did sound a little stressed under his customary tale spinning and Robin never sounded stressed. He'd fallen in with a bad crowd apparently. That made him more like me. Good for him. I didn't want to be the only one. Although vampires and werewolves, tsk, were nothing but fanged and furry trash. I'd stick to demons.

"Who, then? What's the name?"

"Wilder Hun."

"You're kidding," I said incredulously.

"That's what he calls himself. Born Eugene Gleck, so who can blame him." He rattled off an address. "He's also a molester of sorts, out of jail a year now." He would've told me to watch myself, but he knew better.

"A woman." I rapped a fisted hand against the bar. *Of sorts?* What did he mean by *of sorts*?

"No."

"A man?" Less usual, but it happened. More and more, it happened.

"No. Think alcohol, a great deal of it, and a redneck's most faithful companion."

Ah, it was simply Robin being Robin. I didn't roll my eyes—that would be juvenile—but it took effort. "All right. Your random pervert. So no one can say if it might have been consensual?"

"I don't think they had the Pickup Truck Whisperer around to ask, but it wasn't his and I hear the muffler was never quite the same." I heard noises behind his voice. "I've got to go. Wire the money to my account." In the background I heard him say, "I said, get away from her. Salome doesn't like you. You do *not* want to end up down the incinerator like that Great Dane."

He hung up before I could get the news on Salome and what she had against Great Danes; so sue me—I was curious. Born curious and lived every day the same way. Ah well, maybe the next time I talked to Robin I'd get the story on the cranky Salome. I had Wilder Hun, the moronic-named truck molester,. to deal with now.

Wilder lived an hour or so from Vegas in Moapa. That's the thing about Vegas that's so different from other cities. There's no main drag, then suburbs, more suburbs, scattered houses, rural area stretching on and on . . . no. There's Vegas and then there's nothing. Nothing but dirt, sand, tumbleweeds, and the occasional mass of horny tarantulas swarming across the road during mating season. You really have to settle in and drive to find the next signs of life. It ain't cheaper outside town, baby, because there *is* no outside town. You have to haul ass to the next town and watch the gorgeous, brown, flat, dead scenery in between.

When I finally arrived at the Hun Mansion, a shack with a distinct lean, I checked my Smith & Wesson 500 and slid it into the back waistband of my jeans and covered it with my shirt, a Chinese silk and brocade top in reds, golds, and peacock blue. It'd warmed up too much for the sweater. That was Nevada winter weather for you. The shotgun I left covered with a blanket in the backseat of the car. A round or two from my Smith wouldn't do much but annoy a demon, but Hun was most likely no demon, just your run-of-the-mill pervert. And I trusted my judgment enough to play it that way. I also trusted myself to take down any pervert, run-of-the-mill or otherwise.

They say the gun is the great equalizer. Not so. A gun blowing off a guy's balls, *that's* the great equalizer.

I sat on the hood of my car, the metal hot but bearable, and called out to the guy with a hammer banging on the side of his "house." "Hun. I'm looking for a Wilder Hun. Is that you?"

There is ugly, then there's ugly, and then there's your mama hooked up with King Kong. He was tall, six foot seven at best guess, hairy . . . long, scraggly brown hair and beard, tufts of hair sticking out of the collar of his T-shirt. His arms were like prehistoric caterpillars, bristling with spiny fur, even his ankles from under his jeans . . . never mind. Big Foot in a torn T-shirt and dirty jeans, and with eyes the color of algae on pond water.

Take your picture of the desert yeti and move on to something more touristy and a little less nauseating.

He spit on the ground. "That's me. Whatcha want, little girl?"

I get called that a lot. I was five-five, flat-footed, but I was rarely flat-footed. I liked heels, the higher, the better, and it wasn't because of my height. What you can do with a knife you can do just as easily with the three-inch heel of a boot—it only takes more pressure.

You don't need height. Guns, boots, and attitude, that's all you really need.

He started toward me before I could respond to his "little girl" remark, and I held up a hand, then patted the warm metal beside me. "Whoa, Sasquatch. This is my car. It's a very nice car, and I love it. Don't you have some sort of fifty-foot restriction against approaching possible victims?"

The teeth he bared in a snarl weren't in the expected Sasquatch–Big Foot range. They were quite nice. Sparkly, pearly white, and so incredibly perfect, they had to be dentures. I had a feeling jail was only one of the punishments Hun had gotten for his crime. In a parking lot somewhere, cavity-ridden teeth had probably once littered the asphalt. Someone had loved their truck as much as I loved my car and had used either a crowbar or a tire iron to prove it.

I started to comment on his bright, orthodontically perfect nonsmile, but remembered I did want some information from this man, and insulting his postcoital dental repair probably wasn't the way to go. "Just kidding. Just kidding." I smiled brightly myself and patted the hood beside me again. "Have a seat." Grumbling, he sat and the car groaned under his weight. My nose stung under the smell, but I kept talking. "I've come all the way from Vegas to chat with you and I brought some friends." I pulled a small wad of cash out of my pocket, spread the bills out, and waved them like a fan. I gave him geisha-girl eyes over the top edges. Men, even those with excessive monkey genes, never fail to fall for that . . . well, that and the four-inch chrome barrel I shoved in his ribs.

The stick and the carrot.

It was a pretty sad commentary that human society never much got past that stage.

"A friend of mine says you know something about the Light of Life." Griffin had mentioned in passing two years ago that Eden House was looking for it, *had* been looking for it, although he didn't know for how long—but it was important. It was important all right. What they didn't tell him was that it was the most important thing that existed in the world. I was surprised he was able to hear what little he had. He had no idea what it truly was or what it could do. It was hard to say who did know in the House—either Trinity and Goodman or only Trinity. High-level info for high-level jerks.

Neither knew what the Light looked like though. At least I doubted it. I wasn't all that sure myself. It was enough that I knew what it did or what it was supposed to do. If it was everything I'd heard it to be . . . let's just say Trixa knew the value of a thing. Anything. *Every*thing. Griffin and Zeke might be in the dark on this one, but not me.

The Light of Life . . . an impenetrable shield that could protect Heaven or Hell from any attack, any second war. Who could put a price on the ultimate defensive weapon? Who could put a price on invulnerability? On absolutely guaranteed survival?

I could.

Contacts, context, and a knowledge of history—it made me one smart girl.

Money made Hun one cooperative guy.

He looked down at the barrel jammed hard against his ribs, assuming he had any under that thick layer of blubber. Then he looked at the money. It was an easy choice. He reached over and took the money. "I heard of it. Some caver, Jeb, found it in an abandoned mine a few towns over. Don't know why he calls it that. It's not like a diamond or anything. Just a shiny quartz rock as big as your fist. The guy says it glows at night, but what's that worth?" He spit in the dirt. "Nada."

"And why'd he call it the Light of Life?" I didn't move the gun. There'd been many a donkey who'd gotten the carrot and then kicked the crap out of the veggie farmer right after. I was content to wait until our conversation was over and Big Foot was back hammering at his shack.

He frowned, hiding the pearly whites. "I don't know. He just did. From the minute he found it and came over to show it to me. The Light of Life, he kept calling it. But he's a caver and cavers are nuts, so what the hell? He can call it whatever he wants."

By the time I left, I had the revolver under the passenger seat, a layer of dust coating my car's red paint, and a giant gluteus maximus print on the hood. Call the *National Enquirer*. Sasquatch exists and here's the proof—ass-print exclusives, fifty bucks a pop.

I also had Jeb the crazy caver's address and wasn't the day looking brighter and brighter? A particularly loud song blared on the radio and I slapped it off. The Light of Life. It was going to do two things for me. Two rewards rolled into one. It was going to get me something far more valuable than gold or diamonds and at the same time, a whole lot of nasty, *nasty* vengeance on the son of a bitch who'd killed my brother.

You're supposed to take care of your younger brother, no matter how far he strays. Travel was in my family's blood. That was a given. You still take care of your brother. No matter how far he goes. No matter what.

Kimano.

I stared blindly at the road. The black sheep of the family. Lazy, content with beaches and waves. Work could always wait another day. For all the ways he was so different from me, I loved him. Loved the hell out of him. Sure, there was work to be done, but it didn't mean he always had to do it. That's how far gone I was on my baby brother. Me. Bar owner, informant, occasional demon killer, and various other things best not spread around. I edged into the workaholic stage. But to me it had never mattered that my brother wasn't like me. Kimano never failed to make me laugh. In all his life, he never failed . . .

But once.

Smooth brown skin covered with blood and torn to shreds, dark eyes staring blankly at the sky. I hadn't laughed then. I hadn't thought I'd ever laugh again.

Years later I'd learned to, but the true laughing I was waiting on, the laughing I craved with everything in me was the kind I would spill over the body of my brother's killer. We all have days in our lives. The Day. The One. Weddings, births, hopscotching on the moon . . . this would be my day. And my patience was running thin. Now, with this—the Light—things were finally moving. Because they all wanted the Light. The demons—Below. And Eden House, which equaled Above.

Things were going to start moving and moving fast.

I'd listened and pried and questioned a long time now and with what I knew, I could have Kimano's killer. Hell would turn him over in a heartbeat if I promised them the Light. And it had been a demon that had killed my brother. I was as sure of that as I was of anything. A demon kill . . . it wasn't anything you ever forgot. And one dark silver-gray scale left behind.

One was all it took.

The demon wasn't all I wanted. It was what I wanted the most, but still not all. It was asking for a lot, shooting for the moon, but sometimes . . . once in a rare while, you can have your cake and eat it too. I had better uses for the Light than Hell did—and Heaven . . .

They could get in line as well.

Chapter 3

Jeb the Caver.

What was there to be said about Jeb the, assumed by Hun, crazy caver?

Well, for one, he was dead.

Not demon dead, but when you're dead, you're dead, and do the particulars really matter?

I sighed and pulled a ponytail holder out of my jeans pocket and bundled my curls on top of my head, clearing the way for a better look. He was tied to an old kitchen chair with wire that ate into his flesh, once raw and bloody—now dry and stiff. Whoever had done the fancy stuff had used a knife. Knife wounds are quite different from damage made by demon claws. Those are serrated, and while some combat knives are, they're not quite so finely serrated. Jeb had been tortured pretty thoroughly. The Light might have been worthless to a jeweler, but it had meant something to him—touched him somehow, and he wasn't about to give it up. And even with two fingers and an ear missing and a savagely slit throat, I don't think he had. Someone had gone away mad. What a shame.

I searched his house, no bigger or better a shack than Wilder's, and found nothing. I didn't expect to. If anything had been here, the person with a knife would've found it—the same one I would bet was with Eden House.

I'd have said they were ruthless before, without qualms about doing what had to be done. Eden itself had been of the Old Testament, and Eden House didn't much differ. They weren't much into forgiving and *Suffer unto the little children*, but torture? Would they go that far? Would Above allow it? And if it was Eden House, why hadn't they brought a telepath?

Too many questions. It didn't matter who had done it. My link to the Light was gone.

Needless to say my mood was not good when I finally made it home, walking into my bar just in time to see Zeke plant a bullet point-blank in a robber's forehead.

"Wait!" Griffin grabbed Zeke's wrist a split second too late—the "think" cue not quite making it over the finish line.

"What?" Zeke looked confused and a little annoyed. "Wrong?"

"Give me a second," Griffin muttered. "I'm thinking."

"Not too wrong, then," Zeke said with satisfaction.

"Son of a *bitch*!"

Zeke and Griffin looked up from the crumpled body to me and each sidled a step back. They didn't often see me well and truly angry. I was cheerful, I was easygoing, I was . . . I was so pissed, I couldn't see straight. "He was armed," Griffin said immediately in defense of his partner. "He was robbing the place and he had a gun. He could've killed somebody. That guy in the corner. The ones at the pool table. Leo." He jerked his blond head in the direction of my bartender, who stood behind the bar with arms folded. "Your Leo." Leo gave me an "Eh, it could've gone either way" shrug.

"And you like Leo," Zeke pointed out, trying to slide

his gun back under his jacket without being seen. "Everyone likes Leo. I like Leo. He gives me free beer."

Leo instantly disappeared into the back kitchen, no doubt to call 911. Yeah, right. "I run a business here," I shouted after him. "This isn't a soup kitchen or a damn beer kitchen either."

"He would've killed someone," Zeke said as I approached him—and he said it honestly, because truthfully I wasn't sure Zeke had figured out how to lie yet. Either that or he simply didn't have the motivation to be bothered. "I felt it. It was right there, like acid sizzling in his brain."

I ignored the excuse. True or not, it was still an excuse. Zeke could've taken him out without killing him. He . . . I gave an internal sigh and let the ire drain away. No. He couldn't have. He was Zeke, it had happened too fast for him to think it through, and Griffin had been just a moment too late this time. It was a done deal. Now we just had to deal with it.

"You." I shoved Zeke into the nearest chair, but without any real force. "You have a conceal and carry, right?" I was almost positive he did. Eden House liked to avoid trouble as much as possible, and on occasion there was some collateral damage while demon hunting. Shouldn't be, but there was. Eden House or not, the demon chasers were human. They made mistakes or accidents happened. Either way, they could plant guns, knives—hell, samurai swords—on the innocent in seconds to get their own off, if that's what it took.

I didn't wait for his reply. I started to reach for Griffin to give him a shove toward Zeke, but he was already there. "Coach him on what to say," I said, "and how to say it, quick, before the cops get here." The *how* to say it was just as important as the what.

"The rest of you." I took in the room of my regulars with a swing of a pointed finger, short nail frosted red. "You are literally on your hands and knees in relief. This man saved your life. That psycho son of a bitch was going to kill every last one of you for the pennies in your pockets. And he may have mentioned doing things to your dead bodies. Bad things. Really, really bad. You're too scared to remember." Eyes blinked, a mouth or two gaped, and I repeated it a little more loudly, "*Literally* on your knees."

Chairs tipped over. Pool cues dropped to the floor and my grand total of seven clients went down with them.

By the time the cops got there, Zeke had his Glock on a table and his head in his hands. "He made me," he said with a fair imitation of shock. "The bastard wouldn't back down. He was going to kill everyone. Swear to God. Everyone."

It went on an hour or so there as someone came to drag off the carcass in a nice black plastic bag. The cupful of brains they left on the floor. Oh, they took a small sample, but the rest . . . oatmeal gone bad and it was seeping into my ancient wood floor. I had Leo out with a mop and some bleach, but the floors were old and cracked. We'd be spraying that spot with a good shot of potpourri deodorizer every morning for a while.

They took Zeke to the police station for the paperwork. Griffin went with him as his "lawyer friend." No, Griffin wasn't a lawyer. I wasn't quite sure what they were taught when Eden House took them in and trained them, but they were as educated as any college grad. Better yet, they had enough fake ID to walk into the White House, get a Twinkie from the vending machine in the basement, then high-five the Secret Service on their way out. If Griffin told a cop he was a lawyer, I knew he'd backed it up with something.

Zeke had still been doing a good job as he left. You would've thought he actually gave a shit about blowing that guy's head off. The guy was a killer; the guy had a gun; the guy went down. It was Zeke's philosophy about this entire situation, but let a cop see that and, justified or not, he would look at Zeke a little more closely . . . maybe for a long time.

But Griffin had run over it with him a few times before the sirens approached. "You're upset. Yes, he was going to kill you, but you've never killed anyone before. You're shaken up. And throw in a 'Shit, why'd we have to pick this bar? Why didn't we go down the street?'"

Zeke repeated it faithfully under his breath, and damn if he didn't actually look almost distressed when the first cop arrived. Ten years ago, he would've killed the guy, stepped over his body to the bar, ordered a beer, and been unable to fake a twinge. Of course, ten years ago he was fifteen and wouldn't have been served, but the point was the same. And inside he was still the same as he'd been ten years ago; he'd just learned to fake it.

Like I said, I thought he knew right from wrong. No, that wasn't true. I *knew* he knew right from wrong, but he knew it in such a black and white manner—the results often ended up the same as if he didn't. Lack of the gray areas . . . it made for Old Testament justice.

"Hey, whatcha doing? Milking your goat on the Sabbath? Really. Now, where's that nice round rock I'm going to stone you with?" Five minutes later, "By the way, you won't be needing that goat anymore, will you?"

Too bad I didn't need a goat.

Exaggerated, all right, a little. Even with his issues, Zeke wasn't that black and white. Although I was amazed with his problems that Zeke had been able to attach to Leo and me. As for Griffin—it was just a given, as I'd thought before ... the Universe. They were two halves of a deadly whole. Zeke needed Griffin and Griffin needed Zeke. Griffin needed to take care of someone. He was a fixer. Wanted to fix, had to. Was it the way he grew up in foster care, surrounded by the weaker kids? A common-sense answer, but was it the right one?

Apparently Zeke's acting lessons paid off, because four hours later, Griffin called and said tiredly, "It's over. There will be more paperwork and a token appearance in court, but everyone is agreed it's justifiable."

"He held up good, then." I'd finished painting my toenails and was now cleaning the Smith. Both were bright and sparkly.

Deadly too.

"He did good. One cop almost had him slipping, but he caught himself. He's come a long way, you know?"

I loaded the gun silently.

He hesitated. "All right. He hasn't, but he can pretend now and that's more than he could do before."

I slammed the cylinder home and said quietly, "It's not his fault he's the way he is. It's not your fault either, Griffin. You've saved him. If you hadn't been fostered with him for those years, he wouldn't have survived. He certainly wouldn't be free." From what Griffin had insinuated about the seriousness of what had happened when Zeke was fifteen, Zeke would be locked up somewhere. Still.

"Don't be ashamed of him, Griffin," I went on, and

put the gun on the table. "That only makes me ashamed of you."

His voice went dark. "I'm not ashamed. No one else could've survived what he has. No one else could learn to function like he has."

I pulled the ponytail holder from the top of my hair and let my hair fall haphazardly around my shoulders. "Then be proud. Of yourself. You're mostly responsible for that." I disconnected and left him with that thought. Two seconds later I cursed myself. I'd forgotten to ask if they'd blown up a demon or an iguana earlier today. I hovered a hand over the phone, then let it go. One day my curiosity truly was going to be the death of me.

The next day I felt like death would be a relief.

The bar was closed. It closed every year on the same day: the anniversary of Kimano's death. Zeke and Griffin had asked a few times why the closing. They'd never gotten an answer and finally gave up. Message received: Private, so don't come knocking on the door and don't ask why.

Leo stayed those days. Leo had known Kimano. We had history, the three of us. Leo could never miss Kimano like I did, but he did miss and he did mourn him as a brother of the spirit, if not the blood. But even if he hadn't, he would've been there for me. The bottom line was that the two of us were too much alike to ever come together in any permanent way, and we wouldn't belittle what we had with anything temporary. It wouldn't be enough and then there would be regret dimming what was so brilliant between us now—that bond that couldn't be broken.

It was nice, knowing that.

But the potential of what could've been if one of us had been only the slightest bit different was always there. Yet another bond that couldn't be broken. There was a wonderful warmth in knowing that as well.

He slept in bed with me the night before. I woke up to blinds-filtered Nevada sunshine with his arm heavy around my waist, simple solace. He was one of the rare ones who knew sex didn't necessarily equal comfort.

I stayed in bed the entire day and he stayed with me. Other than food and bathroom breaks, we curled up and said nothing. Once in a while he'd chuckle against my shoulder and I'd curl my lips, instinctively knowing just which Kimano memory had come to mind.

We'd done this for years now. At first we talked and laughed about them, but now we knew the routine and the flavor of them so well, that when he laughed, I knew. And when I groaned and covered my eyes, Leo knew. Kimano had never been good at his job, but he'd left more memories behind than if he had been. He was much softer hearted than he should've been. Our mother had raised us to be tough, to do the job at hand, no matter what it was, and do each one as if it were your first, last, and only job. Hold people accountable always. *Be* accountable always. I liked working; it was easy for me. But Kimano let the slackers slide, because he was one himself.

There was a soft, heavy breathing by my ear and a few stands of straight black hair wafting over my cheek. Leo had never failed to stand by me . . . or lie by me, if that's what I needed . . . which was a change for him in his younger days. He'd been big, bad, and full of anger. He'd mellowed over the years. He was still big and bad if you put him to the test, but he'd learned a little more tolerance and a lot more patience. What he did to those who pissed him off in the past . . . well, it made seeing him throw a man through the plaster bathroom wall seem considerably mellow, almost kindly in fact.

I, on the other hand, had gotten a little less mellow with age. Taking care of Kimano's killer might take care of that; it might not. We'd just have to see.

My eyes drifted to the picture on the dresser. A stark black and white—it was Kimano in a patch of grass with his arm slung around the shoulders of a grinning coyote and a sharp-eyed raven on his shoulder. Lenore. He'd written *Arizona* across the back of the photo. He always said I had the worst memory for the fun things, the silly things. Maybe he'd been right, but the bad things . . .

Those I never forgot.

The gold bars from the slats in the window slowly passed across the wall, only a shade lighter color than the wall itself. Then night came, later night, and finally by the clock, midnight. I rolled over to face an already-sleeping Leo, wrapped my arm around his waist, shut my eyes, tucked my face against the blazing heat of his neck, and let the new day begin.

Chapter 4

The first customer through the door the next day was Griffin. He looked like he'd had a hard two nights. Between the cops, justifying Zeke to Eden House, and a possible exploded iguana, he deserved the look. He sat down at a stool as I patted the top of his head and said, "Morning, sunshine."

He swatted at my hand and muttered, "Screwdriver." I looked up at the clock: ten a.m. I shrugged and served it up. At least he was getting his vitamins. He took a drink, then took his first good look at me, and winced.

"Is that a comment on how I look, Griff?" I bent over, folded my arms on the bar, and rested my chin on them to study him expectantly. "I'd think twice before answering, just for your personal safety."

"No." He took another drink. "It's the way you feel. Sad, angry, and a little hormonal. Is your per—" He stopped, very wisely, and took another drink. "Sorry. It's the empath thing. Normally I don't get much off you. Sometimes nothing at all. You must've had a bad day and I must've had a shitty yesterday to even bring all this up."

Since he was right and apologetic, I let it go. He'd told me about being an empath a long time ago, when

Eden House had come looking for him ... their own telepaths and empaths picking up him and Zeke. If burning demons worked, the House would probably be out there scouring for their own little Stephen King fire starters too.

About being an empath, he'd said back then, it's mainly boring. He'd pointed at the people in the bar. Cranky, horny, hungry, horny, pissed off, horny, sad, horny. After a while of that, he'd snorted, it got real old real fast. A thankless talent, I thought. There weren't too many people running around filling the world with joyful vibes. Being an empath would really, well, suck. But it was useful for the job. Demons, they felt nothing like humans. They had one emotion humans didn't have, at least not to this degree. It was murder, greed, and a longing, all wrapped up in one single ribbon of emotion so intense that it didn't have a name. He said when he closed his eyes he could see it ... dark purple with jagged streaks of bile yellow and blood red.

When I asked what Zeke "heard" when he psychically touched demons, Griffin said nothing good. It was all *Kill, eat souls. Weak. He's weak. He'll give his up in a heartbeat.* Zeke could only read the very surface of anyone's thoughts, though. The bigger and badder demons like Solomon ... the more-controlled demons ... could and did pass for humans at times. But Zeke was the strongest telepath Eden House had, just as Griffin was the strongest empath. To my knowledge, the only demon they couldn't pick out *was* Solomon, although they didn't have to, because Solomon had been bold enough to tell Eden House he was setting up shop. That was before Zeke and Griffin's Eden House days. Solomon's human body was probably in his late thirties. A very sexy late thirties.

Yep, they definitely had to pick those bodies out of a catalogue: *Hot Soul Suckers*—check out the discount late-nineties models at the back of the book.

"I heard through the grapevine. Something happened." Griffin finished the screwdriver and exhaled, eyes clearing slightly. "Something about the Light of Life. Remember me telling you about that a few years ago?" He didn't wait for a comment, which was convenient for me. "No one's giving out anything specific. Just that there was a body and no sign of the artifact."

"Of which you still don't know anything—what it actually is or does," I said matter-of-factly. Trinity and Jackson hadn't told them. Then again, neither had I, but that was one case of the less they knew, the better—for everyone. Not that that made my next comment any less manipulative, but sometimes you have to be deceitful to warn those you care about . . . without blowing your own plans. It still felt wrong, a feeling I wasn't used to. "Some trust your House gives you guys. Makes you wonder how badly they're going to paddle your asses if they find out I've been going on demon hunts with you." No House telepath could read them now. Zeke had learned to shield his casual thoughts and taught Griff to do the same. It was one of the few occasions when Zeke was his teacher, not his partner.

Zeke chose that moment to come in. "You must be psychic," he said matter-of-factly as I rolled my eyes, although for him it was a good effort. "Demon hunt tonight. That tip you gave us looks good. Going?" He ordered a Corona while I considered it. I'd heard there was a bar a few miles from mine where people were getting rich, famous, and laid like crazy. That had soul selling all over it, and I'd passed the news along.

Sitting on the stool next to Griffin, Zeke beat his hands in a slow, hypnotic tempo on his legs and frowned when I put the bottle of beer in front of him. "Where's the lime?"

I looked over at Lenore on his perch. "Bird, lime." He flashed a beady eye, flew over, plucked one out of the tray, strutted over, and stuffed it in the mouth of Zeke's bottle.

"There you go." I smiled cheerfully. "Enjoy."

He scowled. "I fight demons. Isn't that enough? I have to take on bird flu too?" But he pushed the lime on down and took his chances. He took a swig, than glanced at Griffin. "You don't look so good. You got up way too damn early. Could hear you banging around in the kitchen."

Griffin and Zeke lived together, a necessity with Zeke's condition. "Some of us had things on our minds," Griffin muttered, rubbing his eyes with the heels of his hands. "Cops, lawyers, court, the House, Mr. Trinity. So sorry I disturbed you."

Zeke hunched his shoulders slightly. "Oh yeah. Sorry." And he was . . . sincerely sorry. Not for what he'd done, but for the trouble it was causing Griffin.

"Hell with it. It'll pass." Griffin exhaled and gestured for another drink, just orange juice this time. "And before we get into the demon hunt issue, Trixa, I'm curious. What would the House do if they found out you went on hunts with us? The first thing would be to probably ask us how you know about demons. I doubt they'd approve of us hanging out with a descendant of the worshippers of pagan gods any more than they'd like hearing about the demon hunts."

"Am I supposed to register surprise here? *Thou shalt not suffer a witch to live* and all that. I'm not a witch and this isn't Salem, but people are still people." I wiped a counter, plastic and cracking, but clean. "And too bad for them anyway. Me and mine might know things even they don't about the big bad world. Certainly things pups like you are in the dark about." I gave them a wink as I finished up with the counter.

"Pups"—Zeke shifted closer—"boys, they just can't help themselves, no matter how many times you remind them, 'not so much. I'm not fifteen anymore.' " He immediately winced at the thought, big and bright, I shot at him that stopped his last word and thought in their tracks. "Ow. Big sister. Hands off. I hear you. You're *loud.*" He rubbed it away. "But there's only six years . . . ow. Okay. Stop. Someone out there won't think of me as a little brother. I'll find them." Great, a mission. Zeke on a mission. That was not good. I didn't call him on the prying as I usually would have, not with this subject. And I knew how to keep my surface thoughts casual and basically bullshit. Griffin had needed lessons; some of us are born with natural bullshitting skills.

"An innocent," I said, warningly. Zeke didn't hurt those who didn't deserve it, but once again . . . with that black and white view of the world, up until now that may have been a case of pure luck. He had to be careful. Who among us was honestly completely innocent? Who among us hasn't deserved a little punishment once or twice? Trouble was, Zeke wasn't so good at doing "little." And with an innocent he would be pushing that luck somewhat less.

"Innocent." That's what I said and "thought" very casually in case Zeke was eavesdropping. At a much deeper level I sent the absolute dead-on emotion of utter denial to his partner. If "never" could be an emotion, this was it. Only for a man, any man—even one as unique as Zeke—there was no such thing as "never" in this department. Zeke was no virgin. He'd had his share of one-night stands, and those women had been fortunate. Either as innocent as I told him to look for now or not bad enough to set him off. I wasn't quite sure what Zeke would do if he ever picked up a murderer, caught a stray thought of something ripe with evil, yet purely human.

Zeke turned to look at his silent partner. "What?" Silent to any onlooker, but not to Zeke. "Oh." His gaze drifted down to his own hands—hands that could kill with or without a weapon. "I get it." His eyes clouded for a moment, then cleared as the obvious solution came to him. "I won't read them. I won't look. Okay?"

"Yeah, partner, that's okay. That's good." Griffin, who'd obviously had the same thoughts I had, sighed and pushed his glass of OJ back toward me for another screwdriver, because both of us knew it was never that easy. "I changed my mind. Load me up." As I did, he leaned back and stretched, muscles no doubt stiff from digging Zeke out of that deeper and deeper hole he'd gotten himself into. No wonder he didn't want to think about any future ones lurking out there. "So?" he asked me. "Going?"

"Maybe," I conceded. "Leo's out today, so he can cover for me tonight. A little hunt might be some fun."

"Good. I can break this in." Zeke, his thoughts of women and one-night stands vanishing instantly in favor of something he loved far more, pulled a revolver the size of an antiaircraft gun out of his jacket and laid it on the bar. "They confiscated my Glock, so I had to get a new gun from the House armory." The armory where they didn't keep grenades, and I was guessing that Zeke actually had authorized access to. "Isn't it something fucking else?" He smiled down at it, grim and satisfied at the thought of all the demon damage that could do. He was like a kid at Christmas . . . a homicidal kid maybe, but . . . "A Colt Anaconda .44 Magnum. The muzzle flare is vented out the muzzle *and* the sides," he said, as proudly as if he'd designed the gun himself. It looked like it was as big as my car. I leaned closer and corrected myself. It looked *bigger* than my car.

I gazed at it, then at his savagely content face, and bit my lip. Patting his arm, I managed to say solemnly, "Oh doll, it couldn't be that small, I promise you. It just isn't physically possible."

Zeke didn't let my psychoanalysis ruin his love affair with his new gun. He brought it that night, concealed in a holster under his jacket. I was surprised the weight of it didn't have him leaning to one side, since it was as heavy as the anchor on the *Titanic*, but it didn't.

Dressed in all black with his hair pulled back into a ponytail, Zeke looked like what he was . . . dangerous. Damn dangerous. He lounged against the wall opposite the emergency door with arms crossed. Bait or the hunter. Zeke loved being both.

Griff and I were dressed the same as Zeke and both of us were carrying shotguns as we crouched in the dark alcove between two Dumpsters near the mouth of the alley—keeping Zeke in sight. The only light in the place was directly opposite him and was a dim bulb mounted over the door, but demons didn't need a lot of light to see. They didn't need a lot of light to kill either. I was guessing that Hell was a dark, dark place.

"Do you ever wonder why they do it?" Griffin

murmured. "Sell their souls? Do they really think a few years of all they could want here could be worth going to Hell? How do they let someone talk them into that?"

"People are stupid, shortsighted, and sometimes just desperate for something more." I had heard there were souls, besides immature ones, that demons wouldn't take. They wouldn't take a soul for a selfless act. Wouldn't or couldn't. No trading your soul for your dying husband or wife, child or brother. No trading it for the cure to cancer. No doing evil to accomplish good. The road to Hell wasn't paved with good intentions after all. "Besides, who's to say Heaven's any better? No shellfish, no pork, no hot guy-on-guy Westerns. No sex at all. Think about that. No sex and no barbecued shrimp. How could Hell be much worse?"

"Is there really no sex in Heaven?" Zeke said aloud, sounding worried. He was listening in to Griffin's thoughts again and being about as stealth conscious as a marching band. We both ignored him.

"Put you one-on-one with a demon and I'll bet you could have him selling his soul to you," Griffin snorted at my ear, then added, "If demons had souls."

"Sweet talker." I jabbed him with my elbow, then tensed as the door opened and a demon walked out, followed by a girl. She was pretty, but not beautiful. Her breasts were small, a B cup, but so were mine. The last thing you needed when running down a demon was a double D smacking you in the face, but that probably wasn't her opinion. She was twenty pounds heavier than the magazines told you she should be with an ass a tad bigger than an anorexic starlet's. In other words, she was normal—which was most likely the worst possible thing to be in her eyes.

And then there was the demon. . . . Picture a male model with empty eyes and a smile as bright as a thousand diamonds—or as predatory as the flashing teeth of a personal injury lawyer. Not all lawyers were demons, but let's say there was a fairly high turnover among the Vegas ones, thanks to Eden House and an endless supply of shotgun slugs.

"Hurry up and run so I can start killing," Zeke told the girl impatiently. He'd pulled out the Colt and pointed it at our prey.

The girl stood frozen. Even in the low light I could see the beat of her pulse, rapid against the pale skin of her throat . . . the beat of her starving heart. She wanted, so badly, all the wrong damn things. I stood, braced the stock of the shotgun against my shoulder, and said, "Listen to him, girl. Try helping others instead of helping yourself. Take your shallow dreams and run to something better, because there *is* better. Go!" She didn't move. *"Run!"* There was a flutter of green silk, fake, and the glitter of diamonds, also fake, and she was gone . . . running past us, out of the alley, and disappearing around the corner. I hoped she believed me. It was true. There was better. She only had to open her eyes and see it.

The demon's smile didn't waver. "Eden House dogs. You . . ."

Zeke shot him between the eyes with three consecutive shots that came so fast, they almost sounded like one. "They always want to talk." He lowered the gun. "Eat your still-beating heart. Skin you alive. Strangle you with your own intestines. Blah-blah. Boring."

The head of the human demon had gone misshapen. Hollow point rounds for maximum damage. Zeke liked his toys to do the job first time around. This time he'd nailed the demon before it even had time to change back to its true form. Scales rippled across its slack face, but it poured downward into a black puddle before it could change any further. No brain, no demon.

Easy. It hadn't been worth taking off my boots and putting on my sneakers. Hell, it wasn't even worth putting on deodorant in case I had to run and sweat.

But that's when we found out why the demon hadn't lost its smile.

I spotted them first . . . on the roof. Five of them and they weren't bothering with human disguises. Bat wings thrashed and they dived at us, transparent teeth bared. Three of them were black, with ebony scales that sucked in the light. You didn't see that color often, and it was never a good time when you did. The other two were a sickening, swamp green-brown, more of what I was used to. They weren't armed with weapons. With their teeth, speed, and claws seven inches long, they were already equipped. And all those teeth, all those talons, they had one target.

"Zeke!" I shouted it and ran, but Griffin was ahead of me. Nothing against Griffin, but I was one fast runner, damn fast. It didn't matter—he was motivated. Unfortunately, that motivation didn't stop Zeke from going down. Not that he didn't take some down with him, because he did—popped two in their heads as they fell from the sky on top of him. It was damn good shooting and from the surprised flare in their red and yellow eyes, unexpected from a human.

Cool, precise, without a hint of nerves. That was Zeke. I doubted he felt his nerves dance with anything other than annoyance when the claws of the third black demon sank into his upper chest and arm, pinning him to the ground and keeping him from reloading.

Griffin stumbled.

Shit. Zeke might not get nerves, but he felt something other than annoyance, all right. He felt pain. And thanks to being an empath, Griffin was feeling it too. Everything his partner felt, he was feeling right along with him. And that was sweet in a bonding, "I feel your pain . . . no, really, I *feel* your pain" kind of way, but it wasn't any use to us now. I grabbed the back of his jacket and kept him upright as we ran. I also gave him a shake. "You have to have some control over your empathy," I snapped. "Use it! You're no help to him like this."

Zeke had his good hand wrapped around the neck of the demon and was holding those haunted-house, shattered-window teeth away from his own throat. I couldn't see the blood on his chest, black was good at hiding that, but I could see a trickle of it run from the corner of his mouth, the red of it on his bared teeth. I didn't need to hear the accompanying wheeze from Griffin to know the demon's claws had at least nicked Zeke's lung.

I stopped running and fired at the black one squatting on top of Zeke. I missed as the head darted forward with uncanny speed—physics-defying speed. Demons were like people. They were all different. Some were fast; some were slow. Some were smart, some not so much, and some beyond idiotic. It was our bad luck to get a smart, fast one; our worse luck that I underestimated him.

But the chest is a bigger target and I was smart and fast myself. I fired the second barrel of the shotgun and hit him dead-on. He was thrown off Zeke into the back of the alley. The talons must not have felt any better coming out than they had going in, because Zeke arched up off the asphalt and this time Griffin did fall. I used one hand and the support of a knee to reload the shotgun, and I used the other hand to slap Griffin's face hard enough to leave an instant hot, red handprint. Then I took a handful of his shirt, pulled him to his feet, and pushed him against the alley wall. The push was as hard as the slap and I saw his eyes focus on me. "Griff, you don't turn it off now and Zeke dies. He *dies*. Turn it off!"

His mouth tightened and he closed his eyes for a split second. His skin was still pale except for the red blotch, but when he lifted the lids, the pupils of his eyes were now normal. Before they had been black with only the thinnest ring of blue; now the blue was back. Dark with rage but back. So was his control, and we'd need it to get out of this trap we'd so stupidly hopped, skipped, and jumped our way into. I couldn't remember all the times I'd been underestimated because I was a woman, but I could count the times I'd underestimated demons. This would be number two and there was no way I was letting it turn out the way the first time had. Not again. Zeke wasn't going to die; Griff wasn't going to . . . none of us were.

"Off?" I asked as one of the brown demons headed for us, crisp air purling under its wings

"It's off," Griffin answered grimly as he turned and fired. The demon fell, one wing shredded. It wasn't off, the empathy, not really. I could see that in the bone white line of his jaw, but he had it under sufficient control to pull a trigger and that was good enough. I hit the other demon swooping at us, this time in the head. A slow one. Good. I deserved a slow one. I also deserved a bubble bath and hot chocolate laced with butterscotch schnapps and topped with whipped cream. But

I didn't have that. What I did have was a one-winged green demon and the black one I'd shot off Zeke. Neither of them looked anywhere near as warm and fuzzy as chocolate and schnapps.

Zeke was pushing up to one elbow, ignoring his own gasps for air as he reloaded using a speed-loader. His chest heaved on one side and didn't move on the other. Pure mission Zeke. Air? Only wimps need air. Just give me something to shoot. It looked like the black demon was going to give him his wish. I was wrong. It passed over its first victim and headed straight for me, wings working furiously. I didn't have time to reload and I'd never played baseball.

There's always time to learn.

I tossed the shotgun, caught the painfully warm end of the barrel, and swung.

This time I got his head with a crash that destroyed the shotgun's stock. Beautifully polished wood splintered and shattered. And all in all, it was about as effective as hitting him with a flyswatter. He did a better job of it with me than I had with him. As I went down, I saw the green demon back up and head for the wounded of the pack. Griffin was right between the two of us, but while Zeke might be almost as ass kicking as he thought he was, with his collapsed lung he was also bleeding and breathing . . . not so good.

"Get Zeke!" I yelled right before the demon fell on me like the MGM Grand and Caesar's all rolled into one. I was good, I was fast, but the human body is only capable of so much. I felt the breath jolt out of my lungs, the rough asphalt scrape through my jacket and shirt as we slid up the alley floor like the aftermath of a motorcycle wreck. Road rash from Hell . . . literally . . . and it hurt. Damn, did it hurt. It might've even come close to how the demon felt when the barrel of my Smith punctured its amber eye. There was a scream of a thousand tortured souls, which he'd probably personally recruited, and then, after I emptied six rounds into its skull, there was silence. Blissful silence.

Then I was covered in disgustingly warm black goo and the emergency door slammed open. A bouncer was framed there. He had no neck and from the steroid acne he had, probably balls the size of raisins. "Something going on out here?"

I pushed up on my elbow, the skin of my back a wildfire of pain at the motion. The green demon was gone. Either Griffin or Zeke had nailed it. Zeke was flat on his back while Griffin, who'd stripped off his jacket and wadded it to apply pressure to his partner's chest, rapped orders into the cell phone cradled between shoulder and jaw. There was blood on his hands, two shotguns on the alley floor, and a gun in my fist.

"No. Not a thing." I holstered the Smith slowly and painfully. "We're good, studly. Thanks for asking."

"Well . . . okay, then. Keep it down." Dull, mean brown eyes, already half crossed, crossed further, and he slammed the door behind him, the only man I would actually *encourage* to trade in his soul. Cerebral cortexes were highly underrated in this town. "Evolution," I groaned as I sat up all the way. "What a myth."

"Trixa, you're hurt." Griffin had let the phone fall, disconnected, and I knew Eden House's own personal ambulance was on the way. They had a medical unit at their headquarters and better doctors and equipment than the local hospitals had. They'd take care of Zeke. He'd be all right, be pissing off Griff and shooting demons again in no time. He would be, because life without Zeke—sociopathically efficient, endearingly psychotic Zeke—wasn't going to happen. It simply wasn't.

I knelt beside him, my own bloody hands cupping his face. I'd made it there and touched his chest without remembering the motion of it. Much as I'd done with Kimano. "Kit, you got to use your big gun. I can practically smell the testosterone on you."

I called him Kit, a baby fox, back when he was fifteen for his fox-colored hair. I'd almost forgotten the nickname in the ten years that had passed.

His eyes, that pale green, were hazy but managed to find me. "Kit." He dragged in several wet breaths. "When . . . do I make . . . full-grown fox?"

"When you know thyself," I said solemnly.

"What the hell's that mean?" Each word was slow and said with bloody lips.

"Ask the fortune cookie company. It came with last night's takeout." I gave him a smile, the best one I could manage when we were surrounded by shadows and the smell of copper and garbage.

A bloody hand gripped my shoulder and my attention. "You're hurt," Griffin repeated.

I already could hear the siren in the distance. Eden House didn't waste any time and they couldn't find me here. It wouldn't be good for Zeke and Griffin and it wouldn't be much better for me. "Superficial. Skin's strictly optional, right?" I already had my own cell phone out. "I'll call Leo. He can take me to the ER." I stood, refusing to bite my lip, but the "Shitshitshit" I didn't bother to hold back. I backed up toward the alley mouth as I made the call, watching the guys— *my* guys. I watched as Zeke closed his eyes, but kept breathing. He kept breathing.

"We walked right into it," Griffin said with dark disgust. He looked down at Zeke and back at me. "Black demons. High-level demons. What were they doing here? Besides making us look like amateurs. Like complacent assholes. We screwed up."

"No. We *fucked* up." It wasn't a word I used often, but the situation called for it. "There's a difference. We won't do it again." High-level demons like Solomon. Well, perhaps not like Solomon, no one was quite like him, but higher than the usual demons we dealt with. "Like Solomon." I couldn't make myself believe that was a coincidence. I stopped at the corner. "Call me and let me know." I didn't need to elaborate. Griffin knew. Then I rounded the corner and walked away, sticking to the shadows to hide the damage to my clothes and back . . . waiting for Leo.

No, I wasn't going to let Griff and Zeke follow Kimano into death.

Never.

Chapter 5

Hospitals were not fun.

My family and I tended to be completely healthy up until the second we were dead; we went out old as hell and wicked as they came. It was a nice quality; saved on health insurance. So this was my first visit to one of the places, and hopefully it would be the last. I waited four hours to get the dirt and bits of asphalt washed out of the raw stretch that was my back by a nurse who thought "gentle touch" was the slogan for some sort of toilet paper. Leo sat with me the entire time, alternately shaking his head and muttering, "This is what happens," and eyeing a blond doctor walking by with intriguing shadows in her violet eyes. Secrets. Leo was a sucker for a secret. For that matter so was I, but certainly not now.

"Thanks for the 'I told you so,' Grandma. Pain pills. You have the pain pills?" I asked as I slowly slid on the scrub top the nurse had given me to replace my shredded one.

"I have the pain pills." He shook a paper bag at me, having gone to the hospital pharmacy while they finished salving my back. "And the antibacterial cream. They didn't have any anti-fuckup pills. Maybe we can check with a Canadian pharmacy online."

"Ass." I didn't put much into the insult. He was right. "And you didn't even look when I put on the top. I know we're not going there, but you could at least boost the ego and *look*."

His stoic lips twitched. "I looked."

"Thank you. It's been a bitch of a night. I lost my strategic skills, almost lost my friends. I'd hate to think I'd lost my sex appeal too." I caught a glimpse of myself in the mirror over the sink in the curtained-off ER cubicle at Desert Springs Hospital. Smeared mascara, absent lipstick, curls stained and coated with demon residue at the ends. And a back that looked like roadkill, but at least that didn't show now. I smiled breezily at him. "Pucker up and get some of this."

He snorted. "Tempting, but as you said, that's not us, and the fact that you smell like demon isn't helping. That"—he closed the magazine on his knee—"is not a good smell."

At that moment, before I could take offense—and I would have—my cell phone rang. It was Griffin. "Zeke?" I said immediately. "Is he all right?"

Griffin's exhausted voice returned. "He's on a ventilator, but should be off in a few days. He has a chest tube and has gotten two transfusions so far, but they say he'll be good as new in a few weeks. He'll be up and taking candy from babies in no time."

To be fair, that kid had stolen that candy from some other child first. It wasn't his candy to begin with. Zeke was merely repossessing stolen goods. That he kept it taught a valuable lesson to the victim about being more careful not to leave your candy lying around.

And Zeke, well, Zeke liked his candy.

"Good," I said, exhaling. "Good. Now go to sleep yourself. And, Griffin, you know you're the strongest empath the House has. Work on it or it'll do you more harm than good." Empaths were rare among humans and the Houses tended to recruit every one of them they could find, but none was close to Griffin's level.

"I know. I made things worse tonight. If you hadn't been there . . . shit." He didn't want to think about that possibility and neither did I.

"Go to sleep," I repeated. "I'm going home now and doing the same."

"Trixa," he said quietly, slowly, "will there be scars?"

It took me a second to grasp what he was asking. "Oh. On my back?" I laughed, winced as the pain spiked through the cotton wool of the pain pills the nurse had already given me, then laughed again. "Griff, I don't care about that. If a guy wouldn't want me because I had scars, why would I want his superficial son of a bitch ass? Now go to bed, all right? And call me in the morning to give me an update on Zeke."

"I will." He hesitated. "You're sure about the scars?"

"Sweetie, I'm not half as vain as you. Sleep," I ordered, then disconnected.

"Vain enough to want me to sneak a look," Leo drawled as he discarded the magazine and stood.

"Well, I'm not vain, but I'm not dead either," I retorted, sliding off the gurney. The shock that ran from my feet to my back was bearable. Yes, pain pills were my friend.

In the car, Leo sat behind the wheel for a few silent seconds and then turned and kissed my temple. "You have to be more careful," he said soberly. "You have to be on your game."

"I know. I do. Those were high-level demons out

there—but I was cocky too." I shook my head. "It's not like me."

He snorted and started the car. "It's exactly like you. It always has been. And you've always gotten away with it. I hope this time's no different."

Back at my apartment I couldn't shower without removing the medicine from my back; at least that was what grizzly-paw nurse had told me. I turned the taps until the water barely fizzled out and I washed my front, slowly and carefully. I bent forward and washed my hair, then stepped outside of the curtain wrapped around the claw-foot tub into a warm towel held by Leo. He made sure it draped only over the front of me and I held it to my shoulders. Sitting on the edge of the bed, I closed my eyes as he dried my hair with a smaller towel and combed it out, careful with the tangles, and I had a ton. The price you paid for wildly curly hair. That and humidity is never your friend. But soon it was its usual damp cascade of waves and corkscrew curls that followed a bath or shower.

He touched the pale gold skin beside my almond-shaped eye and then touched one of my curls, a deep black one with a streak of red and a hint of bronze, pulled at it lightly, and watched as the spiral sprang back. "How can you be so many things at once and make it all work?"

I leaned forward and kissed him beside his mouth . . . kissed him for his help and a little more. "Why are you asking silly questions?" I tugged at a long strand of his hair before sliding under the covers nude, lying on my stomach with the sheet and coverlet only up to my waist. I wanted nothing but air touching my back tonight.

I watched as Leo went to my closet for one of my

many spare shotguns and sat in a chair a little too puffy for his tastes, I was sure, but the reds and golds of the cloth suited him. "Babysitting?" I asked.

"You know Solomon was behind this." He looked over the Browning, semi-automatic and self-loading. He nodded approvingly. It was new. An impulse buy from a basement with a lot of unpleasant men, one of whom didn't appreciate me or my favorite copper-colored boots. He was so damn lucky his blood came out of the fine stitching or I might have gone back to that basement to try out my new purchase.

Just to scare him, of course.

Boots were just boots, not worth a human life. Although, technically, without DNA proof, I wasn't jumping on that guy being on the human bandwagon just yet.

I didn't need DNA to know Solomon wasn't human . . . at least not all of the time.

I doubled the pillow with my arm and rested my head against it. "Probably. No matter how interested he is in me, he might be getting tired of our games and I'm sure the other demons tease him about his human pest problem, pyromaniac cockroaches." My lips curved. "Poor Solomon. No one will do lunch with him anymore or take his calls. I doubt he even makes his soul quota, what with his obsessing over us all the time."

But it wasn't just us or just me. Solomon had another obsession, one I thought we shared. A big powerful demon here these past few years, rumblings at Eden House . . . Solomon had come to Vegas for a reason. Hadn't we all?

The Light of Life.

We all wanted it, only who had it now? Someone had wasted his time torturing that poor old caver. If the demons or the House had it, we'd know about it. I'd know about it. The heavens themselves would know about it. But no one knew. It was still out there. I still had my chance to get it and make things right.

"If he visits tonight, he can spend his time obsessing over his castration," Leo said calmly, breaking open the shotgun to make sure it was loaded. Take no chances . . . that was Leo. "Do what you have to do. Be who you have to be with him. Be true to yourself." His black eyes were darker than Lenore's feathers. "But not tonight. No taunting, no teasing, and none of the other things I don't care to think about. Tonight you sleep."

"If only your father knew," I said, my eyelids already falling fast. "See what you've become inside."

"I doubt my father will ever know me again or care to." He turned out the light on my bedside table. "He can't forget. I was bad . . . evil." Being around demons will show you the real meaning of the word *evil*, and how people so rarely see the real thing even when it's right in front of their faces.

"Not evil." I let my eyes shut, remembering a younger Leo.

He snorted sharply.

"Not good." I gave in a little. "But not evil. You had a . . . wildness in you."

"Evil," he repeated with a sigh. "Don't sugarcoat it. I was what I was. I'm different now. But back then, I was evil."

And, honestly, yes, he had been more than a toe over the Dark Side. More like a California commute over. Hours from the line we all walk. Going, going, gone.

But he'd come back, and while he wasn't now, he had been then—evil. Bad as they came.

"You were." I reached out blindly and rested a hand on his knee. "Love you anyway."

"What about the bad old days? What about then?" Patient, undemanding—all with cold steel across his knees. A quiet and serene hunter.

I told him the truth. I had to. It was Leo. I curled my fingers into the warmth under his knee . . . seconds away from sleep.

"Even then," I whispered.

The next morning, after Leo helped clean and cream up my back again and then left to open the bar, I noticed it. It was the smallest fleck of dark brown in a crease of my knuckle. Could've been dirt, but it wasn't. It was blood. A tiny remnant of Zeke left on me. It had somehow survived two showers, that one stubborn speck. Even his blood was stubborn.

I scrubbed at it thoroughly with a washcloth until it was gone. My skin was red and abraded, but the blood was gone. I shouldn't have let Zeke and Griffin get to me. I'd known that from day one, the day I'd let two wary teenagers into my bar, handed them cleaning supplies and enough money for breakfast until we got the deep fryers going. I'd known I shouldn't get attached. They weren't like puppies you planned to find good homes for. No, I'd known I'd be seeing the wary blond one and his emotionally frozen friend with the lost eyes for a long time. Seeing, yes? But not getting close to.

Not puppies. More like that sweet, sweet neighbor who lived next door. Ninety-five if she was a day. Made you cookies or told you stories or whatever sweet old people did . . . sweet old people who died the moment you got attached. Granted I hadn't had cookie-making neighbors next to the bar, just winos, a porn shop, and a strip club. But I'd seen movies about it, getting attached, and I wasn't going to do it. I had Leo and everything else . . . everyone else was expendable until I found out who killed Kimano. It had to be that way. Had to.

Lying to yourself, it's an art.

That's what I'd thought back then. It hadn't lasted long, a week maybe—a week of feeding them and watching them twitch and duck their heads every time someone walked into the bar. Watching for cops, social services, or a vague but terrifying authority figure only an on-the-run teen could imagine, the one with the icy clamp of hand on the junction of neck and shoulder just when you might think you were safe. Griffin and Zeke had been a thousand times worse than the most vulnerable and cute damn puppy.

I'd gotten attached. And it hurt. It hurt like hell.

"Bitch alert. Bitch alert," Lenore cawed as I came through the door at the base of my apartment stairs.

That only deepened the scowl I felt on my face. "The deep fryer works on more than just cheese, you know, bird," I threatened.

Unimpressed, he cleaned his feathers, then flew to the window, unlocked the catch with his beak, pushed at the glass until it swung sideways, and flew out. There was a shotgun lying on the bar—Leo's way of telling me he was going to be out for a while and I decided that was it. No more. The bar was closed today. Except for clients—I was expecting two or three. The rest of the time I could spend on the phone, trying to get information from my own contacts. Someone somewhere had to know something more about the Light.

I tried Robin again. There was no answer other than an imaginatively erotic, borderline-pornographic voice mail recording. From there I went down the list, hitting every single one I could think of who might know anything—and not have an agenda of their own. That left out Ishiah in New York. He wasn't Eden House, but it was possible he'd swing their way more than mine. I couldn't be sure about him. He was like a lapsed Catholic—you never knew when he might get God again. It wasn't worth the risk. Above could kiss my ass . . . the Light was mine.

In between calls my clients came knocking. One lady wanted to know where her cheating husband had holed up with their money and his mistress. It was a quick ten thousand. "Don't kill the mistress," I said matter-of-factly as I counted the money. "She's nineteen. Stupid. Doesn't know better."

Bitter eyes narrowed behind expensive, tinted sunglasses. "And my husband?"

I smiled coolly. "He most definitely knows better, but you don't want to go to prison, do you, sugar?" He'd also once had a business partner who liked to fly Piper Cubs as a hobby. One day that partner went up and nobody ever found out where he came down. But her husband, he might not have known where, but he knew why. He was a cheat and a liar and, I strongly suspected, a killer. I trusted myself enough that strongly suspected was good enough for me. Give a lady a fish and she eats for the day; teach a lady to fish and she finds the yacht her cheating spouse is living it up on, puts his ass in jail, and lives on their money for a lifetime. Maybe hires a few dancing pool boys—and good for her.

"The guy next door at the porn shop has a brother who's a private detective. Good one too. You might want to have him take a look at your husband's work-related past, especially his deceased partner," I offered as I stacked the bills. "And, Mrs. D?" I added as she stood. "Happiness is the trifecta of no means, no motive, and an unbreakable alibi." I was just full of fortune cookie wisdom these past few days. "I doubt your husband has that lucky ticket."

I dealt with two more clients, fewer fees, and a very small commission from the porn guy—not all clients need just one thing. All in all a good day. Right up until the moment Solomon appeared. He didn't bother with the door. He solidified into the shadows behind the bar and walked forward to pull down a wineglass from the overhead rack. "White, red, or . . . pink?" He raised an eyebrow.

I was fairly certain you weren't supposed to mix alcohol with painkillers. Maybe the serrated combat knife I pulled from my boot and tossed at his chest was a bit of an overreaction to his lack of medical knowledge, and the movement did rip at the nerve endings of my back, but I wasn't sorry either way.

He didn't bother to dodge, only grunted as the knife slammed into him, and then went on to pour himself a glass of red. He drank half of it before he reached down and pulled free the knife, buried blade deep in his chest. He rested it on the top of the bar, where it dripped ebon. "Maybe tea would be better. A teaspoon of honey might improve your mood." He smiled that smoky smile. "Sweeten you up, my Trixa."

I could've gotten up and walked over to the shotgun that lay beside the knife on the bar, but it was far and I was tired. I was also curious. Curious, pissed, wary, and working it. Always working it. "Siccing several demons on me is not the way to my heart, believe it or not."

"I didn't expect them to do that much damage." He furrowed his brow, the dark slashes of eyebrows pulled into a V. "I expected more from you. I definitely didn't expect you to get hurt. You're better than that. At least you always have been. You're not losing your touch, surely?"

"Would you lose interest in me then? If I killed a few fewer demons?" I asked.

"If you were a little less lethal, a little less demonically destructive in your habits? Perhaps my interest would fade. It's an interesting question. I'll have to think on it. Now . . . honey in your tea or not?" he asked pleasantly.

Sighing, I leaned back very carefully and answered, "Four teaspoons of sugar *and* four of honey. And what about the other demons? Some of them were higher level. Why would they work for you?"

"Living life on the diabetic edge, are we?" he said with humor as he started on the tea. "There is high-level and then there's me. You should keep that in mind. Now enjoy your diabetes."

"I will. Life is short. I doubt I need to tell you that, Solomon." I was amused too; it seemed to confuse him, but he wouldn't have admitted it. I'd confused Solomon for years now. It could be one of the reasons he hadn't tried to kill me . . . at least personally. Solomon had been around a long time. Things that confused him, interested him, confounded his devil ass, were bound to be few and far between.

Which was what had kept him focused on me. At least until now, although he could be telling the truth. He could've thought we were up to the fight last night, and if we hadn't been so overly confident, maybe we would have been. I'd not been so sloppy since I could remember. I disgusted myself, but there was a time and a place for self-recrimination, and while facing a demon was not it.

"No, you do not have to tell me about the shortness of life." Stirring the honey into my cup, he added casually, "I doubt you have to tell your friends Griffin and Zeke so either."

"Not the way to get on my good side," I said flatly.

The relationship between Solomon and me was complex . . . if complex grew up and developed a multiple personality.

He'd been in Vegas thirteen years to my ten, from what information I could gather, and had shown up at my place three years ago. I'd known he was a demon the second I saw him. Too handsome, too smooth, too rock star, movie star, too everything. And he couldn't have been more perfectly designed to appeal to me physically. Dark hair, the shadowed eyes, the warmly wicked smile. Leo from a different time . . . a wilder time. I did have a type and demons were nothing if not good at sizing up someone's type. But there was a difference between Leo and Solomon. Leo had been a chaos of blackness, rapids over the rocks, with serious, *serious* father issues. Solomon's darkness was the opposite—the glass-smooth surface of a river with an undertow that would pull you in and drown you in seconds.

I had known that Leo had a spark of light in him. Maybe I exaggerated when I thought goodness . . .

maybe it was more a spark of reason. As for demons, did they have glimmers of good? They were once angels. Did they have the occasional doubt about what they did? And just what was it they did do? Kill, okay. Any sociopath alive could explain why they did that—simply because they wanted to. But bargaining for souls? I was sure plenty of souls ended up "downtown" anyway. Why would they need more?

"What do you do with the souls you bargain for?" I asked, changing the subject to something other than Zeke and Griffin. If I hadn't, I'd have to shoot Solomon, although half the blame was mine, and that wasn't the most delicate way of getting information out of someone. It tended to cut down on their cooperation fairly quickly.

"We eat them." He sat opposite me and set the mug before me. He leaned back in his chair and linked fingers across the dark gray shirt covering his stomach. "Don't look so surprised. We have to get energy from somewhere. Lucifer is but a fallen angel himself. He can't feed us the way the angels are fed by the Glory and the Grace." He almost had a touch of respect as he said the last, still remembering how it had felt. "And some of us require much more energy than those lower demons you kill so easily"—he paused, obviously considering the night before—"usually with ease, at any rate."

"So all demons aren't created equal?" That was interesting—with more power came more need.

"Hardly. The hierarchies that existed above exist below. Those mud- and slime-colored demons that are so prevalent were the lowest of angels. Former messengers. If you'd ripped off their wings, they may as well have been human. Pigeons," he snorted in disdain. "Before the Rebellion came, they might as well have been flying Heaven's Hallmark cards here and there. They have none of our glory."

I guessed in some higher angels' eyes that hanging around with humans was their version of slumming it. But if you were a fallen angel, it became automatic. Ironic. Nope. More like karmic. I drank the tea. If Solomon were going to try to kill me, poisoned honey would not be his weapon of choice.

So Solomon had been a high-and-mighty angel in his day. It figured. He was simply too arrogant to have been anything else. "A soul is just a snack, then." After all that's said and done, it was sad to have that luminous quality ending up as something akin to a Happy Meal. It was a great pity for those who didn't know the value of what lived in them. "At least there's plenty to go around. Billions of humans, but not so many demons. Exactly how many of you guys are there anyway?"

"Not enough, and we can't grow. God can create, but Lucifer cannot." The gray eyes were grim—the ashes of a crusader's loss. "There's a war on. A cold war at the moment, but still a war. Surely you knew that. I know a good little girl like you went to Sunday School."

"Actually I had a problem with shellfish being an abomination." The tea was good, hot and sweet. I smiled and tapped a nail on the table. "I do love my oyster shooters. Hard to respect a god who won't let me have that."

"You're Jewish?" he asked, momentarily distracted.

"No, Solomon, just a smart-ass." I drank more of the tea. It was soothing. I'd had a hard night. I could use a little soothing.

"As if that's news to me," he said with an almost-indulgent smile. "So, what do you know about the Light of Life?"

Ah. Not a routine seduction visit. Hun the pervert had sold me out or else Solomon had followed another rumor. Solomon was here for a reason far from sex and a very good reason it was too. The Light of Life. And why not? Solomon had to be one of Below's top players. Who better to send looking? And as he said, there was a war on. Not an out-and-out war. More of a cold war. No angels storming Hell, no demons assaulting Heaven. Not yet. The demons simply didn't have the numbers, and if you didn't have that, then you needed some other edge. Such as the Light.

"I know you're nowhere near that to me yet." I tilted my gaze over the mug's edge. "Not the light of my life. Not my reason for being. Not my pookie-bear. But you keep trying, Solomon. Maybe one day you'll get there."

He stood in a motion so smooth and fast he put a cheetah to shame. Slamming both hands down on the table, he demanded darkly, "You've been sniffing around. Don't think I don't see that. Don't for an instant think I don't know. Now, *tell* me about the Light."

I nodded at his right hand, where my second combat knife had just been embedded through the flesh and bone into the table beneath it. This time it was the other way around—a demon underestimated me. "I know a Snoopy Band-Aid should take care of that." I also knew the hand was quicker than the human eye. And demons were quicker than that, but not in this case. He appeared sincerely surprised. Why, I wasn't sure. If I had one knife in my one boot for his chest, what did he think I had in the other one? Tickets to *Spamalot*?

Men.

Demons.

I might have miscalculated with the second category last night, but they returned the favor on a daily basis. Although usually not Solomon. Outside of the House of Eden's hunters, I might be the only nondemon he respected. But apparently he didn't respect me quite enough. I thought I'd just changed that and that put me one up on what Solomon thought of Eden House hunters.

Hunters . . . Zeke. Griffin. I put the mug down as Solomon yanked the knife, blood dripping from the serrated edge, from his hand. Pretty. But not pretty enough to make me forget. If Zeke had died, I would've killed Solomon the moment he'd stepped from the shadows. I'd have taken that shotgun and ended whatever this thing was we had between us. I'd tried so hard not to let anything interfere with seeking vengeance for Kimano, but Zeke and Griffin, no matter how much I wanted to deny it, had stepped into a place close to his. To the right, to the left. Not his spot in my heart, but near . . . very near. My brothers, whether I wanted them to be or not—whether they screwed up my plans or not. They had done it and I'd seen it coming, tried to stop it, but in the end . . .

That Zeke was in the same shape made Solomon the luckiest demon alive.

"You really should be Eden House. You're quick. So very quick." He flipped the blade, ignoring the black blood staining his fingers, and offered the handle to me. "For a human."

"I'm a savant. Some are good with music, some math. I'm very, very good with sharp things." I took the knife and gave an internal sigh at the cleaning job lying ahead, bound to clog up the dishwasher. "Some of us might be born hunters, but that doesn't mean it's the path we have to choose. Officially. I like my independence. I don't need any little social clubs like Eden House to back me up." I gave a triple flip of the blade and caught it by the black rubber handle again. "What could they possibly have to offer me except chains?"

His hand had healed in an instant, the same as his chest had. "You're not telling me a thing, are you?"

I waved fingers at him and drank more of my tea. "Don't worry. I'm not telling Eden House anything either. If God wants the Light, Above will have to come begging to me, just like you did. And they'll get the same thing right now. Nothing."

"God?" he repeated, appearing genuinely astonished. "You think God has anything to do with this? With Eden House?"

I frowned. "He doesn't?"

He shook his head. "And you thought you knew it all, didn't you? No. God has been hands-off since the Rebellion. The angels with free will have taken it upon themselves to form a middle management, if you will. To carry on Heaven's work or what they think Heaven's work might be. God didn't start Eden House. Man did. And then angels took advantage of it. Why soil their lily-white hands when they can get Man to do it for them? Why fight demons when Eden House will train soldiers to stand in their place?"

"And what does God think of all this?" I asked.

Shrugging lightly, he replied with a trace of melancholy, "I'm a demon. I don't know God's word or will anymore."

"And the angels?"

"I don't think they know either. God is the sun to

them now, warm, loving, but silent. Distant." He was silent as well for a moment, remembering or thinking, before he finally mused, the gray of his eyes lightened to an almost silver, "You're fortunate that I find you so . . . unique. Be careful of your back, Trixa. You humans, so fragile."

From most demons . . . I would've said all demons up until then . . . that would've sounded like a threat. This didn't sound like that. This sounded different. Like Solomon was different. But what was that difference? There was a thought that kept turning round and round in my head. A little kid's whirligig, spinning. Always spinning. Black, then red, then silver, and which was real? Which was true?

Black.

Red.

Silver.

"I didn't mean for you to be hurt. I didn't mean for our game to go this far," he said softly, eyes inscrutable. "We're angels, you know. Fallen, but still angels."

Then the door opened behind him and he disappeared into the shadow of it. Sank into the puddle of darkness on the floor. Angels . . .

Who ate souls, but had to if he wanted to survive. An angel who bargained for souls, but always gave fair trade. Gave you what you asked for. Even the Better Business Bureau couldn't fault him there.

Angels or demons or both . . . and I had a headache. But I also had a client and this one couldn't wait.

"Did you find him?" She was thirteen years old and not living on the street, but not precisely living off the street either. Her hair was long, lank brown and hadn't been washed in a few days, and her frame was skinny but not too skinny. She was getting food somewhere. She probably hung out around the shelters. I didn't ask her name because I knew it. Alone. She was alone in the world and when she thought of herself, that's probably the only thing she called herself. Alone. Until a few weeks ago, but the past few days had been a return to that alone.

Kimano, Zeke, Griffin, Solomon, the Light . . . they were all things beyond me at the moment, but not this. I grinned and whistled. There was a skittering of paws and a dog just as brown as its owner came speeding out of the kitchen, half a hot dog still hanging from his mouth. Brown, yes. Lank like the girl, no. He was round like a beach ball.

Wary blue eyes turned clear in an instant and she scooped up the homely hound. It snarfed the last of the meat and licked her face enthusiastically. "Koko." She didn't care about her own name, but the dog . . . the dog had a name. She squeezed her eyes shut for a moment as she hugged him and when they opened again, they were just as wary as in the beginning. "How much?"

"This one's pro bono," I said, grinning back at the dog. Two of a kind we were. We saw life and hot dogs and seized the day. Carpe diem. Carpe canis. Beef canis. Pork canis. Kosher canis. As long as it had mustard and relish, we were good. Right, doggy? The tongue lolled at me in what I was sure was agreement.

The girl's forehead wrinkled at the pro bono and I elaborated, "Free."

"Nothing is free," she said with prompt suspicion.

"Just come by next weekend and clean out the alley and we'll call it even." I finished my tea. "And come by any afternoon and my bar guy Leo will feed Koko. I like dogs." I leaned across the table and tickled Koko's belly.

"What about people?" She lowered her head and the brown hair spilled forward, hiding her face.

"People I can take or leave." I moved to the dog's chin and it kicked its back legs ecstatically. "But Leo is a softy. If he likes you, he might even feed you too."

She snorted. "Find my dog for nothing. Free food. You're a sucker."

I laughed. No one . . . *no one*, not in my entire life, had called me a sucker. "Leo will like you all right. He'll feed you breakfast, lunch, and dinner if you want. It'll be greasy, but it'll be food." I jerked a thumb. "Go out the back through the kitchen. If you happen to see any food lying around, help yourself."

She hesitated. "Aren't you going to even ask my name?"

"You don't know your name. When you figure out what it is, then you can tell me," I said with a yawn. "And it's not Alone. That's no kind of name for anyone. So think on it."

She vanished almost as quickly as Solomon had, but I doubt he'd taken a loaf of bread and an industrial-sized package of cheese with him. Too bad. He might have found that tastier than eating souls.

The rest of the day I spent napping and popping one more pain pill. They give you weird dreams, those pills. Bright colors, drifting like the wind. I saw Kimano again, but always out of reach. Always moving away. Always leaving me behind. The same as ever they were, only in brighter colors . . . more real, and if I had been just a little faster, I could've touched him.

Touched his skin. Turned him to see the laughter in his
eyes.

Later that night I flushed the rest of the pills down
the toilet. Numb my back and claw my heart; it wasn't
a good exchange.

Not at all.

Chapter 6

The next morning I went hiking—that would be "hiking" with quotes around it and a good amount of subtext. Leo didn't want to go with me—he said the limp, shuffle, drag of my hiking boots was giving him flashbacks. I wasn't sure if those flashbacks were to the last Mummy movie he'd seen or some previous work he'd had at a nursing home as an orderly. Grumbling and bitching aside, he came along in the end. He also brought snacks and a cooler. At least he was good for something, I told him.

"You'll be begging for that something one day," he challenged, "and I might not give it to you. Ever think of that, 'boss'?"

We swapped glances, both responded "Nah," with a grin, and I started the car. He shrugged and propped his cowboy-booted feet out the window; it was the only way he'd fit in my little racing bug of a car even with the top down. "But there's no denying you've always liked the bad boys. Robin, for example, he couldn't keep it in his pants if an alligator was undoing the zipper."

"Oh, come on. You're exaggerating." He wasn't. "And the donkey thing. That was a complete lie." I was hoping. "Total urban legend." I turned on a country music station. I didn't like country music really, but lately the women singers were stomping the hell out of their cheating, lying, no-good men. Blowing up their trucks, setting their houses on fire . . . righteous vengeance. Maybe I should sign up for Eden House. And, lo, we shall smite the sinner with good old country girl ingenuity—all we need are boots and lighter fluid. "And you're one to talk. You dated that one with the boob job five years ago." I steadied the wheel with both knees while I held out my hands about two feet in front of me. "They were bigger than the Himalayas. I swear I saw a goat grazing in there, and its shepherd probably suffocated on her perfume." I dated the bad. Leo dated the bimbos.

He snorted. "Wake me up when we get there."

In Vegas there are two places: your destination and then the circles of Hell called construction you have to pass through to get there. This time they'd been doing construction under the Spaghetti Bowl, the intersection of I-15 and U.S. 95, for more than a month. Every time I passed through it, I used it as an educational experience to watch the pearification of a man's ass and to practice the curse words of every language I knew, which, considering how much I'd traveled in my youth, were more than a few. Some days it was entertaining if I didn't have anyplace better to be. Some days, as I watched an entire line of men sit on a guardrail and do nothing but swig Gatorade and work on their tans instead of the pavement, it got old.

Today it was old. Very, very old.

Until it wasn't.

I finally wove my way inch by inch through the orange barrels, and had just snailed my way beneath the shadow of the overpass when the squeal was first heard. Failing brakes, the heart-banging crumple-crunch of metal against asphalt, and in my rearview mirror, the truck tumbling over the side. Its cab's front wheels caught at the last minute and out of the back catapulted hundreds of cans of red paint. They hit the asphalt, popped their tops, and geysered the scarlet fluid high in the air . . . into a sudden gust of wind that pushed the flood of it sideways. Every still-unmoving, gaping-mouthed "worker" out there was coated in it.

Now wasn't that lucky?

I put on my brakes and turned for a better look. "Ha!" said the truck driver who'd scrambled to safety. He was pointing down at the workers on the road beneath the overpass. "Take that, you lazy-ass motherfuckers. Next time you hear brakes, I bet you get off that fat ass just like that." He went on ranting as road worker arms were flung out, dripping red, and blank-eyed bodies shambled through a river of red paint. It was pretty as any picture in those fancy art galleries you'd find in the casinos. I tucked the mental picture away for later savoring as I stepped on the gas again, still watching it all in the mirror until it faded from sight.

Blood from the sky. Who knew laziness would trigger the Apocalypse?

Which put me in the mood for some old, cheesy eighties, heavy metal music, and I listened to that all the way up to the caver's hovel. When I stopped the car in a cloud of dust, Leo yawned, lifted his hat, and grunted, "I feel very, very angry and in the need of hair spray and a pentacle-studded leather codpiece. Your doing?"

I ignored him and pointed out the shack. "That's where his body was. I think our best bet is to go into town"—a couple of more shacks and a few mobile homes—"and check out his friends when they come down for supplies." Today was the day everyone stocked up and caught up. I found that out with a little earlier investigation. But there would be one—one who wouldn't show up. That would be the one we'd have to go tracking. Jeb had told Hun; he would've told someone else. Hun couldn't be counted as anyone's best friend and closest and only confidante.

"Too bad your last girlfriend isn't here. The Amazon. She could've piggybacked us into the mountains." I started the car back toward town.

"She wasn't an Amazon. She was a nice girl," he said with a calm that was possibly more annoying than the Amazon had been.

"She was six foot five if she was an inch. She could've taken off that belly ring, put it around my neck, and led me about like one of those little yappy dogs." All right, maybe she'd only been six foot one, but she had been taller than she deserved and her stiletto stripper shoes made her even taller.

"Funny you should say that." His lips curved. "You're not the first."

I narrowed my eyes behind dark sunglasses. "She did not."

"Said you'd be her first shiksa-poo. She could get one for all her friends. They'd be the toast of the temple."

I narrowed my eyes further and a brown finger wagged once. "Nuh uh, little girl." He emphasized "little," the bastard. "That's not how it works. We don't screen one another's hookups or dates. No retaliation, no matter how low our opinion, remember? Which means you can't fill her car with mating tarantulas . . . again."

"Fine. Fine," I said irritably as we pulled into town.

We talked to the dusty locals, who knew all of Jeb the Caver's friends. Turned out Jeb even had a last name: McVann. "One-sixteenth Indian, he was," said one old guy who'd been around long enough for that term to go from politically correct, to incorrect, to back again without any idea things had ever changed. "Get the old sot drunk and he'd go on and on so much, you'd think he'd been the one to stick the arrow in Custer's dick at Little Bighorn himself."

He, one Artie Beaver, served me another canned lemonade at his trailer/refreshment stand. "Yeah, he was all about the land and saving your home. I told him if the Indians had saved their home, fifteen-sixteenths of his ass'd be back in Scotland drinking warm beer and wearing a kilt." He shrugged. Artie was a big guy, happy and helpful, but he didn't know much more than that. He knew Jeb was dead and that his friends would be down today to say a few words, restock, and head back up. And for a few dollars he'd point them out for me. I handed over the money willingly. Artie was working hard entertaining me. He deserved to be paid.

"Guess he just wanted roots." He carefully swiped at my rickety plastic table. If he'd wiped too hard, it probably would've collapsed under the attention. It was older than Methuselah and cheaper than a bleached-blond, teenage pop star. "We all want roots, right?"

But sometimes only the ones we pick. Still, that might have been why Jeb found the Light. He believed in saving and protecting. No better person around here to have found it. Leo and I sat and watched as the day dragged on. It was comfortable. I didn't miss the summer heat. I enjoyed it when it was there and I enjoyed the cooler temperatures when it was gone. Mama had taught us that. Appreciate what you can't change, and change what you can't appreciate. She was as tough as the mountains around us and filled to the brim with common sense. I liked to think she'd passed that on to me, but she'd also said more than once that I wasn't half as clever as I thought I was. Considering what I thought of myself, that still made me pretty damn clever. That attitude had gotten me more than a swat or two when I was younger. I'd learned to temper my self-belief in my quick wits with a dash of caution. It wasn't enough. A swat to my ass was still waiting for me at every family reunion. I yawned, stretched my legs out, and let Leo be my eyes for a while. I didn't nap, but I let the world slide gently out of focus.

"How's your back?" Leo asked.

"Well, I'm off it, unlike your Amazonian ex, so that's something," I retorted, resting a shoulder against the iron pole holding up the canopy.

"This is ridiculous. If you would just . . . ," he started.

"No."

He sighed and passed over two Tylenol, a far stretch from what my back really needed, but it would have to do. "Once, my brother lied and told my father, this was after he and I stopped speaking, that I was spending time with you. . . ." He shook his head, the black braid undulating along his back. "I heard that the old bastard laughed so long and hard that he choked on his venison and passed out at the table."

Our families were familiar with one another, to say the least, and we followed the same general ideological path, had the same long lineage. What my family knew of the world, Leo's knew equally as well. We hadn't grown up next door, hardly anything that mundane with the travel blood so strong in me and mine, but we passed their way now and again. Leo's family had what Jeb had wanted: roots. Leo could follow his family back as long as I could, an oral history that put the most convoluted and far-reaching of family trees to shame. Back to the mammoths and beyond wouldn't be an exaggeration. A historian would be foaming at the mouth to talk to him. Of all of his family, though, only Leo was a wanderer now. When you're kicked out of house and home, you don't have much choice.

"Did he think I would be a little much for you?" I rested my sunglasses in my hair.

"More than that. He thought you'd be the death of me." He pulled off his hat and waved it at a raven far overhead. "And I'm not so sure he would be wrong."

"Chicken," I teased. "Oh, come on. Where's the harm? Lots of twosomes do just fine. Friends or lovers, and living it up." I toasted him with the can of lemonade.

"Like Butch and Sundance?" he said knowingly. "Thelma and Louise? Romeo and Juliet? Nitroglycerin and a pogo stick?"

"Don't be so dramatic," I tsked as I finished the flat lemon drink. "And I think the wake has started. Let's go see who didn't show up."

About six people were there, including the truck molester. We mixed and mingled. I'd dressed down. Leo looked like he looked. We had "good folk" written all over us. After some talking, we discovered the only friend of Jeb's missing was John Wilbur. I'd wriggled directions to the guy's place out of Artie. Normally, he wouldn't have, but I was playing cute and feisty for all I was worth and Leo was dessert from the looks of him. Charisma, Leo and I had it in spades when we wanted. Demons weren't the only ones who could bring out the flash, and even Artie couldn't stand against it. "You'd make great con men," he'd grumbled as we took off.

Isn't it great when your calling and your work are the same?

It was dark by the time we reached John Wilbur's short, squat mobile home. There was a bright generator light flooding the place and the sand around it. In that sand someone had literally drawn the line. And it surrounded the trailer in a circle twice as brilliant as the generator light. My sunglasses were in the glove compartment, although I wished I had them back as I shaded my eyes for a better look. Flakes—minute flakes of glass or crystal made up the circle, and the fact they glowed almost as bright as the sun said one thing and one thing only.

The Light. They came from the Light.

Leo mirrored my frown. "Someone knows something."

There was the faintest of sounds behind us. A whisper of sand. A rustle of cloth against cloth.

"Our Mr. Wilbur is clever . . . for a human." The tone was so bored. So very "have been there and had a stained-glass window designed in my image." So "Why oh why must I suffer the indignity of discoursing with the unfaithful and the sinning?" I turned and considered shooting the angel dead center in his chest. It wouldn't be the first time I'd shot one. But I knew if I did, he would bleed a ray of luminous white light for a few seconds; then he would be whole again. It would be all for nothing. While the angel I had once shot had deserved it, I wasn't sure this one did simply for being annoyingly superior and in the right place at the right time—when I wished he weren't.

"Look at this. Temptation in the desert, but it's not the devil this time—only a parakeet with delusions of grandeur." I kept the gun aimed at him. Truthfully, I wasn't sure you could kill an angel. Then again, maybe the same would hold for them as held for demons. If you could keep their bodies anchored on Earth and blow out their brains ... After all, as Solomon had said, he was an angel too—simply a fallen one. Seemed what would work for one, destruction-wise, would work for the other. I'd never had the need to put it to the test. Yet. But if he got between me and the Light, that might change.

And where did angels and demons go when they "died"? Because it was death, at least for a demon. They didn't go back down to Hell for a little detention and pop up again later. At least, I'd never seen one that had. Once the brain was gone, it was gone for good. What then? Per their doctrine, there was no place higher to step up to for the angels and no lower for the demons, right?

Curious.

So was death really and truly death for them? The nothingness of nonexistence?

Maybe I'd ask this one. "Hey," I started, until a familiar elbow impacted my side. Leo. He knew exactly what I was thinking. He usually did.

"Sorry." I gave in, not graciously, but I did give in. A great woman had once said, *The cure for boredom is curiosity. There is no cure for curiosity.* That did describe me down to the molecular level, but, sadly, there was a time and place. This was not it. I nudged my thoughts back to the more important matter at hand: the Light.

The angel that was here to fetch it was a man in the same way that demons are men. Although, to give credit, demons were women too. Same MO. Female demons were just as drop-dead gorgeous as the males, sweating unbelievable sex appeal, the eye of a hurricane of pheromones—the whole nine yards. Demons were equal-opportunity salespeople. We'll take your soul, male, female; bring whatever you have and we'll be whatever you want. But now that I thought about it, the few angels I'd seen had always been male. It made me a little sorry that I hadn't shot this one after all. Sexist pigeon.

Instead, I asked, "What do you want here?" I knew very well what he wanted. "Never mind," I dismissed him. "Whatever it is, you're not getting it. Take a hike, or a flight, and don't look back. Turning into a pillar of salt would be the least of your concerns."

I hadn't seen his wings, but now I noticed a shimmer of dark purple-blue light hit a curve, almost as if the wings were there but made of glass. Solemn, promising eyes of the same twilight color peered through his white-blond bangs. "Trixa. Leo. We've been waiting for you." Then he smiled and I was *in* that twilight . . . a glorious spring one, warm and silken. Surrounded by it. Caressed.

I looked over to see a faint sweat over the cords of Leo's neck. "Really?" I said, surprised. "You go that way now and again? I had no idea."

"No, I don't. And you do have an attention span. *Use* it," he gritted, flushing lightly before turning his head to the right. "Well, shit," he said in disgust.

Solomon, our Solomon, stepped out of the darkness there. I knew he was up to his neck in this—might've even killed Jeb himself. It hadn't looked like a demon kill—had lacked a certain level of violence and definitely didn't smell like demon—but it wasn't beyond him to fake it to look otherwise. I had no idea who had done Jeb in, Eden House or a demon. Either way, Solomon *was* in the game; that I'd known for some time. "Whatever this molting chicken has to tell you isn't worth hearing," he said, giving a dismissive nod at the angel.

"That's probably true. It's probably true about you too." I met his gray eyes as I took a step toward the curve of light in the sand.

"If that's what you imagine it to be, do you think it will be that easy?" he asked with a shadow of amused arrogance underlying the question.

"You never know. Not until you ask nicely." I did ask—in my mind. I asked quite courteously if I might enter. I heard nothing, saw no mystical signs, but took a chance anyway and stepped over. I felt nothing more than a warm tingle that shimmered from my head to my toes—not to say that wasn't enjoyable and it definitely beat disintegration or slamming into an invisible wall, which the angel promptly did. "Look at that, Solomon," I said, giving the angel a sassy and unrepentant smile as he hauled his holy ass back to his feet. "See where a little politeness will get you? A nice invitation—that's what." I tossed my gun to Leo. It was allowed through the same as I had been. "Stay out here and play duck shoot?"

"Be happy to," he said with a cold smile, and pointed the barrel at Solomon's head.

I rapped politely at the metal door and bent my head

to climb in. John Wilbur was a tiny man sitting on an equally tiny orange and brown couch, his small hands clasped as he rocked back and forth. The desert had withered him to a raisin of a man. Small, dark, and wrinkled.

"I'm Buddhist, you know. Picked it up a few years ago," he said immediately, his voice four times bigger than he was. "They ain't right. I have my own ways. They ought to be leaving me alone. The two of them. Trying to talk me into coming out. Talking and talking and lying and giving me the smooth." The skin around his small eyes spiderwebbed as he gave me a snaggle-toothed grin. "Tossed one of my Buddhas through the window at the one. Surfer boy." That would be our bleached-blond angel. "He had a dent in his head for a good minute." That was good to know. Things could leave our bubble of protection, but nothing could enter, not without permission. Although I didn't think it was Wilbur's permission I had received, I thought that was via the tiny bit of the Light left here, and it was only a tiny bit. From what I'd heard of the Light, this display was a firecracker compared to the atomic bomb. Heaven, Hell, and Earth weren't moving against one another for the ability to protect a trailer.

I looked down at Wilbur, holding a cheerfully green ceramic Buddha in his hand. The place was littered with them. Fat, laughing Buddhas. Skinny, solemn Buddhas. One was even in a hula skirt. I liked that about Buddha. Throughout history he had never minded a laugh at his own expense. He had never minded any good-natured laughter at all. We should all be that happy.

"Good for you." I smiled. "Toss me one and let's see if I can get the dark guy in the high-roller suit."

I missed Solomon with the green Buddha, but only

because he turned to dark mist and sank into the ground. "Cheater," I said under my breath as he immediately rose again.

"You don't throw like no girl." Mr. Wilbur tried for another grin, but it wobbled. "I'm not getting out of this, am I?" He shook his head. "The bastard should've warned me first, but ain't no way I'd take it then, right? Even with his talk of a better world. Making things right. Crazy old bastard. Couldn't understand a damn word he said half the time." He sighed and wiped at an eye. "Twitches now and again," he mumbled. Straightening, he squared his small shoulders and said, "Jeb said after he had time to hide that damn thing away, it'd be no problem. No reason for anyone to come looking for him and it would be safe. The Light would be safe. Well, it might've been gone, but he wasn't. Neither am I."

I didn't know how whoever found Jeb had done it. Whether it was through Wilder Hun, probably, or some other way. But I suspected they had found Wilbur precisely the same way Leo and I had. Demons and angels had been lurking out of sight at Jeb's wake, avoiding the warm lemonade, but getting the same information we had. And wings made better time than my car. Popping in and out of existence wherever you pleased was a quick commute too.

"Who came looking for Jeb?" I interrupted. "Who killed him?"

He shrugged listlessly and shook his head. "I dunno. Doesn't matter now anyway, 'cause here we are. I don't have it. Jeb showed it to me, shiny gewgaw that it was, but he didn't give it to me. Not really. They won't believe me though, those out there."

"No." I met his eyes squarely. Wilbur wasn't completely correct about the Light. A minute amount of it had stayed here, but at least Jeb hadn't given him up. It wouldn't have been much comfort, so I kept the thought to myself. I also thought that whoever had killed Jeb could've had a telepath with him and it wouldn't have mattered. A little Light here, a little Light also in Jeb. I imagined it had left enough of itself in him to hide any information he had on its location. Pretty smart for a rock. Less smart on me as I still didn't know who'd killed Jeb.

"And once those out there find out I don't have it, they'll kill me," Wilbur said bitterly. Then he straightened to tell me earnestly, "But first they could find out." He touched his head. "The Light, I might not have it, but it leaves its voice, like an echo, you know? A trail of bread crumbs to follow, just like the fairy tale. To find where Jeb hid it. He told me he passed the voice on and whoever has it will pass it on. I thought he was talking crazy until the Light talked to me too."

"You're a bread crumb?" I asked skeptically.

He tried for another grin and failed. "Yeah. Not the worst thing I've been in my life."

"So you know where Jeb hid it?"

"No." He shook his head. "Wouldn't be much point to leaving a trail of bread crumbs if I did. And I guess you're who I've been waiting for. The Light let you in. That makes you good people. Good enough anyway, because I'm out of time. Hope you paid attention to that Hansel and Gretel story when you were little. Here's your way to the second crumb." Before I could say anything, he slammed the palm of one hand against my forehead . . . and I felt it.

Felt the Light.
Felt the Life.

The inextricable twist and glitter of them both.

It didn't speak to me; there wasn't enough left of it there for that—not in Wilbur's mind and not in the faint castoff outside surrounding the trailer. There were just sensations. Warmth. Strength. A beckoning finger. And, lastly, the distinct feeling that I was the lesser of a few evils in the mix. Ah well, it wasn't the first time I'd been accused of that.

I rested on my sore back and rubbed my equally sore forehead from where the sheer energy of the Light had actually knocked me flat. As I rubbed, I looked up. The ceiling was interesting. Another Buddha poster with lotuses and a river, bright colors long faded and the serenity of a place far better than here.

"Now they'll hurt me like Jeb was hurt. You and your friend can try to stop them, but I think one way or another I won't be one of the winners." Still on the couch, he looked down and scrubbed at his face.

No. He wouldn't be. Leo and I could get away in my car with the weapons we'd brought, depending on how many angelic and demonic reinforcements they brought in, but protect Wilbur too? Probably not.

"Demons and angels. Watched out for 'em my whole life," he muttered. "One to toss me into the pit and one to catch me. Now what? They torture and kill me like Jeb, leastwise the demons will. And then they have my soul to torture all over again." He bowed his head and rested it against the largest Buddha in the place, the brass one on the coffee table in front of him. "Don't want the angels either, if they could even get hold of me. I've been a bad guy from time to time. There's a whole lot of no-good in me. I know that. And I want to make up, I do, but my way, not theirs."

It seemed Dream Angel out there hadn't made much

of an impression on Wilbur. He hadn't made much of one on me either. I sat up, stood still until I stopped swaying, and then reached up and ripped the poster from the ceiling. Laying it on the table, I pointed to the blue river and said gently, "Then join the river, John. You're a Buddhist." I took his hand and placed it flat on water that almost seemed real. "Rebirth. You flow on. They'll never find you. There are many ways in this world. There's no reason you can't do it your way."

"My way."

As he contemplated the water with the sweep of his thumb, I kissed his bristly cheek. "You and I, John. We are of a kind. Until the day we die and beyond, we'll do it our way."

Five minutes later I was being chased out of a trailer, buckshot singing over my head. Wilbur was yelling and swearing, firing again, and slamming the door shut. It was wild and crazy and I needed Solomon and the angel to buy it for just a second. I passed the first as he was pounding with both fists at air that sparked gold under the impact but didn't give way.

Then the swearing stopped, the buckshot ceased, and there was a long moment of quiet before the sound of one single shot ripped through the night. It sounded like small caliber. Didn't matter really. It just meant it would bounce around the inside of his skull, turning to pudding everything in its path. Wilbur was a mountain man. If he wanted something shot dead, it was shot dead. The glowing circle around the trailer instantly faded, the flakes of crystal crumbling to gray ash.

"Gone," the angel said flatly.

"*Gone*," Solomon said with a little more dark emotion.

Both were right. Wilbur was gone by now. Riding

the river along to his next life. No Heaven, no Hell . . . only the constant stream. His choice. I only hoped he did better next time. That he wasn't so bad. Didn't need so much to atone for. Was a little taller maybe, if that made him happy.

Poor bastard.

I kept running—toward the car. Leo was right behind me. The angel looked up, eyes no longer violet dusk but as bright as tropical water under a high sun . . . waiting. Like a good little GI Joe, Boy Scout, soldier of God . . . or so he thought. Lower management all the way. A GI can't take a piss without the paperwork, and an angel of this caliber wouldn't take a single step without orders from the higher-ups. That meant middle management, angels with free will and what they thought was a license to use it, would be here any second. Lucifer was apparently a little more lax in that entire employee protocol/rules and regulations area because Solomon was already heading in our direction, showing the boss that he had some serious initiative. Running. Not flying. He had never shown me his demon side and I thought he probably never would unless he had to kill me. So no swooping—he ran. That's not to say he couldn't run fast. *Damn* fast.

I dived behind the wheel and had the car moving before Leo was quite in it. "Damn it." He wanted to say I could've waited half a second, but he didn't because he was male, and a guy wouldn't say that if you were taking off in the shuttle while he ran alongside.

"I had faith," I said to his unvoiced bitching.

"Yeah, and it warms my heart," he grunted as he got the shotgun up and nailed Solomon—barely. The demon probably would've disappeared, but Leo had reached out and grabbed his arm before discharging the shotgun. That was the thing about demons and probably angels. They could disappear, back to Heaven or Hell I guess, as long as they weren't anchored to this world. The best thing for anchoring them here was a tight hand and a cranky attitude. Iron or steel seemed to work too, but it was one slow-ass demon that would let even me wriggle him into some cuffs . . . at least without whipping out the leather, teddy, braided whip, and holding back the bile. As for an angel . . . I wanted one of those in chains even less than a demon, although for different reasons. Demons occasionally came alone. Angels almost always had backup.

As Solomon writhed around the end of the shotgun, black blood flew around his neck as the car slid in a circle. Leo let go of him, ready to take a shot at his head, but I grabbed his arm to give Solomon that split second he needed to disappear. I ignored Leo's frown. Solomon would be back—to join his brothers. Sure, demons occasionally came alone, but not this time. What I thought was bumpy terrain beneath was shown to be dozens of brown demons springing from the earth.

And as that happened, the night sky turned to van Gogh's *Starry Night*. There were swirls of scarlet and green and blue and amethyst, but most of all . . . silver and gold. The nearly invisible curves became wings of glass. Red and gold. Green and silver and all variations. The angels floated in the air in their true form . . . their oddly alien faces were narrow with eyes large, almond shaped, and as full of light as the outer edges of their wings. You could see the stars through the glass of those wings, although they rippled because every "feather" was a sharply transparent dagger edged in gemstone color. Their skin was filled with light as well, only slightly cooler than the eyes. It was definitely a different look than surfer angel had been sporting not too long ago. Nothing like their human costumes at all.

I blinked against it all, not sure whether I was seeing angels or an impressionist masterpiece come to life, roiling the night sky—even the stars and moon seemed part of it all.

It was beautiful and it was terrible, all in one.

"You won't have them," Solomon said to the angels, having returned from wherever he'd gone, his face twisted as the car rocketed by.

"Neither will you."

I expected that angelic retort to be the music of battle, the symphony of a storm. What I got was a familiar voice through a bullhorn. Griffin. There was the also the rapid chop of rotor blades behind his voice. Lots of rotor blades. The demons kept coming. Angels and Eden House weren't enough to have them giving up—not when they thought they might have a link to the Light so close. They weren't believing Wilbur's act of running me off as thoroughly as I'd hoped.

Two managed to grab on to the back of the car as I drove over them. They climbed up, hissing like an entire nest of rattlesnakes—pissed and hungry. I could see the mottled, moist inner flesh of their mouths in the rearview mirror. Leo unloaded the other barrel of the shotgun into the face of the one on the right, dropped the empty gun, then pulled a sword from under the blanket covering the back floorboards and turned the second demon into a less than politically correct alligator bag. The head bounced into the front passenger seat, glass teeth still gnashing. Separating the brain from the body worked as well as liquefying the organ.

"A sword?" I swerved the car, smacked a few demons with the side, and shot one in the head as it climbed over the front windshield. Blood and scales sprayed in a fine mist over us. I was going to have to rethink the whole convertible situation. "You and a sword. I am boggled."

"Sometimes you really do have to embrace your roots, just like your lemonade man said." Luckily there were no tourists around to explain that to as Leo gave an unaccustomed grin and swung again as a demon launched itself into the backseat. Another head bounced up front. Now I had two heads with teeth still slowly chomping away. Would they just hurry up and die already? The last thing I wanted was them stripping flesh from my ankle and calf all the way down to the bone like piranha in an old Tarzan movie .

"It's getting crowded up here. Swing the other way, Babe Ruth," I called as I turned the car into another high-speed spin with one hand and used the other to toss the heads out, getting one nice slice across the back of my hand out of it. Bastard. The dead should be dead . . . immediately. No hanging around snapping like ill-tempered, satanic Chihuahuas. I fired again, this time upward as a demon dropped from the sky. My Smith & Wesson 500 was no shotgun, but it knocked him off course. He missed the car. The car did not, however, miss him. There was a very satisfying ka-thump as I careened over the top of him. It wouldn't kill him, but it'd slow him down for a few minutes and make him respect a good American-made car. Or Japanese. Or maybe it was German. I kept forgetting which. I liked pretty things, but I also liked moving on to the next pretty thing fairly quickly. It made it hard to keep track.

Unless the pretty thing was riding on your hood.

"What did he tell you, Trixa?" Solomon said over the rush of the wind from the speeding car. He didn't raise his voice. He didn't have to. I heard him as clearly as if he were at my ear . . . which he suddenly was. He sat in the demon-bloodstained passenger seat and repeated it calmly. "What did he tell you?"

"He didn't tell me a thing." And Wilbur hadn't—not really. It was the Light that had told me.

"Then what did *it* tell you?" he asked, catching on quickly. "Where is it?"

"It told me I was a naughty girl, but the lesser of evils." I smiled brightly. "And while a girl does love hearing a compliment, I have no idea where it is." Sadly, that was true enough.

But I did know how to find it.

Before Solomon could ask any more questions, a helicopter swooped down and hovered right in front of us. I slammed on the brakes. I was wearing a seat belt. Leo, who knew how I drove, was also wearing one, even in the back. Solomon was not. But he disappeared to black smoke as he went through the windshield, cracking it into a spiderweb mansion. "Wonderful," I sighed. "My insurance company already hates me." Then I tried for a look on the bright side. "It might be a sign. Time for a new car."

Leo leaned over the seat as the helicopter landed and the rest of the demons finally gave up and disappeared when men with machine guns jumped out. "So, what did the Light tell you?"

I told him. I had no secrets from Leo. Not about

Kimano. Not about the Light. "The lesser of evils," he snorted. "That doesn't say much for the company we keep, does it?"

"Come on," I protested on my behalf at least . . . but, honestly . . .

It was true.

Chapter 7

The helicopter had brought us to Eden House. They, like everyone else, definitely had a finger in this pie. So here I finally was, and this time it wasn't just hearing Griffin describe its elegant glory of antiques, the library of secret books and documents that historians would give ten years of their lives to see, and the magnificent showcase of ancient demon-fighting weapons.

Or Zeke saying, "Yeah, it's big. Hard to find the bathrooms. Now can I have another beer?" I was here to see it with my own eyes. Unfortunately, the higher-ups knew it. They now knew about Leo and me, and knew that we knew about them . . . worse yet, about the Light. And you can bet they didn't like it—all that knowing. They were probably discussing it right now, their complete and utter dislike of it all.

The hell with it. There was nothing I could do about it now, and I had something far more important right in front of me.

I held Zeke's limp hand and rubbed the pad of my thumb softly across the back of it. He was still out of it, drugged to the gills, but he was off the ventilator and on an oxygen mask. I took that as a good sign. He was in a hospital bed, and for all intents and purposes was in his own hospital ICU. It was in Eden House's basement. He was hooked up to a heart monitor, oxygen, a pulse oximeter to read the level of oxygen in his blood, IVs . . . too many things to count.

A sheet was pulled up to his hospital gown–clad chest. Next to all that white and green, he was gray. The ashy skin next to the color of his gown wasn't a good combination and it made me feel . . . I looked over my shoulder and let Griffin feel that mood. I didn't bury it or hide it as I usually did. I let him feel it because it let him feel it himself—something I didn't think he'd allowed himself. Not until then.

He stood by my side as I sat. "He'll be all right." He was telling himself the same as he was telling me. "The doctors said that he's recovering faster than they anticipated." He reached down and lightly knuckled the top of the unconscious, reddish bronze head. It was the same move a kid would make to another kid—a younger one. It wasn't surprising. They'd been in the same foster home since they were ten and twelve, at least until they came to me five years later. When something had gone drastically wrong. Griffin had always said it was Zeke's story to tell.

He changed his mind.

Why? Could've been any number of reasons. He could've known that Zeke would never tell. It might have been he was still so angry over what had happened back then that he had to tell someone and that someone wasn't going to be a member of Eden House. They valued Zeke for his strong psychic skills, but without Griffin around to keep him in check, Eden House wouldn't have anything to do with Zeke. And I think Griffin had just now realized that. He'd seen them virtually kidnap Leo and me and for a thing his boss refused to elaborate on. He would name it, but he wouldn't explain it.

Kidnapping and secrets. That wasn't the milk of human kindness. That wasn't someone you could rely on to take care of a psychosocially damaged man. If something happened to Griffin, as far as the House was concerned Zeke would be on his own, or worse. A rogue psychic whose sense of judgment didn't allow for shades of gray, who saw the action that needed taking, but not always the consequences of that action . . . a man whose actions might be traced back to them. They wouldn't allow it. Remember Lot's wife? And she'd just looked in the wrong direction.

And that was why Griffin told me, the true reason. He wasn't a stupid man. To the contrary, he was extremely sharp at sizing up people. Now he was sizing up his own people and they were falling short. Should a demon get the better of him, he wanted Zeke taken care of, and Leo and I were the only ones who could do it.

"It was a baby, but he didn't mean to." He bowed his head and rubbed the back of his neck with enough force that I winced for him. "You don't think he'd still hold on to that enough to not come back, do you?"

"He's not leaving us," I said with determination. "That's a promise. And you know I keep my promises, Griffin."

I waited as he straightened and folded his arms to watch the methodical beep beep of Zeke's heart monitor. "His throat." He looked away from the monitor, from Zeke, from everything, and stared at the closed door that led out of the room to the hall. "After he realized what had happened. After he knew." He looked back at me and I saw the eyes of a traumatized seventeen-year-old. Not a twenty-seven-year-old man, but a boy—a boy who'd seen too much death long before he ever knew demons existed. That monsters were real. "He walked into the kitchen. Just walked. Everyone was screaming. Our foster father"—his lip curled—"was so helpfully kicking in the TV screen. I was calling 911 and Zeke just walked past me and went to the drawer by the sink, took out a butcher knife, and tried to cut his throat."

The ugly three-inch furrow across the otherwise-smooth skin had been half healed when they'd shown up at my place. "You stopped him," I said without doubt because Zeke wouldn't have stopped himself. He never did. When he started something, he finished it . . . if he knew what the end was. It was a lucky thing that Zeke had been so young, or he would've cut deep enough to have bled to death even from those few inches. But at fifteen, his killing skills weren't what they were today.

I stood and pushed Griffin into the chair. As much as my back burned, he needed the rest more than I did. "There was a baby and Zeke tried to cut his own throat. Help me out a little, Griffin. I'm lost."

And tired, hungry, and more than a little concerned that Leo and I'd been outed to Eden House by those damn nosy angels at Wilbur the Buddhist's place in the desert. I was assuming that's why the helicopters had shown up so conveniently.

But enough time for that later. Time for this now.

"There was a baby?" I prompted, and leaned against his shoulder.

He exhaled, froze as the heart monitor alarmed for a second, then relaxed again when it quieted back to its rhythmic beeping. "Bob and Angie. Good old bored, fat Bob and good old clueless, even fatter Angie. They were foster parents for a living. That's all they did. Take in kids, especially special kids like Zeke. They were paid more money to take special ones. They had six then, including Zeke and me. The youngest was David. He was one, one and a half. I never was very good at guessing ages of little kids." He leaned back and closed his eyes. "The social workers told them, told our foster *parents*, never to leave Zeke unsupervised with things that could hurt him or others. Told them all about his problems and how long it had taken him to even learn to do things on his own, simple things like dress himself. He had to be told. And when he improved: Turn on the stove; make your macaroni; turn off the stove. Eat macaroni; wash dishes; put them away. The stubborn bastard learned."

He shifted against me restlessly. "He made it to the point he could function almost normally, except for that black and white outlook he has. Because of that, how it affected his decision making, how he couldn't see past the immediate, he still needed supervision and they didn't give it to him. I knew he needed it. All the other kids who were old enough knew it—the only ones who didn't bother to pay fucking attention were the adults."

He went quiet. I waited for nearly ten minutes before I bent and rested my chin on top of his head. "The baby?"

One more minute of silence and he said without emotion, "Angie told him to give the baby a bath. 'Zeke, get off your ass and give that filthy baby a bath,' is probably what she said while she sat on her worthless own fat ass watching her soaps. I was still at school, some

after-hours thing, so Zeke . . . he gave the baby a bath."
He exhaled heavily. "Until two kids got into a fight in
the kitchen."

Violence: Zeke's number-one draw. The flashing red
alarm. Protect the innocent; punish the guilty. My mind
painted the image easily enough. Off he ran, fifteen-
year-old special Zeke, to break up the fight. To keep the
smaller kid from being hurt, to show the bigger one exactly what it was like to be beaten on. By the time that
was over, by the time that developmentally different,
single-minded brain of his remembered . . .

I could see a blue-gray little boy floating facedown in
the cooling bath water when Zeke ran back. Blubbery
Angie heaving her way off the couch to berate him for
making more noise breaking up the fight than the fight
itself. Following him to yell at him for being so damn
loud and drowning out her stories.

Then the screams, the accusations, the shouted, poisonous blame.

Zeke realizing it was his fault . . . no, not realizing,
because it *wasn't* his fault. But Zeke being blamed for
it, being told it was his fault, and going to punish himself. A hand for a hand, an eye for an eye: That's the
only justice Zeke had in him.

"I got home just in time," Griffin went on. "Not for
David, but for Zeke. I stopped him. I took him and ran.
Whom would the social workers believe? Not that it
mattered anyway. That had been his last chance. He'd
gone through too many homes, too many foster parents who didn't give a damn about watching a kid, really watching him. If this last one didn't work out, they
were going to institutionalize him. Stamp him 'not able
to function in the outside world.'"

"But you saved him." I watched Zeke's chest rise and

fall a little more raggedly than made me happy, but at least it still moved. "Did he ever forgive himself?"

"No." He gave a half laugh without an ounce of humor. "It's why he likes fighting demons so much. He says he plans on spending eternity doing it when he dies. Why not get the practice now?"

"Zeke. Kit." I straightened and moved to him, touching a finger to my lips and then to his cheek, the cold plastic of the oxygen mask brushing my skin. "You're not going to Hell. I promise you that." I hoped at some level he heard me. I hoped he believed me. "And you're not going to die either. Do you hear me?"

The door opened and Leo walked in with a tray of food. Eden House might try to dispose of us later, but at least for now they were going to feed us, which was a good thing, because I was starving. I have a high metabolism and when I lost weight, the first thing to go was my ass. I liked my ass; I wanted to keep it. It was great for sitting on and even better at making men do incredibly stupid things. By the time they realized my brain was far bigger, metaphorically speaking, it was usually too late for them. It was cheap and cheating, just a little, but when you're in the information business, you use every asset you have to get the info you want, brain and body. Naturally, they only got to look, not touch, but men . . .

I snorted and took a plate from the tray and said to Leo, "Pigs. You're all pigs." Griffin raised his eyebrows and opened his mouth, but Leo shook his head. "Don't bother," he advised. "It'll only make your head hurt." He handed the tray to Griffin, took his own plate, and found a chair on the other side of Zeke's bed. I joined him. "I have two guards that followed me from the kitchen here. They're stationed outside the door with your guard, Trixa." Black eyes sparked with humor as he took a bite of his sandwich.

"Three whole guards." I dug into my own sandwich. When I finished half of it, I went on, "We're doomed now."

They'd asked for our guns and Leo's Viking-looking sword before we boarded one of the copters and, at that moment, with machine guns being held casually ready for any returning demons or maybe two stubborn barkeeps, turning over our weapons was about the only choice we had. So we did. But only three guards? Insulting and a little less than smart.

"Not everyone is impressed by a bar owner and a jack-of-all-trades," Leo reminded me.

True. Jackson Goodman, their second in command, knew Griffin and Zeke hung around my place, but he didn't know we hunted demons on occasion with them. He definitely didn't know what we were capable of. I would have preferred to keep it that way, but it didn't look like that would be an option. Of course, they no doubt cared less about that now than about the Light of Life. Goodman was probably looking for a saw to cut off the top of my head so he could take a peek at my brain. See what the Light told me for himself. Eden House might not torture me as Jeb the Caver had been tortured, but then again, they might. I still didn't know. And even if they were nice enough not to torture me, they weren't going to let me go either, and that was the surest bet you'd find in Vegas. Not without getting something from me first.

Griffin seemed to know what I was thinking, which wouldn't be hard, as I frowned my way through the second sandwich. "I'll do my best to get you out of this," he said. "I promise you that."

In most cases it's the thought that counts, but this time . . . I shook my head. "You don't have a chance. They think I know where the Light is. They're not going to let me go anywhere."

"The Light of Life, Ms. Iktomi," sounded the voice from the door, which had opened silently, so silently I hadn't heard it, "belongs with us, or rather with him for whom we toil."

And the owner of that voice would have to be Mr. Trinity, who now stood in the doorway. That wasn't his real name. Zeke or Griffin had said that the head of any Eden House anywhere in the world was called Mr. Trinity. It was a title, an honor, a badge signifying whom he served. I wondered if they all had the same presence too, because this guy would make a demon scurry home to his mommy—or daddy as the case may be. He was six feet tall and broad shouldered with thick white hair and a startling slash of thick dark brows. His eyes matched them, the same color as Leo's. He had to be in his early sixties, but his face was strong and unlined. If they made a movie of my life, he'd be played by Sean Connery and he would either seduce me or kick my ass, or both. And, let's be honest, if it were a movie and Sean Connery, I'd let him. Either way, he'd get what he wanted—the Light—and I'd be nothing but a credit at the end.

It was just too bad for Mr. Trinity that this wasn't a movie. Like I would give him the Light. Did he know who killed Kimano? Did he even know my brother had once lived? No. Could he find the demon who had taken his life? Doubtful. They were legion. A human couldn't do it. Only a demon could.

And I had my money on Solomon. He wanted the Light just as badly as Mr. Trinity. It was easy to see why when you knew what it could do.

Like I told Mr. Trinity I knew.

Like I'd told Solomon at the battle.

All's fair in love and war. Now imagine what's reasonable in vengeance and fucking with my family. Mr. Trinity might be a ruthless leader, but I wasn't sure he could quite imagine the things I was willing to do. Solomon was a demon. . . . Solomon might have an idea or two about my limits—as in none.

I patted my mouth with a napkin and folded my hands across my lap like the good girl I was. "Unless you have a red-hot poker in the next room"—I tilted my head just enough to let him know I didn't think it completely beyond him—"you get nothing from me. At least not until I get what I want."

By the way he clenched his fist, if that nonexistent red poker had been in his hand, I thought he would've used it. "And what, foolish, greedy woman, do you want?"

"Greedy." I'd seen the money that went into and never came out of Eden House. It made me wonder . . . when had they forgotten that a camel would pass through the eye of a needle before a rich man entered Heaven? "Well, Mr. Trinity, this foolish woman has all the apples she needs, so I think you'll find my price quite cheap for what the Light can do. It's just one *you* can't pay."

He ignored the price check and focused on the rest of it. "What it can do. You think you know what it does?" Coldly but carefully lacking scorn. If I did know, he didn't want to make me angry—it's a pissed-off cow that gives little milk. I didn't know if there was a folk saying in that exact form, but you could take it on truth in content.

"It's the wall no horn can blow down." Griffin and

Trinity's eyes were fixed on me. Leo's weren't. He already knew what I knew, what I'd known for a while. Trinity would assume I got the information from the Light itself via Wilbur. There was a calculating shift of his eyes—like Goodman, what Trinity wouldn't give to pop the top to my skull and take an ice-pick jab and look for himself.

"If Jericho had the Light, it would still stand. The Light is neither of Heaven nor Hell, but before. Long before."

"Blasphemy." Trinity said it reflexively, without a lot of investment in it. He was more concerned about what I knew than offense to the Lord at the moment.

"It's an unbreakable shield," I went on. "Should war come between Heaven and Hell, whichever side had it would be completely protected."

"What's going on?" Griffin demanded.

"Torture, murder, and a race to the perfect weapon. Invulnerability," Leo said matter-of-factly as he moved on to his next sandwich, unbothered by the violence that constructed those words. "That would make any war a short one."

"God is invulnerable, not a Light," Trinity said this time with a quiet certainty and power.

"Then why do you want the Light?" I didn't even have to ask. Griffin did it for me.

"The Light is for Heaven. That's all you need to know," the older man replied brusquely. For Heaven maybe, but not for God, but no angel was going to tell the Eden Houses around the world that. Lose their human servants? Where was the benefit there?

"No one will stop us in obtaining it. Not a woman and not a demon," he went on. Demon singular, as in Solomon, Trinity's equal in Vegas. "Or hordes of demons. Every hell-spawn in existence can stand against us and it will not matter. Eden House has its orders."

"Good for Eden House." I stood and put the tray on the chair. "We should be going. Thanks for the hospitality, but I have a business to run and a Light to find."

"I think not." Mr. Trinity didn't move, just as the three guards outside the door wouldn't move—unless we made them. Then there would be reinforcements, and although I knew without a doubt that Griffin would back up Leo and me, someone would get hurt. And Zeke wasn't even conscious. Griffin wouldn't leave him if the fight went badly. *I* wouldn't leave him.

It didn't leave me with much choice. I didn't trust Trinity, but maybe I should put a little trust in someone else—Solomon. Trust that when I finally came to the Light, he'd be right there for the bidding. He was involved. He'd shown that by appearing at Wilbur's. I'd had to wonder why a demon stayed so long in one place, stayed so long in Vegas. Not simply for seducing me. I had ego, but I wasn't a fool. It'd be nice to think all the eligible men and demons were after nothing more than my brain and smart-ass self, but it'd be nice to keep on breathing and living too. Delusion wasn't very compatible with survival.

"I guess we have to negotiate, then." I smiled with confident cheer. And I shouldn't be so quick to assume Trinity couldn't track down a demon. I shouldn't be putting all my eggs in one basket with Solomon. I couldn't afford to make a mistake. "Good thing I specialize in that."

Trinity smiled back. There wasn't any cheer in it at all. "Yes . . . good thing."

The room I was provided with in Eden House was plush. No surprise there. Even if I weren't quite as good at bargaining as I knew I was, Mr. Trinity wasn't likely to put me in some sort of basement cell. He was too much of a gentleman for that. He might think I was a greedy woman. He might kill me Old Testament style, but bad manners? Never.

Once I'd made it clear that I didn't know the Light's location, only the whereabouts of the next bread crumb in a trail I didn't know how long, and once I'd promised to deliver him to the Light and then talk price, he had let Leo go in a show of good faith. And Leo had gone in another show of good faith: that I could take care of myself.

Truthfully, I didn't have to hit Trinity as hard as I'd thought with my skills of negotiation. I'd told him he couldn't pay my price, but he hadn't believed it. The head of Eden House was just like a common demon: He assumed everyone had a price and he could meet it. Shame on me—I was looking forward to seeing his expression when he was proven wrong. Then again, maybe he'd prove me wrong and do what I was depending on Solomon to do. Life is full of surprises that way. I'd had past plans combined with a smug attitude come back to bite me in the ass before. Best to stay open-minded . . . for Kimano.

I showered in a bathroom easily as large as my bedroom. Unbelievably thick towels in deep blues and greens, a whirlpool tub that could host a hot tub party. Soft lighting, a sea glass tile floor, and cool, creamy walls, it was beautiful and tasteful—a little too tasteful for me. It had no fire, no life. Although with all the colors of the ocean, Kimano would've liked it.

Close now, little brother, I thought as I wrapped myself in a towel and opened the bathroom door. My lips curved. So close.

"Such an evil smile. I don't believe I could do any better myself."

Solomon was on the large bed—dressed at least—back against the headboard, fingers laced across his stomach, legs crossed casually at the ankles. His gray eyes were amused as I dripped in the doorway and his smile was anything but evil. It was appreciative and full of heat.

I had to be reluctantly appreciative as well—at his sheer blazing audacity. "I had no idea demons had a death wish. This is Eden House. *Eden* House. Full of psychics and empaths. They'll be on their way right now."

"You know that's not true." His smile widened to show a flash of teeth. "Although you could scream. I'll try not to enjoy it too much."

"I wouldn't hold my breath." And he was right. It wasn't true. A demon as powerful as Solomon could block any psychic or empath. But he couldn't block me if I cared to give a verbal shout of "Demon." I didn't. I kept my thoughts and emotions as carefully neutral as Solomon was keeping his. After all, this was what I wanted—him there when I found the Light.

I moved forward and sat on the foot of the bed. I was grateful he was wearing clothes, because I could all too easily feel the lack of mine. "Could you find a demon for me? A particular demon?"

"You? Asking me for a favor? I'm staggered." The amused look faded to calculation. "I'm quite sure. I assume you know there would be a price for that. What are you offering?"

Now I was the one to smile. "I think you know that, Solomon. You're not a stupid man . . . or demon."

"Your soul or the Light." He held out both hands, raising and lowering each like scales. "I know which

I'd prefer, but unfortunately I answer to a higher ... rather *lower* power. The Light it is." He leaned forward toward me, one of those big hands resting above my knee, the fire of it burning through the thick cloth of the towel as if it weren't there. "Tell me where it is and I'll deliver up any demon you wish. A hundred if you have that much ammunition."

"And you don't even want to know why?" I asked as the hand slowly kneaded my leg until I felt that fire intensify and seep through every inch of flesh under his broad palm and caressing fingers.

"I don't care. I care only about the Light." He was right there—his breath mine. His mouth mine. And it wasn't that of a monster ... a demon. The breath was that of a man touched with the faintest smoky taste of whiskey. The lips were slowly lazy as the drip of honey and artful. Extremely, amazingly, unbelievably artful. This time not a man's—unless that man had lived thousands of years with the sole purpose of learning to please a woman with a single kiss. It could make you forget where you were, who he was, who *you* were. If he could do all that with one kiss, I could see why some women might find souls overrated.

Some women.

When he pulled back, his eyes were gleaming with success ... gleaming almost as brightly, in fact, as the blade I held against his throat. Then only my blade was gleaming. Solomon's amusement, his seduction, it all disappeared behind a veil of tarnished gray. Anger. "Where is the Light?" he demanded darkly.

"I don't know. I only know where the next stepping-stone is. Follow me, Solomon, while I follow the path. It'll be just like *The Wizard of Oz*. We'll follow the yellow brick road. I'll be Dorothy." I pressed the blade harder. "And you'll be Toto after a visit to the vet's office—snip snip . . . so don't push me."

"Trust me, Trixa. I'll follow you," he promised, reluctant respect surfacing behind the anger—that of a warrior for another warrior. "There's no place on Earth you can go that I can't find you." Despite the metal at his throat, he kissed me again. It was the barest touch of skin against skin.

Then he was gone.

It was just me and my trusty letter opener that I'd borrowed from the desk in the corner and hidden under the mattress. Good enough for paper, but too dull by far for slicing a throat. What Solomon didn't know wouldn't get me eaten—at least eaten in the bad way. I fell back on the bed and felt the tingle that prickled with a quicksilver burn up and down every nerve ending.

Why was it always the bad boys?

Chapter 8

"This is it?"

Griffin looked skeptical. Trinity didn't bother. He just kept that black gaze on me, patient as a spider. The five other men were hidden behind sunglasses and I didn't waste a look to see what their reaction was. I didn't care. They were extras in this little play.

"This is it," I said, "this" being the aquarium at Mandalay Bay Casino. I didn't like aquariums any more than I liked zoos, but the Light was calling me here. As for who the next person was who had a bread crumb deposited in their brain, I'd discovered the Light had a sense of humor. "This way."

I waited while one of Eden House's version of MIBs, Men in Bulgaria sunglasses, paid for our admission. I wasn't paying for my own kidnapping. Mr. Trinity wouldn't dirty his godly hands with filthy sinful money—never mind he was rolling in it, and Griffin was distracted. He didn't like being away from his partner's side and it showed. He didn't trust Trinity completely anymore if he trusted him at all, but that didn't show, not to anyone but me. If the other five were empaths or psychics, it wouldn't matter. It wouldn't show to them either. Griffin was better than they were. He and Zeke were the prizes of this particular House. They had no equals there.

Leo was back at the bar feeding scrawny girls and their pudgy dogs. She gave most of her food to her dog. She deserved the help, just as Zeke and Griffin had years ago. "She left with a garbage bag full of food," he'd said placidly when I'd called him on the phone before we left Eden House for the aquarium. "If she does come back to help clean, we may have to roll her through the mouth of the alley."

"You never know," I'd said sweetly. "Angels disguise themselves to test the generosity of us sinful mortals. You may have earned a spot in Heaven." With a snort and no comment, he had hung up on me.

"Miss Leo?" Griffin said in a low tone at my ear, picking up on the emotion that I hadn't bothered to try to conceal. Griffin was missing his own partner as well, I knew.

"Maybe some. He's certainly going to be sorry he missed this." I sighed.

The eight of us moved through a mass of tourists— some pudgy, some thin, and all seemingly dressed from a 1992 JC Penney catalogue. They'd obviously broken out their best for Vegas. Plastic clothes for a plastic town. We went through the underwater ship and then through the tunnel where fish and sharks swam over our heads. One swam especially close, bumped his bullet nose against the glass above us, and rolled—the traditional shark move for taking his prey down. "I think we made a friend." I waved at it and mentally cursed the Light for at least the fifth time.

After we exited the tunnel, I stood for a second, my head cocked to one side . . . listening, but not really.

More like feeling a tickle in my brain leading me along. "This way."

"This way" turned out to be a door marked NO ENTRY. Griffin kicked it in, using as little force as he could so the splintering of the jamb wouldn't be spotted from the outside hall. Inside the room was a walkway over the shark tank. Netting rose from the rail to well above six feet. Didn't want the employees accidentally tumbling in and ruining ticket sales with their blood and snackable entrails.

"All right." I leaned against the netting to watch the sea life, and then sucked in my breath, stripped off my shirt and jeans down to panties and bra, and said, "Someone give me a knife or cut me a door."

Griffin's mouth fell open. For such a bright, intelligent, and serious guy, it wasn't such a good look for him. "You. . . . down there? I thought it'd be one of the trainers or guides. You mean the Light planted a clue in some sea bass's tiny little brain?" He moved forward, stepping on my clothes without awareness. "And, please God, tell me it's a sea bass."

"Did I ever tell you my brother liked sharks? And not so much planted a clue as left a trail." One of the MIB was slicing an opening through the mesh and Mr. Trinity didn't seem concerned in the slightest if I lost a body part or two. Big surprise. "He thought they were the beauties of the ocean. Not dolphins or orcas, he just had a thing about sharks. He even swam with them."

"Your brother swam with sharks." Griffin followed my gaze downward. "He wasn't any smarter than you, then, was he?"

I smiled, kissed his cheek, and was through the netting and diving into the water below before he could grab my arm. Not that he didn't try. A very good friend, Griffin.

The water was cooler than I expected. Not cold, but not warm either, but the salt in it burned my raw back like battery acid. I ignored it as best I could and began swimming down. I didn't have to go too far. With eyes wide open I saw electric blue and yellow fish come to nibble at my knees and toes curiously. I saw the wavering faces of tourists who were getting a far better show than they paid for and then I saw it, the same seven-foot-long shark that had bumped and grinned at me—you haven't seen a true grin until you've seen a shark grin.

Seven feet isn't really all that big for a shark. They've seen them twelve feet long, but right now seven feet was fine by me. Nothing bigger required. It was one of the few cases when smaller was better.

It swam up to me slowly, black eyes round and familiar. It looped around me until I felt the sandpaper scrape of its skin against mine. I reminded myself it had something to give me, to pass on. That's why I hadn't brought a knife borrowed from one of the MIB. That's why I didn't open my mouth for a gurgly "Oh shit," not that drowning while being eaten is much better than simply being eaten. I had faith in the Light, which was odd, as I had so little faith in so many other things. I also had faith in the elemental soul of the shark. Kimano had, and for all his lazy ways, he'd been a good judge of character. Sharks weren't the villains movies painted them. In all likelihood they weren't half as savage as your average teacup poodle.

I rested a hand on the blunt head and thought of my brother and then of the Light.

It was there, only the tiniest bit—the barest molecule. But even that lit me up. Filled me from the inside out with safety and home and unending warmth.

Neither Above nor Below deserved the Light.

But hadn't I known that all along? Yet business was business, and few knew backroom negotiations like I did. I knew how to get what I wanted—*everything* I wanted. My house of cards wasn't going to tumble down now. There was no way that I would let that happen.

After the warmth and the light came two faces. The first was Jeb—alive, whole, the torture and death a thing of his future. I saw him through shark eyes as he stared back, cradling a large paper bag in the crook of his arm. From the paper bag came a glow—didn't they say you shouldn't hide your Light under a bushel? Or in a bag? Then Jeb moved, and a second face appeared, probably that of the next person who caught the shark's attention. It could've been hours later or a day later; who knew? The face was unfamiliar, but I knew it wouldn't stay that way. He had stared at the shark, mesmerized. Jeb had brought the Light to the shark, and it had passed something along to the giant fish. The shark had in turn passed it along to the second man. The Light hadn't been shy about leaving a bit of itself in the shark to go poking about in the guy's thoughts. Who, where, what? The Light obtained it all . . . and that was what was given to me.

Whatever the Light had given to the second man, however, was gone from the shark's brain now. I was assuming that missing information would be the location of the Light. Assuming, hoping. But all I received was where to look next—or rather, whom to look *in*.

Clever. I knew where to look for the next trail marker,

but the final resting place of the Light, that I still didn't know.

Next thing I knew, I was standing on the back of a shark and being pulled upward, back through the netting. I wrapped my arms around Griffin's free one and literally climbed back up him to the catwalk. Up at the top, I shivered, looked down, and then wrapped my arms around my bare breasts. I glared down at the shark, which was diving playfully with a red lace bra caught in his teeth. Then I laughed. What else could I do? And in my mind Kimano stood at my shoulder, laughing even harder. Black hair, black eyes, sun-browned skin, and a grin brighter than the sun on the Pacific.

"Funny, is it?" Griffin was trying to control a smile of his own as he disentangled himself from the netting and handed me his jacket.

I bundled up in it and wrung out my wet hair with a reminiscent curve of my lips. "Just nice to see it isn't only people who have a little bit of the joker in them." I leaned back against the netting and called down to the water. "Quite the trickster, aren't you, Nemo?" I dressed back in my dry clothes, using Griffin's jacket as a shield.

"So where is the Light?" Mr. Trinity demanded as we moved on, hopefully before security arrived.

"Oh, it's hardly that easy. For a smart man, you underestimate the Light. It's not like we're talking a sixty-watt-bulb worth of intelligence or anything. We have a ways to go. The giant guppy just pointed me in the right direction, to the next bread crumb."

"And where is that?" Griffin asked curiously. It was better than the harsh demand that had been ready to cross Trinity's lips.

"Details." I offered his jacket back. "Details. Give my brain a chance to sort it out."

Trinity didn't look especially pleased with that and turned to the nearest bodyguard, because that's what they were: a body for him; just plain guard for me. He tapped his shoulder and pointed down into the water. "Go. See if it tells you anything."

The bodyguard's mouth gave a faint twitch. It wasn't a happy twitch. He looked at me and I could see him calculating that if I could do it, a glorified bartender about a third his weight, then how dangerous could it be? The sharks must be tame from captivity and daily feedings and, yes, he so didn't have a clue. He stripped to boxer briefs, which, I had to admit he wore well, and dived in as I had. He came out—the newspapers said later—with a red bra wrapped around his neck and missing a chunk of his calf. We didn't stay around long enough for the live version. Once the thrashing and bubbling screams from the tank and security started rattling at the door that Griffin had jury-rigged shut behind us, we left. I heard later from Griffin, that aside from the bra and missing flesh, the bodyguard had gotten nothing out of the shark. I was still Eden House's hole card.

Before that information had come my way, we'd passed out of the casino into the sun, making our escape as Trinity went on, wasting no thought on the man left behind. "Where is the next step, Iktomi? I assume the Light passed its next bit of the puzzle to you. There is no other reason to be discussing it."

"I don't know." It wasn't completely a lie. The winter sun, mildly warm, felt good against my skin and I held my face up to it. "It's all sliding through my head. One big, jumbled puzzle of letters and identity. It hasn't come together yet. It might not for a day or two. I'm not quite used to telepathic Lights playing with my brain or its carrier leaving me with a huge appetite for raw fish." I let the tourists swell around us on the sidewalk. "I want to go home. You can leave your pit bulls behind to watch the place if that's what you want, but being at home, being someplace familiar will help me get my brain unknotted." I looked down. "Besides, I have bras there. And while I like to consider myself a free spirit, I'm not that free."

I wasn't sure if it was the bra argument or the little regard Trinity had for me, but he had me dropped off back at the bar with men taking turns watching the place, two at a time. I didn't offer them any food or shelter. Their car was more plush than my place anyway. Griffin was torn, but not so torn he didn't go back to Zeke's side—which was the way it should be. More than ever his partner needed protection . . . from injury, from himself, and maybe from Eden House.

I walked into the bar and Lenore was pecking, bored at the countertop. A bright eye flashed at me and he cawed, "Boom chika boom."

"I'm not Dolly Parton, you horny crow. It's not that noticeable," I retorted, then went upstairs to change into some sweats and take a nap. You'd think it would be swimming with the sharks that would take it out of you, but that wasn't it. It was the Light. It weighed down every thought, buzzing like a swarm of bees setting up camp there—every gray cell a honey cell. I took a quick shower before changing, getting the aquarium salt off me, pulled on the softest sweats I owned, and climbed into bed. It was only then I noticed a sprinkling of brown dog hair on the foot of my bed. I took a quick glance around the room. Nothing was missing. The girl hadn't been up here, but her fat friend had taken advantage of a soft bed for a nap of his own.

I clucked my tongue, but I wasn't mad. If I were a fat little dog, I think I probably would've done the same. It was a comfortable bed. He had good taste. I rolled my hand into a loose fist and tucked it under my chin, closed my eyes, and drifted. I dreamed of family. Of traveling the world, as we always had—as our ancestors had—seeing mountains, forests, oceans or water and sand, seeing people of every color and language. Of coming together with my mother, brother, and cousins, laughing and swapping stories, then going our separate ways again. It was a good life, and though each of us was born a wanderer, we kept close—coming together again and again. They were always the best of times, except the last time. Without Kimano.

"Sorry about that," Kimano said in my dream. He lounged in the chair in the room's corner, legs sprawled, wearing bathing trunks with a shell necklace around his neck. I could even see the beads of Pacific Ocean water on him. "I'll bet I deprived Mama of some prime bitching about my work ethic."

"What work ethic?" Sleep was good. Sleep was wonderful. It was the only place I saw Kimano since that bloody beach.

"True." He shook his dripping hair as if he were a wet dog, then combed his fingers through it. "But you can work and play at the same time."

"You could, but you never did, and Mama knew that." In the dream I sat with my legs tucked under me on the bed, wearing a bikini with plumeria flowers in my hair. Their scent, so unmistakable . . . more of Heaven than Heaven itself . . . filled the air. "But you were still her favorite." I tried to scowl, but couldn't pull it off, not in the face of his teasing pleasure.

"The squeaky wheel gets the grease." He tapped his foot on the side of the chair, dumping a rain of sand on my rug.

"The lazy wheel, you mean, and cut that out." But once again I didn't mean it, not really. Kimano was Kimano. It would be like getting angry at the wind or the moon. He was what he was and I liked that. I loved that. I missed that. I missed that so much.

"I'm gone, you know," he said abruptly, sitting up with serious eyes. "All this you're doing, all that you're risking, it won't bring me back, *kaikuahine*," Hawaiian for sister. He'd traveled too, but always back to the islands as I always tended to return to the desert. "But I think . . ." He leaned and held out his hand. I did the same and our fingers just brushed. "I think we'll see each other again. And if we do, I hope my lazy ass doesn't keep you waiting too long while I'm off wandering. Have a mai tai until I show up."

No one can lie to you like your own mind can. I woke up, dry-eyed in a way that was beyond pain. I wanted to think I'd see my brother again, but I didn't know. I did know Heaven or Hell wasn't for the likes of me. The Buddha-loving Wilbur and I had that in common. Where did my kind go? The free spirits, the wanderers, the gypsies at heart? We turn our backs on Heaven, refuse Hell—and occasionally kick demon ass while we do it. There was a place for us—I did know that—but whether I deserved the same eternity as my brother, I wasn't as sure.

I heard a pounding on the floor, Leo slamming his fist on the ceiling below. "Trixa, get your ass down here!"

Leo was not in a good mood. It would have been "your beautiful ass" or "your gorgeous ass" if he had been. I sighed, rolled over, and checked the alarm clock. It was just past eight p.m. Considering the day I'd had, I felt I deserved to sleep around the clock, but that particular timbre of pounding meant something was up. And by the time I made it downstairs, that something was up all right, in full force.

Zeke.

Zeke and Griffin, to be more specific, but Zeke was the one making all the trouble, as usual. It was his gift. He was still drugged as he'd been in Eden House's minihospital, but he was conscious this time. In a way. Griffin was holding him up—Griffin and the hair of a customer with his face smashed against his small table. "Tip . . . your . . . server," Zeke slurred. Lank strands of his hair fell over a completely bloodless face and the green of his eyes was almost completely obscured by the huge black of his pupils. He was dressed in hospital scrubs and sneakers, no socks.

"You were going to tip Leo but good, weren't you, sir?" I managed to pry Zeke's fingers from the unfortunate cheap bastard's hair. A small trail of blood crept down from the man's right nostril to pool onto his upper lip.

"Tip. Yeah, tip. Was about to do that." He wiped at the smear of red, left a wad of bills for Leo on the table, and bolted for the door.

"What the hell?" I helped Griffin ease Zeke into the just-vacated chair. Barely in time, too. His legs melted like butter and he collapsed into the wooden framework without a single moan. Yes, very, very good drugs. You couldn't look as transparently pale as he did, with Tim Burtonesque charcoal smudges under his eyes, without being host to a shitload of pain. I hoped Griffin had brought some of those excellent painkillers with him, because Zeke was going to need them for a few more days at least. "I've heard of bad doctors, Griff, but not even a chiropractor with an online degree would've let Zeke out of bed, much less into a slightly less than sterile bar."

"Eden House kicked us out. Trinity said we're tainted by our association with you and painted as liars for keeping your demon hunting a secret." His fine suit jacket rumpled beyond repair, he crouched beside Zeke to keep him upright in the chair. His eyes looked up at me with perfect candor layered like frosting over the perfect lie. He didn't bother to give me a little empathic jolt. I'd read him like a book when he was a kid, and I'd only gotten better at it over the years. He knew I'd grasped the real reason right away.

Eden House had sent two spies to keep an eye on me, sent their two best men. The trouble for Mr. Trinity was I'd gotten hold of those men . . . boys then . . . first. I had fed them and sheltered them and I hadn't used them in the meantime. Trinity couldn't say the same. Now in return for his emotionless employment, lies, and icy coldness, he had two double agents. They simply were double agents for me.

I touched blond hair as mussed as I'd ever seen it. Griffin was riding a thin line. Being betrayed by his employers, his partner injured, more or less at a loss as to what was really going on, he had had a hard day. Knowing I'd gotten what he'd been trying to tell me, he turned a haggard face toward Zeke . . . a thin face. Leo and I had eaten at Eden House, but I didn't recall Griffin doing so. "Come on." I motioned Leo over.

"We'll get Zeke up to my bed and get you both some food."

Leo and I took Zeke's weight from Griffin—probably the first time that had happened in days, physically or emotionally. We basically carried him up the stairs. His legs made uncoordinated motions that were more unhelpful than anything, but he did make an effort. Griffin followed us. By the time we reached the bed, Zeke's jaws had begun to tighten and he was shaking in our grip. We got him under the covers while Griffin went to the bathroom for a glass of water to go with the two pills he'd fished from the amber bottle in his pocket.

By the time I returned upstairs barely fifteen minutes later with food, Zeke was out, his profile marble pale against the deep red of my sheets. The bedspread was pulled up to his chest and his right hand was curled upright against the fiery colors . . . still as stone. His chest moving was the only thing that let me know he was breathing. Beside him, on top of the covers, Griffin was out too, as deeply unconscious without the drugs. I wasn't surprised. Who knew the last time he'd slept. Before Zeke had been sliced to pieces, I was sure. I left the food, meat loaf and mashed potatoes from the deli down the street, on the bedside table. Ear-length, light blond hair covered Griffin's closed eyes, and there were deep brackets besides his mouth. Poor damn guy. I covered him up with an extra blanket.

"You and your strays," Leo commented as he touched Zeke's forehead to check for fever.

"Yes, so glad I'm not as hard-hearted as you." I didn't roll my eyes. Instead, I used them to look around the room for a place to sleep. It looked like it was the bathtub for me, as Leo would no doubt be taking the couch downstairs in my office. I could take care of myself, but Zeke and Griffin couldn't say the same, not right now.

"I'll take the couch tonight," he said, a virtual echo of my thoughts. As predictable as the Vegas summer sun and as predictable as me. I wouldn't have left him either.

"He's too sick to be here," Griffin said in the morning. "He's too sick to be anyplace but the hospital."

The pills the Eden House doctors had given to Griffin weren't touching Zeke's pain. Only morphine and sedation would have. He'd fisted the sheets and covers beneath his hands and was sweating profusely. "F-fine," he stuttered between clenched teeth. "I'm . . . fine."

"Which is why I feel like I'm fucking dying," Griffin spat, hand clamped tightly around Zeke's wrist as if he wished he could take the pain instead of only feel it. "God." His other hand was tangled in his hair and he looked like he needed a shower in the worst way since I'd first seen his dirty, scrawny seventeen-year-old frame.

"No hospital." Zeke transferred his grip from the sheets to Griffin's leg, the fingers biting in hard. "They'll know. They'll recognize me. Fingerprints."

He was paranoid. Although his fingerprints were in the juvy system, they wouldn't have made it to the adult one. And even if they had, the hospital wasn't going to fingerprint him. You couldn't tell him that though, couldn't get him to believe it. After what he'd gone through as a child, I wouldn't have believed it either. Not to mention the fact that Eden House had planned this. They'd seen Zeke getting stronger and stronger with his psychic abilities. They'd set Griffin up as a spy and if Zeke ended up in a psych ward from what he babbled under the IV drugs at a hospital—well, was that so bad?

"When can he have more pills?" I asked Griffin.

"Three more hours." Torture was relative, but no matter how you looked at it, for Zeke—for Griffin, three hours was more than a long time. It was forever.

I pried Zeke's fingers from Griffin's arm and Griffin's hand from Zeke's wrist. "Take a shower. I'll take care of Zeke."

Griffin looked at Zeke's gray face, tightly screwed eyes, then back at me doubtfully, a little hopelessly. "How?"

"Because I will. Now go. Robe and towels in the closet to the right." He followed my directions blankly after gripping his partner's shoulder lightly. He didn't pay attention to the fact that the bedroom and bathroom were one room and that he was showering feet away from us, the shadowed silhouette of his body showing through the curtain. Too far gone to care or flirt. And he moved like an old man . . . an old man in a lot of pain. A harsh shadow of Zeke's pain.

"We're here."

I was holding Zeke's hand now, feeling my bones creak under the desperate pressure as I looked up to see Leo, the no-name girl, and her fat dog in the doorway. Both had been coming by every day for food as I'd invited them to. Leo said she hadn't been by yet this morning. I'd known it wouldn't be long before she showed up. Koko's round stomach needed maintaining. The girl might be able to hold off on breakfast herself, but he wouldn't be willing to. Little pig. The dog grinned as if he knew what I was thinking and wriggled his butt in a spring for the bed. I shook my head at him. That motion would have Zeke screaming in pain. "Later, Koko."

He sighed, then made for the nearest rug and rolled a good handful of brown hair on it, then rested on his back, happy as happy can be. All across his pink stomach were scars, crisscrossed . . . everywhere. Too many for even the best vet to fix. I'd seen that the first day I'd spotted the girl and her dog. I'd known then what she could do. "So you fixed Franken-doggy, did you?" I said to her.

The brown hair fell like a curtain, barely concealing her suspicious blue eyes. "He was like that when I found him."

"Sure he was," I said lightly. I'd known all along she was special, just as Zeke and Griffin were special. I had a knack for that; our whole family did—passed from generation to wandering generation. We'd seen it all in the way that only those who wanted to, *had* to cross every hill they saw could. If it existed, one of us had seen it. "Come over here, would you?"

I don't think she would have, but Leo was at her back and she wasn't leaving her dog. Not for anything. She moved closer to the bed. "Figure out your name yet?" I asked.

"No." She hesitated and moved closer. "Your friend. He's sick. He's getting better, but he's still really sick."

"Yes, he is." I patted the air above the bed and she slowly and carefully sat. Even so, Zeke's teeth went through his bottom lip, blood welling, and I heard Griffin stagger in the shower. "It would be an amazing thing, a wonderful thing if you could do to him what you did to Franken-pup. He hurts, Whisper. He hurts. . . ."

"So much," she finished in a stronger voice than

her name. "And how did you know that's my name? I didn't even know."

"You whisper the pain away. That's what healers do." I reached over and took her slightly grubby hand and laid it on Zeke's chest. "Whisper our friend's away. Please."

And after a brief pause, she did. She leaned in and whispered in his ear. I couldn't hear what she said. If I could have, I'm not sure it would've made sense to me. I wasn't a healer . . . far from it. Her hand continued to rest on his chest as she whispered. It started to shake for a moment, but I rested mine on top of hers and kept it in place. The power that hummed under my skin was incredible. It took a long time, or maybe it only seemed that way. An hour or minutes. I hadn't checked the clock. The first thing that let me know it was over was not Zeke; it was Griffin. I heard an exhalation so deep and sharp that I wasn't surprised to hear him fall against the porcelain next. It sounded like his knees that hit. I assumed he was all right when I heard him breathe his partner's name in pure relief.

Zeke opened his eyes. Not in surprise or shock or even curiosity at being healed or the sudden lack of pain. Because that was Zeke, living . . . no, *existing* in the moment. "I'm hungry," he announced. He looked at the girl. "Are you hungry?"

Small white teeth flashed as she nodded. "Me, and Koko too."

We sent out for pizza while the dog ate the leftover meat loaf and Zeke took the next shower, squeezing his partner's shoulder through the robe as he passed him, silently saying what Zeke himself had trouble even understanding. Griffin hit the bed and was asleep literally in midair. He hadn't woken up long ago, but the relief from pain had him out again. The girl . . . Whisper . . . watched Zeke walk to the tub with something like awe and fear. "He's strange—inside his head. Different than everyone else." She brushed a strand of hair behind her ear marked with multiple piercings. "I couldn't fix that."

"Good," I said matter-of-factly, sitting on the rug and rubbing the dog's belly. "Some things can't be fixed and some things shouldn't be fixed and some things aren't yours *to* fix."

"So . . ." She knelt beside me and tickled under Koko's chin. "You've seen someone like me before. Someone who can fix animals and people."

"Once. But she was really old and gone by now, I think." Her eyes dulled in disappointment. "But," I went on, "this sort of thing tends to run in families. I was thinking about sending you down there. Louisiana. Her family likes me. They'll take you in. Teach you what they know if they have any other healers there, and I imagine they do. It's a big family."

"You'd do that? You'd do that for me?" she said with a huge amount of suspicion and only a sprinkling of hope.

"Why not?" I grabbed Koko's nose and gave it a good shake. "If I'd help those two troublemakers." I nodded toward a snoring Griffin and a wet, naked Zeke. "Damn it, Zeke. The shower curtain?"

"Oh. Sorry." He pulled the curtain around the tub, then stuck his head back out, hair soaking. "I am supposed to be sorry, right?" He took my glare as a yes and jerked his head back in.

"If I'd help them," I snorted, "why in the world wouldn't I help you? Besides, I've already needed a healer once. I might need one again someday and you'll owe me."

"Maybe *you'll* owe *me* for healing the naked guy," she shot back, and folded her arms defiantly.

"I like you." I smiled widely. "Damned if I don't. And you know what? Maybe I will."

In a few hours I had her cleaned up with a suitcase of new clothes, a bus ticket to Louisiana, and a bright red collar for Koko along with a brand-spanking-new carrier. It had cushions and toys. All the bells and whistles. I could've lived in that thing. I also gave her three hundred dollars and a knife. "Put the money in your shoe," I ordered. "And the knife . . ." I held it up to the sun. It was transparent and gleamed bright enough to make you shield your eyes. "It's glass, so it won't set off any metal detectors. Use it if you have to and run like hell if you do. Cops are an aggravation you don't need."

She slipped it into the waistband of her jeans and pulled her shirt over it before zipping up the bottom half of her jacket. The authorities might search her bag, but they wouldn't search her. Not a thirteen-year-old, who looked more like eleven and who, I was betting, could cry crocodile tears of fake fear at the drop of a hat. "The world's not a very nice place, is it?"

I considered that for a moment. It was something I hadn't had the luxury to really think about in a while . . . not with Kimano and the Light. "I think that it's not nice but it's not that bad either. It's like a peach. There are some bad spots, a few just mushy ones, and then some really great juicy bites."

Blue eyes ringed with a thick line of deep, dark purple liner—kids—took that in and she sighed. "That was so lame."

I tugged at the red streak I'd dyed at the front of her light brown hair a few hours before. I'd called ahead, but I told her this way they'd know she was from me for sure. Red was my signature. I tended to leave it wherever I went. I said, "When you've got a better one, come back and tell me."

Her bus was due at the terminal soon and I left her at the curb with a backpack of clothes, my number curled in one hand, and the handle of Koko's carrier in the other. I could've parked and gone and waited for the bus with her, but in this life she was going to have to be strong. Now was the time to start. Because she was right . . . the peach thing was lame. The world was a whirlwind of life and excitement and danger and death, a kite soaring high or plummeting to a crumpled wreck on the ground. You had to be prepared . . . from day one. This was her day one.

I watched her walk away and then started what was left of my crumpled little car, with its cracked windshield and sand scars along the side. I patted the buttery leather steering wheel under my hand. "You were a good girl. The best."

"Odd. It doesn't get around downstairs that you know much about being good."

The voice was as buttery and smooth as the leather. I turned to see a new demon sitting in the passenger seat beside me. Definitely a demon, and definitely also fresh from Hell. The shimmer of heat that hung around him was slow to dissipate. "Eligos." He dipped his head slightly in a bow. "You can call me Eli. And the less you know about good, the better in my book. I like wicked women." Where Solomon was the smoldering, mysterious section of the catalogue, Eli had gone with the charismatic naughty boy. The grin he flashed was so bright and happily predatory that women walking on the sidewalk actually stopped and looked around as if they could feel the warmth of it.

He had brown hair, halfway between tousled and spiky and streaked with dark blond, hazel eyes, a strong chin, and a dimple beside a mouth that was simply too perfect to exist in nature. He had a thin upper lip and a full lower lip. I was as much a sucker for that look as for the Latin lips Solomon sported. Both were sexy as . . . well . . . Hell, obviously. Eli's clothes were casual but expensive and he had a brown leather jacket that made him look ready to hop on a motorcycle or in the cockpit of a plane at a moment's notice . . . with a very heavy emphasis on cock. Like all demons, looking far too good to be true was part of his business.

"So, Trixa, what's it going to take to get you to Light up my life?"

"I've gone through all this Light thing with Solomon. Don't you guys have meetings down there? Send e-mails? Doesn't the left hand of evil know what the even more left hand is doing?" I started the car and pulled away from the curb.

"Ohhh, you think we're all friends down there. That's sweet." He leaned back and whistled a few notes of "Why Can't We Be Friends?" "That is so cute. No, sweetheart, we hate one another, almost as much as they hate us upstairs. We're competitive, we loathe all other demons, and in our scaly little hearts we'd all like to be the one to bring the Morning Star down and take his place." The grin, if anything, got wider and more playful. "Evil, remember? There's a bookstore two blocks up if you need a dictionary." He pulled sunglasses out of his pocket and slid them on. "How about we grab some Chinese and talk? I'm starving.

Souls are like Chinese, you know. Eat one and you're hungry for more two hours later."

I should've shot him. I had my Smith tucked in my back waistband holster. But he was right. I'd assumed Hell was united in this. If they weren't, at least this one might keep the others off my back. And truthfully enough . . . I was hungry. It crossed my mind that I was getting a little too comfortable in the company of demons. It also crossed my mind they were getting a little too comfortable in the company of me, which meant they underestimated me.

That was a mistake I could live with.

I cultivated that warm vengeful glow in the pit of my stomach. It kept me on target and blunted the undeniable edge of Eligos's charisma. It didn't take long to find the nearest Chinese restaurant with edible cuisine. I'd been there once before and it was an excellent one. That was important. All I needed was a demon mutilating the chef because the dim sum wasn't up to his standards. We were shown to a booth by a gorgeous Asian woman who tripped twice, unable to take her eyes from Eligos—there was no conceivable way I was going to call him Eli.

"Tell me, Eli"—damn it—"what's your story, then?" I asked as he stretched his arms along the back of the booth. "Solomon says he can pay my price if I find the Light. Can you?"

The hazel eyes were suddenly empty of that uncanny magnetism, empty of the seemingly ever-present humor and sexuality, empty of any emotion at all. They may as well have been the eyes of a dead man or the empty shine of skillfully painted glass. "I can give you anything Solomon can. Anything and more."

"Promises. Promises." I drank the lemon-flavored water.

"I know you're not too fond of him making Vegas his home. Give me the Light and I'll give you whatever you want, plus remove Solomon from your backyard . . . permanently." He ordered without looking at the menu. I took my time, to get to him—letting a demon push you was the first step down a slippery slope with a bottom you did not want to see or experience.

Finally, I made my selection, then leaned back in casual imitation of his pose. "Solomon's a pretty powerful demon, from what I've seen. Are you saying you play in his league?"

His eyes filled up again, like an empty glass, but it wasn't with the wild and exciting emotions of before. It was as he said . . . evil, remember? Dark and savage and utterly confident. "Let's just say he only wishes he could play in mine."

I didn't know if Solomon would agree with that, but Eligos exuded enough self-assurance that although I knew a demon couldn't open his mouth without telling a lie, I almost believed it myself. "Let me see you," I said abruptly. "The real you."

The eyebrows rose. "Aren't we the kinky one? I really am going to like you." There was a flicker, so fast no one else in the restaurant saw it. There were copper scales, eyes like copper-flecked tar. . . . They sucked down the dinosaurs; they'd sucked down souls as well, claws the same dense black, a forked and mottled tongue seen through the waver of clouded glass teeth. The wings of a pterodactyl. Demons weren't pretty, but they weren't ugly either. Like a mixture of Komodo dragon body combined with a raptor that brought death from the skies and the calculating, cold, endlessly patient eyes of a python. Nature: deadly, terrifying, but not ugly.

The flash passed and he was Eli again, white teeth replacing glass daggers. "Which is sexier? Ever want to take a walk on that wild side, babe? Because I can accommodate you there."

"Thanks, but I don't think they make birth control for what you're packing." Although I knew demons, as well as angels, were asexual, they could choose any sexual human form—at least the demons could female-wise. I still didn't know if angels couldn't put on a female costume or were just gender biased. But I did know both angels and demons were sterile, contradicting both the Bible and Hollywood. It didn't matter. I still liked to put it to them once in a while.

"*Rosemary's Baby.*" He snorted. "*The Omen.* Two movies and we never live it down." He adjusted the blinds and blocked the sun. It seemed more appropriate to talk about these things in the dark. "What do you want, Trixa? For the Light, what do you want?"

I pulled out the scale. I kept it with me always, tucked away in a tiny gold locket on my bracelet. "This came from the one who killed my brother. I want him."

I laid the scale on the table between us and he touched it with one careful finger, soaking in its essence . . . its signature. He raised an eyebrow. "You want him dead?"

Something curled my lips, but it was the farthest thing from a smile there was. "I want him. Don't worry about killing him. That pleasure is all mine."

"Hmm." He leaned back and I returned the pewter scale to its place. "There are many demons that color. Hundreds, maybe even a thousand."

"Does that mean you can't do it?" I challenged.

"Sweetheart, there is *nothing* I can't do." He shared that smile with the waitress who'd arrived with our food. "I excel at all things. I achieve all things. In other words, I'm one amazing son of a bitch . . . so to speak. Not literally of course." The smile sharpened as the waitress backed away, legs trembling and eyes both fascinated and fearful. Trapped. And if he wanted her, she *would* be trapped. She didn't have it in her to step away if he had but crooked a finger.

"Besides, I have his essence now. His scent. I'll find him. I'll deliver him, and I'll destroy Solomon if you want, just as the cherry on top." He dug into the food, took a few bites, then made a seesaw motion of his hand. It looked like I hadn't picked the restaurant well enough after all. "Good, but could be better. I think I'll make a deal with the cook on my way out. You keep looking for the Light; I'll scour the earth to locate your brother's fiendish killer." He put his hand on his chest and gave me his perfect profile. "Do I look noble when I say things like that? I feel noble. Straight out of a John Wayne Western or Errol Flynn flick. Before your time though. Pity." He called the waitress over and drawled, "Sweetheart, we're not going to pay for this. Is that all right with you?"

She swallowed, eyes glassy with a good girl's version of lust, and nodded. "I will pay myself, sir."

"Thanks. You're a doll." He gave her the grin, the up-and-down look, until I thought her skin would actually burst into flame, and then he shooed her off. "I'll check in later," he said to me, suddenly all business. "Tracking killers. Damning souls. I might have to forgo running over puppies. This is going to be an entertaining day."

"I was wondering," I asked before he got up, sincerely hoping he was kidding about the puppies. "How many years do people get to enjoy what you demons give them for their souls?"

"Interesting question." He rested his chin in his hand and the smile returned. . . . It was more blinding than the sunlight the blinds had blocked. "Most demons give you five years, some fifteen, some twenty. Arbitrary, really, depending on whom you're dealing with and how hungry they are. Now me, I give my clients the entire span of their natural lives."

Clients. He was something, this one. "Really?" I said skeptically. "Because you're so generous?"

"No, darlin'." The hazel eyes hosted swirls of black. "I do it because that gives them hope. They think, if I live my life and do good things, share my wealth and good fortune, give to the church, God will forgive me . . . take me in when I go. And eventually they even forget for months, sometimes years at a time. What an imagination I had when I was younger. How stupid of me to think something so crazy." The smile had gone from sun to jagged, smoky crystal. "And then, when they're ninety, and it's all just a memory, I show up and drag them down. Sometimes I eat them right away and sometimes I let them suffer years and years in the fire, but the look on their face when I first show up . . ." Scales rippled across the back of his hands; then he was all human again, sexy, happy smile back in place. "It's so much damn *fun*, it should be illegal."

"Instead of immoral?" I said, quelling a ripple of disgust.

"You say to*ma*to, I say to*mah*to." He clapped his hands together once. "And I'll have the best Chinese food in the world right here anytime I want. See you later." He got up and headed straight for the kitchen. I

TRICK OF THE LIGHT

didn't try to stop him as I would've if he'd been on his way to simply kill the cook. I could save the man's life, but I couldn't make his decisions for him.

Free will. God giveth and the devil laughs all the way to the bank.

Chapter 9

I broke the news about the new demon to Leo that night when we were readying the bar for the night owls—they tended to be messier than the daytime crowd. His eyes narrowed as though it was somehow my fault, but he only grunted, "Harems went out of style a while ago."

I started emptying the dishwasher and hanging glasses above the bar. "Please," I said scornfully, "I'm hardly some leather-wearing monster killer with a cadre of hot men and demons waiting on my every sexual whim." I paused, a glass held in midair. Leo started to speak and I held up a finger on my free hand. "Wait a minute. I'm still contemplating why I'm not that and wondering how to change it."

He snapped a bar towel against my ass. "Spare me. Your tawdry fantasies are not something I want to think about."

"Tawdry?" I hung the glass and admitted it. "Okay, tawdry, but I'll make you head harem boy. First in my heart and loins."

"Harem *man*," he corrected, "and no thanks. I don't look good in pantaloons."

"Oh, the harem goes naked at all times . . . unless buttless chaps are involved." I gave him a wink and finished with the glasses. "All the better to serve my depraved needs."

"You're depraved, all right; I'm just not sure it's sexually," he grunted as the door opened to admit the first alcoholic of the evening. "And you're wearing leather right now."

I looked down at the rich color of the brown pants I was wearing. "It's faux. That doesn't count. They don't let you in the club of Monster Layers of America unless you wear the real cow. It's in the bylaws. You also have to like male-on-male porn. That's even above owning your own whip." I poured a whiskey for the customer. "Too bad I only qualify for one out of three."

Leo held his hand up. "Don't tell me. Please. I'll beg if you really push it, but please don't tell me. There's a reason straight men call it a devil's threesome and it has nothing to do with demons."

It was teasing between us. Long honed from an even longer history. The temptation was always there, but Leo and I both knew it couldn't last, and the fact that we might outdo nuclear explosions before we separated still wouldn't be worth losing what we had now. We might not be together sexually, but we were *together* in so many other ways—in all other ways. We were friends and family and lately warriors shoulder to shoulder. That was much better than a harem.

As for the Monster Layers of America . . .

Besides, stare into the abyss and it stares back into you. Follow that to its natural conclusion when it came to sleeping with demons. And that's what Solomon and Eli were, no matter their charm and appeal. One of their kind had killed Kimano . . . as so many of them killed others, over and over. Solomon seemed to think the fact that he limited himself to just taking souls made him a

saint. To hear him talk, it was no worse than a person
eating a hot dog. At least Solomon's meal had agreed to
it—the pig hadn't. And I was far from being a vegetar-
ian; I'd yet to come up with a good answer to that one.
That people were better and more deserving of life than
animals wasn't it. I'd never met a dog I didn't like. I'd
met plenty of people I couldn't say the same about.

Solomon said he didn't kill, but . . . demons lie. All
demons.

Didn't they?

Now Eli . . . Eli definitely lied and he definitely
killed. That I knew as surely as anything. Souls would
never be enough for him. He was a demon—as much
as he looked like a man—who would crave variety, in-
finite and in any fashion he could get it. Eli existed for
every experience he could get, because for him life was
the opposite of short. Instead, life was endless. How to
fill the millions of hours . . . days . . . years.

Why, sweetheart—I could see that disarming grin—
anyway I can.

The night was unusually quiet despite our prepara-
tion. No demonic hordes. No wounded friends in pain.
No wispy little girls and fat, waddling dogs. It was just
half the number of the usual drinkers, sports fans glued
to the TV, and the occasional hooker. Not legal inside
the city limits, but if they could put up with what they
did for the few bucks they needed to survive, I wasn't
going to kick them out. "Nice night," Leo observed.

And it stayed that way until I was escorting a wobbly
patron to his cab. Getting the door open with one hand,
I used the other to grab his waistband as he started to
go down and tossed him in the back with one heave.
"Damn, lady, you got some muscle on you," the cabbie
observed.

"Pilates," I responded. "I like a good workout."

"You work out killing my brethren." Solomon's dark velvet voice came from behind me.

I turned as the cab drove away, folded one arm under my breasts, and kept the other free in case I needed my gun. "From what I hear, I'm not the only one." Not that he was wrong. Fighting demons was great for toning. I should've bought an infomercial. "You'd just as soon kill one another. You higher demons anyway." The mud-colored demons, the lowest of the former angels, seemed to follow the orders of the other demons. Like Solomon had said, or the equivalent of, if you were a mail clerk in Heaven, you were a mail clerk in Hell. "Or so Eligos tells me. Don't tell me you haven't been completely open with me, Solomon. Where is the trust there?"

"As if you ever gave me an ounce of it to begin with." His face was blank. I wasn't sure I'd seen it that way before, a canvas empty of seduction, anger, manipulation, and the darkness. "If you play with Eligos, Trixa, if you give him the smallest pinhole of an opening, you'll only wish he'd killed you."

"I don't know." The moon was high above us, almost the same orange as the Vegas night sky. "He seemed more honest than you. A killer, I'm sure. But I learned more about demons at a lunch with him than I learned in years of knowing you. And here I thought you were all on the same side, one netherworld united under god—god of darkness anyway. But that's not so. I've been negotiating with you when I could've opened the field to all bidders. Why didn't you tell me that, Solomon?"

"I'm a *demon*," he growled. I noticed they used that justification quite a bit. "Self-interest is part of the package, believe it or not. I'm not a killer, but I'm not perfect either. Are you?"

I knew that, naturally—it was hard to forget some-one was a demon—but it opened him up. That can-vas was painted with all sorts of emotion now. It had taken me a while to determine that demons did have real emotions outside murderous rage and homicidal hunger, but they did. They had pride, envy, boredom, fun . . . unfortunately, the fun was a result of the rage and hunger the majority of the time.

"And you don't know Eligos. The things he's done. The ambitions he has. He would raze this entire city with blood and fire and a thousand demons to get what he wants," he warned, stepping closer to me, his hand reaching out to cup my cheek. I let him. Why? A question best answered later when I couldn't feel the beat of his pulse through his palm. "He would take you apart inch by inch, slice by slice. He would make death seem like the rarest and most wonderful dream you could fathom. He would do anything to get the Light. Anything."

"And you wouldn't?" I said softly.

His hand dropped away from my face, but I could still feel the warm imprint of it. A demon's touch was never cold, or maybe that was just Solomon's. "There are things I wouldn't do. I know you don't believe me, but it's the truth." He gave a rueful smile. "A demon can speak it once in a while." He stepped back, asphalt scraping under his black boots. "Perhaps if you would tell me what you want for the Light, we could gain a little more trust between us. A demon, but which demon? And why?" His eyes sharpened on me. "Did you tell Eligos?"

"I did, but you . . . " I looked at him with skepticism,

distrust, and an emotion I doubted he could guess, even with all the souls he'd taken over the years. He may have devoured them, but that didn't mean he understood me. "You, I've known a lot longer. Distrusted a lot longer. When we find the Light, then I'll tell you what I want. Who and why. It'll keep you hungry and sharp, and that in turn will provide a check to Eden House and Eli."

"You play us all against one another." His smile was grim. "You would make a good demon, Trixa. Eating you would be a waste of a good soldier." He moved closer, his breath as warm as his hand. "A waste of an incomparable soul."

The door to the bar opened and Solomon slipped a card into my hand. "Have dinner with me tonight. In an hour." He hesitated, then added a word I would've guessed he didn't even know. "Please." Then he was gone in a minitornado of black smoke. Showy bastard.

Leo stood in the doorway with a shotgun. "Either you're playing games, and you might die because of it. Or you're not playing games—and you will die because of it."

I followed him back inside. "Trust me. I know what I'm doing." Dinner. That was a new one. After three years, maybe he thought he'd try a different approach than threats or straight seduction. It might be interesting.

"I do trust you." He flipped the bar towel over his shoulder and put the shotgun back behind the bar. "You're the only one I trust, but I've seen you lose your temper. And what you feel about Kimano is far beyond simply losing your temper. You could lose your mind before this is all over."

I touched the Pele's tear that hung around my neck, and thought to myself, Who says I haven't already? To

Leo I said, "I have to go change. I have a date." Ignoring his exasperated sigh, I disappeared up the stairs and reappeared a half hour later.

Leo was still waiting, propped on a bar stool with arms crossed. "Nice," he rumbled. "Red dress, tight, lots of perfume. Not like a hooker at all."

"It's not perfume. It's deodorant." And the dress was not that tight. "You think I should try to charm information out of him with my faded T-shirt, holey jeans, and the sweet smell of perspiration?"

"Your idea of charm is to shoot a demon in the head instead of the dick," he said dryly. "But I know better than to try to stop you. Go seduce away. Sleep with him if you think you need to, but think about what Kimano would say about that."

"I am not sleeping with him." I shot him a poisonous glare. "If I had a bumper sticker, it would read, 'Demon slayer, not demon layer.' "

"Your mouth says no, but your cleavage says yes."

I looked down automatically, but saw the same as usual. I was a medium B cup. The only way I was going to get "yes" cleavage was with a fifty-dollar bra or the Army Corps of Engineers. "You are such an ass."

"That's better than what I used to be." He flashed a grin and started closing up the bar. He waited until I was at the door before he said, "Be careful."

I gave him a grin just as bright. "You should've given that advice to Solomon." He simply shook his head in resignation and finished turning out the lights as I opened the front door to pass through. Unlike most Vegas bars, we closed when we felt like it. Usually at one or two. Tonight had been fairly empty, and we'd closed at midnight. That was a little late for a dinner, but in Vegas, time has no meaning. The card Solomon had given me was of a very upscale, difficult-to-get-into restaurant that served until four a.m. And miracle of miracles, it wasn't on the Strip.

Soon enough I was handing my much-abused car over to a dubious valet. The restaurant was called Green Silk. Green wasn't my color, but I appreciated the atmosphere. Candles and candles alone lit the dining room. It made each table seem like the only one there. Once I was escorted to Solomon's table, we were promptly deserted. Usually in a place like this you would have a waiter hovering by your table in case a crumb should fall or you should need a single drop of wine to restore the liquid in your glass to the perfect level. Privacy was a nice change, although when it came down to it, I preferred pizza joints, Greek food, Ethiopian, a hot dog stand . . . anything run by people, real people—not mannequins. Places where you could laugh and not shatter the paper-thin crystal glasses at your table.

Solomon had stood as I was seated, then sat again. "You look. . . ." He smiled and raised his glass, already filled with wine. "I have no words."

"Funny. Leo had quite a few words." I tasted my wine. It was the good stuff, as they say, very, very good. There were some advantages to the high life.

"But you came anyway." Solomon put his glass down. "Have you ever listened to anyone in your life, Trixa?"

"Oh, I listen and then I do what I want, but I do listen. I'm not rude." I had another sip and savored the cherry and spice flavor of it.

"Homicidal, seemingly suicidal at times, with a smart mouth you never bother to rein in, but not rude. I see." His eyes were warm in the candlelight. "In all my years, and they have been many, I've not met any-one quite like you."

"No?" Food was placed before me. Solomon had taken the liberty of ordering before I'd arrived—I hated it when dates did that, but this wasn't a date, I reminded myself. And as it was a small, enormously thick, and extremely tender piece of steak, I let it go. "I still think I've met plenty like you. So, tell me, Solomon—make me truly believe you aren't like all your kin. Tell me. . . ." I thought for a moment. "Tell me about the Fall. The real story, not the made-for-TV version."

His eyes went from warm to somber. "It's not as different as you might think." He looked at his own steak but didn't cut it. It seemed his appetite was gone. Slowly, he started. "Lucifer was best loved by God, when he was an angel. You've heard that, I know. But fathers shouldn't do that. They shouldn't love one of their offspring more than the others. And that's what we thought we were . . . children of God—not tools. But actually we were creations with a purpose, no more a child than a television or a car. Lucifer was the first to tell us it wasn't right. He told us that if he ruled Heaven, he'd be our father and he would love us as children and love us all the same."

"And did he mean it?"

He shook his head. "I don't know. At the time I was sure that he did. God didn't deny what he said. He said nothing and left it up to us . . . with our precious free will . . . to decide. In the face of that silence, it didn't cross my mind that Lucifer might lie, that God might be testing us." Solomon was looking into my eyes, but I didn't think I was the one he saw. "Lucifer was an angel. Angels do not lie, or didn't then, and, truthfully, we thought him the best and brightest of us all. If you could have seen him. His face was the sun, his wings the moon, and now"—his lips pressed tightly together and he drained his glass—"you would die. One glimpse of him and you would die. When we fell, we all became the opposite of what we were. He changed most of all. Our would-be father was turned into something so hideous, even we demons can only glance at him from the corner of our eye. The Morning Star fell, and an endlessly hungry Abyss came to life. Destroying him would've been much kinder. But perhaps he deserves it for taking us all with him."

I was quiet for a moment as he abruptly turned and called for more wine. When he had it and was making his way through it with a grim intensity that had a passing waiter wincing at the lack of appreciation for its age and taste, I asked, "You said free will. I've always wondered how there could be a revolution in Heaven if angels had no free will. That doesn't make any sense. How could you rise up without wills of your own? I know angels learn it eventually if they spend enough time among humans, but the Fall was a long time ago."

He put the glass down and gave a faint smile, pleased to be one up on me for once. "Contrary to popular argument, angels did have free will in the beginning. It was after we were cast down that God stripped free will from the remaining angels. Not much of a reward for loyalty, is it?"

Or perhaps he thought it was like a fast car and a sixteen-year-old new driver. Dangerously beyond their control. Not that it mattered. The angels that interacted with humans on a regular basis regained the will they'd lost. I'd seen it, seen them. It didn't automatically make them the Precious Moments angels with the oh-so-cute tipped halo. Free will can make you a saint or a bastard. There were no guarantees. "So demons didn't learn free will on their own. They had it all along?"

He raised his glass. "We did and we kept it. The one single parting gift left to us by God. Which is ironic. Since with our free will many of us wanted to return home."

"Even if you had had to lose that free will if He let you in?"

"To be in his grace again, it would be worth it. Even without, even as not best loved." He pushed his untouched plate away.

Give up my free will? There was no grace worth that. He read my face. "You don't know. You can't know." For a second, bleak misery flickered behind the gray as his hand fisted on the table. "Grace and home, I'll never have either again."

There were two sides to every story—three sides on some occasions, but I couldn't say that to him, not then. Instead I reached over to rest my hand over his fist. He turned his hand under mine to clasp my wrist lightly. "I want the Light, Trixa, but I want you too. I always have. To talk with you, laugh with you, to sleep late in cool sheets with you." His pupils dilated. "To be inside you. To be one with you."

"Clichéd," I said, a faint flush warming my face. "So very clichéd."

"But effective?" he smiled.

We didn't talk about the Light as I'd expected. We didn't talk about anything else at all. We sat and stared at each other before he kissed my wrist and let me go. I went. I hesitated at the table and I looked back at him halfway across the room, but I went. As I took my last look at the strong planes of his face years familiar now, I thought. . . .

Solomon, whut am I going to do with you?

It was a good thing that I flew the "Slayer Not Layer" flag, because when I did get home, my bed wasn't empty. There wasn't room for Solomon. There wasn't room for me either.

Zeke was sitting cross-legged in the middle of my bed, unloading and reloading his gun. I blinked. No, he was really there. He and Griffin had gone back to their house earlier. They had a dingy box of a house in a concrete alley in a neighborhood over by Lake Mead in North Vegas. It was a perfect choice for them—a part of town so bad that an occasional gunshot from a demon attack wouldn't be investigated by their neighbors or the police.

I was sure Griffin would've preferred something more like the District at Green Valley where expensive condos were located over the top of expensive stores, all painted a rainbow of pastel colors that reminded me of the houses known as Painted Ladies in Charleston, South Carolina. Gracious Southern living brought to the West. Griffin did like the finer things in life, the things he'd never had as a foster kid. But personally I felt my brain twitch at the thought of shotgun-toting Zeke living above a Pottery Barn or a Williams-Sonoma.

The outside of their current shack might have been for work, but the inside was the dream bachelor retreat. Huge flat-screen TV mounted on the wall, surround sound, slate floor, leather couch and chairs, spartan glass and bamboo wood kitchen, all in desert colors. Griffin had gone all out, although the TV was probably Zeke's baby. If Griffin couldn't live where he wanted location wise, he'd make the inside up to his standards. Then it had been a simple matter of Zeke using his telepathy to pick out the dealers and thieves in the neighborhood, knock on their door, and stick a shotgun muzzle in their face with a matter-of-fact, "Do not fuck with our house. Do not fuck with our car. Do not fuck with the blond guy." Thanks in advance for your cooperation and lack of future bloodstains on our driveway. I doubted he'd actually added the last sentence. Politeness wasn't one of Zeke's strong points. I also knew Griffin didn't need Zeke acting as his bodyguard. He was as deadly a fighter in his own right. He didn't need babysitting.

I looked at him now on my bed, and thought to myself that it could be there was an exception to that. They must've come up the back stairs sometime in the last few hours. "You'd better not get gun oil on my bedspread," I warned Zeke.

He didn't look up. He'd heard me come up the stairs and open the door. Probably heard me breathing. Zeke was uncanny that way. So was Griffin. Eden House training or natural talent? I was betting on the latter. "Griffin is sleeping," he said unnecessarily.

And he was, as I'd noticed. In my bed like Goldilocks. I'd seen he was lying beside Zeke when I'd walked into my bedroom, but I hadn't really wanted to notice or see, so I'd managed to push it to the back of my mind. The bathtub, believe it or not, was not a comfortable place to spend the night and I was seeing that in my future again. "I see that. And why aren't you both asleep at home in your own place?"

"Because all he does is sleep. I had to drag him here." Zeke finished with the gun and holstered it. "He won't eat. He won't get up. He just sleeps. And if he just sleeps, he's not there to help me know what to do. He's not there to talk to me. He's"—his light eyes darkened with the slightest edge of panic—"not there."

I sat on the other side of him, although there wasn't much room. I wrapped an arm around his shoulder. It was a lot like embracing a cactus. He only allowed Griffin to touch him without tensing up, at least while conscious. But I gave him a few minutes and he relaxed minutely under my touch. "You were out of it for two days. The drugs knocked you out, but the pain was still there. Not to mention the worry. Griffin didn't know if you'd make it. The doctors said yes and there was a good chance, but things happen. Griffin has been with you . . . what? Since he was ten and you were eight? That must feel like his whole life that he's looked after you. He felt like he failed you when the demons took you down; he felt all your pain even when you were out. If he slept for a week, I wouldn't be surprised. His body is exhausted and so is his mind. Whisper didn't heal him like she did you."

He was silent for a moment, then asked belligerently, "Why not?"

"Because healing bodies is simple for a healer, but healing minds isn't. At least that's what a healing friend of mine said a long time ago. It's just the way things are." I smoothed his hair and tugged at the short copper ponytail. "You want to stay here tonight?" I asked.

His eyes moved over to Griffin and he laid a hand on the slowly rising and falling back. "I want . . ." He stopped and started over, more honestly. "I need help to watch him. If the demons come, he won't be ready. Not as ready as he needs to be. I have to protect him."

Like he protects you. I understood perfectly. "Okay. No problem." I waited for him to offer to sleep in the tub since Leo was still sleeping on the couch downstairs. And I kept waiting. Finally, I said, "How about I sleep with Griffin and you take the tub and some blankets."

"No." He went for one of his knives this time, one from an ankle holster, and began polishing it—with *my* bedspread. My expensive, well-loved bedspread.

"Zeke . . ."

"No." This time he scowled. "He's *my* partner. I'll guard him. Understand?"

Indeed I did. More than he himself, I thought. I looked at the tub and grumbled under my breath. I really was too softhearted for my own good . . . no matter how many demons I'd killed. I grabbed blankets, enough for a thick pseudomattress and one to cover me. I also took a pillow and climbed in. It was a huge, roomy tub, but it still wasn't a bed. "You owe me, you know?" I told Zeke over the edge before pulling the curtain and changing into pajamas.

"I know," he answered without emotion. "I owe you everything I have in my life. I won't ever forget that."

"But I still can't sleep with Griffin?" I groused, as I tried to find a comfortable position.

"No." This time he sounded faintly amused. I pushed the curtain back and peered over the porcelain edge just in time to see the small smile disappear.

Sneaky dog. I curled up in the fetal position, felt for the gun under my pillow, and dozed off. Whether Zeke slept at all I wasn't sure, but when I woke up in the morning he was in the same position and this time cleaning my weapons. At least he wasn't using my bedspread this round. It was an improvement. I don't, as a rule, get attached to things. That was the way of the traveler, but I'd been in Vegas longer than I'd been anywhere else. Things started to creep in. Bedspreads. Whimsically carved beds. A large hunk of amber encasing a trapped spider from long ago. That was actually to remind me. I might be in a cage now, one of my own making, but I'd get out eventually, when I'd accomplished everything I'd set out to do. Then again, the amber was a particularly fine orange-gold. Like being cradled by the sun—comfortable and warm. Maybe it wasn't such a bad thing to stick around a place for a while. Oh, hell, what was I thinking?

I'd been here ten years. That was a record for my family. Apparently it was taking a toll on my sanity, along with everything else that was going on. I was a wanderer, born and bred. I had to give it up temporarily for the Light and for Kimano, but I'd wander again. It was my nature, and natures don't change. Hair color, breast size, houses, cars, schools, and jobs—all of it changed. Every second of every day there was change, but never the spots. You were born with spots and you died with the exact same ones.

I looked at Griffin and Zeke. Then again, there was always the occasional exception to trip you up.

"He's still not up?" I climbed out of the tub, the wrinkles falling out of the silk pajamas as I stood.

"No." He sat there with two of my guns in my lap; his hands had stopped moving. "Maybe he'd rather stay where he is. I'm nothing more than a damn anchor around his neck."

He sounded defeated and angry and neither emotion was like Zeke. There were long stretches where someone who didn't know him would wonder if he had any emotion at all. He did. He just kept it buried in a dark place, a place I thought was probably host to cold bathwater and a drowned baby. The way he was showing it now was an indication of how truly upset he was.

"You're his friend, Zeke, and you're his purpose. He's lucky to have you, more than you know. Knowing your true purpose in life, that's a miracle." I padded over to the bed. "I'll show you." I put a hand on Griffin's shoulder and shook him. "Wake up, sleepyhead."

His head was turned on the pillow facing Zeke. His eyes flickered instead of snapping open immediately, evidence of his exhaustion, but when they did open, they fixed on Zeke first and foremost. They showed instant relief; then he frowned. "Is it morning? Have you had breakfast?"

Zeke returned to the guns as if he hadn't been worried, as if he didn't even know what worry was, but I saw his jaw relax. "No. I was cleaning Trixa's guns."

The frown intensified. "Did you eat supper last night?"

"No. I was cleaning my guns. Guns are more important than food."

Griffin sat up. "You woke me up and made me eat something. I wouldn't call it food, but it was microwaved, so I'm guessing you would."

"That was lunch. I couldn't wake you up for supper. And someone has to take care of you. You're weak and frail," Zeke said with a sardonic twist of his lips—there and gone so quickly you could convince yourself that you imagined it. "Like a little girl. You asked for a pudding cup."

"I did *not*," Griffin growled. Griffin of the fine food and fine clothes, who had given up the pedestrian things of a foster child life the moment Eden House had showered him with money. The words "pudding cup" almost literally horrified him. We all do our best to deal in different ways.

"All this codependency is bringing a tear to my eye, but get up and go eat, the both of you," I ordered. "At the diner around the corner. I'm ready for a little alone time." I hadn't had any in quite a few days. I wanted it, I needed it, and despite them obeying me, I still didn't get much.

Fifteen minutes after Griffin and Zeke had gone, Leo was calling for me. I came down the stairs to see Mr. Trinity and his entourage. I was still in my pajamas, but while silk, they covered me neck to ankle. I doubted it would've made any difference if I'd come down stark naked or with tasseled pasties rotating like propellers. I didn't think Mr. Trinity was into sex . . . with either gender. He was an asexual pillar of ice. I didn't even know that I was a person to him instead of just a thing to accomplish his goal. It seemed all of him, every speck, molecule, iota, belonged to his Creator. His focus lay in serving him and only him. And pardon my political incorrectness, but it was creepy as hell. What was worse was imagining how he might feel if he knew God wasn't giving him his orders . . . angels were, angels who were using him as a windup tin soldier and didn't necessarily have a clue as to what God wanted.

"You've had your time," he said, charcoal suit impeccably tailored. "Where is the next signpost?"

"Orange juice," I told Leo, who was standing behind the bar. He poured and handed it to me and I was grateful for the slug of vodka he'd included. He was a man who really knew how to read a woman, especially one who wasn't particularly a morning person when the night before was spent in the bathtub. I drank the squat glass down and sighed. Better. I turned back to Mr. Trinity with his four men dressed a little more casually, although certainly not Zeke-casual, but enough for fighting demons if they had to. "San Diego. The next bread crumb is in San Diego."

"We leave this afternoon. I'll have someone pick you up at four," he said flatly. Then he turned and, followed by his loyal dogs, was gone.

I sat on a bar stool and raised my eyebrows. "If only my trips to the gynecologist were that quick and efficient."

"On that note, I'm going to balance the books and puncture my eardrums." Leo tossed his towel onto the bar. "Do you want me to come to San Diego with you?"

"No. I'll be surrounded by Eden House's second best and most anal." I tried for the dregs of the OJ. "I'll most likely be safe from our downstairs neighbors. Will you be okay? I'm leaving Zeke and Griffin to stay here with you. Considering the time they've had, their place might not be the best place for them. Besides, they can act as your bodyguards," I teased.

"Don't insult me." He snorted. "You want me to look after them, I take it? You're aware my paycheck doesn't cover babysitting."

"Pretend they're family." I handed him the glass and he put it in the dishwasher.

"You do remember how I got along with my family in the days when they were still speaking to me?" he asked wryly.

True. His family was definitely not my family. They lived at one another's throats and Leo was the worst of them all. Or he had been. He'd changed over the years. Well, not changed so much as mellowed a few thousand degrees. Same spots but greatly faded. I hoped one day they would give him a chance to prove that. But the bad blood between Leo and his father was very bad indeed. Bile, black and acidic. That kind of burn would take a long time to cool. Either that or a catastrophe.

Later, I'd be thinking how hindsight was such the bitch.

"Someday"—I pulled at the black braid that trailed down his chest—"someday they'll see you for what you are now . . . if I have to kick the ass of each and every one. I promise."

"That might be the one thing that does it. They fear you almost as much as they did me." He returned the favor by wrapping one of my messy curls around his finger. "And with good reason."

"You always were one with a compliment." I slapped his chest and ordered, "And treat Zeke and Griffin like my family, then, not yours." I told him this, but I didn't need to. Leo had treated them just that way, just as I had, from day one. Strays who needed help; strays who'd become adopted family because if we didn't do it, no one else would. And honestly no one else was as qualified as we were. Just because I sold information that occasionally led to the end of a rotten, cheating, and abusive soul didn't mean I also didn't have sympathy for those who deserved it.

Although these days, fewer and fewer seemed to. Maybe it was the crowd I'd started running with. Demons and the lackeys of angels. I was no one's lackey.

And despite what Mr. Trinity thought when he arrived to pick me up, I certainly wasn't his.

Chapter 10

The House had their own jet. No surprise there. It was only a four-hour drive, but I suspected the last thing Mr. Trinity wanted was to be cooped up in a car, no matter how large and opulent, for that long with a bar owner. An annoyingly low-class bar owner with unsuitably tousled waves of streaked hair, equally unsuitable red jacket and pants, and the rude habit of demanding food and pomegranate martinis on an hour-long flight.

At least Eden House had connections far above and beyond the government, because I boarded their plane without showing ID and carrying my gun. And a few knives. I could've carried in a shotgun if I'd wanted. I didn't want. I wanted another martini, but we landed before I was able to order one. Mr. Trinity hadn't exchanged one word during the flight. His second in command, along for the ride, Jackson Goodman, was less restrained. "Greed and gluttony," he said disapprovingly. "While we're on . . ."

"A mission from God?" I smiled winningly. Old movies, I loved them. I'd been waiting a long time to use that line with Eden House.

After that, Goodman didn't speak to me anymore while we were on the plane. It was for the best. He annoyed me, and I couldn't spare the concentration right now to think of ways to annoy him back. Not that he didn't think that I annoyed him already. Poor Jackie. He had no idea what I could do if I put my mind to it. But there was a time for everything.

We disembarked in San Diego to blue skies, the imagined smell of the ocean, and a slowly falling sun. I liked San Diego. I liked the cold, salty ocean, the wet sand, Old Town, the Gaslamp Quarter, the seals flapping and snorting seawater. It was a great place to visit, a great place to live if you could afford it, and apparently a great place to drop a bread crumb. That face, that name, their plans . . . someone had visited the aquarium in Vegas and stared at a particular shark through the glass—and that someone had ended up here. They had good taste.

Maybe I could pack in a minivacation while scooping up a tiny portion of the Light. I ignored the diesel fumes on the tarmac and turned toward the ocean. It wasn't in view, but I could imagine it. Now, if I actually could get to see it and eat seafood on the docks, it would be a great day. A fabulous day.

I wasn't holding my breath.

"Where is the next step?" Mr. Trinity said behind me, his voice the drip of a frigid icicle. I'd be willing to bet his greatest regret was that he hadn't been born in the time of the Inquisition or witch burning. Not that Eden House was Catholic . . . they were an order of their own making, unknown by the public, unaffiliated, and were around before BC clicked over to AD. Ancient indeed.

"I'm not exactly sure. Sharks aren't as verbal in their communication as people, even with the Light's help. It took me a while to get his name, Butch—so imaginative—but I can't get a last name. But I did get this general location. . . . I know he's here. Somewhere. I'm just not exactly sure where." I saw it again, a blurry vision of the man through water and a thick layer of glass. Almost unwillingly he'd put his hand up to the glass and the shark had rested its blunt nose on the other side. The trail to the Light had passed. The picture was waving in my head like seaweed—a man, not a very attractive one. He looked like the kind of man who'd toss a hair dryer into his ancient mother's bathtub to get a measly inheritance—just enough to buy a truly gorgeous guitar. He'd find a band, then, who would take him. They'd all see. I could see the frayed towels, the rubbery flowers on the bottom of the tub to keep the elderly from slipping. A big ratty hair dryer from the eighties bought for twenty-five cents at a yard sale. A smirking grandson who'd kill a neighborhood cat if he could catch it. Sparks flying. The lights going out.

I'm known for my imagination.

Then again, knowing he was in a band wasn't my imagination. The shark told me that, the Light told me that, the same as it told me to go here. So it could be that Grandma had shuffled off her mortal coil just as I pictured it.

Butch's smirk in the aquarium had been combined with dyed black hair, a narrow face, weasel eyes, and silver canine teeth flashing in an uneasy grimace as the smirk slid away. Hard to blame him. It wasn't every day a shark shoved something into your brain. Drugs, it had to be the drugs; I could hear the echo of the thought through the Light. He moved away from the glass, snarling and showing those inlaid silver canines again. See? Look at me. It's just a stupid shark.

I'm not scared of it or the cold, saltwater thoughts in my head.

I saw him brush by a man with a two-year-old tucked in his arms. The little boy looked at the silver teeth and whimpered. "Bogeyman."

Oh, sugar, I thought with sympathetic amusement, not hardly. Here's hoping that's the worst thing you see in your life, that pathetic monster wannabe.

"We need to go that way." I pointed. "Toward the Gaslamp Quarter. He's there somewhere."

"Can you be a little more specific?" Goodman spoke up stiffly for the first time in forty minutes. Dressed in a suit an undertaker would've found darkly grim, with washed-out blue eyes and hair neither brown nor blond, he barely looked like a human being at all. More of a wax figure that didn't make the grade and was tossed to molder in Madame Tussaud's basement. In every way, he was far more frightening than the wannabe with the black hair and silver teeth. That guy had an identity, as pathetic as it was. Goodman looked like an identity vampire. Like he would suck up the essence of everything that made you *you*, to fill up the hollow figure he was . . . fill up what he was missing inside. What was he missing? From the looks of him and the shimmer of what seemed like almost a vacuum around him, that might just be every single thing that made a human human.

"I'm not a bloodhound. Get me closer and hopefully I'll get more specific. Or the Light will."

By the time the hired car took us to the Gaslamp Quarter, I did have it narrowed down. Unfortunately it wasn't in one of the great seafood restaurants, but rather the looming presence of Petco Stadium. There was a concert coming up in two hours and the teenagers were already rowdy, shouting and cursing good-naturedly as the line curved around the stadium.

Goodman flashed his ID—CIA, FBI, Homeland Security; whatever Eden House provided him with got us through the door and past the crowds. I took the lead, a glowing thread reeling me in. I walked through the circular halls and past security guards and bodyguards, all who stepped back as if whatever laminated card Goodman continued to flash was kryptonite. Several bands were playing here tonight and our goth-emo-imitation monster from the aquarium was no doubt in one of them. Finally reaching a door relatively untrampled by headset-wearing men and women who seemed frantic just for the love of the emotion, I opened the door without knocking. No one would've heard me anyway. It was a party. Drugs, alcohol, and underage girls galore. I grabbed a beer from a table and waded in. I looked over my shoulder to see that Mr. Trinity and his entourage had decided to wait in the hall out of the crush. Wimps. Demons they'd take on. Sweaty, half-naked, puking groupies were a little too much for them.

I moved through the room, ears deafened by bad music—this band's music. Had to be. I came to an unconscious guy on the floor and bent for a closer look. Not my guy, not Butch. I stepped over him and kept going. I finally found the weasel on a couch with four women, two sandwiched on either side of him. He looked unbearably smug and rapacious. He thought he was a predator surrounded by his prey—a ferret with small, silver fangs.

Since the couch was full, I plopped on his lap and flashed him a smile, wide, sexy, and stupid as they came. "Hi." I had to fit in with everyone else for the few seconds this was going to take. I needed him to hold still. The passing of the way to the Light was disorienting. I didn't need him having a shark/aquarium flashback and freaking out. Then I'd have to knock him unconscious and that was more work than I wanted to invest in.

"Hey," he said back, trying to fake being bored and cool during our scintillating, monosyllabic conversation.

I reached a hand up and touched his hair as if I were going to comb my fingers through the limp strands. Instead, I clamped my fingers on the curve of his skull and let the shining bit of Light pass into me. It poured out of the drug-soaked brain into mine. It was like before, running to the edge of the cliff and jumping, arms spread. Flying for a split second, and then falling. Falling and falling. Forever. On top of whatever drugs he was on, it had to be ten times worse for him than for me. His mouth dropped open. He gurgled, then started to yell. I slammed my hand over the chapped, cracked lips of his mouth. Kissing him would've been more convincing to those around us.

Not in this lifetime.

I closed my eyes and let the Light flash through my brain around and around and then curl up like a cozy cat. If the Light had emotions, this tiny molecule of it was probably glad of the new, less drug-addled home. The ferret screamed under my hand. No one heard him. It was too loud, my hand was too tight, and the alcohol had flowed like a river in this room.

"Sharks and guitars," I whispered to him. "Which is real? One or both?"

His thin chest heaved and the breath died against my palm. I pulled my hand away and he gagged in disbelief, "I'm high. I'm so high."

"Depends on what standards you're going by." I moved off his lap, one of the better shifts in location I'd made all day, and headed back for the door.

"We're on. Let's go!"

Someone from the band actually said it. It was like a rockumentary, a very bad, fake rockumentary. I stepped to the side as the room emptied in a rush, all the bad music lemmings flowing out into the hall. I waited until they were gone and followed. Trinity, Goodman, and the others were waiting, completely wrinkle and rumple free. Untouched. Quick of foot, force field of holier-than-thou superiority—either way it was impressive.

"I have it," I told Mr. Trinity. "It's not telling me anything yet, but I have it."

"Good," he said, as if he expected nothing less. There couldn't be too many failures among the agents of Eden House. Trinity wouldn't tolerate it, which is why he didn't suspect Griffin and Zeke of being double agents. He couldn't imagine anyone going against his authority, especially not for the likes of Leo and me.

I leaned against the wall and folded my arms. "Give me a second. I'm still a little dizzy."

Goodman looked impatient, Trinity was impassive, as usual, and the minions were as blank of face as they'd been throughout the entire trip. I bowed my head and studied the toes of my boots for several minutes before I said, "All right, I'm ready." I straightened, stepped away from the wall, and started down the hall. Goodman was ahead of us with his magic card in hand, parting the Red Sea. We were almost out when I heard the band start tuning up out on the field. I turned and saw them on the stage set in the grass. Singer, bassist, drummer, and my friend, the guitarist. He did have a gorgeous guitar as I'd seen, the one the Light had said Grandma had paid her life for. It was red. Of course I was sure he had lots of guitars, all colors. He just happened to pick my favorite color. Wasn't that ironic?

What was more ironic was when his fingers touched the strings, there was an arc of white fire that arched him up on his toes with his back bowed and his head thrown back with tongue jutting forth. Not a pretty sight. Fortunately, the roadies were bright enough not to touch him, but it was a few seconds before they managed to turn off the electricity. They tried CPR, but he was gone, just like Grandma had been.

"Damn," I murmured to Mr. Trinity, "a real act of God. I'd never seen one before. You guys . . . sometimes Hell takes too long, huh?"

He looked at me blandly, as if he didn't know what I was talking about, but that symmetry? Grandma and grandson going out the exact same way? Justice. It couldn't be denied, and I certainly wasn't going to. There was power behind this. Real power, the kind to be respected.

Trinity didn't bother to discuss it, turning and walking away. His men stayed behind me, keeping me in sight. Keeping me in line, they thought. One seemed to think I wasn't moving quickly enough and gave me a push. I whirled quickly enough that none of them had a chance to slide a hand inside their jackets. I punched the one who thought he could put his hands on me uninvited hard enough to knock him flat. I turned back and kept walking. "You shouldn't take things for granted, especially not women who work in bars. Sometimes we have to act as our own bouncers," I said over my shoulder. "Sometimes we have pervert dates."

"And sometimes you even face demons." Trinity slowed until I moved up even with him. "And that," he said flatly, "is something civilians don't do." Not shouldn't do or couldn't do, but didn't do. Mr. Trinity and the House of Eden had plans for me after this was all done. It wasn't so far-fetched. The firstborn wiped out, the cities destroyed, angels had been God's warriors in the Old Testament—Eden House had taken it on themselves to do that job now, and no middle-management Gabriel or Raphael had bothered to tell them differently.

While Trinity must have known every word of the Bible, I thought he rarely spent much time mulling over the love and forgiveness in the New Testament. Whatever he thought he was going to do to me, none of it would give the man a second's pause or a single night's bad sleep. After all, wasn't it God's will? Did anyone know that will better than Trinity? That doubt couldn't exist in his mind. I knew that for a fact. He didn't need to check it out first with any dagger-feathered angel; he already knew. Superiority, arrogance . . .

Pride. We all knew whose fall that went before. Mr. Trinity knew his Bible, but did he *know* his Bible?

Probably not.

Yes, Trinity no doubt had plans for me or just one in particular. A swift and ruthless one. It was entirely too bad for him, because he simply wasn't man enough for the job.

"Hawkins and Reese may have foolishly trusted you, but I know differently. Whatever your reasons for killing demons, they aren't ours. You don't know the greater good."

It was far too cuddly to call your employees by their first names, but I so rarely heard their last names—Zeke

Hawkins, Griffin Reese—that I often had to think twice when I did hear them, just to remember who was being referred to. It was easy to forget. Just like Trinity would be quick to forget them once they were gone. His plans for them weren't any better than the one he had for me. Regardless of whether they were true double agents on his side and not mine, watching Leo and me for Eden House and ready to help drag us in at any moment, their fates still wouldn't have been any better. Working with outsiders? That was worse than failure to Trinity. That was treachery, intended or not.

Griffin and Zeke knew they were in trouble, knew they were playing with fire, but I wasn't sure they knew how far their boss would go. When all was said and done at the end of this, they were the same as demons to their House. We all were.

The greater good, as they saw themselves, didn't want us.

When I got home just after nightfall, the place was empty. The bar was closed and dark. Leo had hung his version of a Gone Fishing sign on the door—black marker on white cardboard that said GO THE FUCK AWAY. There are men of few words and then there are men of perfect words. Leo was the latter.

I let myself in, waving at a car parked across the street that held two Eden House agents. Trinity's cover for Zeke and Griffin, and a check because it never paid to trust anyone too much, not even your own "double agents." Our Mr. Trinity was so untrusting.

Flipping on the light behind the counter, I looked for a note. Not that Leo and I usually kept that close an eye on each other. We knew we could each take care of ourselves, and our social lives weren't crossing paths.

Leo's taste in women—except for me—didn't lead to double-dating. Amazons and bimbos with IQs half their cup size. Leo's bad taste aside, this situation was a little different. I'd asked him to watch Zeke and Griffin. If he had left, there'd be a good reason. There'd be a note.

There was. It was held down by a bottle of bourbon and a shot glass. That wasn't a good sign. I read it and sighed. I was lucky Leo had applied the antibiotic ointment to my back that morning, because it didn't look like he'd be here to do it tonight or to bunk on the couch again. I folded the note on the words *Family emergency. The dog is loose. Back tomorrow.* In a way though, it *was* a good sign. Leo's family was reaching out. It might only be to use him, but that was better than the past years of not speaking to or acknowledging him at all. And that dog was mean, mean enough that no one but Leo could deal with it, but mean or not, it was family too. They'd simply have to catch it before it ate anyone.

"Want to share the bourbon?"

I looked up to see Griffin on the stairs. "Still hanging around, you two?"

"Zeke still thinks I'm off my game. Besides, how could Zeke and I send Trixa reports back to Eden House if we're not here to actually watch you?"

He still looked tired, gray smudges under his eyes. No, Zeke wouldn't be happy with that, and an unhappy Zeke could rarely be budged. "So your fellow demon hunters outside don't have a clue, then, I take it?" I retrieved another glass and poured him a shot as he sat down beside me.

"No." He rolled the glass between his hands, then tossed it back. "You and Leo are damn good at keeping your thoughts and emotions under wraps. The agents outside aren't as strong as Zeke and I. No one in the

House is, and you two are the most self-possessed people I've come across. You don't give off anything you don't want to give off. I didn't pick up on you while I was upstairs until you walked through the door. Normally I can pick up on someone I know or a demon a good three blocks away. Even now I'm not sure exactly how things went in San Diego, except you're not disappointed."

"I'm not disappointed. You're right there." I drank my own shot. "As for giving off thoughts and emotions, having a psychic and an empath hanging around the place will teach you better. Especially when it comes to Zeke. He wouldn't see the harm in watching my last date in his head like it was rent-a-porn."

"Your last date was that good, eh?" He held out his glass for another.

"Since the last man in my bed was you, drooling and unconscious, with Zeke nobly defending your virtue, not especially." I poured, then stretched out the kinks from the two plane rides. My back protested and I gave myself another shot of my own. Purely medicinal.

"I don't drool." He tried for outrage, but with his weariness couldn't quite pull it off.

"Maybe not, but your virtue did survive the night intact," I pointed out, putting the bourbon away. It might be medicinal for me, but it would only make Griffin more tired. I didn't need den mother Zeke down here trying to kick my ass.

"Thanks for that, Zeke," he said glumly.

"He was very cute—in an unsocialized–pit bull kind of way." I patted him on the back. "Now, pack up your things and move them down to the office. The two of you are sleeping on the couch. I want my bedroom back."

"I don't think the two of us are going to fit on your couch," he said dryly.

"Spoon." I gave him a light shove toward the stairs. "Or one of you can sleep on the floor. It all depends on how secure in your masculinity you are. Either way, I'm sleeping in my own bed."

"It'll be hard to get Zeke to give up all that decadence, but I'll do my best. And no one is that secure in their masculinity," he finished as he headed for the stairs.

"I wish I'd taken a picture last night. Curled up like puppies in a basket," I lied without a qualm. As for Zeke, his appreciation of my décor went as far as cleaning weapons with it.

"You are truly evil." He disappeared, but I heard the repeated, "Evil," as he went.

Several seconds later someone added from behind me, "I like that in a woman. Malevolence is good too. Do you have that on tap, Miss Trixa?"

I swiveled on my stool, automatically training the gun pulled from my waistband directly at Eli's head. He was leaning against the end of the bar and was every inch as I remembered him. Gorgeous and charismatic. Also deceptively deadly, and that didn't bear forgetting. I didn't need the take-out box of noodles he held in one hand to remind me.

He used the chopsticks in his other hand to point at the container. "Want some? Best in the world . . . now."

Was making the ultimate sweet-and-sour worth your soul? I didn't think so, but apparently the restaurant chef had. "No thanks." I kept the gun pointed. "If I want food of the damned, I'll just microwave a Hot Pocket." Griffin and Zeke didn't come running down the stairs, shotguns in hand, which meant Eli was as powerful as he said he was—or at least equally as powerful as Solomon. He couldn't be "seen" by a psychic or empath, no matter how good. He was simply better. Stronger.

"Suit yourself, and I'm assuming you usually do." He stabbed the chopsticks into the noodles and set the cardboard box on the bar. "I don't have to ask if you found the next step to the Light. I can see it, glowing around you like a halo, which, by the way, is a huge turnoff."

"Sorry about that." Not quite. "Do you have any information for me or are you here for the ambience?"

He looked around at the scarred tables, dartboard, small pool table, TV mounted over the bar and shrugged. "Add a floor of knives and air of pure unholy fire and it'd be just like home. Except for the TV. We don't have satellite yet. The boonies are always the last to get it." He peeled off his jacket and tossed it over a stool. "Actually, I'm here to dance."

Leo's radio behind the bar came on and jumped from station to station until a slow song came on. "Once again, before your time," he observed. "A flash from the past, but it's easy to move to . . . vertically. Horizontally too, if one were in the mood."

"Which I'm assuming you always are." I considered the situation, then replaced the gun in the back waistband of my pants. If he wanted to play, I could do that. In fact I was rather good at that. Demon good? I guess we'd have to see. "And the halo?"

"I'll close my eyes." He gave me that smile, far more warm and intimate than a monster had any right to, as he held out a hand. I took it as he looped an arm around my waist, deftly avoiding my gun. We moved to the music. "Amazing. You can dance like you're all grown-up." He whirled me around slowly.

"I'm thirty-one. I've been to a dance or two. Hit the floor at weddings with more than one grandpa."

"Ouch." He tilted his head down to look at me. "Are you going to hold a million years or so against me?"

He smelled nice, which wasn't fair. There was no clichéd whiff of the traditional sulfur and brimstone. He smelled clean—like soap and wet spring grass with the faintest trace of ozone. Of lightning and a thunderstorm in the distance, ready to wash over you to bury you in rain and shake the ground like an earthquake. I could play all right, but he wasn't an amateur by any stretch of the imagination.

"I've dated older men before. Age doesn't matter." We did another slow turn as I added, "It's the killing innocent people and the taking of souls I have a problem with."

"I'm sure they weren't all innocent. I mean, really, what are the odds of that? Three out of ten might be *mostly* innocent, I'll give you that. But all of them? Statistically impossible for the human race." He dipped me and smiled as he hung over me. "And surely you're not claiming innocence, Trixa. I see things behind your eyes that tell a different story. A far more interesting story, by the way. Innocence is so boring."

"Speaking of boring, if you don't have any information for me, then that's all you're doing." I mirrored his smile, my back twinging from the dip. "Boring the hell out of me."

"You do make a demon work for his due." He straightened, pulling me upright, and let go of me. The radio shut off. "When did this demon kill your brother and where? The one you want so badly?"

"If you need that to do your job, you're not half as good as you say you are." I sat back down. My back was healing, had healed quite a bit in the past few days, but the dancing hadn't done it much good. I'd thought of having Whisper heal it when she healed Zeke, but it was just scraped and torn skin already mending on its own. Zeke's pain had been out of control. My pain was more of an inconvenience. When you find inconveniences too much to handle, then you'll find life to be exactly the same.

"Oh, I'm good and I'll find him, but I could find him more quickly if you'd be a little less of a bitch and a little more cooperative." He said "bitch" the same way he would've said "sugar" or "honey" or "darling"—as if it were an endearment. He really was something.

"You're a straight talker, I'll give you that. And only that." I retrieved the bourbon, poured him a shot in my glass, and slid it down the bar about four feet to him. "I'm not here to help you. You're here to help me . . . that is, if you want the Light. If I make things too easy for you, Eligos, who's to say you'll wait for me to find the Light? Who's to say you won't try to take me from Trinity and put me on your own leash?"

"Who is to say?" he echoed blandly before he swallowed the shot quickly and smoothly, sitting down himself. "I might be transparent to your eye, but that doesn't mean it wouldn't be easier and quicker for both of us."

"Quick or easy—it doesn't matter, because it's not going to happen," came a new voice, deep and rough.

Which was all we needed to make a party.

Solomon.

He stood by the door, not that he'd needed to use it. His gray eyes were slits. I'd been right when I'd guessed that Solomon wouldn't care for Eli any more than Eli cared for him. "This is my territory, Eligos. This place is mine. *She* is mine. You can leave now, whole and intact, or you can leave it in a spray of blood and flesh. A pool of rotting fluid on the floor." The gray blazed to silver, the first physical hint of demon I'd ever seen in Solomon—the first true loss of temper.

"He's a cranky son of a bitch, isn't he?" Eli turned over the shot glass and tapped it once, to all appearances bored. Certainly the farthest thing from intimidated without actually dozing off. "Tell me you never found him entertaining. No one's taste could be that bad. The brooding. The smoldering. He'd fit in fine on the soap opera channel or a vampire movie, but real life?" He raised a disbelieving eyebrow. "Real sex? You'd be better off with a Ken doll. Same personality, and probably the same equipment."

I'd felt differently when Solomon had paid me that uninvited visit several nights ago, straddling me in bed. And I do mean *felt* it. But true or not, it was enough to tip Solomon over the line from temper to rage. I'd never seen him angry; I'd only seen the imitation of it. Solomon didn't care that much about his club and our arson of it. He played as if he had emotions, because that's all Solomon had ever done with me—play. With Eli he was serious—the kind of serious that would end with demon blood and entrails on my floor, neither of which could be put right with your average household cleanser.

The fight wasn't a surprise. The surprise was Solomon pulling a gun from under his jacket and nailing Eli with several shots midchest. The two that should've hit him in the head missed and for one reason only, because Eli could move that fast. It was a flicker of brown so quick that my eye only caught an afterimage of it. Caught it from the floor, by the way, where I was crouching below the bullet path. I was good, but I wasn't a fool.

"Please. You're kidding, right?" Eli brushed at the front of his shirt that had turned black with demonic blood. "A gun? Oh, I get it. You don't want the girl-friend to see you for what you really are, warts and all. Or should I say scales and all?" He didn't move from the stool. Instead he grinned, gloating and smug. "I have news for you, Solomon. She likes that. There's a whole level to her you didn't even suspect." He looked back at me as I waited ready on one knee with my own gun drawn. "What do you say, Trixa? Want to see the real thing fighting over you? You want to see scales and fangs and everything we truly are as we rip each other to shreds?"

First, it wasn't me they were fighting over. It was the Light. If I forgot that, I'd be another puddle on the floor that Leo would have to Clorox the hell out of. Second, it appeared my system of hell-spawn checks and balances might go all the way to balancing each other out altogether. That wouldn't do me any good when it came to Kimano's killer.

Third, Zeke wasn't going to let any fight go down that he wasn't part of. He came down the stairs in a rush, followed by Griffin. Both had shotguns, but only Griffin was polite enough to tell me to duck right before they fired. Both went for head shots, the surest way to put a demon down; both missed. And that, that was unheard of. If nothing else, it showed that all the demons we'd killed in Vegas, except for the black ones that had taken Zeke down, were nowhere near as powerful and inconceivably quick as the two that were in my bar now.

Eli swiveled on the stool to take in the two partners. The slugs that should've blown through his skull had instead blown through one of the wooden posts that went from counter to ceiling. "Pets, Trixa?" he drawled. "You should have them neutered. Makes them less likely to piss on your rug."

I ignored him, ignored Zeke and Griffin who were reloading, and looked at Solomon. "What happened to the two guys in the car out front? The two who were watching me." Why hadn't they come running at the shots as Zeke and Griffin had?

The silver darkened back to gray and his eyes focused on Eli. "I imagine he killed them. That's what he does, Trixa. I take the willing souls. He takes it all."

Eli shrugged. "Right, as if you don't. But if those two angel ass-wipers are dead out there, Solomon did it. He likes easy targets, the fish-in-the-barrel types. Lazy, lazy. I prefer a challenge."

"Liar." Solomon had let his gun fall to the floor. That he had even tried the weapon meant he hadn't known Eli was equally as good as he was. He'd suspected maybe, but he hadn't known. From the animosity between them, it couldn't be their first battle, but it could be their first one in human form. Solomon could've thought he'd have the advantage there for some reason, or that he'd simply surprise Eli with something as outrageous as an actual human weapon. If that were the case, he'd been wrong.

"Of course I'm a liar. I'm a demon, just like you, Solomon. Or have you played human so long, you've forgotten what you really are? Pathetic." He turned his gaze on me as I slowly stood from my crouched position. "If those men out there were sliced and diced by yours truly, I wouldn't deny it. I'd brag on it. I might lie about most things, like all good demons, but I never lie about my body count or the notches on my bedpost. Some things are sacred. Right, darlin'?"

"I don't notch my bedpost." I put my gun away. It wouldn't have done me any good anyway. "I cut off their tackle and hang it from my rearview mirror."

"Damn, you must taste great," Eli said with admiration. The trouble with that admiration was I didn't know if he thought I would taste great sexually or in a culinary sense. Probably both.

"Go. Get out. The both of you. I'm tired and going to bed. Alone." I stood up. "And one of you take the bodies and the car with you. I've had my fill of cops around here."

"Bossy, bossy, bossy," Eli sighed as he slid off the stool. "Rather fun being on the receiving end of it for once." He passed a hand over his shirt and it was pristine again. "I'll take the car. Like I said, the Chinese doesn't stay with you. Not when you have an appetite like mine." If anyone was going to have the last sexual innuendo, it was going to be Eli. He waved a hand and went to the door and through it, passing so close to Solomon that their shoulders brushed. Solomon briefly bared his teeth in a snarl; then his eyes met mine intently for several seconds before he silently disappeared.

"I should've opened a women's shoe store. Demonic visitors don't just drop into a women's shoe store." I went and locked up.

Zeke was studying his shotgun with a furrowed brow and an annoyed lift of his upper lip. It was his equivalent of a man finding his wife in bed with the mailman *and* the local Jehovah's Witness before falling to the floor, shouting, "Betrayed!" to the skies. Griffin took in the expression and elbowed him. "Don't be so melodramatic." He looked at me. "We've never been up against anything like them before. I've never seen demons move like that."

"No." I turned out all the lights but one. "So no going after them alone."

"The demon was right. You are bossy." Zeke transferred the disgruntled look from his weapon to me.

"I've babysat your scrawny asses for ten years. I've a right to be bossy," I retorted, shooing them toward the back office and the couch. "Now, go cuddle."

"Four years," Griffin muttered as he moved into the back and out of sight, but I heard the last words. "You're only four years older, Trixa. It hardly merits a salute."

"Cuddle?" Zeke looked after him, then back at me, a mildly panicked expression replacing the aggravation. "We have to cuddle? I'm pretty sure I don't want to cuddle."

I patted his cheek as I passed him on the stairs. "You never know until you try." I made sure I locked my bedroom door behind me in case a pissed-off and forcibly cuddled Griffin stormed up. It didn't happen. It made me wonder who slept on the floor or who was the big spoon and who was the little spoon. When I woke up the next morning, it was to see Zeke standing at my bureau holding my picture of Kimano.

"When did you get so good at picking locks?" I would've woken up had any stranger tried to enter the room. But I could sense Griffin and Zeke. The psychic and empath thing. The raising them for a few years thing. A hundred other things. Take your pick, but I knew when they were around, the same as I knew when Leo was around, and the building still felt empty. He hadn't come back yet.

"Since you taught me." He continued to study the picture.

"You talk like I'm not always on the side of the good and noble law. Like I'm an actual criminal. Shame on you. I fed you fried cheese to your heart's content when you were a boy." I pushed my hair back and climbed out of bed. Still in silk, but a knee-length nighty this time. I did love silk beyond all things. I walked over and took the picture frame and folded it against my chest. I had a world of deceits in me, too many to count. My wandering and slightly unlawful ways called for them, but that protective movement I couldn't have stopped if I'd tried.

"You don't look alike," he commented.

It was perceptive of him. The hair, except for my streaks and his being straight to my curly, and the skin color, were both on the money from what you could tell from a black-and-white picture, but, no, we shared none of the same features. "Our family's that way. No peas in a pod among us."

He then picked up one of my knives that had been lying close to the picture, opened a drawer, and began to polish it with a pair of my underwear. And from the tilt of his head he knew exactly what he was doing and the degree to which he was annoying me. "Leo told us a long time ago a demon killed your brother. He told us you didn't like to talk about it."

"Leo should've kept his mouth shut and what exactly do you think you're doing now?" I said grimly as I snatched the panties away from him with my other hand. Revenge for the cuddle remark, had to be. He normally wasn't suicidal. Homicidal, yes, but not suicidal. At least not since he was fifteen, the scar on his neck reminded me.

"Talking about it." He flipped the blade and caught it. "Griffin says you're too stubborn to realize how dangerous those two demons are. He says you're so focused on revenge—on your mission—that you're blind. He says you're acting like me." He looked down. "Nice legs." He bent over slightly to get a better look.

I kicked him hard in the shin with the heel of my bare foot. It probably stung me more than him, but it was worth it. I grabbed the knife he was still tossing as it was midair in another flip. Holding it by the point, I tossed it at my headboard, nailing a cheetah in the eye. The panties swung cheerfully from the blade. I'd keep it there as a reminder. These things were temporary. Once the killer was dead, I was gone, and if it felt like I was leaving two other brothers behind . . . I'd get over it. Because for all his irritating ways, let me count the thousands, I did love Zeke. And I loved Griffin. It was something I never counted on. Leo would leave too. He was staying only because of me and my mission, as Zeke called it. What would happen to them then? They were men, all grown-up, but there was Eden House and then there was the truth. . . .

I sighed and pulled him down by his shirt until I could rest my forehead against his. "Who better to tell me if I get too Zeke-like, then, right? But trust me, I know what I'm doing."

"You are too Zeke-like," he countered immediately, resting a tentative hand on my back. "But I trust you."

"Honestly?" I smiled. Absolute, full trust from Zeke . . . that was huge.

"Right behind Griffin." He paused a beat before adding, "He tells me I should."

I groaned and reached around to swat his butt. "Ass," I repeated fondly before turning him and pushing him toward the door. "I'm going out to shop for the bar. Plus, I have no desire to see your boss today. If he shows up asking where we go next, tell him I still don't know. I still haven't sorted it out yet. That guy was so high I'm having trouble telling where his hallucinations begin and the Light ends. As for the two missing guys out front . . ." I shook my head. "Tell them the truth, but just say it was Solomon. They already know about him and how he likes to hang around here and harass me."

"Demonic dick," he grunted. "But he's good. Too good. You really are being too much like me. Can't you stop it?"

I didn't answer, only shoved him out the door and closed it behind him. But the truth was I couldn't stop it, any more than he could have. Griffin's training, it wouldn't work on me, and Leo knew better than to try talking me out of it. I had my mission.

Because I didn't have my brother.

Chapter 11

Las Vegas Springs Preserve was my favorite park in the city and a good place to think. Close to Meadows Mall, it lacked the stark beauty of Red Rock Canyon outside Vegas or the wild burros that roamed free. On the upside it had cottonwood trees and winding paths, and your chances of seeing a tarantula were a little less. Not that I had anything against spiders. They were just out to make a living too and make the occasional connection with another creature . . . whether it was to screw it or suck it dry. It wasn't the prettiest way of putting it, but the most honest. We all had to eat. I suppose we all didn't have to have sex. Nuns managed, after all, but they had more self-control than spiders and probably more than I did too. Although it had been quite a while since I'd dated anyone casually or seriously, even if Solomon was doing his best to make that choice difficult.

But I had too much to do for casual dating . . . with a nice, normal nondemon . . . even if most of what I'd been doing was waiting. Once I'd found out about the Light, it was just a matter of waiting for it to show up. I'd searched for years, but the Light had turned out to be good at hiding—which only made it more mysterious. I knew what it did, but where it came from originally, I'd never been able to find out. Was it a living creature or more some sort of sentient artifact? I didn't know. Even with part of it living in my head, I still didn't know. Alien maybe? Technology from before the dawn of time? A night-light from Atlantis?

I sat on a bench in the garden by the Desert Living Center and gave an inner snort at that. As if demons and angels weren't enough, let's go straight to the tabloid trash route. I also didn't know why the Light had chosen now to pop up, or if it really had been just a fluke that a caver had tripped across it. It didn't matter which though, because it was helping me find the other thing I hadn't been able to locate on my own no matter how long I'd looked: Kimano's killer. I knew the Light would help me do what I couldn't manage alone, and I'd been willing to wait as long as it took.

And that was now. I'd waited until now. I felt the fierce satisfaction. It warmed me more than the winter sun, but it would never warm me as much as my brother's presence would have. Revenge had kept me moving when I'd wanted to lie down on the bloody sand beside Kimano and die with him; revenge had kept me sane when it would've been so much easier to drop off a cliff into a mental chaos that would swallow me for all my life. Revenge was good for those things, but it wasn't his warm laughter, his rose-colored-glasses view of the world, his incredibly warped sense of humor, and it wasn't anywhere close to replacing how he'd loved me best.

You should love your family all the same, but of course you don't. Just as Mama had loved her black sheep, squeaky-wheel boy best, Kimano and I had loved each other best. I would give up anything, give up the rest of my life to have him sit beside me on that bench for just five minutes. To hold my hand, to tell me his last silly prank, laugh at himself about how it had all gone wrong and he'd been the one to end up with egg on his face. To call me sister and say he loved me anyway, despite my workaholic ways.

He'd actually thought I was a workaholic. He was laziness incarnate, my baby brother, and gone so long. . . .

No more. Time to concentrate. That's why I was here. The open sky, nature, peace—it would help me go where I needed to be. I closed my eyes and let Vegas disappear. I let the Light come into my consciousness, the tiny speck of the stuff—buzzing around my brain like a meadow bee sleepy with sun and pollen. Where did the trail point to next? Where had that musician passed off the gatepost to something more amazing that he could've ever understood, no matter how many drugged-up dimensions he passed through? The buzzing was slightly annoyed. I thought the shark had probably been easier for the Light to work with than that guy had been.

The buzzing went on and on, spinning in circles, trying to find in my brain what it needed to show me . . . to draw a mental picture for me. To lead . . .

And there it was. Sort of. Now I knew why there was a "Just say no to drugs" slogan. This was going to be more work than the others. It was going to require research. I really needed to look into getting an intern. Being caught in a battle between angels and demons had to be worth at least three college credits.

As I stood, I took in a last breath of spring-scented air, listened to the birdsong, and then saw a member of wildlife the conservationists hadn't planned on reviving in this place.

A perv in a white shirt and polyester pants. A standard hide-in-the-bushes-and-whack-it perv. Fat and balding, it was as appealing as watching a giant marshmallow go at it. That would put any teen who saw it off sex a thousand times more efficiently than any school's abstinence campaign. And from the school buses in the parking lot I'd seen on the way in, he was waiting for a happy-go-lucky line of kiddies to come skipping by to see what he was selling. I sighed. I didn't have the time to do anything truly interesting about it. Too bad. I had to settle for walking over and pointing the muzzle of my gun at his chest. It kept my eyes away from far most nauseating sights as I said, "You've ruined my sex life for the foreseeable future. Now take that thing that's catastrophically failing at masquerading as a penis and go away."

He did. Smart marshmallow. Then I went shopping for supplies as I'd told Zeke and followed it up with a trip to the library.

I didn't get home by dark. I was still at the library when my cell phone rang. It was on vibrate to escape the wrath of the library police. Flipping it open, I didn't get a chance to say hello before Griffin's urgent voice was telling me Eden House was under attack and he and Zeke were on their way. I told him I'd meet them there, jammed the book I'd been looking through into my bag, and ran for my car. I ignored the ringing alarm as the library doors slammed shut behind me. Some things didn't allow time for proper procedure, such as checking out books. Eden House's coming under attack was one of them. The only other time I'd heard of that happening to one of their chapters had been the House in NYC. The demons had brought down a five-story building. To this day, there was no Eden House in New York. For that matter, there were no demons there any longer either. Certain creatures didn't like that sort of attention brought to their city, as my fellow info source, Robin, had pointed out while wallowing in epic party memories. Demons weren't the only thing to fear in the dark, and a good majority of those night dwellers lived in New York. Enough to make it uncomfortable enough for demons that they chose to hunt and seduce in easier locations.

Las Vegas wasn't New York. Demons and angels had a balance here. As far as I knew, they had for as long as there were enough souls to bother fighting over. It was hard to believe the demons would suddenly try to shift that balance, especially as I didn't think Eli or Solomon had clued any of their kin in on the Light—the only reason I could think of for them to instigate an out-and-out war.

Eden House was located in Spanish Trails, one of the oldest gated communities in Vegas . . . fifteen minutes from the Strip, which was hard to believe. There may have been a more expensive neighborhood in the city, but Spanish Trails was still an architect's wet dream. It was one of the very few places in Vegas you could have a lot of privacy, the eight-million-dollar-compound type of privacy. The main house itself was three stories high and set on five acres. Hell, they even had grass. The governor wished he had it so good. An eight-foot-high white wall surrounded the property with an iron gate painted the same color to keep out the unworthy, the disreputable, and the uninvited. I fit all those categories, but I had never let that sort of thing stop me before, and with the gate wide open, I didn't have to let it stop me now.

I careened the car through the thick posts that supported the gate, slid into the curve hidden by tall oleander bushes, and ran over a demon crouched in the driveway. It had been distracted by the arm it had cradled to its chest as it gnawed—a human arm with only half its flesh still clinging to the bone. I'd thought the battle would be over by the time I arrived from the twenty-minute drive, but if it was, it hadn't gone the way I'd wanted it to. Zeke and Griffin might be persona non grata in pretense and reality, but that wouldn't stop them from going to the aid of the people they'd worked with for several years. Trinity and Goodman might be dicks for the greater good, but all of the House weren't like them. Some had the hearts of my boys. Some had compassion, imagination, and that spark that I would call a soul. Those were the ones I didn't want to see fall. Trinity and Goodman might keep their souls in freezers, but not all of Eden Housers did. I'd fight for them.

And I'd kill for Griffin and Zeke.

I slammed on the brakes and vaulted out of the car to pull my HK from the trunk. It was a beauty—an MP5, fully suppressed and illegal as they came—not available at your local 7-Eleven. And, better than being pretty, it was able to take out a shitload of demons without waking the neighbors. It was just in time to nail the demon that snarled and clawed its way out from beneath the undercarriage. I put six sound-muted slugs in its skull, turning its brain and then its entire body into instant pudding. I stepped over it and started running toward the house.

Most, like Griffin and Zeke, had their own houses, condos, or apartments, but the House kept a minimum of twenty members on-site at all times with five guards watching the building and grounds from nightfall until morning. But those were details I'd heard from the guys. My first official look I'd gotten at the place was when I'd been kidnapped the other night.

The look I was getting now was far different.

From opulence, armories, and medical facilities to blood and death. It was a war zone and Eden House had lost this battle. Once I ran through the gaping, double front doors, I could see that. They were still fighting it, trying to stand their ground, but it was over. If the demons had a flag, they would've been minutes from planting it. And there wasn't a single angel in sight. Maybe that didn't shake the faith of those still alive and fighting, but it pissed me off. Do our dirty work, fight our earthly battles, die for us, but consider our number unlisted. Work miracles for us, but don't expect the same in return. Those days are over. Our convenience, not yours. But still stick us on top of your Christmas trees. We like that.

There were flames flickering inside, concealed from the outside by steel blinds, and there were too few people to put them out. No one was about to call 911 either. Eden House took care of Eden House business, even if it meant that Eden House would burn.

Human bodies littered the foyer. Huge with arched doorways, the space now had its marble floor marred with the dead, blood, and puddles of black ichor that had once been demons. I hesitated. Should I search the ground floor first or head up? The sudden voices from above made that decision for me. I ran up the wide stairs that opened off the foyer. The staircase split off near the first floor, curving to the left and right. I took the right and when I reached the top, I snatched a quick glance around the rotunda. Still nothing but dead bodies, some hanging over the wrought-iron rail.

The voices had stopped and this was getting me nowhere fast. "Griffin!" I shouted. "Zeke!"

I heard it then—not Zeke or Griffin, but the clatter of claws behind me. I turned, twisted sideways, and slammed my boot into the midsection of a fungus green demon. Bright red eyes flared with irritation as the metal-enforced heel passed through the softer belly scales and into firm flesh. Then the force of the kick threw him down the stairs tumbling head over tail, but he was back in seconds—this time flying. I didn't get to see demons fly often. Despite their wings, they tended to keep close to the ground when they fought, slithering like snakes and lizards. Maybe flying reminded them too much of what they'd once been and had. Then again, I might assume too much. They might not miss the grace and glory. Unlike Solomon who said he did, but he was the only one saying so.

Being evil for so very long, could you ever be what you were before that? Would you even want to? The great thing about being evil is you don't *care* that you're evil. As a matter of fact, you probably enjoyed the hell out of it . . . no pun intended.

The downside of being evil is when someone like me shoots your dragon wings to tatters before ramming a gun muzzle in your open, fanged mouth and liquefying your brain. I grabbed another clip from my bag, slammed it home, and started searching for the voices I'd heard earlier. I was about to call for Griffin again, when I heard him. I ran, following the circular hall. Another demon came at me. I hit the floor and rolled as it passed in a rush over me. Swiveling, I shot it in the back of the head, turned, and kept running until I came to what I vaguely remembered as a banquet room for those who lived in the house. Chandeliers and the finest china, it was all crushed to ivory splinters and crystal dust now. That dust glittered along wings and snake heads, giving the demons the air of something else to be put on a Christmas tree—a very dark, gothic Christmas tree.

There were ten demons and Zeke and Griffin were facing them while standing back to back. They'd been here fighting long enough they'd gone through all their ammo and were now down to knives. That didn't make them any less dangerous. Zeke was a stone-cold demon killer with a combat knife, because he had no fear, not for himself. No fear of pain or being hurt or even death. Zeke's mind didn't allow multitasking. When he was fighting, he was fighting. Period. The only other thought he was capable of was to protect his friends. Kill and protect. In the heat of battle, nothing else existed for him. The Japanese Bushido philosophy said the greatest warrior was one who didn't fear his own death. Zeke went a step further with not even *knowing* that he could die. Because he lived in the moment, he didn't have enough focus left over to consider mortality.

He was in that moment now. He was covered with slashes of demonic claws, but he was also covered from the waist down in black demon blood. As I stepped into the room, he had just slashed a demon's neck so forcefully with the serrated edge of his blade that the spinal column split and the demon became a black rain.

Griffin was deadly himself, quick as a demon, and smart enough to think like them if he had to—to anticipate their moves. Zeke couldn't multitask at all, but Griffin was the king of it. He rammed his blade through the eye of one demon, while using his other hand to slash an identical blade across the gut of the brown demon hurtling toward him from the side. A mass of entrails spilled free. It wouldn't kill the creature, but it was enough to have it tumbling back temporarily.

My boys the killers. I couldn't have been more proud.

But ten demons . . . now eight and a half. And scattered among the green and brown lesser demons were two gray and one the cyanotic purple-blue of a strangled corpse. Higher demons. Thanks to Solomon, we now knew these were the ones to watch out for—not demon-lite. Those wouldn't be so easy to kill.

"Guys!" I tossed them two Glock .40s out of my messenger bag. Mary Poppins had her endless supply of goodies in her purse. I had an endless supply of goodies too, and they were more useful than tea and freshly baked biscuits. They both dropped one knife apiece and caught the guns. I stepped back out into the hall to give them a clean line of fire and called as I did, "You, grape gecko, want to play?"

The suffocation-colored demon whipped around and undulated itself toward me with a speed that made a viper look as if it were moving through three feet of tar. It hit me. There was no way to avoid it. No way for a human, at least. Here was another one that if he wasn't in Solomon and Eli's league, he was damn close. I did manage to dive to the side quickly enough that although it clipped my side, it didn't hit me head-on. It did flip me over the rail, the iron hitting me in the ribs. I caught myself with one arm hooking around an arabesque. I hung in midair, my shoulder creaking, and I discovered that my Barney-colored new demon friend might have been almost as fast as Solomon and Eli, but it wasn't as smart. It perched on the rail above me, baring smoky quartz teeth at me in an arrogantly rapacious grin. It was nice of him to savor the moment. It gave me the opportunity to take its head off at the shoulders. The sound suppressor on the MP5 was only good for one clip. These shots rang loud and true. No matter how big the compound was, someone was bound to hear that and call the police. I coughed as the smoke billowed more thickly and wiped at my dripping face to clear my vision of what had once been a demon who'd thought a little too much of himself.

Tossing the gun up and over the rail, I used both hands to follow after it. I snagged one foot in a curl of metal and vaulted over the rail with several feet to spare. A member of Eden House stood there, a shocked look on his pale face. "Yoga," I explained. "It's good for more than making your way through the Kama Sutra."

But it turned out his shock wasn't for me and my gymnastic ways. As I picked up my gun, he said numbly, "They're dead. Everyone's dead." He had dark blond hair, rumpled from the battle and darkened by the smoke, and a face marked with demon blood and devastation. It made me wish I'd kept my smart mouth shut.

"Not everyone." I grabbed his arm and pulled him into the room I'd only just left. I'd heard the barrage of shots. When I passed through the door, I saw what I expected—a floor awash in dark fluid, the remains of the brown and green demons. The two gray ones were still very much in the game. That changed when they heard us come in behind them. One of them turned in time to see me pull the trigger. It turned to smoke before the bullets left my weapon. The other demon left on its own, disappearing as well. I didn't know if it was from fear or the fact that its job was as good as completed. From what I could tell, I was standing with the last of Eden House Las Vegas—Zeke, Griffin, and this poor bastard whose own gun slipped from his hand to fall to the floor.

"Our house has fallen." He rubbed his eyes against the smoke that continued to thicken. "How could that happen?"

Griffin moved up, turned the man around, and pushed him back out into the hall and toward the stairs. "We have to get out, Thomas. The authorities won't be a problem, but burning to death will. Let's go."

The authorities wouldn't be a problem. That meant one thing. "Trinity wasn't here, then," I stated as I followed them, coughing again. We all were. If we weren't so close to the front door, there wouldn't have been enough oxygen to make it. If Trinity wasn't here, he would definitely clear things with the Vegas authorities. They either worked for him and Eden House or he owned them, one way or the other.

"No," Griffin said as he continued to guide the dazed Thomas as we clattered down the stairs. "Neither is Goodman. They left for Miami. A meeting of the heads of the Houses." So they were alive, and an alive Trinity was capable of covering up anything.

"The rats always know when a ship is sinking," Zeke grunted.

"You think they knew this was coming?" I reached behind me to take Zeke's wrist and pull him along faster. You'd think the man was meandering down to the kitchen for a snack.

"No. I think the Universe sucks. The dicks are eating steak and drinking wine while their soldiers die." Zeke saw the warning glance Griffin shot from him to Thomas, but I didn't think Thomas heard a word as we passed out of the house into clean night air. He was young, so young that he had to be newly recruited. His survival had been nothing more than a fluke or maybe he'd hidden during the battle. If so, I didn't blame him. He looked like he'd never fought a single demon, much less a horde of them.

Outside we discovered there were a few more left, both demons and survivors like Thomas. The human survivors were only a handful, but they were holding their own for the moment. It was a very small and passing moment, though. They might have been fighting, but they were seconds away from being lunch meat. The three of us moved toward them and the ring of demons that surrounded them as Thomas fell to his knees and vomited. If they rebuilt Eden House here, I didn't think he'd be a part of it. All the empathic or telepathic talent in the world doesn't make you a fighter. Genes, a screwed-up childhood, or training did that, but sometimes none of the three worked. Thomas would never be a warrior and I also suspected Thomas would never sleep through the night again.

But there were more urgent matters right now—to keep what remained of the House alive. The demons spotted us as we moved up behind them. The circle opened as half of them scattered to face us, while the other half moved in on the other six survivors. I aimed the MP5 at the two demons rushing me when Solomon appeared between us.

"Stop!" He was in human form as always, but his voice was anything but. It was the roar of a lion—the largest and most lethal one on the plains.

The demons hesitated, but the next thundering "Go!" left nothing but wisps of murky vapor floating in the air. Solomon turned to me. "I didn't do this."

I scrubbed the rest of the demon blood from my face with the sleeve of my shirt. "You think I care? You think whether or not you did makes a difference? Do you think I even believe you?" I checked my clip automatically and avoided grim gray eyes. You could've even said they were sympathetic . . . if you were that gullible. I never had been. I couldn't afford to be. "Because we both know if you had a reason to take out Eden House, you would."

"You think the Light is my reason." He stepped closer, close enough to rest a hand on my arm. I heard Zeke growl, but Griffin must've held him back. "I'm more subtle in my tactics. Mass slaughter's not my way. Murder isn't my way. I'm different than the rest. I have control. I would *not* do this."

"What about Eligos?" I demanded as the warm thumb rubbed the tender skin on the underside of my arm.

"He could . . . easily, but," he added with obvious reluctance, "I don't know that he did. I've heard nothing about a plan to destroy Eden House. All know this is my territory. No one beneath me would attempt anything like this without consulting me first. With my equals, I think I would have heard rumors. Gossip is a minor sin after all. We embrace it. This may have come from above."

"There are demons above you and Eli besides the big guy?" I pulled from his grip, but not as quickly as I should have. I couldn't deny the warmth felt good against my skin. "I'm surprised you'd admit it."

"We have brothers who couldn't come to Earth without setting the ground to flame beneath each footstep. Whose gaze would kill anything it fell on." His lips curled cynically. "Once far above archangels, now princes in Hell."

"And you're still waiting on the promotion." I shoved my gun in my bag. I could hear the distant wail of sirens.

"A half million souls wouldn't get me there." The sirens were closer. "I'll find out what I can." He was gone as unexpectedly as he came. The sirens were closer. Our vanishing act wasn't as darkly mystical as Solomon's had been. Ours was more of the piling into my car, spinning in a circle, and peeling out of the driveway. I took my boys and the rest of the survivors ran to cars of their own. Trinity could deal with the explanation of the dead bodies—if he had to bother to explain at all. Eden House had tentacles in all levels of government, local and federal. For all I knew, they'd invented the concept of government . . . they or Lucifer.

The flames flickered in my rearview mirror, reminding me of all the times we'd burned Solomon's club to the ground. Things come and things go, but one thing remained constant:

Fire consumed it all.

Chapter 12

They had been mostly dead when Griffin and Zeke had gotten to the House, their brothers and sisters in arms, Griffin told me that night while we'd cleaned our slashes and slices. He'd told me while Zeke had said nothing at all—not since we'd left the ruins of Eden House. They'd lost another home. They'd realized it was gone when Trinity had found out about their bringing outsiders into Eden House business— their "calling" from his point of view. But knowing it and seeing it burn before you, that was different. And knowing it and seeing those you'd fought side by side with for years die nearly to the man, that was so beyond different, and it had hit Zeke hard. A dead baby, dead companions . . . it was a lot to lose in such a short lifetime. Only twenty-five years old, and Zeke had already seen so much death—and considered himself the cause of a part of it. The fall of Eden House was pain all in itself and a painful reminder of what had happened in that bathtub ten years ago.

Dead and gone, all of it.

"We fought, but it was too late." Griffin had slid a washcloth down both arms, washing away red and black blood. "Too many were already gone. They'd called all of us back home, but there were too many demons for them." That had to be a lot of demons . . . except for the newer recruits like Thomas, all those that served Eden House had been good fighters. Not Griffin and Zeke good, but damn good nonetheless.

As for home, the two of them obviously never really considered their house home. It had been Eden House to a certain extent, and here. All in all, they certainly spent more time at my bar than Eden House or their place combined.

"This is home," I'd reminded him firmly, and after I'd used it first, I let them use my bath to get cleaned up. They'd fought much longer than I had in the battle and had been banged up more as a consequence. So, giving person that I was—a giving person who was probably never going to reclaim her own softly comfortable bed, I had ended up spending the night on the couch in Leo's office without a single person in sight to spoon with.

Sometimes you needed it—the touch, the comfort. Just another living creature who cared for you. Sometimes you got it.

Sometimes you didn't.

I woke up with a crick in my neck and my gun under the pillow I'd brought from downstairs the night before. Leo was still gone. I knew it the second I opened my eyes. His family trouble must've been more than he'd expected. Or they'd lured him into an anger management intervention he hadn't needed for a long time now. Now there was a mental picture. Leo in a circle of relatives all trying to turn him from wolf to lamb. He'd never be a lamb, but he was a good wolf now . . . or far less likely to bite anyway. Although getting his family to believe that wouldn't be easy. They'd be trying to put the more mellow carnivore in a pink rhinestone collar. Poor Leo.

I rolled up and off the couch, stretched, and looked down at the rumpled pajamas. Not silk, my standby favorite, but a present from Griffin and Zeke from last Christmas—thin cotton footy pajamas covered with nursery rhyme figures. For the Mother Goose in me, they'd said, as I was always trying to take care of them. I couldn't deny they were comfortable. I also couldn't deny that when I walked out into the bar, wild halo of bed hair, cotton jammies and all, I might not have looked my best. Stunning was definitely out the window.

Not that the angel sitting at the bar seemed to care. He, on the other hand, was immaculate in human form. They always were, the few I'd seen, just like the demons. This one had straight silver hair to his shoulders. The gleam was a stark contrast to his younger face. His eyes were the same pale silver and empty. Cool and disinterested. If he had a single emotion in him, I'd let him have for free that glass of red wine he was drinking.

"If you're here looking for a virgin, I can't help you." I put the gun under the counter and rooted around in one cabinet for a breakfast bar. It didn't look like I was going to have time for much else today.

He ran a smoothing hand down the light gray suit and ignored my humor or blasphemy, depending on your point of view. "Eden House Las Vegas is no more."

I opened the wrapper and took a bite of chocolate and granola. It didn't sit particularly well as the memory of the dead bodies from last night hit me. "You could say that. Thanks for the help, by the way. It really turned the tide." I took another bite, this one grimly savage. "Bastard. They were your followers and you let them die without lifting a finger to help them. Or a feather."

He looked over his shoulder as if he expected his hidden wings were showing before turning back to face me. "They serve Heaven. Heaven does not serve them."

"That makes it better. Thanks for that. How about they're in a better place now. Don't forget that one." I discarded the granola bar. I couldn't stomach it. Demons were bad enough, killers and liars through and through, but most angels were cold. Not all of them, but most of them. Superior egos carved from ice. They had the charisma in human form that the demons did, when they wanted, but the majority of them rarely used it. You could almost understand demons before you could an angel. I glared at him and folded my arms, equally disinterested in him as he pretended to be in me.

"If they lived lives of purity and servitude, then, yes, they are." He sipped his ruby-colored wine. "I am Oriphiel."

I had a feeling the surfer angel who *had* bothered to toss the appeal and magnetism our way in the desert had been demoted for his failure to get the fragment of the Light that I'd beaten him to. "Middle management, lower management, I could care less." I dismissed him, although I knew that the name Oriphiel meant he was an archangel. So it was written. Somewhere. You needed a flowchart to keep it all straight.

From the looks of this guy, he considered the title of archangel and himself to be pretty hot shit—certainly not one to take orders. He gave them. "Go find Trinity," I told him. "He belongs to you. I don't."

"Trinity is returning today. We will speak, but the Light is too important to be left to an unsupervised human, even one of Eden House." He said "human" as if he were saying "pet" and, worse yet, the kind of pet that takes a year to learn how to use the cat door and another year to figure out the flap moves both ways. His pale face was as beautiful as marble and as unmoving. I wished Lenore were there to give him a lesson in pet respect, but I was here to give him the human version.

"If you think I'm going to put up with your hanging around, you're wrong. Trinity's putting me on a leash is more than enough." I took the glass of wine out of his hand. "And cops drink for free. Stuck-up pigeons don't."

"The Light is for Above. Even one such as you couldn't think it was better in the hands of the Abyss. Trinity says you know what it does. Can you imagine what will happen to the earth if we fail to obtain it? You will be at their mercy."

"From what I could tell last night, we already are. I think it's your feathered asses you're worried about. I don't think you give much of a damn about us, only about spiting Hell."

"You have no idea what Heaven is, no idea what we are. You couldn't understand if you wanted to," he said serenely.

So smug, so damn superior. I poured the rest of the wine into the sink, but it was a struggle not to pour it over his silver head instead. "I've read the Bible. I think I know a thing or two." I had read the Bible as well as several other holy books. I was familiar, you could say, with quite a few religions. Mama made sure her children were educated on a wide variety of subjects. When you traveled the world, she said, you needed to know how to stay out of trouble or how to get into it, depending on your mood.

"You're like a worm given a molecule of a blade of

grass, an electron microscope, and expected to extrapolate what the world looks like . . . its mountains and oceans, lakes and rivers, trees and plains, and all the creatures that inhabit it. The Bible"—he steepled his fingers—"that is your molecule. And you, the worm, you can't even find the microscope."

"Maybe that would've come across better with a blare of trumpets or if you'd descended from the sky surrounded by a veil of golden light, but you know what it sounded like just now?" I rested my elbows on the counter, steepled my fingers in the mirror image of his, and rested my chin on them as I faced him. "It sounded like you just screwing yourself, because there is no way in hell, or heaven for that matter, that I'll ever help you now."

He frowned. Finally, a ripple of emotion. "You have no choice."

"I refer you to that molecule you were talking about on the subject of free will. So when I tell you to kiss my ass, it's only because God was kind enough to give humans that choice." Although truthfully the Bible, theology, and Solomon were all contradictory on the subject, I didn't feel the need to bring that up. I was free and I knew it. I flattened my hands on the bar and was about to tell him to get the hell out of my bar when Hell decided to tell him itself.

"You really do let anyone in this place, darlin'. You need a good exterminator." A coil of black smoke reared behind the angel to form into Eligos. He draped a black-clad arm over the shoulders covered in gray and leaned heavily, his lips touching the silver hair. "Oriphiel, pal, buddy, friend o' mine. How's it hanging?" His other hand dropped into the angel's lap. "Or is it like the old days when you didn't invest in that part when you came to Earth? Too afraid of temptation. I have to say, Ori, you were right. The temptation is so consuming, *so* damn good, you never would've made it." He lifted his hand back up with a sigh of disappointment. "Yep, like the old days. Still not packing. You should give it a try, at least once. You are missing out like you would not believe. Let me tell you. . . ." His lips moved to Oriphiel's ears. I couldn't hear what he said to the angel, but I saw the results.

It was more than a ripple of emotion this time. I saw shock, distaste, and even a trace of fear before Oriphiel was gone, not in a coil of smoke, but a blaze of light bright enough to trigger a headache. Great. I rubbed my forehead. "You could've warned me. Sunglasses would've been nice."

"Show-offs. They don't get to do much else these days, what with humans fighting in their place. All bark and no bite. No more flaming swords. No more throwing down of the rebels. Warriors of God? Ha! Pussies," he snorted. "And you know what? I think they stuck it to themselves but good. I think they miss it. Who wouldn't? We might lie to everyone else, Miss Trixa, but they lie to themselves and that makes them equally as dangerous as us." He grinned. "Not that I'm dangerous. Never. Just very, very interesting." He jerked his head toward the pool table. "Let's play a game." He tossed his leather jacket over a stool and flashed that cocky, sexy smile I was inexplicably getting used to. Then I pictured the dead bodies from last night and put that smile into perspective. The teeth of a carnivore. Period. Unrepentant and loving every minute of his blood-soaked existence. "But we have to bet. There's no point in playing a game if there's nothing to win . . . or lose."

"Don't even bring up my soul." I followed him, bringing my gun with me. Why did I follow? Because at the moment, spending time with a degenerate killer demon was a breath of fresh air compared to the creature that had just sat at my bar. Oriphiel and Eligos were flip sides of the same coin, only Eli bothered to fake the charm. And charm as manipulation was deceitful, obviously, but it was better than assuming I was a servant to anyone, even Heaven. If an independent creature like me had a pet peeve—or had to pick one among many—that would be it.

"Trust me, I'd never be that clichéd." The hazel eyes were more copper and green than brown and green. "How 'bout we play for those PJs, little girl? I have a whole set of fantasies already going about those. And spankings are way too vanilla to make it through the door." He cracked his knuckles. "Do you have any teddy bears upstairs?"

"Don't be sick or I'll put the pool cue where you won't like it."

"'Don't be sick'? I'm fallen. Pure evil. Demonic spawn from the depths of Hell. Why do I have to keep reminding you of that? Do I need a tattoo or maybe a T-shirt? Tacky, but it would show my pecs. And as for the pool cue, you never know. I might more than like it." He racked the balls, then waved his hand, flaring to life the overhead light. "Ladies first."

I placed the Smith on the side of the table and chalked my cue. "We haven't established what I get if *I* win."

"You'll really throw the PJs in the pot?" He rocked back on his heels. "I'm impressed. Okay, big spender, that deserves something equally worthy. You win and I'll tell you who was behind nuking Eden House. That has to be worth a little full-frontal nudity."

"How'd you . . . Never mind." I liked to sleep free and unencumbered under my sleepwear. So sue me. "You know who did it? Solomon didn't know."

"Solomon *told* you he didn't know. Don't tell me you believed him." He tossed his cue lazily from hand to hand. "I know you're not that naïve."

"I don't believe anything a demon says, but he sounded less like a liar than usual." I broke and proceeded to wipe the floor with his demonic ass. He barely got a chance to get on the table, poor baby. It was an honest game on his end, obviously, but only because he knew I wouldn't live up to my end of the bet if he cheated. Actually, I wouldn't have lived up to my end if he had won. He'd get a limb before he got my pajamas. In the end, it'd be less catastrophic for me. It wasn't only demons who could lie.

"How'd you get so good? I've played pool longer than you've been alive." He scowled. For the first time that sexy, crazy, roguishly cheerful smile was replaced with something real. Disappointment with a good dose of spite.

"Don't pout. It doesn't look good on a hell-spawn." I boosted myself up to sit on the edge of the table. "And I'm good at everything. Physics included." Good at everything except keeping my little brother alive, and winning a pool game with a demon didn't quite make up for that, did it? I touched the black teardrop at my throat. No, it hardly did.

Eli had put away the spite, which I thought was most likely an act anyway. He wanted to tell me about Eden House. That was the reason he'd shown up. He might not have cheated to win, but he'd been prepared to cheat to lose. It simply turned out he didn't have to. Quite a surprise for him. It was one reason I never hustled pool. It was too easy and rather boring to watch grown men sulk like little boys. It wasn't worth the money for the win or the irritation as they tried to look down my shirt whenever I made a shot.

"Pool is more than physics," Eli went on with outraged passion. I rolled a ball idly across the table, then played with the pool cue a few seconds before laying it beside me to watch the show. For all that Eli was a self-invention of pure ego, he was entertaining, and I didn't mind the distraction. It was better than thinking of how no matter how many things I succeeded at, it couldn't make up for my one heart-killing failure. "It's more than a game. It's war. It's sex on green felt if you do it right. That quick is not doing it right." I tuned out after that. He was amusing and fun and six feet of pure, unadulterated sex, but as much as I wanted to be distracted, it wasn't happening.

"You aren't afraid of me." Abruptly his face was in mine, so close I felt his breath, saw the minute flecks of copper swimming in his now-ebony eyes, felt the fall of brindled brown hair against my forehead. "You should be," he said softly. "Oh, little girl, you should be."

"Why?" I didn't pull back. This was my place, my territory, and nobody would make me afraid here. Nobody. "You can't kill me. You'd lose the Light."

"Maybe. Maybe I can't kill you." The metallic flecks swirled. "But I could always torture you." He lifted his upper lip and this smile was neither sexy nor amusing. "I'm good at that. First in my class. Plaques on the wall. And, even better, I really, *really* enjoy doing it."

"And I'd tell you everything I know." My eyes weren't as copper as the flecks in his, but I had a feeling what lurked behind them was as dark as the blackness of his.

"Everything you know and every invention you could possibly scream from what was left of your throat." His voice wasn't human anymore.

"I have to say, this is your worst attempt at seduction yet." I nipped his full lower lip and then rammed the pool cue through his stomach. I missed the spine . . . on purpose. At that level it wouldn't have killed him and the effect of two feet of polished and gore-stained wood coming out of his back was showier. I liked showy. It tended to make lessons stick with the one on the receiving end. When he was comparing pool to everything except a game, I'd removed the tip and ferrule from my personal cue to reveal a nice sharp metal point beneath it. This turned a perfectly good pool cue into an even better spear, and if Eli had been too busy showing how sexy and clever he was to notice what I was doing, well . . . at least he was still sexy. Or would be once he cleaned up.

He stepped back and glowered at the length of wood impaling him. "You just get bitchier and bitchier all the time, don't you?" But it was said with reluctant admiration. If Eli was too fast for a bullet to hit, he was certainly fast enough to avoid a pool cue through the abdomen. But when you're strutting your demonic stuff for a woman, getting turned on with the torture talk, and carrying an ego the size of Hell itself, you do make the occasional mistake. He flicked a finger against the polished wood with a light thunk. "Excessive violence doesn't go well with the footy pajamas. It's a behavioral and fashion faux pas all rolled into one."

I held on to the cue. As long as I held on to it, he was held to Earth in his physical form, although he could have turned demon if he'd wanted. But he'd still be pinned like a dead bug in an insect collector's display case. "And the threatening me with torture, that was entirely kosher?"

He held his arms wide as his eyes turned from black and copper to penny and forest hazel. "At least I'm dressed for it. You have to give me that." He was. Black shirt. Black pants. Black jacket thrown to the side.

"Yeah, you're the demonic Darth Vader. I'm beyond impressed." I turned my head to Griffin and Zeke who'd been sitting on the bottom step of the stairs with the door propped wide for quite some time now. The angel might've been too high-level for them to sense and I knew Eli was, but they could hear. As soon as the pool game started, they'd come down, both with shotguns and bad morning attitudes. "What do you think, guys? Should we—"

"Shoot him," they said simultaneously, interrupting me.

"You don't seem to be as charismatic as you think you are, Eli," I commented. "Isn't that a shame?" I was still sitting on the pool table, but I was ready to jump to the floor and try to hold him here if he decided to fight. There was more room between us now, about two feet. Even for a demon, a makeshift spear through the guts will have you staggering back a pace or two.

The smile was back . . . as cocky, and almost as warm. If he was pissed, and I imagined he was, he hid it well. Then again when you claim to have been around millions of years, how mind-numbingly boring that would be. A few thousand years, sure. Maybe even ten, but after that, things were bound to get boring. Eli considered me surprising and I don't think he was often surprised. "If you shoot me, I can't tell you who ordered Eden House smote to the ground. 'Smote.' I haven't gotten to use that word since my days upstairs. I kind of miss it. Lots of pomp and circumstance in a word like that." He tapped his chin as the smile became sly. "Downstairs we just say slaughter or massacre or team-building exercise."

"Who, then?" Too bad the pool cue wasn't barbed along its length; I would've twisted it. It wouldn't have done much good. Demons, especially these high-level demons we were suddenly seeing so much of, had a high tolerance for pain. "Tell me and maybe Zeke and Griffin won't turn your head into history and the rest of you into a pool of ecological disaster that'll have the EPA beside themselves."

"All right. All right. What a sore winner," he grumbled. It was all just another show. As I'd thought, he wanted to tell me. He'd come here to tell me. Putting up a fight wasn't on his agenda . . . for now. "Beleth ordered it. And guess who works under Beleth. Way under. As in 'He's my boss, but I just sit and wait for his memos and gaze dreamily at his photo on my desk.'"

"Solomon." I'd read books other than holy ones. I had the list of the higher demons memorized to the last duke, assuming humans got it right when they wrote it all down, and that was a big assumption. Beleth was supposedly a king in Hell. There was only one step above a king downstairs. "Beleth wants to take over? Push Lucifer aside?"

"I told you, darlin', we *all* do. But he's one of the ones with the best shot. And if he obtained the Light, he could start a rebellion. Another rebellion, rather. Arrogance and pride were the downfall for us all. We all want to sit in the big chair someday." He shrugged. "Solomon is personal assistant material. It's beyond him, but if he brought the Light to Beleth, swing! One

big-ass promotion and a giant step closer to the throne
for himself."

Solomon had seemed sincere in his denial of knowledge about the fall of Eden House, but Solomon always seemed sincere. He was good at what he did,
but a demon that gave up killing? I shouldn't buy
it. Couldn't, not if I wanted to do what needed to be
done. "And whom do you work for, Eli? Who sent you
for the Light?"

"Nobody. I'm a free agent. I sell to the highest bidder." He grasped the pool cue and within seconds
pulled it loose. I let him, dropping it from my hands.
"Like you, Trixa. We're one in the same. Well, I might
be slightly more sexy, but basically one in the same.
We're all business when it comes to the Light." He
handed the cue back to me with a small bow. "But all
pleasure when it comes to everything else."

He held out his hand and a box, wreathed in a wisp
of smoke, rested in his palm. The same size as his
hand, it was plum-colored with a thin silver bow. Very
elegant. "For you. Call me if you decide I'm a lighter
touch on the leash than Trinity."

"Call you?" Sexier, my ass. I leaned back and crossed
pajama-covered ankles. I couldn't help but take him
in and admit to myself, all right, maybe a tad sexier.
Just a tiny bit. Vain bastard. But he wasn't smarter, no
matter what he thought. "As in say your name and
poof—here you are?"

"Hardly. I'm not a genie. I'm a demon, and my hearing isn't in the superhero range. Call my cell." He
whipped out a card and passed it over. "Here's my
number."

I didn't bother to look at it. "I'm guessing 666-
6666."

"Oh, right. As if that number weren't snatched up decades ago." The sarcasm hung in the air, but he was gone. Even his jacket was gone.

Damn, what a long morning.

"You never let us play anymore," Zeke grumped from his position on the stairs. He'd been well behaved and waited on my signal as to whether to shoot or not. He was getting better and better at grasping the intricacies of mental battles versus physical ones—even if he thought the former were rather pointless.

"I still need him, Kit. Between Solomon, Trinity, and the angel that showed up this morning, I need a wild card to play if things don't go my way." I carefully undid the bow—I did love presents—and pulled off the lid of the box.

It was a finger.

Definitely not the kind of present I was looking for. My stomach rolled. Griffin and Zeke had already moved to my side to ask about the angel. They didn't get the chance.

"Leo?" Griffin's voice was hoarse and black with rage. I rested a hand on his shoulder and squeezed.

"No. Not Leo." I closed the box and retied the ribbon with a savage twist. I had no idea what I'd do with it. There was no point in turning it into the police. Whoever it belonged to was no doubt dead by now, and if he wasn't, he was far beyond the reach of any authorities.

"How do you know?" he asked incredulously. "It could be. It looked . . ."

It looked like Leo's. The same color red-brown skin, large . . . there was blood on the white velvet beneath it, indicating it had been taken off a living human being. Poor damn bastard, whoever he was or had been . . . but the finger didn't belong to Leo.

"I know. But it's not, not that it makes it any less horrible." I put the box on the pool table before standing and going to the bar, where I picked up the phone and dialed the number on the card. I got Eligos's voice mail. It figured. I always thought that an invention of Hell anyway.

"Eligos, find my brother's killer and only then do you get the Light. As for the finger—I'm giving it to you right now." I disconnected, although throwing the phone across the room instead was very tempting.

No, he wasn't half as smart as he thought he was. All he'd done was succeed in pissing me off—and I had a long list of people who could tell him that wasn't a good thing. Mama said never hold a grudge against a man; hold his balls instead and yank them off. Saved the both of you time. Aggravation time for you . . . recovery time for him. Eli had better watch his back and his sac from now on, because I was through with playing. This girl was going to make him sorry he'd ever stepped one foot outside Hell.

"How do you know for sure it isn't Leo's?" Griffin persisted. "I didn't see any marks or scars, so how can you know?"

"I just do." Back at the table, I retrieved the pool cue, put it back to its less lethal form, and cleaned the black blood from it with angry strokes of a bar rag.

"Can't you call him and make sure?"

Griffin, in his own way, could be as inflexible as his partner. And he'd known Leo as long as he'd known me—gotten his male bonding from the bartender. Leo had been and still probably was his role model. It was understandable Griffin would be worried, but he'd have to trust me on this. "Because there's no coverage where he is. And before you ask, his family doesn't have a land line."

"What are they? Native American Amish?" Zeke asked, annoyed. Annoyance was one of the few emotions he was genuinely good at. But that wasn't fair. He was as worried about Leo as his partner; he just had trouble showing it.

"They like their privacy. Now leave it alone. Leo is fine. And, Griffin, don't ask me again how I know that finger isn't his. You're giving me a headache. I just know, all right? How I know, you don't need to know. Got it?" I said, patience thinning. I wasn't proud of it. But everything was coming together now after so long. I needed to concentrate, not squabble.

"No, I don't have it," he snapped back. "And what about the angel you said was here? What angel? What did he want?"

At least that I could tell him. "Oriphiel," I sighed. "I know you had to learn enough from the House to know he's up there, no mild-mannered little Christmas angel. He's come to hold Trinity's leash while Trinity thinks he holds mine."

At that moment Lenore winged through out of nowhere, as usual, swooped down toward the pool table, and snatched the bow to the box in his beak. He then flew toward the back office. I'd decided to drive to the desert and bury the finger, but I could see that wasn't in the cards for me after all, which was for the best. I still wasn't done with my research on what the seed of Light had flashed through my brain. "I'm taking a shower. Take Lenny and my car"—what was left of it—"and get rid of the finger, would you? My keys are on Leo's desk." I softened it further, adding, "Please?

Bury it. Treat it with respect." Although I knew Griffin didn't need to be told that. "And if any more boxes show up, don't open them. There's no point."

"But how . . ."

I went up the stairs, leaving the questions I couldn't answer and the poignantly pitiful body part behind. The next time I faced an angel, demon, or human ice cube like Trinity, I wanted to be at my best. Having to fight in cotton, Mother Goose pajamas didn't have me feeling quite at my peak. I could do the same damage, but as a samurai went into battle in his armor, I preferred to go in my clothes. Mark Twain would've understood. He'd once said, *Clothes make the man. Naked people have little or no influence on society.* My interpretation ran along the lines of naked people had limited options on where to hide their weapons. Thin cotton jammies weren't much better. And weapons? They had a great deal of influence on society.

Human and demonic.

Chapter 13

The day was shot. I'd known that from the beginning. Angels, demons, severed fingers, Griffin irritated with me and with every reason, more boring research to be done, and now this.

I cupped my cheek where Trinity, swear to my best pair of high-heeled demon-stabbing boots, had just bitch slapped me. "You said you could do this," he said, reaching into his suit pocket for a handkerchief to wipe off his hand as if I were contaminated. I was surprised he didn't pull out a bottle of antibacterial wash and scrub up like a surgeon. "And you are not living up to your claims."

"You slapped me." Bemused and stunned, I said it as if the sky had abruptly turned green and promptly fallen on my head,. "You actually slapped me." Never mind I'd punched one of his men two days ago. That had to be done . . . as a lesson not to imagine they could force me under their control, that they couldn't push me. I didn't think they learned it, because this was pushing. I didn't think I'd ever been slapped in my life. Hit, kicked, thrown against a wall, thrown *over* a wall, clawed, and stabbed . . . a demon carrying a mundane switchblade . . . I hadn't seen that coming. All understandable with what I did. But slapped? I was insulted.

No, I was *furious*, which might be why I lost my temper. Completely. A luxury I rarely allowed myself.

"What are you, Iktomi? Thirty? Thirty-one?" He knew exactly how old I was per any documents on file with the city. He would've investigated me thoroughly the second he found out I was involved with Griffin and Zeke's hunts, and more important, connected to the Light. He was only demonstrating how little I mattered by pretending to forget such routine information. "You are a child compared to the long history of Eden House, a child in this war."

"And let me guess, 'Spare the rod, spoil the child.'" I pulled my Smith from the holster at the back waistband of my black jeans and pressed the muzzle hard, right between his cold eyes. "What about 'Spare the bullet'? Ever heard that one, Mr. Trinity?"

We were up in my room, where I was doing the research I'd planned on. Books and on the Internet. I hadn't found what I was looking for yet, but I was close. Trinity had one of his two men kick open the door downstairs. I'd heard it and not been particularly surprised. Picking the lock would've been more subtle, but Trinity wasn't in the mood for subtlety now. He was only in the mood for results.

They'd ascended the stairs as I stood up from the chair at my desk, fully expecting who it was. What I didn't expect was for him to walk over and, without a word, slap me across the face. It was a slap full of contempt and no anticipation that you'd raise a pinky in self-defense ... or revenge. How unfortunate for him that he was that lacking in perception. I decided a gun was too good for him and much more than I needed to take both him and attitude down.

I must have still had my mama's advice on my mind

as I moved the gun, aiming it at the men with him. I then gave him a swift knee to his crotch, swept his legs from beneath him to drop him on his side, and rammed the knuckles of my left balled-up hand onto the floor hard and fast. It was so close to the front of his neck that I brushed his skin and he knew, for a nicely unpalatable fact, I could've crushed his larynx if I'd wanted. It was a move I'd picked up in Israel, where the martial arts aren't meant to be pretty and color coordinated—they're meant to kill.

"It's been a long time since you fought any demons hand to hand, hasn't it, Mr. Trinity?" I asked as his eyes closed tightly in pain as he struggled not to embarrass himself by cupping his damaged-during-delivery package. "I fought one last night."

His two men moved closer, then backed away when I narrowed my eyes and aimed the gun at them. "I'll bet it's been thirty years since you actually faced one down," I added. "I kill demons all the time. I can kill you with a lot less effort, time, and firepower. And don't think your boss is sending anyone to help you. Heaven let Eden House burn. Why would they save you?" I stood from my half crouch beside him. "Besides, I talked to Oriphiel this morning. It seems he has the same confidence in you that you have in me. I doubt he'll care if he loses his middleman. How many Eden Houses are there anyway? How many Mr. Trinitys? I sincerely doubt you're irreplaceable." I put a booted foot on his leg and rolled him over from his side onto his back. "But I am. I'm the only one the Light speaks to. And you know what? That should have you kissing my feet, if not other parts of me."

I walked to the bed, took the book I'd "borrowed" from the library, and said casually, "When you're done writhing in pain and self-pity, I'll be downstairs and maybe . . . *maybe* we'll talk. If you puke, avoid my rug and have one of your pathetic minions clean it up, and when you start plotting your revenge"—I smiled—"and I know you will, be sure you wait until after you have the Light to carry it out. Otherwise, Mr. Trinity, *you'll* be carried out by Eden House pallbearers. As far as I can tell, you're no better than a demon. If I don't have a problem with killing them, why would I have one with killing you?"

I certainly didn't have a problem beating the crap out of an old guy. I suppose that made me a bad, bad girl. But the fact that he was in his late sixties, early seventies, didn't make it harder mentally and only easier physically. A bad girl, but a practical one. He might have the Sean Connery look, but Connery never would've gone down that easily. Mr. Trinity was a disgrace to his profession. As they say in so many professions, there are no retired demon hunters, only dead ones. Trinity might not have gone soft, but he'd gotten slow.

But slow or not, he hadn't forgotten how to use a shotgun.

He pulled the trigger as he stepped through the door at the bottom of the stairs. The slug from the gun of one of his bootlickers hit the ceiling directly above me, causing plaster dust to drift down onto me. It landed in my coffee as well; black with six sugars, extra sweet like me, but it had gone cold anyway in the twenty minutes I'd sat there thumbing through the book. I looked up, brushed at the black and copper swirls of my shirt, and ran a hand through my hair to see white dust fly. I won't deny a shiver passed down my spine. I was relatively sure he wouldn't shoot me off the bat.

I was tough, but I had nerve endings like anyone else, and they had minds of their own when it came to the sounds of massive booms near my body. Feeling it and showing it though were two different things. "You know"—I pushed the ruined coffee away—"I'm surprised you had the balls to do that . . . especially considering what I did to them upstairs."

"You think I can't kill you, Ms. Iktomi," he said levelly. "But I can hurt you. Cripple you if I like. You will give me the Light, and you will not make such unseemly trouble again or I'll shatter one, perhaps two kneecaps, and watch you crawl to the Light, leaving a trail of blood and screams behind you. Do we have an agreement?"

I opened my mouth, then closed it as he pulled more ammunition from his suit pocket and reloaded the shotgun. A little slower than he'd once been, but not soft, and still a man to be reckoned with. "I think we might." I nodded, reluctant, but you can't play two sides against each other if you don't have both sides present. Kimano would've told me that justice wasn't worth my life, but it wasn't justice—it was vengeance, pure and simple. And Kimano wasn't here to tell me anything.

"Although some respect on your side would help quite a bit," I added pointedly.

"That is unfortunate as I've yet to see any reason you deserve it. You're a mediocre merchant of mediocre alcohol in a less than mediocre establishment. You live and run a business designed to promote nothing but sin. Why two members of my House found you in any way worthy enough to join them in fighting an evil beyond your limited comprehension, I cannot fathom." He aimed the shotgun again, this time at my chest. "If I do kill you, the House of Eden might not find the Light in my lifetime, but neither will any demon. Think upon that."

What a way with a compliment he had. At least he didn't call me a harlot or Jezebel or Whore of Babylon. It was an unexpected and pleasant surprise. "Don't think they won't be pissed about that, Mr. Trinity. I already have two jockeying for it." From the tightening of his lips, this was apparently news to him. Good. "You're right. If you kill me, they won't have the Light—they'll only have you. Are you that anxious to go meet your big boss? With your ironclad, I'm sure, faith, I bet you can't wait . . . even if you have to be skinned alive strip by bloody strip and your internal organs eaten while your heart still beats to get there." I shifted my view back to the book and turned another page. "I admire a man of your conviction."

I heard the metal of the gun's muzzle clink once, twice, three times against the floor. Trinity was thinking, but what? He was a fanatic. Fanatics are almost impossible to reason with or outthink. " 'Thou shall not kill,' " I reminded him softly, my eyes still on the book.

"We honor 'Thou shall not murder,' and killing a soldier in a war is not murder, especially if that soldier is fighting against God." I heard his footsteps slow and measured.

"I'm not a soldier." Any demon could tell him that wasn't true. "And I'm not fighting against God." Heaven maybe, but not God.

"But are you fighting for him?"

He had me there. No, I wasn't precisely fighting for him. I was fighting for myself and my own. Luckily, I found a way around answering his question, not that I didn't have a lie ready and waiting on the tip of my tongue. "There." The thrill that ran through me this time was triumphant. There it was. Finally. I ran my fingers over the glossy black-and-white picture. At least it had once been black and white. Now it was black and a pale yellow. "I've found it. The next signpost. The last signpost."

For a moment he forgot to care whom I was fighting for and moved close enough for a look at the picture himself. "This is where the Light is?"

"No." It was a bleak picture, but beautiful as well. "But this is where the last bread crumb lies, the one that tells us where that caver Jeb hid the Light." The caver who had been tortured to death . . . by whom, I still didn't know. I had no evidence that Mr. Trinity had anything to do with it, but I wasn't about to jump to the conclusion that he wasn't capable of having it done either. Look what he was willing to do to me.

It made sense that Jeb, the Light—the mixed-up conglomeration of the two of them—would choose this. I thought the shark had been all the Light's idea—it seemed to have a wicked sense of humor—and all this, leaving a difficult and annoying trail, seemed more than sentient enough for humor to exist in the Light. But with this, the Light had let Jeb have his way. Cavers were desert to their heart and bones. And deserts were rock and sand, caves and scorpions, mines and ghost towns. Rhyolite was one of the bigger ghost towns in Nevada.

There was information everywhere on it, but that drugged-out musician couldn't make things that easy. Couldn't give me a name or a glimpse of a highway sign or even a feeling in one particular direction. All I was able to get was the flash of the inside of a building and not even a clear flash. Just a haze of sunlight dancing in different colors of amber and green, so much of it that it almost reminded me of the light seen through a stained-glass church window. That was all I saw—a blurry amber and green glow, a wood floor beneath my feet, and the sense of an L-shaped building. Small. I must have looked at the same place in twenty different pictures before I realized it was the semi-famous Bottle House of Rhyolite. Built mainly out of beer and medicine bottles, it was one of the star attractions in the ghost town. But I hadn't been there and none of the pictures showed what the inside of the building was like. After so many times of looking at photos of the peculiar thing, it had finally hit me. The sun was shining through the bottles. Our drugged-out, french-fried friend had been standing inside the Bottle House bathed in that odd light. Sightseeing, he'd probably thought. I knew he had no idea an ancient caver and a far more ancient crystal had anything to do with the fact he'd ended up there to drop the last bit of Light that wasn't in me or tied into the crystal's whole.

I leaned back in my chair as the overwhelming sense of relief hit me. Not only were the House, the demons, and I pushing me, the Light was also pushing. It wanted to be found. Soon. It wasn't entirely safe from discovery where it was, not for long. It needed to be in hands that understood it; knew what it was made to do. It had whispered I was the lesser of evils when it first curled into a corner of my brain. I hoped it hadn't changed its mind. I rubbed at my eyes and slammed the book shut. "Thank—"

"God?" Oriphiel's smooth voice was back. And he wasn't alone. Two more angels of the same silver persuasion stood behind him. I wondered if that was what happened when silver angels fell . . . They became gray demons.

I glared at him as he stood beside Trinity. There had been no flash of light this time. One second he wasn't there; the next he was. It was kinder on the retinas, I had to say. Trinity himself took four steps back when the angels appeared, to put himself firmly where he belonged—in the shadow of Heaven's hand. "No," I contradicted. "Thank me. I'm the only one doing the heavy lifting of the three of us. So how about a little prayer of gratitude aimed in my direction."

"Blasphemy." Trinity murmured the accusation more harshly than he had days ago.

Oriphiel wasn't as upset. Why be upset with the ant that waves its antennae at you in rage when you crush his hill? How pointless. "You do as you were created to do. If you find the Light, it's only because Heaven wishes you to find the Light. How amusing you think yourself that important. You exist only to do Heaven's work. Or you can choose Hell, if you haven't already with this pitiful life. As you said, you have free will." His smile was carved with an ice pick. He made the ever-frozen Trinity seem like a raging bonfire. "As much as we would like the Light, I cannot help but hope you've chosen the latter. Writhing in hellfire, devoured by a demon, that seems as right for you as a serpent-tainted apple."

Could you call someone a prick if he didn't actually manifest one when he was on Earth? Ah well, if the sentiment was there . . . "Don't be a prick if you don't have one to back it up with." I pushed the chair back and stood. "As for the original tattletale crying to Daddy, it's a shame God came up with man before he did spines. Must've been a lot of flopping around in the garden for a while.

"And if you think we're going yet, you had better pull up a bar stool and wait. If you want more wine, you'll have to go somewhere else. I'm not serving you. Or you." I added those two words in address to Trinity. "Until my friends are back, I'm not going anywhere. Oh, and Mr. Trinity?" I said as I passed him. "My friends aren't your friends anymore and they haven't been for a while. I'm sure you've been around long enough to block telepathic or empathic probes, but my boys aren't stupid. They fight demons because it's right. They worked for you to accomplish that, but they learned over the years."

"Learned what?" he said stonily.

"That Oriphiel isn't the only prick in town."

When I reached the phone, I hit REDIAL and pretended to order a pizza into another wretched voice mail recording. Not much in the way of breakfast food and I hoped the son of a bitch actually sent one as a cover story. As much as Eli had angered me right now, he was the only demon I could get in contact with. Solomon had, much like a married man, never left his number and his club was still burned to the ground, so no go there. I didn't want to be standing with Griffin and Zeke at the Light's last clue if Eden House went postal, the three of us surrounded by the holy choir— Heaven's wrath on one side, Trinity's blazing Eden House shotguns on the other.

Eligos was trying to mess with my head with the fear that he had Leo. I knew he didn't have Leo. That didn't change the fact that I'd known the demon was a killer all along, but if he followed us to Rhyolite, at least that would be one more knife up our sleeve. I didn't have to like Eli. In fact, I could despise him for the murdering monster he was. It didn't change the fact that I could also use him and respect what he brought to the table. I'd seen Oriphiel's face when Eli had whispered in his ear. The angel was afraid of the demon, which made Eli serious shit, a deadly weapon, and a good advantage. As long as I didn't forget he didn't care whom he killed to get the Light—angels, humans, or me.

As for Solomon? Who knew? He'd tell you he cared, that he didn't want to kill, but would that stop him?

Sooner or later, I would find out.

Zeke and Griffin arrived back from burying the finger about two hours later, an hour after the pizza had shown up. It was a double garlic anchovy special. Eli—smugness incarnate. Too bad for him that I rather liked garlic and I loved anchovies. It did keep Trinity, Goodman—who'd shown up not long after the angels—and the other two Eden Housers at a distance. The angels kept their distance as well, but I doubted it had anything to do with the pizza. It could've been any number of things. Some angels, like Oriphiel, had superiority complexes and considered humans just a bundle of walking sin waiting to happen. Others were mystified by the entire mammal experience; still others were following orders of middle management . . . there to do the job and not get involved with the natives. It was the rare angel that wanted to hang around and chat. They existed, but you didn't often see them with Eden Housers.

These angels took a table in the corner, folded their hands, and froze into three identical positions. Communing silently with one another over the plan or taking a nap. Who knew? The only difference between the other two and Oriphiel was eye color. Oriphiel's were as silver as his hair. The angel to his right had pale brown eyes and the one to his left dark blue. The rest was the same: faces, suits, hair. Like a cluster of Stepford Angels, which made me think Oriphiel was the sole middle-management angel of the group. The other two were there for orders only. No equal, free-will birds here to divide the glory with. It was all for Oriphiel . . . oh, and Heaven too.

Oriphiel was so much more like humans than he ever knew. I didn't see Trinity sharing any of the information about the Light with the other Houses or there would be out-of-state Trinitys here. It spoke volumes that there weren't.

"Fuck," Zeke said succinctly at the sight of Trinity and the angels. Swatting in annoyance at Lenny who was perched on his shoulder, tugging at the random stray copper strand, he repeated it. "Fuck."

"Couldn't have said it better myself." I sighed, then nodded at the now-cold pizza. "Want a slice? Keep the vampires away."

"Vampires do not fear garlic." One of the angels had come out of his coma.

Griffin frowned. "Don't go there. There are no such things as vampires. Demons are enough, all right? So shut up about any damn vampires." He was right. For Griffin, demons were more than enough evil in this world. It would be cruel, with the loss of his brothers and sisters in arms to tell him differently. He didn't need to know and it wouldn't do him any good, not now.

Griffin's mood, normally easygoing, had not improved with the burial detail or what he saw before him. "And for that matter, why the hell do you bother to show up now? The House is gone. Most everyone's dead. If you can't show up when we need you, why do you come down here slumming with your dirty servants at all?"

Zeke shook his head as Lenore flew off to pick at what was left of the pizza. "Leo." He retwisted his braid that the bird had done his best to destroy. "You should tell him."

Tell him how I knew Leo was safe. Griffin needed that. He needed one less of his friends to be dead. But I couldn't tell him how I knew. Leo had been in on my plan for a long time now. He wouldn't want me endangering it with loose lips about where he might be. I could do something else for Griffin though. Hopefully it would be enough. "Griffin." I turned him away from the angels of whom his opinion seemed to drop drastically. He was losing it all. His House. His friends. His faith. "Griffin," I repeated. "I can't tell you where Leo is or how I know he's safe, but touch me. Know that I'm telling you the truth."

He focused on me. "You'd let me?"

"You deserve it and you need it, so go on." I dropped my shield just a fraction, the one I'd long ago built up against telepaths and empaths. I waited until I felt the lightest of touches as he felt the truth.

He smiled, weary face relieved. "He is all right. You do know."

"I do." I smiled, just as I slammed the shield back up in time to have an angel's psychic probe hit and bounce off. One of the silver boys winced as if he had a headache. "That's what you get for trying to walk in uninvited," I said with satisfaction. "It must just kill you that humans have it too: telepathy, empathy, and even other psychic talents you don't have." Fire starting didn't mix well with feathers.

Eden House had always said it was God's plan, giving humans those powers—to fight the demons on even ground. More and more it was clear they didn't have a clue what God's plan was and never had. This was the most prime of examples. An Eden House rogue board president, Trinity, meets Above's middle management while the CEOs are on vacation, and a merger is born. Any big corporation could tell you how that worked—it didn't.

Zeke had moved to stand at Griffin's shoulder, but his gaze wasn't on demons. It was on Trinity and the other three Eden Housers. "How was Florida?" he said without emotion. "Bring us a postcard?" Griffin might have come to see what Trinity was . . . not a good man, no matter that was the side he claimed. But there had been good people in the Vegas House, and he had liked them, felt as if he'd belonged. Griffin was a social creature and he hated Trinity now. Trinity had tried to use him while planning on rejecting him and didn't seem to give a damn his own House had burned.

Zeke had considered those in the House comrades, but he couldn't go further than that. His bonding emotions extended to Griffin and to a lesser degree to Leo and me. He missed his comrades, but he had never had emotions for Trinity one way or the other—until now. He didn't care if Trinity and all the Houses of the world rejected him—as long as he had Griffin. He did care, however, how it made his partner feel. He cared a great deal. As Griffin looked after him, he looked after Griffin . . . although in a slightly more homicidal way. "We missed you at the battle," he went on, and his Colt Anaconda was in his hand. I had a feeling Zeke didn't plan on missing Trinity now . . . or a good chunk of the wall behind him.

If he killed Trinity, Goodman and the two others would be at his throat in an instant. Truthfully, I wouldn't put my money on them. Shotguns against the Anaconda, that didn't really matter. Them against Zeke, that was the meat of the matter. And meat was what Zeke would make of them. But there were the angels—at least one a high-level angel—and whether they could take Zeke or not, I didn't know.

Nor was there any need to find out. When I found the Light, I wanted a virtual crowd around me. Demons, angels, humans. Whatever it took to muddy the waters. If they were preoccupied with one another, they wouldn't be concentrating on me. If Eli showed up with the price I was charging for the Light, if Solomon showed up to demonstrate what side he was really on—angels, demons, humans—it was going to be one massive brawl.

Finally, after all these years, Kimano could rest. I could rest.

As for Heaven, Hell, and Earth . . . let the pieces fall where they may.

My way.

I looked at Griffin and he wrapped his fingers around Zeke's wrist. He didn't say "Safety on" to halt Zeke, but I imagine he thought it loudly enough that Zeke heard it in his mind. He had to have because he growled and moved away from them all, not showing them his vulnerable back once. Lenore had flown back to his shoulder with a shred of anchovy in his beak and was eyeing the angels with suspicious, beady eyes. He swallowed the bit of fish and squawked at the angels, "Whom the angels named Lenore." But these angels hadn't named Lenore. He had more or less named himself, and he definitely didn't consider himself birds of a feather with them. "Nevermore. *Never*more," he hissed with dark emphasis. That the angels didn't give him a second glance was their mistake, a huge one. Forgive me if I didn't bring it to their attention.

We waited a few more hours. What I had to do might be better done in the dark with no tourists around. Better safe than sorry. It gave me a chance to get the rest of the plaster dust out of my hair and pull it up in a twist with loose curls springing everywhere. It also let me brush my teeth free of garlic, because offending Trinity wasn't worth offending myself and half the city to boot. I didn't bother with makeup this time. If I was going to wear war paint at the end of this day, it would be made of blood. But hopefully we'd get past this last bread crumb without a fight. Don't get me wrong. There *would* be a fight, but I wanted it at the end . . . when I claimed the Light. When everyone tried to buy it from me or take it from me.

Then there would be blood.

Finally we left, and "finally" truly was the word for it. Except for Griffin, Zeke, and Lenore, the company wasn't entertaining. The angels and their servants didn't play pool or darts. Or talk. Or do much other than blink balefully at us (that would be Goodman), coldly (Trinity), and not at all (the angels). It made my eyes water to watch the latter; unmoving, unblinking, they were like silver and marble statues, nothing like Malibu Angel from Wilbur's place. I don't think they even breathed—although in human form they would have to. At least, I thought they would.

Zeke spent his time gathering up weapons, some of his that he kept here and some of mine. Since he seemed to have enough for Griffin and me as well as him, including three shotguns, I stuck with my Smith.

I did make sure to slip several speed loaders in my messenger bag just in case. I expected Trinity or at least Goodman to protest, but they didn't. I guess having three shining warriors of Heaven on your side evened the odds and then some from their point of view.

Rhyolite was about two and a half to three hours north of Vegas, taking U.S. 95. There were ten of us. We took three cars—mine, held together by once-shiny red paint and sheer hope, and two of the Eden House cars, big, black, and official looking. "Why aren't they white?" I asked Griffin, who sat beside me in the passenger seat. "Isn't white all that is holy and good? Pearly gates? Fluffy-white-cloud cities?"

"Too hard to keep clean with all the dust and sand," he grunted, sliding down and pushing the seat back to close his eyes. "And demon blood."

"So cleanliness is *better* than godliness, not just next to it? The things you learn." I looked at the brown-gold skin of my hands on the steering wheel and grinned. "And pure white isn't all that. I could've told you."

"I was born pasty. It's not my fault," Zeke grumbled from the backseat.

I reached back with one hand and smoothed his copper hair. "No, sugar, none of this has ever been your fault."

He looked confused for a moment, then did what Zeke did best with confusion—he ignored it. "What are you going to do with the Light when you get it?"

"More to the point, do you think either side will let you keep it or choose whom to give it to?" Griffin murmured, his eyes still shut, obviously still wiped from the night before. Emotionally and physically. The death of so many comrades. That was triply hard on an empath as it was on the rest of us. "It's going to be a massacre."

"Yes, indeed it is." My grin tightened to something with very little humor. I put my sunglasses on and ramped the speed up to ninety.

"Sounds fun," Zeke said seriously. "Can I kill Trinity then?"

"Kit, when the time comes, you can kill anyone you want," I promised. Griffin opened his eyes and shot me a questioning glance, but I didn't answer. When it was time, he'd see—see if he'd still serve Heaven or serve anyone but Zeke and himself. I wasn't the only one whose life was going to change. He and Zeke were going to have to make a choice, and I had to say I was really curious to know the way they were going to go. Maybe even worried. You try and raise them right, but in the end, they have to make their own way. Make their own decisions. I shook my head.

Kids.

Chapter 14

Rhyolite was a few miles from a tiny town called Beatty. I stopped there at a little gas station. I didn't need gas, but I was thirsty and a candy bar wouldn't kill me. Mainly, though, it was to irk the rest of the wagon train behind us. There was a bigger place, the Death Valley Nut and Candy Company on the north end of town, but they were so big, bright, and shiny that I figured they had all the business they needed. I liked giving my business to someone who actually could use it, and this ramshackle place looked like it could use all the help it could get.

I got out of the car and headed in, smiling at the actual rusty ding of a bell overhead. Didn't hear that much anymore. I touched a dreamcatcher hanging from the ceiling and gave it a gentle push. Inside, an American Indian teenager slouched over the counter, thumbing slowly through a magazine. He had short black hair, copper skin, and a long-sleeved T-shirt that used to be black but now was faded gray. "What you want?" he said, with such incredible boredom that I was amazed he could keep his heart pumping from the sheer weight of the tedium of it all.

"Food, water, peace on Earth." I spread my arms, braced my hands on the counter, and gave him a big smile as a reference point. "And service with a smile maybe?"

He looked up when he heard my voice . . . female— ding . . . and smiled back. Smirked, rather—a genuine, horny sixteen-year-old smirk. I might have passed the big three-O, but I still had it. I laughed at myself— which is some of the very best laughter there is. "I've got more than a smile for—" A dark wrinkled hand smacked the back of his head hard. His grandfather or great-grandfather stepped up beside him.

"You show respect, Aaron. You show it to every visitor. You never know who might walk through our door." With iron gray hair streaked with white and tied back into a long ponytail, the man bowed his head. "I apologize for my grandson's slothful, rude ways. I am Samuel Blackhawk. Welcome."

By this time, Griffin and Zeke were wandering the whole two aisles of the store and Trinity and his men stood behind me. I gave Trinity and the others a dismissive look over my shoulder. "I'm hungry. So wait here or wait in the car. Up to you." Then I turned my attention back to Samuel Blackhawk and held out my hand. He hesitated for a second, then took it with exquisite care.

"Your eyes—I remember them." His own dark eyes flickered. "You are beautiful. You are terrifying."

"And you're a wise man with a silver tongue and one who knows how to treat a lady." I gripped his hand. Because I wasn't beautiful in the physical sense. My mixture of races made me striking, unusual, and definitely eye-catching. I was happier with that. Why be beautiful like so many when you can be uncommon? When you can stand out like the single exotic glow of a garnet in a field of tacky gold? As for terrifying, there were some demons and others on my shit list that could testify to that too. "Samuel Blackhawk, I would like three bottles of water and six candy bars. What would you like?" I released his hand and held up a finger as he began to demur. "I like you, Samuel, and I want to give you a present. And those men behind me with sour faces and even more sour dispositions are going to pay for it. Now, what would you like?"

He smiled then, showing one missing tooth at the bottom, and the look he gave Trinity and his crew wasn't the respectful one he gave me. "A truck. I would like a new truck. Mine only runs when it rains." Which out here was to say never.

I turned, pushed up, and sat on the counter. "Well? Someone go buy Mr. Blackhawk a truck. It's a small town, but I'm sure someone has something for sale." They didn't move. Neither did I, other than to examine my nails. I kept them short, but the bronze was still chipping. Considering the week I'd had, I wasn't surprised. I'd gone with the red first, but, no, the bronze was better, I thought. In fact . . .

"The Light," Trinity said tightly.

I raised my eyes. Who was pulling whose leash now? "When we have the truck."

He could have shot me. He wanted to, I knew. But there were Griffin and Zeke and civilians. He wasn't running the show anymore, not that he would admit it. He turned, back straight, and left the store to confer with his men. Thirty minutes later Samuel had his new truck. It was big, desert worthy, and a dark metallic green. I frowned, but took the keys from Goodman's stiff fingers and handed them to Samuel.

"Paint it red," I said. "Red is my color. Red is good luck. Red will always bring *you* good luck."

He nodded instantly. "I will."

The teenager, Aaron, protested, "But that's a cool-ass green. Why should we—" He received another smack on the back of the head.

I took the bag of water and sugar and started back toward the door. I gave one last smile over my shoulder. "I liked you, Samuel Blackhawk. I still do."

Outside it was full dark and it seemed as if the stars should've been dancing as the cool wind blew through. "I thought you said you'd never been to Rhyolite," Griffin said.

It was true. I'd mentioned it in the car. "I haven't, but I've traveled around the desert. Just because I didn't stop at a tourist trap ghost town doesn't mean I don't know where the good-looking men are." I winked back at the door where Samuel stood and waved. Back on the road, we headed west to the ghost town, and Zeke ate all our candy bars.

"Killing takes a lot of energy. Sugar gives you energy," he said as he avoided Griffin's grab at the last bar.

"So killing and sugar go hand in hand? Is that what you're saying?" Griffin snorted.

"That is what I'm saying," came the answer, without a shred of doubt. Lenny, sitting on the top of the backseat, leaned closer and reached for a nut with his black beak. Zeke, who'd just denied one of the most prolific demon killers other than himself the chocolate bar, hesitated, then let him pick out a peanut and crunch placidly on it.

"Zeke, swear to God. You're not afraid of a demon, but you're afraid of a bird. I have so lost any respect I ever had for you." Griffin shook his head and swiveled to face the windshield again.

"No, you haven't." Unconcerned, Zeke finished the chocolate.

"And how do you know that?" Griffin fiddled with the radio before shutting it off

"If you had, you would've shot me and taken the candy bar."

The side of Griffin's mouth curled. "True."

"This is all entertaining," and it was, "but I'm hoping we can go for no killing tonight. I want to find the Light itself before any moves are made. This isn't the Light, only the last step before we get there. So be good boys. Don't kill the jackasses."

"Which is everyone in this convoy but us?"

I leaned over and opened the glove compartment to pull out a PayDay I'd been saving for emergencies and tossed it back to Zeke. "Good answer."

Griffin glared, a very much out of sorts Griffin indeed. The worst I'd seen him. In his life I'd seen him scared, sad, confident, in pain, angry, amused, happy, but I don't think I'd ever seen him quite this pissed. We had had some bad, bad days this week, and he'd taken the brunt of it—literally feeling the pain of his partner being wounded, not knowing if he would live on top of it, losing more friends—even if he would've lost them anyway when Eden House kicked him out or put a bullet in the back of his skull. It was a lot to deal with. I reopened the compartment and gave him two PayDays and a kiss on the jaw.

"I'll always be your family, Griffin. Leo and I, as long as you want us." I would travel again, but there was no reason Griffin and Zeke couldn't come with me if they wanted. A newly rebuilt Vegas House wouldn't want them anymore and that was if they weren't actively trying to kill them for betraying House secrets. "You and Zeke will never be alone." Or lost as they'd been those seven years in foster care, when they'd had only each other. "Now, have some sugar, Sugar. We have work to do."

I don't know if the candy bar or the hand that I saw Zeke secretively place on Griffin's shoulder helped him more. They might be able to block out other human empaths and telepaths as well as the angel and demon variety, but I don't think since they'd come into their powers they'd ever put that to the test. I thought they were most likely wide open with one another, and that was what helped them survive before they knew what empathy and telepathy were. Before Eden House had come to clue them in, and once they did know, why close the barn door when the horses are jumping the fences and running for freedom? They were whole together in a way they couldn't be apart. Zeke needed Griffin to keep him human, to meet society's and the mental health system's definition anyway, and Griffin needed to be needed. Most of all he needed to save Zeke, but he also needed to save people, to save everyone he could, to save the world in essence. Why?

It was a good question, and like all good questions had to wait until the end of class. Or the end of it all.

Whatever emotion Zeke passed on to Griffin through his touch, it worked. The stiff shoulders slowly relaxed as did the bunched muscle of his jaw, and his eyes, hard as stone, returned to the blue warmth I was used to. "Thanks," I heard him murmur softly. Then I heard him think it as well. Not in my head, but I felt the shimmer of it pass through the air back to Zeke, the gratitude in it so strong that the night air itself reflected it.

"Wuss." Zeke grinned. "You'll make me cry."

Although he never had. A baby died and he tried to

slit his throat, but he hadn't cried. I didn't think Zeke was capable of crying, not yet. Self-mutilation and suicide, yes, but crying was far down the spectrum when one had to learn the full range of human emotions instead of being born with them. Suicide was easy; crying wasn't. It was a thousand small suicides scattered throughout your life. It made the big one, the only one, more logical—at least to the teenage Zeke, who was mystified by most emotions every moment of the day. He was still mystified, but he was better. Much better. Without Griffin, he would've been a sociopath. I knew it. But look at him now. I did just that, glancing at him in the rearview mirror.

"Ass." But Griffin passed back one of the PayDays.

I laughed and shook my head. Both of them scowled at me this time. "What's so funny?" Zeke demanded as he clutched the candy bar possessively.

"Just something I saw on the Discovery Channel once." I turned into Rhyolite. "Are you coming with us, Kit, or are you going to stay in the car and play with your shiny pebble?" I nodded at the PayDay.

They were both confused now, but I didn't have time to explain it. I also had no future plans of explaining it. They'd have to stumble their way through this on their own. I wasn't going to rob them of the thrill, the excitement of their entirely ridiculous and oblivious natures.

Rhyolite wasn't much to see at night. There was a caretaker, but Goodman and his magic encyclopedia of fake IDs took care of him. With Eden House though, they may not have been fake. Everyone might be as genuine as my knife in a demon's gut. We moved past the ruins of a foundation, some kind of miner's building, and stopped at the Bottle House. The train station and abandoned Cook Bank were farther down the gravelly dirt road.

The Bottle House was fenced in, sadly enough, with chain-link topped with barbed wire and the saddest paddock lock I'd seen in my life. A five-year-old could've strolled through in less than thirty seconds, although I imagined our guitarist had climbed the fence and vaulted the wire. A five-year-old probably could've done that as well, the security was that half-hearted.

On the front of the gate was a plaque telling us that it had been originally built by a Tom Kelly in 1906. All the bottles, set in concrete, were beer or medicine bottles. Tom Kelly must have spent most of the early 1900s in a happy haze. The house had fallen to ruin once and since been redone—just a tiny L-shaped structure with the walls of bottles of clear green and amber glass. All the round bottoms of the bottles faced outward. It wasn't particularly attractive or interesting, not to me, but Jeb had liked it for some reason. Griffin popped the fence lock with the universal key—a pair of bolt cutters. The windows were boarded up and I tried the door. It was locked or relocked after the guitarist had broken in, and Goodman had sent away the caretaker with the key.

I sighed and dug in my pocket. Within seconds I was picking the lock, which was quite a chore considering the difference between locks now and then. I'd have been better off picking it with a fork than my tiny instruments. "Why not just kick it in?" Zeke asked, already losing his patience. No demons, no gunfire—what a waste of time in his opinion.

"Because, unlike some"—I tossed a narrow-eyed glance at Trinity, who stood to the side—"I respect other people's property." There were two things wrong with that statement. Granted, Trinity had one of his Eden Housers kick down my door, but I burned down Solomon's nightclub anytime I couldn't find anything good on late-night TV. That was the first thing. The second thing came in a matter of minutes, and it wasn't my fault. I could do a lot of things, but predicting the future wasn't one of them.

Once I was able to get the door open, Griffin, Zeke, Trinity, Goodman, Oriphiel, and I all went inside. It was a tight squeeze for just the six of us and the others were sent back to the cars. As Griffin turned on a small flashlight from his pocket and Zeke pumped a slug into his shotgun, Goodman moved in front of Trinity and raised a shotgun of his own.

"Stop with the testosterone. I'm trying to concentrate," I said absently. I could feel it—a sliver of the Light. But where? Before it had been easy. Touch a shark's brain, touch a drug addict's melting mind, but this—this was different. The Light wasn't in anything organic. It was here and everywhere, but I couldn't pin it down. I knelt down and touched a hand to the wooden floor. No. Here, everywhere, but not there.

I stood and looked around as Griffin's flashlight hit one of the thousands of bottles that made up the wall. It shone in the light like diamonds. In the Light. That was it. . . . That was where it was. The last sign. The last stepping-stone to the Light and vengeance. Awed, almost unbelieving after all this time, I stepped forward and placed a hand against the cool glass of the bottles.

That's when the house blew up.

Technically, not true. The house blew outward, every bit of it. Had it simply blown up, I doubt too many would've been left, sliced to pieces, to tell the tale. It sounded as if the roof landed in two or three sections several hundred feet away, and the walls . . . those incredible walls of glass . . . how had I not seen how beautiful they were? The glass poured outward into the night like a sideways rainfall. And every fragment of them, every piece, every shard, glowed like a white-hot sun.

Trinity and Goodman had dived to the floor. The angel had disappeared. Griffin and Zeke flanked me as I stared at my hand that glowed as brightly as the flying glass. None of the three of us had a single cut. The shattered glass hung in the air for nearly a minute, shimmering brilliantly, before finally settling in the sand like the glitter of thousands of falling stars; the glow faded away slowly as it did in my hand. But I could still feel it. Warm, powerful, mine.

If anyone lurking around had seen that, we'd just created a new Roswell—Elvis-loving aliens welcome. Either that or they'd think something had made it out of Area 51. It was only about one hundred miles northeast—a short hop for escaping aliens.

Zeke looked around at the debris: the scattered glass, the pieces of roof—all the remains of a miracle of light and destruction. "Huh. Cool." Then he shrugged, walked back over the now-flattened door, and headed for our car. And probably that PayDay. Mysteries of the universe, yeah, whatever, was his attitude. Job done. Let's go. There were times I almost envied Zeke's been-there, done-that, live-in-the-moment attitude. Not the consequences of it, but the escape it could be.

"Holy shit," Griffin said, scanning the space where the walls had once been, then up to see sky where a roof once was, and finally back down at the floor still sturdy beneath our feet—and beneath Trinity's and

Goodman's bellies. "You . . . Damn . . . Holy shit," he repeated, and managed to slide it by without comment as Goodman, normally our "Thou shall not blaspheme" enthusiast, was still covering his head and praying fervently under his breath. Although I didn't think "holy shit" counted as a true blasphemy.

"Not me," I denied. "The Light." If such a minute bit of the Light could do that, what kind of power would the entire thing hold? I knew if I was wondering that, Trinity was as well. Savoring it. Picturing the moment he held it in his hands, although I didn't think the now-absent Oriphiel was picturing the same thing. Let a mere human touch such a glory? I couldn't see him allowing it.

But back to business. "Whatever card Goodman flashed the caretaker, I don't think is going to cover this without a lot of talking. And it's almost bedtime." I stepped over Goodman on the floor, saw the chilly bite of Trinity's eyes, and kept walking. Griffin followed me, still shaking his head in awe as glass crunched under his shoes. "Just be thankful Zeke didn't ask me to do it again," I said as I gave him a light shove to the shoulder.

I climbed back into the car, this time in the passenger seat, and Lenore hopped onto my shoulder. "Nevermore?" he cawed doubtfully.

"No, Lenny. No nevermore. Now. The time is now." I propped my knees against the dashboard.

"Now," he repeated, and squatted up against the warmth of my neck. He sounded as grimly contented as I felt. "Now."

We made it ten miles, Griffin driving this time, before Eli materialized in the backseat next to Zeke. If it had been daylight, we could've cruised through Death Valley, past the Artists Palette, a chunk of mountain striped in pastel greens, yellows, blues, and pinks, or seen the Devil's Golf Course, a salt flat that had cracked and bubbled with escaping air until it looked like the surface of an alien moon. But it was night and instead of nature-made tourist attractions, we were given Eli. I definitely did not consider it a fair trade.

I knew he was there before I turned my head. I smelled him. Not sulfur or death. No, I smelled freshly popped and buttered popcorn. I turned to see him toss a few dripping yellow kernels into his mouth. "Thanks for the invite. That was quite a show." He grinned. "Heaven, Hell, and a fireworks extravaganza. What more could you want? I'll bet you scared the ass feathers off those parrots from Upstairs."

Zeke had put his hand on his shotgun by his leg, but then I could see the memory in his pale green eyes of what had happened at the bar the last time he'd fired at Eli and Solomon. He could fire as often as he liked and he still wouldn't hit the demon. Solomon and Eli were simply too quick for a human body's actions and reactions—when they were prepared. There was no chance that Eli wasn't prepared now. He, like Solomon, had already made that mistake once before with me and ended up with a pool cue through his abdomen. He wasn't going to be unprepared again. Zeke knew it and only rested his hand on the gun instead of yanking it up to fire. Eli's grin became mock solemn. "You can learn. Not fast, but you can learn. Good for you." He extended the bag of popcorn toward Zeke. "Treat? Go on. A nummy-num for positive reinforcement?" Zeke ignored him, and you truly haven't been ignored until you've been ignored by Zeke. As far as he was concerned, Eli had been plucked from the fabric of existence itself. The seat was empty and a demon called Eligos didn't exist. Never had. Unless he made a hostile move.

Eli offered the popcorn to me instead. Who knew where his hands had been, besides down his own pants? No thanks. I turned back and watched him in the rearview mirror. "Trixa, you were a star. You glowed like the most brilliant of supernovas."

"Mmmm?" I raised an eyebrow suspiciously. It seemed rather lame for Eli. Slick for a science geek maybe, but that wasn't the kind of sexy Eli liked to put out. "You think?"

"One of those amazing ones that wipe out entire peaceful civilizations. Billions of lives gone in one matter-destroying radioactive glare of cosmic poison. You were magnificent." Happy as a serial killer with a full dungeon in his basement and a week off work to enjoy it, he slid down in the seat and continued with the popcorn and watching the stars above us. The convertible top was down and the sky was spectacular; I had to give him that.

Or maybe he wasn't watching the stars; maybe he was watching for something else. Someone else—someone bright and silver. I didn't think exploding glass would scare off angels long. "I don't think I've ever been so . . . damn . . . *elated* before," he said, before continuing nostalgically. "Well, there was that time with one damn unlucky bastard; a red-hot poker; four horses aimed north, south, east, and west; and the crowd cheering me on. The Coliseum was always a great place to go on vacation. Reinvigorated you. Taught you the little things in life can still make it all worthwhile."

"As much as I'm loving the trip down memory lane,"

I said glacially, "stop sending me body parts. I already hate your kind. You don't want me hating you specifically, Eligos. Trust me on that."

"My full name." He flashed his teeth at me, unabashed. "Makes me feel like I've been a bad boy. I need some punishment. Up for that?" When I didn't respond, he crumpled the bag into a ball and sighed. "Ah well. And I really hoped that would work. I searched for someone who resembled your friend, and he's a big guy—it took some time. Dulled my best carving knife, but the hell with Thanksgiving, I said, and this is what I get? Not only you don't fall for it, but you don't appreciate the effort I put into it. That's just uncivil." He leaned forward again. "How'd you know? He hasn't come back. I have a few low-level flunkies watching the place. Did he call? I stole his cell phone the last time I was around him so you couldn't call him, but there was always the chance he'd call you. I was playing the odds."

"And you crapped out big-time." I wasn't about to tell him how I knew.

He drummed the back of Griffin's seat with one hand and tossed the red and white paper bag out the window. He could've made it disappear, but littering was a little sinful, right? You took them where you could get them, I guessed. Even the tiny sins. "It doesn't matter . . . although it was still a daring plan; you have to admit that."

"No, I don't. And why doesn't it matter?"

This smile was gloating. This smile said he had me right where he wanted me. "I found your brother's killer."

I'd known it. Felt it. The Light, Eden House, angels and demons, all of it converging together after all this time. It left only one thing—Kimano's killer. There was a synchronicity to it, an inevitability. The moment I'd heard that demon I'd killed whisper of the Light with his last worthless breath, I knew it would bring Kimano's murderer to me, because it was the only thing that everyone would want. Do anything to possess. Above and Below. Someone would be willing to pay the price.

I turned again and smiled at him. You wouldn't think a demon, especially one of Eli's rank and caliber, would flinch at the simple curve of two human lips. And he didn't . . . quite, but he shifted his shoulders and puffed up as all male creatures do to ward off predators. "He'll be there, then? When I find the Light?" I asked.

"He'll be there. I'd swear to it, but we both know that would just be fun and games in futility." He frowned, puzzled. It put a crease between his eyebrows I doubt he'd have been fond of had he been human and that crease permanent. But demons don't need Botox, and Eli didn't need any sign of weakness from me. "Don't you want to know the name? Don't you want to know, even if I won't trade him until you give me the Light?"

"No." I turned back and studied the stars again. "Think of it as a surprise present, Eli. So much more fun to open those than the ones you already know."

Griffin snatched a glance off the road at me when I used the word "open." I knew what he was thinking. If the demon was as high-level as Eli or Solomon, opening him might be more difficult than I made it sound. But he didn't say anything and he didn't ask me about the Light, whether I really would turn it over to Hell. I answered the last unasked question anyway. "I'm not as pure as you think I am, Griffin. Not as good. Not without a little sin myself. Maybe a lot, considering whom you're asking."

"I never thought you were pure." He reached for my hand and squeezed it. "But you're our family. You can do no wrong."

I squeezed back and let all the feeling I had for him and Zeke show in my face . . . in my eyes. "My miracle, who went so good when your life could've turned you so bad." One last grip to his hand and I added, "Angels aren't on the state of Nevada's endangered list, are they?"

Griffin jerked his eyes back to the road just past the time he could've avoided plowing into a creature of glass, holy light, and a pissy attitude. I was fairly sure he didn't bother to brake, but the car stopped nonetheless. Whiteless silver eyes glowed as did the sweep of hair brighter than platinum. The glass wings and body were filled with a cool white light, and it still amazed me that something that should've been so beautiful—a crystal, metal, and glass work of art—could be so starkly forbidding when it wanted to be.

Fingers of glass imbedded themselves in the hood of my car as the engine revved futilely. "Griffin, there's barely anything left of her now. Give my baby a break," I said lightly.

If it had been Zeke, he would've ignored me and gunned it. Griffin, scowling, but obedient, listened. He slammed on the brakes until the car was stopped by good old human technology and not the angelic equivalent of the Terminator. "Where is the Light?" Oriphiel demanded in a voice less like trumpets and more like the sound of fire raining down.

Eli once again proved himself useful for more than

tracking murderers, stealing souls, and setting the standards for seducers and male models/gigolos everywhere. Overhead, missing us by inches, copper scales passed on a long serpentine body propelled by the wings of a dragon. Eligos settled on the hood of the car, between the archangel and us. His lizard head snaked forward and, despite the forked tongue, I understood every word. It wasn't trumpets either. It was the last breath of a dying man twisted with the hiss of a boa guarding its prey.

"The Light is not yours." Eligos's sibilant denial split the air. Jet-black claws punctured the hood precisely, blocking the angel's fingers.

"It will never be yours," Oriphiel hissed back, sounding not far from a demon himself.

Two sets of wings thrashed through the air, raptors— both of them. Harpy eagles they were, ready to fight to the death for the right of prey. "There is no bet this time. No job. This is an auction. The Light goes to the highest bidder, Oriphiel." The snake tongue curled around the name with salacious glee. "What do you have to offer? What do you have to give but sanctimonious bullshit?"

"Meet me at the bar tomorrow." I stood and leaned over the windshield to address them both. "We'll leave from there. Make sure Eden House has a helicopter ready to go. I know both sides will make sure I get a good night's sleep. I don't care how many of you winged bastards fly around my bar tonight, watching one another. If nothing else, you'll balance each other out. As for you, Oriphiel, you'd better come up with what I want for the Light." Eli had already come through there, or so he said, but better safe than sorry. "And what I want is my brother's killer." I sat back down. "Now, I'm tired and I'm going home. Eligos, you move the angel and you get first bid."

Eli already knew he had the only bid at the moment, but it didn't stop him from leaping onto Oriphiel. They lurched through the air, a mass of scales, glass, and roars. They hit the sand beside the road and Griffin slammed his foot on the gas, leaving behind deep-throated screams and the sounds of ripping flesh and shattering glass.

"Do you really think we'll survive this?" Griffin asked as the unsettling sounds faded to silence behind us. He didn't look back at Zeke, but I knew what he was thinking. He could protect his partner from many things in this world, but what would go down tomorrow? It was hard for him to imagine any of us walking away. If the demons didn't kill us, Eden House would be right behind them to take the next-best shot. That would be a best-case scenario. Worst case: We'd be caught in a cross fire of—well, to quote another great, older movie—*biblical proportions*. Bloodbath. Massacre. Whatever name you wanted to put on it, tomorrow was going to make the infamous Rasputin think he'd been in a playground scuffle.

"You and Zeke don't have to come. This isn't your fight. This is about Kimano and his killer, about the Light and me. You two can walk away and start a life somewhere else, safe. I wouldn't think any less of you. I'd rather you lived, if worse comes to worst for me tomorrow." There was a lie in there, but I didn't let Griffin feel it or Zeke read it. I kept my wall up and let them make their own decision. That they had to make it without all the facts wasn't fair, but I couldn't change that.

"We're going," Zeke said with nothing more than

mild anticipation in his voice. "Trinity won't let us walk away."

"It's true," Griffin agreed. "No matter what happens, Trinity will want us dead. He considers us traitors and he's old-school, to say the very least, when it comes to betrayal. However this is resolved, we may as well resolve it tomorrow rather than wait around."

"And family doesn't desert family," Zeke said solidly.

I couldn't have said it any more eloquently.

Finally home, with Zeke and Griffin taking their turns sleeping downstairs on the couch. I didn't peek, but I pictured them reluctantly spooned—I really needed to get a camera shot of that—before I went upstairs and turned on the light in my bedroom to see Solomon in my bed. He was bare chested, but wore pajama bottoms of dark gray silk. We'd come some distance from weeks ago when I'd been ready to shoot him for the same thing.

"Wonderful," I sighed as Lenny flew past me to roost on the headboard, his shiny, suspicious eyes fixed on the demon.

"*The power of Christ compels thee,*" the raven croaked balefully. I wasn't the only one who could quote old movies.

"Amusing," Solomon said dryly before dismissing the bird to take me in. "Long day at the office, I see."

"Less amusing." I sifted through a dresser drawer for pajamas of my own. They happened to be silk as well. I didn't know if that meant Solomon and I had similar tastes or he copied mine . . . seeking any advantage that he could. That was the mind of a demon or a manipulative man. I treated Solomon as if he were either—or both—and confronted him. "Eli says you were responsible for the fall of Eden House and you work for Beleth. That you want the Light for him. Any comments?"

I changed in front of him, leaving my underwear on this time. It was no more revealing than a skimpy bathing suit and I made it a short show. He watched silently, but it didn't distract him enough to catch him in a lie. I wasn't stupid enough to think it would. I was just tired. Too tired to leave my bedroom to change. Too tired to care. Too tired to play his games. Tomorrow was the end. It should have invigorated me, that thought, but it didn't. It exhausted me, as if all those years of searching and mourning had caught up with me in one crushing moment.

"I do work for Beleth," he admitted after I slipped the top on. "In Hell, everyone bows to someone else—all except the Morning Star. And he does want the Light. But I wouldn't hurt you for it and I did not take out Eden House. Why would I?"

"Because they are after the Light as well, with backup from the Heavenly Host with the Most—Oriphiel. Getting rid of the competition makes all the sense in the world." I pulled the clip from my hair and let it spring free.

"That holds true for Eli as well as me," he pointed out, then exhaled. "I fell, Trixa, but we all make mistakes. Murderers serve life or die for their crimes. I was merely a rebel. I would repent, given the chance. Being made into a monster for all eternity, forced to make deals with greedy, stupid humans to be able to survive, how can that be just? I don't kill. I don't murder, and if I didn't need the souls to survive, I'd never make another deal again or consume the souls who find Hell on their own wicked path."

"Would you give the Light to Beleth?" I folded my arms tightly, hugging myself, exhaustion chilling me.

"I would give the Light to Heaven if they would take me back, but I know they would not," he said. "So, yes, I would give it to Beleth. I wouldn't have much choice." He slid under the covers and held them back for me. "But I would never harm you for it. I would only take it if you gave it of your own free will." His lips twisted at the last two words. "Odd, how the blessed and cursed of God share that one thing. Free will." His eyes were regretful, colored with what he'd lost. I didn't look any further. We all made our choices. We all lived with them.

I climbed into bed, turned on my side away from him, and pulled the covers over my shoulder. He moved up behind me and wrapped his arm around my waist. He was warmth all along my length and that warmth soothed my aches from a week filled with battles. I felt the nuzzle in my hair and the even warmer kiss on the nape of my neck as that hair was pushed aside. I closed my eyes at the sensation. It had been a while since I'd felt the touch of lips there. "I've watched you, played with you, wished for you for three years now. I've never hurt you. I don't think I could, even if Lucifer himself ordered it. And I didn't mean to hurt your friends. A game gone wrong." He exhaled. "The only way you noticed me. Trixa, I want very much to be noticed by you." He rested a large hand against my stomach. "Sleep," he said softly. "Tomorrow it'll be done. One way or the other. Then you can truly rest."

"Tomorrow when I tell you which demon I want for the Light?" I murmured, my fingers interlocking with his.

"I said I can give you anything or anyone. I will. Now sleep."

I did sleep, with Lenore and Solomon watching. Circling outside the bar there were probably more angels and demons than Elvises in Vegas, but I didn't care. Tonight was my last night as this Trixa: vengeance seeking, mourning, looking for a light . . . not the Light, but any light. Tomorrow I could be myself again. Kimano would rest. Mama would rest. I would rest.

The world would be the world again. My life again, not the one I'd faked for so long. I would be free.

I woke up with lips on mine, clever and so very practiced; yet they seemed meant only for me. I opened my eyes to see gray ones fade away along with Solomon himself. But the "Be mine" hung in the air. "When this is done, be mine."

I rolled onto my back and pushed my hair away from my face. Shiny eyes looked down on me, but for once Lenore said nothing. "He makes you want to believe him, doesn't he?" I said as the sun striped across the bed. Lenny remained silent.

I touched my lips. "He really does," I murmured, staring past Lenore at the ceiling.

Chapter 15

I gave up on my red that morning and went with Kimano's colors, the black of the lava sand beach, the black of his hair, the black of a shark's eyes. This was his day. A snug, black long-sleeved, thin sweater; black pants; and black climbing boots. When I went downstairs, Griffin and Zeke were dressed much the same, only with more weapons. I shook my head. "Trinity won't let you take the guns." Zeke scowled as heavily as a toddler whose security blanket had been cruelly yanked away. "We'll see," he said stubbornly.

"He's your partner," I pointed out to Griffin. "Prod a few of his brain cells if you can. I'm calling for breakfast. What do you guys want?"

Griffin sat on a stool, lowering his head enough that the long sides of his blond hair fell into his eyes. He looked annoyed and he looked dangerous. Truthfully, he was probably both. Being dangerous was the only way he might survive the day. As for annoyance, I guessed he slept on the floor instead of spooning on the couch. His loss. "I don't think breakfast is that important right now."

"Then you think wrong." I called the diner—I didn't want to walk even a block with what winged things might be hovering out there. I ordered three breakfasts and when they arrived a half hour later, I ate all three of them. Omelet, hash browns, toast, two fried eggs, three slices of ham, scrambled eggs, bacon, three do-nuts, and about half a gallon of milk. Lenny clucked disapprovingly and disappeared for a while. Scrounging up his own breakfast.

"What are you doing? Do you have a hidden con-joined twin you're feeding too?" Griffin watched in disbelief as I ate bite after bite.

"This is the endgame, Griff. I'm going to need my energy. You might want to rethink it yourself."

But it was too late for that. Trinity was at the door with Goodman, two other men, and Oriphiel, who was back in one piece after whatever Eligos had done to him last night. His human form didn't have a scratch. It worked that way when you could remake yourself from angel or demon to human and back. If you could reform yourself, you could banish any wounds—provided you'd survived those wounds. There wasn't much reforming after the death of your scaly body, and I still wasn't sure angels could die. I'd never tried to kill one . . . not that hard, anyway. "It's time to go. Would you care to fill us in as to where that would be, as we have a helicopter in a parking lot two blocks down."

"Leviathan Cave." No research needed. It had come to me crystal clear as the Bottle House exploded around me. "Leviathan, a devil's name . . . appropriate, don't you think? That can't be a coincidence." I finished a last swallow of a bottle of orange juice. "Seems to tip the scales more toward your downstairs brothers."

Trinity seemed less than pleased at the news, but asked blandly, "You are sure?"

"Oh, I'm sure." I pushed away from the table. "I couldn't be more sure."

Leviathan Cave is north of Rachel, Nevada, about three hours from Vegas. A gigantic sinkhole, one entrance, was on the flank of Meeker Peak in the Worthington Mountain Range, and was big enough for a helicopter to set down in. Convenient, as I didn't have any desire to make a strenuous four-mile climb up the side. As the cave itself wasn't even one-fourth of a mile long, I didn't think the Light would be hard to find when we arrived. Hard to hold on to?

We'd see.

I didn't see any more angels on the walk to the helicopter or Eligos or Solomon, but I knew that at least the latter two would show up even if they didn't ride along with us. Oriphiel did ride, surprisingly enough. He didn't disappear into a ray of the morning sun or a flash of bright glory, but I expected he wanted to keep an eye on my friends and me. Try to run one angel down with a car and they become distrustful. Where was the spirit of forgiveness, I ask you? As for cranky Zeke, it was as I said it was. Trinity, Goodman, and the others wouldn't allow any of their weapons aboard, at least not until they were secured in a locked strongbox. "Traitors have no weapon rights," Goodman said as he held out his hand for Zeke's beloved Colt Anaconda. If Zeke hadn't respected his gun so much, I thought Goodman might have a colonoscopy without the benefit of hospital equipment and anesthesia and instead the use of something that vented muzzle fire. Not too pleasant, but Zeke certainly seemed to think he deserved it.

But with my encouragement, the partners grudgingly turned over their guns and knives. Big trust in me, huge. I'd do everything I could to make sure I came through for them. Trinity and his men kept their weapons and didn't bother to hide the fact. The helicopter was big . . . not military big, but larger than your average traffic copter. We all fit. Even Lenore, who had returned to ride on my shoulder.

"And that is?" Goodman sniped.

"Moral support." I climbed into the middle row of seats with Zeke and Griffin. Goodman flew with Trinity beside him. Oriphiel and the other two House members sat in the last row behind us. Sandwiched between the holy and the holier-than-thou. As the helicopter took off, I looked out of the right window in the side door. I thought I saw a flicker of wings. Copper or gray-silver, I couldn't be sure—it was too quick. I smiled. It didn't matter which. They would both show. Greed—humans hadn't cornered the market on that. My demons would be there. And at least one of them was as murderous as they came.

I continued to look at the pink and blue sky as I sang lightly under my breath. My voice wasn't the best, but that was all right. As long as it was sung, that's what counted. Lenore crooned lightly on my shoulder. His voice was worse than mine, and that made it even better. Kimano would've laughed himself sick that his *mele kani kau*, his mourning song, was sung by his tone-deaf sister and a croaking raven.

"What are you singing?" Griffin asked. That he could hear me was testament to the luxury and soundproofing of the helicopter. The president wished he had one so nice.

"A song for my *kaikunane*." *Kaikunane*—my brother. I finished up the Hawaiian good-bye and watched as Vegas passed beneath us. I might have stayed in Las Vegas ten years and considered that the longest any of my family stuck around a place, but Kimano had returned to Hawaii so many times, he may as well have lived there. Mama probably wondered how she'd gone so wrong with the both of us.

"It was . . . nice," Zeke said, making the effort, as uncomfortable as it was for him. He meant it too. No mocking of my lack of singing talent.

"Thanks, Kit." I reached over Griffin and patted the denim over Zeke's knee.

"Would your brother have liked us, you think?" Griffin folded his arms and slanted his gaze at me. "I mean, you treat us like younger brothers," he snorted, not all that appreciative of the younger part, apparently. "Do you think your brother would've liked us?"

An interesting question. "Once he got to know you," I mused—once he had genuinely, deeply got to know them—"then, yes, he would've liked you. He liked almost everyone."

There was a long moment of silence except for the muted whirring of the rotor blades. Zeke kicked the back of the seat in front of him. "I want my gun," he growled flatly.

"Make that little brothers, not younger ones," I said dryly. "And me with no PayDays this time."

"It's all right. It's time for a tutor session. That'll distract him. Zeke loves tutoring." Griffin gave a faint, mocking smile.

Zeke just snarled and slouched further down in the seat. "You suck. We could die today and you want to tutor me?"

Griffin smiled blissfully, and with that blond hair and blue eyes, his expression was as blissful as on Michelangelo's *David* and then some. He crossed his arms, reciting, "A grandmother with a stroller carrying twin babies and a cocker spaniel puppy are crossing the road. They're about to be hit by a bus. About two blocks down the street, a low-level demon is eating breakfast at an outdoor café and reading the paper. Do you save Granny, kiddies, and pup, or go kill the demon?"

The scowl on Zeke's face deepened as he thought, and from the furrowing of his brow, he thought hard. After nearly three minutes, long ones, he asked, "There's a puppy in the stroller?"

"Yes." Griffin said in an aside to me, "This is why we have the tutoring."

"Is it cute?" Zeke asked.

Patiently, his partner answered, "It's a spaniel puppy. On a scale of one to ten, it's a ten in cute, and, yes, ten is the highest level of cute you can get."

"Damn." He couldn't slouch any further, although he gave it his best try. "The demon's two blocks away. Do I have a clear shot?"

"No."

By the time we arrived at the Worthington Mountain Range, nearly an hour later, Granny, tots, and the world's cutest puppy had just been flattened by a city bus. But a demon had had his breakfast rudely interrupted with a shotgun slug to the head. "I think you got that one wrong," I said as the copter hovered above the giant entrance to Leviathan Cave.

"It's the puppy," Zeke muttered. "I know I should always go with the puppy, but I like shooting things." Demons, robbers, whatever the occasion provided. "Why did God make the NRA if shooting isn't always the right answer? And grandmas shouldn't push strollers. They're too damn slow." He knocked on the glass of his window, an idea obviously having struck him. "What if I shot the bus driver, then . . ."

Griffin and I said together, *"No."* If anyone was expecting a commentary on Zeke's slightly psychopathic decision-making skills from the angel Oriphiel behind us, they didn't get it. If a demon had been sitting back there though, assuming it wasn't the hypothetical one having breakfast and reading the paper, I imagine Zeke would've gotten a cheerful thumbs-up on the hat trick of granny/puppy/kiddy squashing.

"What now?" asked Goodman from the front.

"Land inside the opening. It should be big enough," I said.

It was and then some. With a name like Leviathan and the massive size of the sinkhole entrance, you almost could believe it was the open gates of Hell itself. But it wasn't. It was only a cave and a rather beautiful one at that.

The copter sat down mostly easy, tilted about six inches due to a rock formation that couldn't be avoided. Outside were deep pink and gray stalagmites and stalactites and a torrent of light from the opening almost twenty feet above. I opened the door once the rotors stopped and stepped out to look up at the circle of sky. I could imagine that's how being born felt like if a baby could remember that far back. A light, colors you hadn't dreamed existed, and a brand-new world. If only they could hold on to that moment forever, because there would never be another like it—that moment when everything is new, and evil is just a word you haven't learned yet.

Griffin passed me, eyes cast upward—blue reflecting blue. As he moved on, I took Zeke's arm when he started to follow him and whispered softly in his ear. "Choices are hard, Kit. Someone's always telling you you're wrong. But there'll come a time today that you'll have to make one and almost everyone around you will tell you what to do. What they say might seem like the right thing, maybe the only thing, but some choices, Zeke, you have to make yourself. Don't listen to what anyone else says—not to them, not even to me. You do what you feel . . . what you *know* is right."

"You think I can?" he said dubiously.

"I do." I meant it. I hoped it.

"Even after the puppy?"

"You will this time. I know you will." I pinched his ribs hard. "Besides, don't think I didn't know you were yanking Griffin's chain with the babies and puppy thing."

He smirked. "I was." The smirk faded and the next words were utterly serious. "I always know about babies. I screw up most of the time. Robbers. Cab drivers. The jackass who cuts in front of me at McDonald's. But I always know about babies."

"I know." I touched the scar on his neck. "Remember, I have faith in you. Griffin has faith in you. Just have faith in yourself." He gave a hesitant and confused nod, then trailed after his partner. It would have to do and was all I could do.

Lenore shifted on my shoulder and gave what suspiciously sounded like a dubious mumble at my ear. "You're just a bird, Lenny," I warned. "Don't forget it or I'll put a bow around your neck and let the tourists take pictures with you." Not that the first was close to being true, but ears were everywhere, and not that there would be any more tourists for me once this was over, but Lenore pretended to take the threat to heart nonetheless and winged away, circling the huge cavern.

"The Light," came a voice from behind me. I didn't need the incipient frostbite to know who it was.

"You're not a patient man, Mr. Trinity." I turned and, wishing I'd worn a jacket, folded my arms against the cold. To give the man credit, it wasn't actually him lowering the temperature. The air in the cave was in the low fifties and I was a woman who preferred the warmer climates. I'd been all over, but Kimano and I both had been sun lovers. I'd done my share of traveling up north, sometimes far up north, but insulation was my friend when I went there. Sometimes you'd be hard-pressed to tell the difference between a polar bear and me if I saw a single snowflake.

"You're still alive. I consider that to be exceedingly patient of me. Now, where is the Light?" He and the three other Eden Housers cradled shotguns. Oriphiel stood apart from them, the big boss waiting for his mocha latte no foam to be delivered to him. He was in human form, the same pale gray suit, the same silver hair and eyes, pale skin. The light from above hit him, turning him into a molten metal statue, peaceful . . . not the crystal warrior who'd gouged holes in the metal of my car last night. I couldn't see him carrying a flaming sword in the old days. A crystal one that shimmered with the light of the moon—I could see that. Could see it cutting a mountain in half or an army of the wicked. All that power, all that lack of empathy for those he should protect. Maybe the best and brightest didn't make up the middle management that watched the earth. God could be teaching them a lesson in his silence. The lesson might be compassion, or at the very least, that humans had value. And some did learn. They had to—it was the law of averages.

"Around." I looked back up at the sky. Kimano hadn't seen the sky when he had died. He'd been killed in his sleep. The demonic bastard that had murdered him had done it while my brother slept. I didn't know which was worse: that my brother hadn't had a chance to defend himself or that he would've been awake and died anyway. He'd been good—in spirit and heart, the way the word should be used. Not a fighter unless he absolutely had to. Genuinely too good to be part of our ragtag, scrappy family. When children thought of angels, they thought of someone like Kimano, not the Silver Surfer standing over there.

Strange, how I remembered that, the Silver Surfer, Iron Man, Superman, but Zeke read a lot of comic books—or graphic novels as he called them—when he was fifteen. Always the superheroes. He'd wanted to fly like they did. Don't we all?

"Then I suggest you look *around* and find it, before I retire Reese or Hawkins now. I will let you choose which one if you like," he offered, his finger resting on the trigger. "I'd suggest Hawkins as first choice. An excellent telepath, but an inferior everything else. Our gardener never quite recovered from the punch in the face and the subsequent mauling by an angry rodent. Plastic surgery can only do so much."

I was with Zeke. Gophers deserved living more than the rich deserved a smooth lawn of Spanish Trails grass. But I moved to play my part. Trixa the Bloodhound. Only this bloodhound was about to gnaw through that Eden House leash and start the action and the auction.

I looked at Zeke and Griffith across the cavern. They were ready. They might not have weapons, but that didn't make them not dangerous. It only put them at a disadvantage. "Even having all of Heaven on your side can't keep your House whole or get your panties out of that massive wad. What a shame." I started away from them. "It's this way."

There were several offshoots, crawl spaces, off the main cave, and I passed three of them before stopping at the fourth. It was just big enough to wriggle through, if you were five feet five and average size. Trinity and his boys were paying the price now for their testosterone- and milk-pushing mothers. They weren't going to make it. Jeb himself, the caver who'd originally found the Light, wouldn't have either. He must've rolled it in as far as it would go. It turned out to be pretty far. And then there it was.

The Light of Life.

That which could protect anything. Keep anything or anyone in the world safe. It sat on the stone and it looked like . . . like nothing I'd ever seen. I'd felt it in my head for days now, but I hadn't pictured it. It was a crystal, but it was alive. I didn't need it in my head to tell me that. It was the size of a cantaloupe with too many facets to guess at first glance and each facet was a different color. Gold, green, blue, purple . . . until I touched it, and then it glowed the purest white. It wasn't a blazing light to hurt the eyes, but a soft radiance. It went through you . . . the soft give of a mother's breast against a baby's cheek. First love. Last love. Lying alone under a blanket of summer stars and knowing at the moment that was enough, that was everything.

"The lesser of evils. Truly?" I smiled and placed my hand on top of it and it was home. To a traveler like me, home was where you stopped moving for more than a day. Almost a dirty word. Something you turned your nose up at, although Vegas had managed to show me that a home could be not so bad . . . for a few years maybe. But the Light gave the word new meaning. You could live in that light, that love, that hope, float there cradled in warmth forever. "You like me," I murmured, my hand tingling pleasantly, "don't lie."

"Iktomi!" The hard shout came from behind me. "Is it there?"

"You can call me Trixa if you want," I told the Light. "It's for friends. You and I, we will be the best of friends." My name was shouted again. I sighed, "For as long as you're around. Let's go. You have quite the crowd waiting to meet you."

"I can't back out," I shouted back. "Too many stone projections. But I think the tunnel curves back around into the main cavern. I'll see you there." I added under my breath, "Ass." I ignored the further shouts behind me and scooped up the light and held it against my chest as I awkwardly crawled on, using one arm and two tired knees.

It wasn't that far, but it took me almost fifteen minutes of inching along, the Light humming against my chest, a subtle vibration I could feel even in the muscle of my beating heart. Its glow was the only light for several minutes before I saw the illumination of an opening ahead. "And here we go," I murmured. "Are you ready for this, because it's going to be all sorts of interesting."

I received the intriguing sensation of a swat inside my brain. My mama would've swatted me the same, actually. She would've swatted me for taking so long. I wasn't sure, but I thought the Light thought I was taking unnecessary risks . . . although its thoughts weren't quite that concrete. They were expressed in concepts more fluid than those in my mind. But if that's what it was thinking, it was right. Kimano would have his day and I didn't care about risk. It was mine to take. Griffin and Zeke weren't quite as at risk as Mr. Trinity thought. Mr. Trinity, while ruthless and a pain in every body part I owned, wasn't quite as smart as he imagined he was. Maybe those panties of his were cutting off his circulation and not letting enough blood to his brain.

Wasn't he wondering where the demons were? Did he think he and the other three with shotguns would do the trick . . . against higher demons? No. And he had to know about the higher demons. He was first in Vegas Eden House. He knew about Solomon, if not about Eligos, although Oriphiel could've informed him about Eli. In this situation, even a lowly human such as Trinity needed all the information possible. On the other hand, angels liked to play it close to the chest. Oriphiel thought no human was worthy of the Light—not even to hold it, not for a single moment—I knew that. He could actually be right this time.

I crawled out into the main cavern, black pants smeared with dirt, as was the palm of my hand. I happened to come out closer to Griffin and Zeke, which was no accident. They were almost as powerful as demons and angels in their empathy and telepathy, and they knew me. Had known me for years. That put them up on the one angel there. They felt me coming and stood on each side of me as I stood up. Lenore flew down to land on my shoulder.

"That's it?" Zeke peered at it curiously. "It's a giant lightbulb. What's the big deal?" Then the hard jade of his eyes softened. "Oh." He touched it with a reverent finger. "That's . . . nice."

I didn't think I'd ever heard Zeke say *nice* unless it related to a gun or an explosion or two, which made this moment nice indeed. Griffin only studied it with that line between his brows, and he didn't touch it—as if he thought he wasn't good enough. It was an odd change of places for the two, and I knew Griffin. He was more than good enough. I wiped off my hand on my pants and took his hand to place it on the faceted surface. He started to pull away as if he'd been burned, but then let his hand rest there. And he smiled—one of those rare smiles of an utterly innocent child seeing his first swarm of lightning bugs at twilight.

Delight.

Magic.

Of course, Trinity had to ruin it. He had an incredible knack for ruining nearly everything. "Give me the Light." He stood across the cavern about twenty feet away, now holding a Desert Eagle, which was pointed, not surprisingly, at us. Behind him with shotguns stood Goodman and the other two. They were grouped a little close and that wasn't good. Respect for their boss equaled bad tactics.

Especially when your boss turns around and puts two bullets in the head of each of you. Oriphiel, still bathed in the sun streaming through the opening, came to life. I didn't think I'd often seen an angel surprised, but he was. "What have you done?" he demanded, all glass and silver again—Heaven's warrior. Human façade gone. He hadn't known what Trinity was about to do, which meant Trinity had a shield as good as mine or it meant . . .

Solomon appeared beside Trinity, as if a clot of shadows from the corners of the cave had joined together to make a demon. "Ready to be a duke in Hell, Trinity?" he asked pleasantly. "You led me to the Light; you gave up Trixa; you've more than bought your way."

It meant he had help.

Trinity's face showed the first emotion I'd seen beyond disgust, ruthlessness, disdain. It showed pure satisfaction. A prince in Hell. Better than a peon, a nobody soul in Heaven. He wasn't the first one to think so, but apparently the lesson of the story had escaped him. "Give me the Light," he repeated, ignoring Oriphiel's flat, "Damned. You are damned."

"No." I shook my head. "You can't have it, and if you think you'll be anything more than a side order of fries to some random demon downstairs, you're the most idiotic man alive." Speaking of alive, I didn't think he'd be that way for long.

"*Give* it to me," he spat before firing the gun. I would've thought that after the "Give it to me," I would've perhaps had the chance to actually give it to him. I wouldn't have, but he could've waited. But that was a man for you—always shooting his wad early.

Dark humor, dirty humor, any kind of humor—it made you feel better when you were lying on your back with a .50-caliber bullet in your stomach. It didn't hurt though, not yet. My abdomen only felt bruised and cold. Not the stereotypical kicked-by-a-mule feeling—kicked by an elephant was more like it. Griffin and Zeke's faces hung over mine as they knelt beside me. Griffin's was twisted, bloodlessly white. He knew. You didn't survive this—a gut shot this far from a hospital, you simply didn't make it. Zeke . . . Zeke just didn't understand. Besides Griffin, Leo, and I were the only ones in his world. No one else existed for him, not really. People didn't understand him, didn't know how alien and lost he was. They were strangers and mysteries, and they didn't want to have anything to do with him. Zeke had the three of us and that's all he had. He couldn't have lost Griffin and survived. I know he didn't want to lose me.

"Trixa?" He said my name in denial, as if it weren't truly me lying bleeding to death on a stone floor. I was a fake, a prop, and the real Trixa would walk in at any moment. Or it was a trick, a game, but not a funny one. Not damn funny at all. Not to him.

I kept the Light cradled to my chest as a soft light bloomed around the three of us, a protective light, but one that was a little late when it came to stopping Trinity's Eagle. I used the bloodstained hand I'd covered my stomach with to grab Zeke's arm. "Get me up. Help me sit."

On the other side Griffin said thickly, "Trixa . . ."

"It won't make any difference," I said to him gently. "You know that. Now sit me up." He swallowed, but with the help of a silent and utterly white Zeke he eased me up to sitting position. Lenore moved from Griffin's shoulder to mine, then sat utterly still.

Trinity bared his teeth at me in a contorted grin. "I've wanted to do that since the day I met you, Jezebel trash." I'd almost made it through Trinity's time on Earth without hearing one of the big three biblical curses for women too. He turned to Solomon. "Go. Take it. It's yours. And you can give me what is mine."

"Power?" Solomon said, eyes on me.

"Yes," Trinity agreed with a hunger to equal any demon's. "Power. Endless power. To rule over the lesser demons. To rule them for eternity as you promised."

Solomon gave him a warm smile. "But, Mr. Trinity, I lied." Then he broke Trinity's neck in a motion so fast, human eyes could barely see it.

As Trinity's body crumpled to the ground, the betrayer of his own House, Solomon looked back at me, his smile gone, to extend his hand toward me and say urgently, "Give me the Light, Trixa. I'll make you whole. I'll heal you. Don't die over politics. Over a thing. And please—please don't die before we know what we could have between us. Give me the Light and be with me. Tell me your price. Tell me the demon you want."

I shook my head again. It was answer enough.

Solomon dropped his hand and took in all three of us with a gaze that was suddenly far from the desperate concern that had only just flashed there—so very far, answering everything I needed to know. Oriphiel, fifteen feet from the demon, did the same, but without any fading false worry over my bleeding out on the cave floor. As one, Griffin and Zeke stood slowly, one on each side of me. Protecting me.

"Zerachiel," came the voice of the angel, the voice of the Tower of Babel falling, "know thyself."

"Glasya-Labolas," ordered Solomon, so swiftly that it could've been an echo of the angel's command, "come forth."

They did, the both of them. They became what they served and what they fought and death might've been a kinder thing. Zeke, Zerachiel, turned to glass. Copper metal hair, oval eyes of pale green light. There was more light in the curves and jagged edges of his wings. The shimmer of copper and a paler bronze that lit his body from within. Griffin, Glasya-Labolas, was a deeply tarnished gold demon, eyes the milky pale blue of a winter sky, his wings spread back like those of a pterodactyl dipped in bronze. Glass teeth, serpent tongue, and whipping serpentine tail.

My boys.

Zerachiel, the angel of children . . . the irony could break your heart.

Glasya-Labolas, in medieval literature, a demon that

looked like a dog with the wings of a griffin. Medieval literature had been wrong, but apparently the name Griffin had been liked by someone in charge . . . either Solomon or Griffin himself.

They had never known, since they'd been formed into the bodies of children, Zeke's eight years old and Griffin's ten, and dumped in Vegas, children with false memories of a past they'd never experienced. I'd known though. I was always one to keep an eye on my competition, and I recognized what had been dropped into the town I'd planned on eventually setting up base—the disguises of children over the spies of Heaven and Hell. But I had soon realized they weren't *aware* undercover spies. They had no idea what they were, where they came from. They thought they were human. Sleeper agents to the nth degree. I also realized after years passed that they weren't an angel and demon anymore. They *were* human, as human as they thought they were—a deeply flawed human in Zeke's case, but human all the same.

One small nudge with two social workers and Zeke and Griffin had ended up placed in the same home within a week of their arrival. It was easier to keep an eye on them if they were both in one place. Hell and Heaven, so smug. As if demon and angel children could appear in Vegas and I wouldn't know about it, no matter how human their bodies. Please. I also knew they'd need each other. They were both living among an alien species, for all intents and purposes. Griffin coped much better; he'd dealt with humans for who knows how many thousands of years before being turned human, but Zeke . . . angels were different. Unless they spent an equal amount of time with humans, they couldn't pull off an imitation to save their wings, much less be the real thing. And from the looks of it, Zeke hadn't spent much time on Earth before being given this assignment. Free will was beyond him for the most part. Decisions, a mystery. Living on his own, impossible. It could be that's why Oriphiel had chosen him, for that lack of free will. He thought Zeke wouldn't question orders when he underwent a transformation that would startle anyone. Oriphiel probably thought he was clever in that respect.

Like I'd thought I was so clever. I knew Zeke would need guidance from the social worker's very first report when they were found—a simple matter of doing what I did best, con and trick, to gain access to the office and scanning both their files. I knew he would need a partner, someone to take care of him, and was self-satisfied I'd had the forethought to have them placed together. And the irony of having a demon look after an angel only made it better.

I'd been such an ass, a dangerously ignorant one.

I'd returned to Vegas seven years later and found out Zeke had needed more help than anyone could give him, though Griffin had tried his best. Zeke could blame Heaven, he could blame Hell, but most of all, he could blame me for that dead baby, but he should never blame himself.

Then Eden House had come for him after he and Griffin had been with me for a few years. No coincidence there, either. A raven had led their way to me. Recruitment had always been the eventual plan. Hell's and Heaven's. It seemed Heaven didn't trust their own House. It had turned out with Trinity that they were right. That Eden House had found an empath along with telepathic Zeke seemed only lucky to them. Hell's luck. My luck, my doing. Trinity would be raging internally that Solomon hadn't let him in on that part of the plan . . . if he'd still been alive.

"Bring me the Light, Zerachiel," Oriphiel demanded. "Serve your Heaven. Serve your God. The Light belongs to us. You belong to us."

I'd told Zeke he'd have a choice to make, one only he could decide. Here it was: the blind obedience he'd known the majority of his existence or . . . something else. The green glow of his gaze, that same rare flash on the sea's sunset horizon, turned to Griffin—Glasya—and was met with a pale blue that could herald a killing blizzard. The sleek lizard face, the jaw that could rip a human into pieces and no doubt in its time had. Demon. A creature Zeke had fought all his life, Above and on Earth.

"No," Zeke said firmly and without hesitation as he held out his hand.

"Glasya-Labolas." From Solomon's mouth the name was stone. "Bring me the Light. You who have slain thousands and laughed as their blood fell thick as rain, seize who you are. Seize the Light for Hell. Beleth will reward us both."

Griffin moved, and it was our Griffin, not Glasya-Labolas. It was the Griffin who needed to be needed, needed to protect the innocent, to save whom he could, to take care of Zeke until his dying day. The one who tried so hard to make up, but for what he didn't know . . . until now. He clasped the arm held out to him, hand to forearm. "No," he said as solidly as Zeke. "Never." An angel and a demon joined together. And neither Above nor Below had been able to stop it.

Now we were missing only one thing, one promise to keep. I covered the wound in my stomach again. I held back the blood well. Not a trickle seeped through.

"Eligos, it's your party," I said to the air, showing no pain or breathlessness. No such satisfaction for Oriphiel or Solomon.

He appeared behind Oriphiel and, with a massive swing, cut off the angel's head with one stroke of those flaming swords I'd been thinking of earlier. He gave that cocky grin that was almost permanently carved into his face. "Souvenir from the Penthouse. They're a dime a dozen up there."

Oriphiel's body disintegrated into thousands and thousands of crystalline pieces with the sound of glass bells ringing in their own deaths. Eli dropped the sword, flames dying away, on top of the pile of glass and raised his eyebrows at Zeke. "A spy in their own House? Not very trusting, to be so wholesome and holy and chock-full of choirboy goodness." He looked down at Trinity's crumpled body. "Although apparently the pigeons had every right to be suspicious. I'm surprised they were that smart."

I didn't care about Trinity or Oriphiel right now. I cared about one thing. "You have proof?"

"You guessed, then. Spoilsport." He held out a hand toward me, and my bracelet jerked free of my wrist and flew across the twenty feet to rest on his palm. "I have your proof."

"Leo, take the Light." I pulled it away from my chest and held it up. Lenny/Leo left my shoulder, spread his wings, and grew—twice the size of a pterodactyl. One black foot closed around the Light, while one wing curled around Zeke and Griffin—I couldn't think of them as Zerachiel or Glasya—and scooped them off to the side while keeping aloft with the thrashing of one wing. The two didn't struggle. After all of this and a brand-new history dumped into their brains, I'd be surprised if either of them could form a coherent thought.

"Show me," I told Eli.

"Darlin', I'd say be prepared to be as astounded and surprised as if you'd seen my equipment at work, insert porn music here, but I have a feeling you knew all along." Eli opened the tiny locket and balanced the scale on his finger as he muttered a few indecipherable words under his breath. The scale spun slowly, then faster and faster before finally flying through the air to hit Solomon in the throat. For a second, less maybe, I saw him as he was—like he'd refused to let me see him before. He was a dark gray demon dappled with silver and eyes that were bright, shining, wholly empty mirrors—empty and cold—and then he was human again. Human and moving toward me with those human teeth bared.

He could now. Neither he nor Oriphiel had tried before because I had held the Light—the one shield absolutely nothing could breach. They couldn't take it from me, thanks to Trinity's activating it by shooting me, but Zeke and Griffin had been touching me, inside its protection. They could have.

They hadn't.

But Leo held it now and the soft clear light enclosed him and Zeke and Griffin while Solomon moved closer to me. The human form he'd gone back to didn't extend to the eyes. They were still pools of mercury as silver as a heart-piercing dagger. Appropriate. He'd torn out my heart long ago. He kept coming right up until the moment Eli asked me curiously, "Why aren't you in shock?" You might also say he topped that curiosity with a healthy dose of suspicion. I had no illusions he was actually concerned for my health, and he didn't bother to fake it as Solomon had.

At Eli's words, Solomon stopped.

"As a matter of fact, why aren't you dead by now?" Eli tilted his head, the blond streaks in his brown hair gleaming in the sun. As he went on to talk about death, he glittered like an angel himself. "You should've bled to death, at the least gone comatose or had a seizure or two. I've inflicted my share of those deaths. I'm more than familiar with how they go." He frowned. "We have a deal, remember? No flopping around like an out-of-water fish until I get what you promised me."

I took my hand away from my stomach and waggled fingers at him. There was no blood on my hand, none on my stomach. I gave him the same answer Solomon had given Trinity. "I lied. That's what I do, Sunshine. That's who I am." I shifted and lifted my eyes to Solomon and said with mock solemnity, "And didn't I do such a good job? The years of 'Will she or won't she'? All that unresolved sexual tension. Pushing you away, but never *completely* away. The kiss, the reluctant pulling from your touch, savoring your warmth despite my weak little self, letting you sleep with me. Hold me. I was trusting as a lamb, so vulnerable. Wasn't that sweet? Who would be so good as to fool you, a demon? Only my kind, only me . . . the ultimate liar."

"Trickster," Solomon snarled, all pretense at being the most regretful of the Fallen, the demon who was fluffy and warm as the Easter Bunny and never spilled a drop of blood, was gone. Gone every bit as quickly as the snap of Trinity's neck.

" 'To every thing there is a season, and a time to every purpose under the heaven,' " I quoted. "And above Hell," I added.

I stood and stretched, felt that lifetime-familiar electricity spread through me; my hair lifting in a most nonangelic halo around my face. "So easily you forget us pagan-kind, forget the *païens*." I was pagan all right, as I'd told the boys—so pagan that I was one of those that the pagan humans had worshipped . . . for thousands of years until these Johnny-come-latelies had spread their way far and wide. "You forget that we belong here too, but that doesn't stop you from casually killing us if given the chance. You thought our season was over." I pointed. "You, Solomon, are especially fond of killing our kind if you can. I've studied you. It's a hobby for you, isn't it? Four hundred of us have you destroyed over the past two thousand years," I growled. Not a female growl, not even a human one. "To you and the angels we are nothing but leftover vermin from a world you refuse to share." I fixed my eyes on the demon, who didn't move. Didn't blink. That was smart of him.

"But this is our world too, and if you won't leave us in peace, then we will be protected from the likes of you all. An abomination to Heaven, a nuisance to Hell. But with the Light, the shield"—it continued to glow around Leo—"neither of you will touch my kind again. We will have sanctuary if we want it. We've been looking for it a long time and now it comes home with us."

"You?" A wave of boredom passed over Solomon's human face. His acting hadn't gotten any better, no matter what Shakespeare had told him. "You plan on leaving with the Light? Little Trixa? And Leo who cleans your bathrooms?"

"Little Trixa." I smiled. Leo's wings began to thrash, creating a wind tunnel in the cavern. "Leo." I knew the pupils of my eyes were dilating as the kill approached. "Not so, Solomon. For you, we are so much more. For you and the shield, my people sent in the big guns. Sent in the heavyweights. The varsity team. The gunslingers. Leo went by Loki for a while. Loki, the Norse god. You have heard of him, right?" Leo's mocking cry split the air like a siren. "He almost ended the world once just to liven up a tedious afternoon. He's mellowed since then. Slightly."

I stepped toward Solomon. "I, little Trixa, have been called Coyote." I went to all fours and became a coyote, one the size of a bear. "Kitsune." My fur turned fox red. "Crow." Massive black feathered wings sprouted from my shoulders. "Akamataa." My tail turned to a scaled, thick whip of a lizard. "Amaguq." The coyote eyes turned to wolf. "Iktomi." The two yellow wolf eyes multiplied to a spider's eight.

My voice wasn't human anymore and neither was my smile, the teeth changing shape to almost perfect triangles. "But a girl gives so many names out, she begins to forget a few. Too bad you didn't pay attention in demon school." I held a clawed paw high. "Gods." I dropped the paw a little lower. "Tricksters." I dropped it considerably lower. "Demons." I couldn't smile coldly with my changed jaw, but I showed my teeth. "Leo looks down on me for not being a god like him, but I'm happy enough." I wasn't a woman any more than Leo was a man—not the human kind. Although the majority of tricksters, like me, *are* born male or female. I might not be a human woman, but I was a woman through and through. I'd said I was born thirty-one years ago. Another lie. That body had been created just ten years past in Vegas and a good one it was. I liked it a lot. Apparently Solomon had too, much more than the one he was facing now.

"What, Solomon? Am I not sexy now?" I took another

step, claws scoring the stone. "Don't I turn you on anymore?" I bared the teeth of a shark—the *Ka-poe-kina-mano* trickster. My brother's favorite form. He had considered Hawaii his home for a long, long time. It was only right that part of him should be here now. Killing Solomon as Solomon had killed him on that black sand beach while he slept in a human form. He had been young, the trickster version of a teenager, and hadn't yet learned to shield his mind and aura from the higher demons. Trusting. The only trusting trickster I'd ever known. Easy prey. And Solomon had been the willing predator. His *hobby* had spilled my brother's blood. The demon hadn't chosen him on purpose. He had only crossed his path and did what Solomon did best. Murder. For fun.

It had been pure chance. Entirely catastrophically bad luck . . . for my brother.

Now for Solomon too.

I hoped Solomon wouldn't make it easy. I hoped he lasted a long time. He was a powerful demon . . . high-level with the speed and skill that went with that.

Which might have mattered in the end if he were up against another demon, but guess what? He wasn't. Demonic levels were meaningless to me. We were going by a different sort of rank . . . demons, tricksters, gods. And this bastard was outranked. He'd killed my helpless-in-sleep baby brother, but I was no baby.

And I had never been helpless.

My predator grin widened, the backward curving teeth broadening my coyote jaws even further with the crunch of bone. "Don't you want me? You once said you wanted to be inside me," I said, my voice thick from my jaw's changed shape, "and I want you inside me too, Solomon, but I think we have very different ideas of where."

He started to shimmer, to travel back to Hell, but I was on him first, taking him to the cave floor, physically pinning him to this world as my claws punched through his shoulders. And that's when he changed to his true form.

Demon. Wings, scales, jagged smoky teeth. Eyes that were poisonous silver whirlpools that threatened to suck you down to Hell.

Scary.

Not.

"And I bet you thought *you* were the monster of this little fairy tale," I said through twisted vocal cords. "I've searched for you for fifty years. The killer of my brother. The darkest sorrow of my family. Do you remember? A black sand beach in Hawaii? A trickster in human form sleeping on the sand and you slaughtered him before he even had a chance to wake. Eli did say you liked shooting fish in a barrel. *Coward*." His teeth snapped at my throat. I met them with my own teeth. "I thought it was you, handsome Solomon. Mysterious Solomon. For at least thirty years I thought it was you as I followed you from place to place, but I needed to know for certain. There were other demons it could've been, others who have your same hobby. Those of the same color, although none had your reputation, your sheer numbers of *païen* killings. I had to be sure.

"I lie, but I lie to make others see the error of their ways." I removed the claws from one of his shoulders and shredded his right wing. "I trick to make things right. I even kill, if I have to, to balance the scales. But I need proof. Now I have it. Now you will balance Kimano."

Although it would take a thousand demons to balance the shining heart of my brother. But every journey begins with a single step and killing Solomon was that step. I roared and buried my teeth in his chest. Black blood pumped free and tasted of fire and bile. His two back feet came up beneath me and clawed at my fur-covered underbelly. The claws were sharp and I felt them tear through my skin. It was good, the pain. Good because it let me know Kimano's justice had come. I dug my teeth deeper into Solomon's chest and yanked my head sideways, ripping the flesh away in a massive hunk just as a shark would. It flew and landed across the cave with a meaty thump. I saw obsidian bones, but no heart beneath it.

I wasn't surprised.

He might manufacture one in human form—I had felt it beat against my back last night when Leo as Lenore had stood watch over me—but Solomon had no heart. I'd known that all along. Not even the spiritual equivalent of one. He surged underneath me, throwing me back, but I didn't let go of him. He wasn't escaping to Hell. If I had only one tooth left, one claw remaining, I'd hold him here to his death. His teeth buried in my shoulder and he removed my flesh as well. I tucked my wings tight against me and rolled to my side, then up again and lifted into the air, my massive crow wings flapping with a pure surge of muscle. I still had Solomon's one shoulder hooked firmly on the claws of my Akamataa shape, the dragon. They had passed through his scales and flesh and come out the other side to catch like barbed fishhooks.

He rose in the air with me, fighting me every inch of the way. His wings thrashed as he tried to pull himself away from me. The rended wing had been remaking itself quickly, but with the gaping hole that stretched the width of his chest, the wing had to get in line. Black flesh and ebon and silver scales began to reform over the ribs. "I hated you," he spat, all that velvety charm gone. All that sweet, sweet care for me now a ghost. "The only thing I thought of you when we touched is how your flesh would taste as I tore you to a pile of gore and scraps. I only wanted the Light from you, bitch. Three years ago I knew you were looking for it. I heard the whispers."

"Were they only whispers?" I laughed ... coyote/ wolf howled—it was all the same. "I told every demon I let live for years and years, many more than three. Until it went full circle and one *told* me. I'd thought more than whispers. I'd thought they'd been shouts for all the rumor spreading I did. I knew it was somewhere in this vast desert. I could wait for you to catch up before I circled in on it. So I could have my cake and eat it too.

"And hated me, my Solomon? Hated me? How you hurt my feelings."

But it certainly didn't hurt as much as what came next.

His wings tried but they couldn't do it. He bit and clawed at me. It wasn't enough. Fifteen feet in the air, I folded my wings back and let us fall. I twisted to one side as he was impaled on a stalagmite that rose up from the cave floor. It passed through his back and thrust its way through his stomach. Fluid gurgled in his throat and his tail undulated sluggishly, but that wasn't enough to kill a lower demon. It definitely wasn't enough to kill Solomon—until I fastened my jaws around his serpentine neck and tore his head from his shoulders with one ripping motion. My four feet on the ground again, I let the head drop before me and stared into eyes that were still aware ... if only for a moment. "For Kimano, you bastard. For my brother."

The silver hate didn't fade until the head as well as the body melted to black sludge. That's when I lifted my gaze and saw it. I saw Kimano standing in the volcanic sand, hand upright in acknowledgment, his grin as happy and bright as always. It wasn't true, but I wanted it to be so badly that I did what I'd done for the past fifty years and pretended that I saw him. I pretended hard enough that maybe I almost did. Almost. It didn't matter. You take what you can get in this life. If almost was all I could have, then almost was what I would take.

I turned my heavy head toward Eli, who stood frozen in place, his normally nonstop sexy mouth slightly agape. I grinned the shark grin that dripped black demon blood. "You still want to hit this or what, Sunshine?" Eli disappeared in an instant, so fast he left a tiny sonic boom in the space where he had stood.

My crow wings fell away and vanished. Eligos hadn't even complained I'd not lived up to my end of the bargain: handing over the Light, not that I'd ever truly planned to. He was more concerned with making sure that gorgeous ass of his wasn't grass. My tail disappeared and my jaw began to change and change again. The demons had learned to lie when they fell, but it was a trickster who had told the very first lie. Demons . . . they were nothing more than amateurs. Although Solomon getting to Trinity, that had been unexpected, actually a little clever. I hadn't looked beyond Griffin for the demon-touched in Eden House. Shame on me. My fur disappeared, my eyes back to two, then from gold to dark amber.

And I was Trixa again. Trixa in black pants and a sweater that had never been hit by a bullet. A Trixa who wavered and fell unceremoniously on her butt. Ah well, things never go quite as you picture them.

I looked at the angel and the demon who were shielded by Leo's wings, and a light more alluring than the sun that came through the cave entrance. Glowing green eyes and moonstone blue ones looked at me. "You told Heaven and Hell no," I said, my voice a little hoarse, but mostly Trixa's normal voice. "Heaven won't have you now, Zeke, even if you changed your mind. And, Griffin, Hell would have you, but you wouldn't like it much. They would unmake you and remake you over and over until the last star in the sky winked out." He would scream for an eternity . . . a literal one.

Their hands still clasped the other's arm and if anything, their grip tightened. "Screw Heaven," Zeke said, oblivious to those words coming from an angel's crystal carved mouth. "I want to stay. I don't want to be one of them. I want here. I want Griffin." The angelman who loved to kill the demons the most, yet not once would he deny his demonic partner. It didn't even cross his mind. I would've loved Zeke for that, if I didn't already love him.

And Griffin . . . a high-level demon. Not as high as Solomon or it would've been him on the outside and Solomon undercover, but still high-level. Who knew how many he'd killed? How many souls he'd damned? The Light didn't let him know. I still felt a small tickle of it in my head. I felt how it took Hell from Griffin's mind and Heaven from Zeke's, took those memories away forever. Griffin wouldn't know what he'd done, so he'd be free to be the good man he was now. And Zeke would be able to hold on to the scrap of free will he'd managed to wrangle for his own and keep working on it. Who knew? Someday . . . a long time . . . but someday, he'd learn, he'd get it right. They looked up as the Light, which existed to protect, protected them from themselves. It brightened as it rained down on them. Glass and scales became flesh. They became human again.

Except for the wings.

Zeke's glass and crystal turned to the very traditional feathered kind—all copper as his hair with only the faintest barring of cream at the bottom. Griffin's were the same dragon wings of before, only less tarnished . . . a brighter gold. They were beautiful, the both of them, just as they'd always been.

"Leo." I met brown raven eyes the size of lemons. "Take the Light to the Hearth." Hearth and home. We would have a home now. A safe harbor. A place no angel or demon could breach, one where they could never kill one of our kind again—where the very first who'd walked this world could be the very last as well. One eye winked and he was gone, the wind from his wings nearly knocking us all from our feet. It would have if I hadn't already been sitting, courtesy of my wobbly legs. I felt the Light caress my mind, saying good-bye, holding me as I imagined Kimano doing; then it was gone . . . every last mote of it. Off to its new home.

Sanctuary. Finally. No more Kimanos. No more *païen* dead.

Of course, that's not to say one *had* to go there right away. Yes, if all out-and-out war came between the three: angels, demons, and the *païens*. Or if you needed a rest after a hard hundred years of work tricking those who deserved it. You could go at any time. It didn't mean you had to stay, hidden from the world if you didn't want to . . . sheltered from the tricks and the dangers. The surly girls and fat dogs. The desert wind and an old Indian who never forgot you, no matter if you were coyote or human. The bar fights and the pool games. The red balloons left tied to benches. The fields of spring flowers and the tsunamis that drowned islands beneath the sea. You didn't have to give up the good, the bad, and the miles and miles of everything else that stretched between.

I mean, where would be the fun in that?

Chapter 16

Getting out of Leviathan turned out to be relatively simple, although none of us knew how to fly a helicopter.

"How old are you? Really?" Griffin asked. "You told us you were twenty-one ten years ago, but you said you'd been looking for Solomon a damn sight longer than that. So that picture you have of your brother in your room, the black and white—"

"Was taken when black and white was your only option, about sixty years ago." It was Kimano, Leo, and I. Leo had been the raven, as usual. I think he did it to irritate his father who had two ravens of his own, annoying little spies that they were, sitting on Odin's shoulders. I'd been the coyote in the picture, and it had been the old American Indian who'd recognized me at the gas station yesterday who'd taken the photo for us. It was nice when someone remembered the old ways. I'd given him a red silk bandana for that, clutched in a pointed furry muzzle then. I'd given him a truck for it yesterday.

"And I'm old enough to know you don't need to know." I waved my arms at them imperiously to be helped up. "Still young and hot, got it?" The two of them let each other go, reluctantly if my eyes were good, and they were.

"I just liked to think if I'm older than you, that I could finally give you shit instead of the other way around, *big* sister," Griffin drawled.

"Look at the ex-demon with his big-boy pants on now," I snorted. I took his hand and Zeke's with my other and managed to get upright and stay that way. "It's not the age of the brain cells, boys; it's how you use them. Do you want to talk about what you did with yours before you came to Vegas?"

He grimaced. "No."

"I didn't think so." But I let go of his hand to give him a sympathetic rub of his back. It would take a lot of processing to come to grips with being what you imagined to be the worst evil in existence. They actually weren't. Only the second most evil, but there was no need to get into that and it probably wouldn't make him feel much better anyway.

We *païens* had our own version of demons, but oh so much worse.

"So we're all old. Any of us know how to fly a helicopter?" Zeke said, more to the point than anything Griffin and I had brought up.

"Never needed one. Wind beneath my wings and all that." I held out my arms beside me and shook my head. "But that's over. I won't have my own again for a while."

"Why?" Griffin took his turn and asked, the thick hair a tangle from the wind of Leo's flight.

I shrugged a little uncomfortably. "I showed off a little. I didn't just want Solomon dead. I wanted him afraid, terrified, and I wanted him to suffer. For my brother. I pulled together a lot of forms at once. Too many. My battery has been drained for a while." I wasn't sorry I'd done it, but there are consequences for everything. Especially vengeance—big vengeance. I'd known the price. Kimano was worth paying that price.

"Then you're stuck in your original form?"

I laughed as I touched his gold wing. It felt like silk strung between smooth metal. "This isn't me. It has been one of my favorite forms though. And I'm only stuck in human form for four or five years or so. It's not that long." It wasn't. Although the human vulnerability rather sucked—no healing, no making wounds disappear as I shifted form. All human. I did like this Trixa though. I'd thought carefully about who she'd be. I'd wanted to be all things, not just one. I wanted to be literally all ethnic varieties on the planet. I might appear mostly Asian and African, but I hadn't stopped there. You named it and it was in me. Caucasian, Arabic, Polynesian, Aborigine . . . everything. It was rather clever: If there is a pheromone component to race and gender, anyone would be naturally inclined to trust me or be attracted to me, because in a small genetic way, they were family. To have your foot already in the door with everyone you met, what more could a trickster want?

Not that it seemed to work with Leo's bimbos of the moment. Nothing could penetrate their own Light, their own shield—one of stupidity.

"You can choose any form you want?" Zeke asked curiously. "Why not one with bigger boob—" Griffin elbowed him hard and we were back to where we'd been weeks ago. Zeke without an internal filter and Griffin saving his ass. It was . . . wonderful. The best.

"You better go get your guns out of the helicopter," I ordered, "if you're going to talk trash like that, and be-

cause the two of you are about to take your first flight.
The first one you'll remember anyway."

While Zeke cursed inside the copter trying to get the
weapons locker open and cursed Leo while he was at it
for not waiting to give us a ride, Griffin at my side said
quietly, "I'm a demon."

"No, you were a demon," I corrected, cupping his
face. "You've been human since you first came to Vegas
to watch over Zeke for literally all of your human lives.
That proves that you, Griffin, are one of the most hon-
orable and truly good men I know." He opened his
mouth, doubt written all over his face. "And," I added,
"you wanted to know how old I am? More than six
thousand years old. Old enough to have known many
good men. More bad men, but many good ones too.
You rank at the top. I promise you that."

"Hard to imagine how that happened," he said,
frowning at the sight of his own wings.

"You are how it happened. You were given a second
chance. With that chance, you chose good, and you
chose Zeke. Remember that." If he didn't, I'd remind
him until it finally took. It might take a lot of work, but
I was up for it.

It turned out Zeke and Griffin were up to it as well.
Both took an arm and we flew, the wings of a falcon
beating in perfect harmony with the wings of a dragon.
At the base of the mountain Zeke was grinning, the
grin of a happy five-year-old who'd flown his first kite.
"This is going to be fun." He looked at the Colt Ana-
conda in one hand and his wings and grinned wider.
"Really fun."

"No, no. With flight and massive firepower comes re-
sponsibility. The last thing we need is a guided missile

with feathers. You'll have to earn your license first." I ignored his glare as I went on. "Put the wings away. It's a fifteen-mile walk back to Rachel. We don't want any roadside conversions on the way. No shrines, not unless they're to Elvis. It's the Nevada law."

"How?" Zeke touched the feathers over his shoulder with a curious finger and said skeptically, "Seems pretty solid."

"Just . . ." I hesitated as I thought of the last time I'd talked to a peri, pulling my sleeves down over my hands. Despite the bright winter sun, it wasn't warm. "Think them away, I guess." It seemed like that's what the peri had said. "Tell them to go. They are yours. They should listen."

It took a few minutes, but they were able to get the hang of it. Copper and gold flickered in and out of existence with glints of gold light until finally they disappeared altogether. Zeke reached over his shoulder and slapped his back. There was nothing but the meaty thump of flesh. "Will they come back? Where'd they go?"

"When you want them to, yes. As for the rest"—I shifted my shoulders in an unknowing shrug—"I've no idea. Next time you see a peri, ask him."

"A peri?" Griffin bent down and picked up a stray red-gold feather of Zeke's that had fallen to the ground and stayed when the wings had gone.

"Yes, a peri. Zeke is a peri now. I think." I started walking down the dusty road. "Not that I've run into one like him before. All other peris have Heaven's stamp of approval on their green cards. Mythology says peris are half angel, half demon. Remember this, guys," I said firmly, "mythology is most often wrong. Sometimes it's close, but in the end never completely right." I hooked my arms through theirs and pulled them close for warmth. "Some angels who lived on Earth among humans for hundreds or thousands of years, watching, doing whatever it is they did, they tended to want to stay on Earth when it was their time to go home. They'd get a taste of free will and the native life. So they'd ask permission to 'retire' . . . to become expatriates of Heaven, if you will. I emphasize they *asked* permission; they didn't give Heaven the metaphorical finger like Zeke did."

Zeke didn't look sorry. He actually looked rather pleased with himself. "What's Griffin?"

"I don't know. What the hell, for once we'll close our eyes and buy into a little mythology. Griffin can be a peri too—the demon half instead of the angel one. He'd be the only one I'd ever heard of." I pulled them closer, more body heat. "Which makes you as special as you always thought you were, at least from the way you dress. If Eden House doesn't rebuild in Vegas, you'll lose the bit paycheck and be shopping at Wal-Mart, Mr. Metrosexual, and then what will you do?"

Griffin started to stay something indignant but let it go as I leaned against his arm. "God, trickster, demon," he said. "Trickster trumps a demon, eh?"

"Mmmm." I rested my head on his shoulder and yawned.

"Especially a pissed-off trickster?" he continued.

"Especially," I agreed wearily with another heavy yawn and a desire to eat the nearest buffet in its entirety. No sharing. I'd carb loaded at breakfast for all the changing I knew I'd do, all the energy I'd need. Now I was drained, had a fifteen-mile walk ahead of me, and couldn't decide whether I'd rather sleep for days or eat for hours. Too bad I couldn't do both at the same time.

By the time we made it back to Rachel, population less than a hundred, I gave up on the idea of "borrowing" a car and heading back to Vegas. We stopped at the Little A'Le'Inn. With Area 51 being so close, aliens were the only tourist attraction and business that kept this tiny town going. The inn's restaurant didn't have the buffet I'd been wanting to devour from beginning to end. I settled for five burgers, five sides of fries, and three milkshakes. I'd have to start watching it from now on. I couldn't just melt the fat away anymore or turn it into more hair or height. I sighed and enjoyed my final burger to every last bite.

"So, your sanctuary—you called it the Hearth?" Griffin fiddled with his tuna on toast. He didn't seem too enthralled with it. He was more into sushi or the expensive restaurants.

"The Hearth." I nodded, and dipped a fry in ketchup. "I was for Haven myself and Sanctuary is far too cliched, but we had a committee and voted. You never heard so much bitching over a name. And some of the members kept trying to eat the other—" I stopped at the look in Griffin's eyes. It wasn't panic. It wasn't fear. It was the resignation of "Here comes yet one more nightmare in the world." He didn't need that, knowing the whole of what lived in the shadows of this world. He was dealing with enough.

"All different kinds of tricksters, you know?" I changed smoothly. "We don't always get along." I finished my fry hastily.

"So it's just angels, demons, and what did you call your kind? *Païens*?"

"Drink your juice. It's good for you," I ordered. "Yes, angels, demons, and the *païens*." As we tricksters tended to call all the supernatural creatures that inhabited the world. But Zeke and Griffin didn't need to peek that far under the covers into the dark. Demons were enough, especially with them coping with their new lives. Humans with wings, telepathy, and empathy . . . the Light had left them all three. Whether they would live as long as the other peris did . . . thousands and thousands of years, I didn't know. If not . . . a gray-haired Zeke in a rocking chair with a marmalade cat in his lap, shooting at the annoying neighborhood kids with a BB gun might be amusing. I almost choked at the mental picture.

"Will you be leaving now? Will you be taking off and leaving us like you always said you would?" Zeke demanded, grabbing Griffin's sandwich when his partner didn't make any progress on it. He gave me a similar look, as if he wanted to grab on to me the same way and keep me there.

I always had said it to the boys, warned them, although I hadn't known exactly what would happen to them when this was over. I'd hoped I could save them. The Light had done more than hope. The Light and my guys had saved themselves.

I was a traveler. Travel came with the job. Very few of us settled down in one spot long. I'd avenged Kimano. I doubted Hell's lapdog, Trinity, had told the other Houses about Griffin and Zeke letting me hunt with them. I doubted he'd told any other House anything at all in those last days. I thought they'd be safe. They could stay here with a new Eden House or have my bar or come with me if they wanted. Or . . .

Or I could stick around awhile. It was only four or five years. I still had my bar, still had my business on the side; I could still even do my trickster work. I didn't have to change form to do that. It made things much easier if I'd been able to, definitely, but I could do it.

"Who knows?" I sucked up the last of the strawberry shake. "I might stay around . . . if you stop shooting up my bar. What's the difference between ten years and fourteen or fifteen? I can see it. Kicking demon ass with you guys for a while longer." It was hard to take brothers for granted when you'd already lost one. I was born to travel, but I was born into a family too, and then I'd chosen one of my own. I'd gotten used to them. Stay in one place long enough and that'll happen. Mama would be so disappointed in me, but, you know what? Mama could kiss . . . Get over it, I changed hastily in my mind. What I'd done to Solomon, Mama could do to me and call it a spanking for a dirty mouth. "Maybe I will stick around and hunt demons with you guys. It's good exercise."

Zeke took in the five empty plates. "You're going to need it if you keep shoveling it down like a starved hippo."

I didn't stab him with my fork, but it was a close call. "I have to crash. Let's get one of the motel rooms, because I have about five minutes before I go comatose for at least a day."

It was a lovely hotel room. I fell face-first on the nearest bed. Actually it could've been the grotto at Hef's mansion for all I knew. I didn't know if there were pictures of flying saucers on the wall or soap shaped like an alien's head or a shag carpet that devoured small pets. Nothing registered but sleep and the vaguely distant grumbling of Zeke and Griffin standing beside the other twin bed, all that was available.

"I'm tired of being the big spoon."

"You're taller than I am. It just works that way."

It went on from there I was sure, but I was long gone, so buried under a blanket of sleep that an entire horde of demons couldn't have woken me up. But what felt like a week later later, the squabbling that put demonic cursing into perspective did.

"You could've slept in the bathtub."

"You could have too, partner. Might have earned you some more halo points. You can't throw omelets at the cook. Hot melted cheese is like napalm. The guy will probably need skin grafts." Griffin's hand was on my shoulder shaking lightly.

"He spit in it." I imagined Zeke's eyes narrowing. Telepathy had always given Zeke more reasons to be cranky than he usually had—as if he needed more. "I 'heard' it. Because he thought I was rude."

"You *are* rude."

"So? He was an ugly son of a bitch who cheats on his wife and I didn't spit on *him*."

"No. You just scarred him for life with a molten-hot dairy product."

All of which made perfect sense and that could only mean I needed more food and a shower. I sat up and saw nothing but black, bronze, and russet tangles. Swearing, I swept back the mop of hair and asked Griffin, "How long has it been?"

"About twenty hours. And we've got to be out in another two. Big alien convention in town. Thirty whole people. They're booked solid." He handed me a plate of scrambled eggs, bacon, and toast. "No spitting on this one, I swear."

"Good to know." I took a big bite of greasy diner scrambled eggs, greasier bacon, and loved every second of it.

"Is Leo coming back?"

I looked up at Zeke and took pity on his foodless state. Handing him my toast, I answered, "I don't know. Loki . . . Leo's not as much of a wanderer as I am. He's a trickster not by race but by choice, by calling, and he's been at odds with his family for a long time. Now that it sounds like he made up with them when he went back to catch the dog, he might want to stay with them awhile."

"The dog?" Griffin said grimly. "He left us in that clusterfuck to go home and catch a dog?"

"Well, Fenris is a little more than just a dog." I took another bite of eggs. "He might not be able to swallow the sun like Norse legend says, but he could wipe out a few hundred—maybe thousand—people if he made it to civilization. And he only likes Leo, so, there you go." I wiped my hands on the napkins Griffin had brought. "Anyway, I don't know if Leo will want to go back for some family time or not. It's up to him. He's been with me ten years straight now. He might need a break."

"He'll come back," Zeke said as he ate the toast, looking not the slightest less lethal in his new black T-shirt that read AREA 51—DEADLY FORCE AUTHORIZED, the sentiment emblazoned beneath the words by a small green alien in army camos and aiming an M-16. "He will," he reiterated with a confidence that couldn't be shaken. "I know it."

Because Leo had to come back. Because the four of us were family, belonged together, and Zeke couldn't see it any other way.

"Maybe so, Kit." I deposited my plate on the bed, kissed the top of his copper hair where he sat on the next bed, and headed for the bathroom. "I need fifteen minutes. Either of you gentlemen up to 'borrowing' a car?" I peered around the bathroom door. Two rooms shared one bathroom, but I'd lucked out. Whoever had rented the other room was out alien hunting or practicing his Klingon at the café. "But only from someone who deserves it."

An hour later we were on the road, listening to static, which was more entertaining than country music, and riding in the saddest Winnebago I'd ever seen. But per Zeke, the owner had been the worst kid-slapping, wife-beating, cheating-on-his-taxes, drunken bastard in Rachel, Nevada. If he thought getting his Winnebago ripped off was just deserts, he had no idea whom he was screwing with. Within a week he'd be in prison— the bad kind where he'd learn what it was like to be a beaten wife himself.

"So this guy deserved it," Griffin mused as he drove. "Who else has deserved it lately? You didn't retire from being a trickster while looking for the Light, did you? That doesn't seem like you."

I slid down in the passenger seat and tried to look sheepish, but I couldn't. I quirked my lips. "Well, there was the zoo."

Zeke leaned forward. "The zoo? Where the wolves ate the perv? Really?"

I was amused by his excitement. "It wasn't hard to get him over by the wolf habitat. Very secluded. He did seem pretty surprised that such a little girl could toss him over a fence that high and convince a wolf pack that they were hungrier than they thought they were. I left my signature: the red balloon tied to the bench."

"That truck of red paint overturning on the road crew that did nothing for weeks in a row but sit on their asses." Griffin shook his head. "You didn't go ahead and tip it all the way over the overpass and crush them?"

I frowned. "They were lazy, not evil. The punishment matches the crime. I'm fair. Mostly." I switched off the radio. "Then there was the guitarist. I electrocuted him, but gave the credit to Trinity and Heaven. That had that bastard's eyes crossing in confusion." I tapped my finger on the glass of the window. "That the guitar happened to be red was just the perfect touch. If I were a church-going woman"—which by now I thought was apparent was not the case—"I would've thought it a sign from the angel factory." I stopped tapping and pointed up.

"You electrocuted him?" Griffin hissed, swerving around a desert tortoise in the road. "Why?"

"Was it a bad song?" Zeke added helpfully. "Did he suck?"

"No." I groaned, reached, and pushed his face back. "He threw a toaster in his mother's bath for the insurance money. Probably paid for that guitar with it. He had it coming."

"So you're judge, jury, and executioner."

Griffin . . . how he had become so damn good, I would never know. It was a miracle, if you believed in those things, but now he was irritating me with his Eagle Scout tone. I pinched his ribs. "Yes, I am. Just like the two of you were . . . the executioner part anyway."

He shut up after that. There wasn't much he could say to it. We all choose . . . for good or for bad, and we all pay the piper. There were simply a lot more of us pipers out there than he was able to remember. "What about Eligos?" he said quietly after several minutes. "If he knows you're human, even if only for a couple of years . . ."

"I know," I said, brooding. "It's going to be a long few years if he hangs around." Long for him, maybe not so much for me. Eligos would make me his personal project of pain and torture if he found out I wasn't the same Trixa from the cave. God, trickster, demon . . . human. I'd tumbled a few ranks. I might still be trickster at heart, but the body was human for now.

"I have a feeling he will stay. Take over Vegas now that Solomon is dead."

"I have a feeling you're right," I agreed with my Eagle Scout, and a very glum and disagreeable feeling it was too. "Vegas seems like Eli's kind of town. So how about we not let him know about me being more or less human, although one with amazing taste and style. I really don't want to end up a notch on his impaling post."

That ended the conversation for a while as I reassured myself silently that I was a trickster. No one could outthink me, manipulate me, lie to me, fool me, and no one but no one could trip me up on a lie of my own. Eli would believe I could turn him into a Solomon PEZ dispenser if the mood struck me, because I wouldn't let him think anything else.

An hour from Vegas, Zeke had sprawled in the back of the Winnebago and was snoring lightly. I slid in an old-style cassette tape and listened to ABBA. Yes, the wife beater listened to ABBA. I ejected it hurriedly and started digging in the floor for something a little less nauseating and much more current. "I'm curious," I said to Griffin as I kicked the garbage around. "I've never measured you, but I think Zeke is taller. So does that make him the big spoon?"

He didn't give me the cold shoulder or the frozen blue eyes, which rather worried me. He just kept driving, hands flexing on the steering wheel. "I'm a demon," he said suddenly. "After all I've seen them do, and that's what I turn out to be? A killer, a stealer of souls, a monster?"

"You're not a demon." I sat up. I was surprised it had taken him this long to crack. Griffin, always in control . . . calm, collected, ready, but no one was ready for this.

"Fine. I *was* a demon then. I *was* a murderer, a soul eater, a hell-spawn," he said bitterly, keeping his voice low so as not to wake our napping ex-angel. The last thing he wanted Zeke doing was worrying about his partner's mental health. Zeke's security in his own mental health wasn't that high.

"No. You are not a demon and you weren't a demon. Glasya-Labolas is dead. You killed him and you killed every horrific deed he ever did. You're Griffin Reese. You were born at the age of ten with a few false memories of parents who abandoned you and you were born human. A human with extra empathy, but lots of humans are born that way. They made you all human, or an angel would've known. Just as they made Zeke all human, or a demon would've known. Only a trickster like me or a god like Leo had known. Switching your body whenever you cared to taught you to see when a change had been made in others. The low can't recognize the high-level, but a high-level can recognize any angel or demon of equal or lower rank." I rested my hand on his tense leg. "You were and are human. Because you chose to be," I finished quietly. "Then when Solomon pushed the demon back into you in the cave, you still chose to be human, you still chose to be a man, and you still chose to be good. And if that's not the greatest accomplishment since the world appeared out of the darkness, I don't know what is."

I squeezed his leg and let go with a pat. "I don't know that I could've done it. I honestly don't. To give up all that power, to become something a demon has nothing but contempt for?"

"But you did." His fingers relaxed on the steering wheel. "Not the contempt, but you gave up your power for your brother. Not for as long maybe, but you gave it up. Sometimes there are things . . . people worth giving it up for." He automatically turned his head to check on a still-sleeping Zeke.

"Big spoon or little spoon?" I asked coyly.

"Oh, shut up," he shot back, but not as crossly as I'd expected, and when I put in the cassette, of the *Eighties' Greatest Hits*, the best the floor had to offer, he tapped his fingers on the steering wheel along in time with "Duran Duran . . . Yes, Duran Duran." Those were the days. They *all* were the days.

"An old Sicilian proverb says, 'Only the spoon knows what is stirring in the pot,'" I said with a grin. "So what's cooking?"

"On-the-bench trickster or annoyed peri with a Louisville Slugger, who ranks there?" He gave his lips a none-of-your-business quirk as he patted the bat leaning against his door.

"Truthfully, I don't know." I smiled and leaned my seat back farther, ready to join Zeke in a nap. "Who could say?"

Me.

I could say.

On the bench or not. Griffin's memories—or those of the demon Glasya—were gone because the demon was gone. But my memories? I still had them. Six thousand years of doing bad things to very bad people. Not to mention some of the best tricksters in the world

couldn't change shape. . . . In fact there is one race of
tricksters who all have the same shape—clones of one
another. One of them had actually ruled Greece for a
while, although most were car salesmen now. I'd be
damned if I let a puck like Robin Goodfellow think he
was better than I was. Eli didn't stand a chance.

I waited almost ten minutes before I said it:

"You're the little spoon, aren't you?"

Chapter 17

It was good to be home, and I didn't feel the need to bite my tongue at the word. Incredible. Home. I looked around the bar. Same stained floor. Same pool table and dartboard. Same beat-up tables and chairs. Despite myself, I was fond of it. Oh hell, I loved it. It beat Ramses II's palace hands down. Forget gold, carnelian, or lapis lazuli; this was better. This was home, the first one I'd ever known and the first one I'd ever wanted. It wasn't the dirty word I'd always thought it. I think Kimano had figured that out before he died, as much time as he spent in Hawaii. Not a fighter, not close to being a halfway good trickster, but he'd been smart in a way I hadn't. He'd known what a home could do for you—what it could be—when I hadn't had a clue.

"You'll be all right?"

I looked over my shoulder at Griffin. "More than all right. Go home, boys. You'll get to sleep in your own beds tonight. No sharing and no napping in bathtubs." I was a good little trickster and didn't say any more, although I did measure them with my eyes. Yes, Zeke was definitely an inch or two taller. Big spoon all the way.

Griffin walked over to the bar, took a bottle of whiskey, and said in explanation, "It's been one hell of a week. Put it on my tab, would you?"

"As if your money's any good here." I waved him off.

"Your money would've been good replacing my ostrich skin jacket you ruined," he grumbled halfheartedly, but nodded and disappeared out the front door.

Then there was Zeke. He stood there, looking the same as he'd always been. But could he be? Finding out he'd been an angel, and that's what had made his human brain different from others, not a drug-addicted mother. Discovering his partner and best friend had been a demon—the one thing he lived and breathed to kill, his one and only purpose. Learning the head of his House was a traitor in Hell's pocket. Seeing that his friend/surrogate big sister wasn't human and had been involved in some elaborate plot of revenge and espionage for more than fifty years—what was he thinking? Behind those placid eyes and blank face, how did all of that impact on someone like him?

"He really liked that jacket," he said disapprovingly.

I laughed. I couldn't help it. Of all of us, I thought Zeke might have the healthiest outlook on this whole situation, whether he believed it or not. I hugged him hard. "I think it's your turn to take care of Griffin. He has a lot to brood about. Don't let him think he's any different now than he was yesterday. He's not. He's a good, *good* man."

"The best." The placid bottle-glass green went fierce. "The best in the whole goddamn world."

"Make sure he knows it." I let go and nudged him toward the door. "And I'll have you know a B cup is the perfect size. Dick."

He waffled his hand back and forth. "Eh, but the ass. Now *that* . . ." I pushed him through the door and slammed it after him before I was forced to hear the rest. I wasn't in the mood for any more violence this soon.

The quiet left behind was perfect. As was my bubble bath, toes with nails painted bronze peering from mountains of pink foam, followed by my silk pajamas, my own bed, my overstuffed pillows. I turned on my side and let my eyes drift over the piece of amber resting on my bedside table. It glinted faintly in the streetlamp's light that came through the half-open blinds. I couldn't see the imprisoned spider clearly. It was only a shadow. "You're not trapped," I murmured. "You're just taking a break. Resting." Long dead, it probably didn't care. "Anyway, get used to it." Because I had. I felt for the shotgun, closed my eyes, and slept.

In the morning I woke up and Leo was there.

Not right there. Not sitting on the bed or looming like a window-peeping pervert. But he was back. I knew the way I always knew—it was the way I couldn't tell Griffin when he'd thought Leo had been kidnapped by Eli. Tricksters always know other tricksters. We usually know all other supernatural creatures. *Païens*. Not always, but the majority of the time. Some you don't know until you're face-to-face, assuming they look human. If they don't look human, you obviously don't need any special sense to recognize them. Some *païens* you could feel a block away. Those were usually the ones you didn't *want* to see face-to-face like the others. No chatting with them or passing on gossip if you were in the boonies far from a cluster of other *païens*.

Don't get me wrong. Tricksters, no matter which kind, were bad-ass. I wasn't going to be shy and retiring, modest little Trixa. No. I was damn proud of our rep. You messed with a trickster, you took your life into your own hands, paws, claws, whatever. We would mess you up six ways from Sunday and then we'd call in our friends and family to decide how to put you back together again. Puzzles can be fun, right?

But . . .

And there's always a but. There were things out there that even tricksters didn't care to get too close to. So it was a nice evolutionary benefit we'd developed. It was rather a mixture of an angel's telepathy and a demon's empathy. You knew who was *païen* or you could feel them coming. That was how I always knew whether Leo was in the bar or gone.

As for knowing whether Eli had kidnapped him and was chopping bits off him . . . just as Solomon had been no match for me, Eli was no match for Loki the Lie-Smith, the Sly-God, the Sky Traveler. He'd have been ended in seconds. Of course, in the old days, Loki and Eli probably shared a few interests and might have tossed back a few meads together. Now, though, Loki was Leo, and Leo would've made short work of Eli. I'd known Eli didn't have him, but I couldn't tell Griffin that, not then.

"Trixa, are you going to sleep all damn morning or not?"

Sometimes feeling Leo wasn't necessary either. I could wait for him to yell for me to get my butt in gear instead. I showered, dressed, did the whole hair-makeup thing. It really is easier when you're covered with fur or scales, but the effort was worth it. Primping could be entertaining at times. Other times it was a pain in the ass, and then it was a ponytail and lucky-to-put-on-a-bra kind of day. But today was a good day. A great day. If there was an all-out war, our people would survive it. Kimano's killer was never going to destroy a family again. More than fifty years of searching and planning had brought me to this moment. Victory. Success. For the first time in five decades I wasn't bent on vengeance *and* finding a way to save all supernatural kind, all at once. For the first time I was free to do what I wanted, no agenda, no undercover work. I was free.

Leo found me sitting on the stairs. I'd made it halfway down before my legs gave out. "What are you doing?" he asked, the dark copper skin beside his eyes crinkled in exasperation.

"I have no idea." I wasn't panicking. I wasn't. The last fifty years had been a drop in the bucket compared to my lifetime. For someone like me it wasn't long enough to build up habits or, worse yet, a rut so deep you couldn't see the top of it. Okay . . . maybe a little panic. "I have *no* idea, Leo. What do I do now? It's over. Solomon's dead. We have the Light. What the hell do I do now?"

He sat beside me. "Trick the stupid, criminal, and unwary as always."

"Yes, right. I can do that." As I'd thought yesterday, even in human form I could deliver just deserts.

"Serve drinks."

I nodded. "Five more years of slinging alcohol. I can handle it." His glossy black braid lay on his chest and I wrapped it around my hand like a lifeline.

"Keep Zeke and Griffin out of trouble," he went on. "You know they'll need it," he said dryly.

That was true.

"Torment my future girlfriends," he added.

"You're staying, then?" I asked, surprised. I'd told the guys he wasn't a traveler like me and he wasn't, but he'd been here ten years. I thought he'd at the very least want a vacation for a few decades or so, or that he'd want to spend more time with his family since they were at least speaking enough to ask for his help.

He frowned. "I may as well. I don't have much choice. The Light seemed to think, like my family, that you're a good influence on me."

What did that mean? "And? Since when did you listen to anyone or anything you didn't want to?"

"Since this." The braid disappeared from around my hand and Lenore gave a harsh croak at me from the step. A second later Leo was back in place. "That's it. That is the sum total of my changing ability until you get yours back."

I laughed. "The great and powerful Loki and you're stuck as a Poe joke and a bartender. That is damn priceless. Your family will never let you live it down. Never."

"Look who's talking. You can't even change into a bird. You're a bartender. Period. With what I hear aren't especially large breasts," he mocked. "And you think I have it bad?"

I was going to kill Zeke if he did not shut up about my breasts, but it didn't change the fact Leo was right. He was one bird up on me. I groaned and lay back on the stairs. Leo leaned over me and warm hands undid the necklace with the Pele's tear from around my neck. "But I was going to stay anyway, regardless of the Light's own little trick. I wouldn't leave you defenseless for five years. I was going to stay to watch your back."

He would have, too. With no urging from the Light needed. But . . . "Defenseless?" We both grinned wolfishly at each other. Even in human form we were nowhere near defenseless. "What are you doing?" I asked as he put Kimano's black tear in his jeans pocket and then dangled another necklace before my eyes. It was a miniature sun with a garnet in the middle. Red. For me, always red.

"The time for crying is over. Now is the time for sun," he said simply.

I sat up to make it easier to put the chain around my neck. I touched the gold and red with a reverent finger. Odd that Leo had come from a place of unimaginable cold and darkness—his place of birth and what lived inside him for so long—yet he had always been my sun. I would've said thanks, but with the thousands of years between us . . . he knew what he was to me. Just as I knew what I was to him.

"Now." He settled the sun in place on my chest. "What you need is a project. A mission."

I did need something. A purpose beyond the average trickster job requirements. I was used to it now—like a pastime, albeit a potentially fatal one. "Like what?"

"Let's see." He stood and held a hand down for me. "How about driving every last demon from Vegas? Eden House here couldn't, but the *païens* in New York did. Do you want them thinking they're better than we are?"

The thousands of *païens* in New York had sent their demons packing, as Robin Goodfellow had been reminiscing on the phone when I'd talked to him. He was my fellow trickster, sometime informant, and had also been known as Pan and Puck in the day. I'd been surprised he hadn't brought up the days of the Kin's rule of Vegas when we had talked. The Kin was the werewolf version of the Mafia and had worked hand-in-paw with the real Mafia back in the Bugsy Siegel days up all the way until the Mob lost its hold in the seventies. Not that the human Mafia had ever known whom they were partnered up with. People, the ones blind to the real world, rarely did. In the end I thought that the Kin was glad to leave Vegas. All that fur? Far too hot. They'd probably panted even in their human form.

Demons were enough to deal with anyway. Of course there were only Leo, Griffin, Zeke, and me versus the entire population of those demons. I smiled to myself. It seemed like a fair contest. "Sure, why not? It ought to keep me busy for the first two years anyway. What will I do with the other three?"

"At least you won't have people asking to take their pictures with you or trying to give you money for stealing your land," he grunted, pushing the door open and tugging me along behind him.

"You chose the form; I have no sympathy. Besides, you're a trickster. You know more than enough about Native American lore to fool any tourist, Leo Rain of Eagle Droppings. You *created* some of the lore yourself," I pointed out. He preferred the North, but like every other trickster, Leo had done his work in every continent and occupied island on the face of the planet.

"I know. I screwed myself," he rumbled in complaint. "It was entertaining in the beginning. I hate tourists. Making asses of them made my day, but it's getting old. Next one I'll offer to reenact Custer's Last Stand in extremely vivid detail. Waivers and death insurance included. Worse yet, now I have this." He lifted his shirt. On his chest was something new: a tattoo of a raven, tribal and stark, arrowing toward the sky, its wings spread.

"The Light really spanked you but good." I laughed, tracing the outline.

"I'm just lucky it didn't put Lenore beneath it," he rumbled in resignation.

The front door opened and two early birds came in. Paunchy, balding, and pink husband. Pudgy, bleached-blond petrified curls, and pinker wife. Both sets of watery blue eyes fixed on him and the tattoo, and the cameras came out. "I'm starting with them," he growled. "Go write up the waivers." I laughed again, pulled down his shirt, and shoved him toward the bar.

The rest of the day blended from afternoon to evening and it was the same as it had always been. The same work, same fried food, same regulars. I hummed and sang the entire time. Once again, my voice isn't the best, but my regulars are usually drunk enough not to care. I could've been an opera singer for all they could tell. Leo eventually couldn't take it anymore and turned the TV up loud enough to drown me out.

I ignored him, except for flipping him off, and kept singing. About eight p.m., Zeke and Griffin came in. Zeke looked like Zeke, and Griffin looked . . . good. He seemed all right. I smiled at him. He was strong and I knew he'd be strong enough for this, because I wasn't losing him to despair any more than I was losing him to death. I went to his table as Zeke went to the TV and turned it off.

I sat to the right of Griff. "Is everything all right? You look good." I patted his cheek. "Good color. Bright eyes. We can get a vet in here to check to see if your nose is cold and wet, but otherwise you look great." He did. He looked better than he had before the Leviathan thing had gone down.

Zeke sat on the other side of Griffin and put his hand on the other man's shoulder. It wasn't a squeeze or warning or reassurance, just the comfortable curl of a resting place for his hand. "We're doing it," he suddenly announced aloud to the entire bar. The kind of aloud that penetrates through the wall to the bathroom stalls. I mean, it wasn't precisely out of nowhere, the information, but he could've worked up to it a little. That wasn't Zeke though. "We're not just screwing either. We're in a *relationship*." He said the last word very carefully, as if he'd never said it. He may never have.

Meanwhile Griffin dropped his head into his hands and groaned. "You are?" I asked him, amused. I'd seen how proprietary they were of each other and that had nothing to do with being partners. Then there had been Zeke refusing to let me share a bed with Griffin. The whole spooning thing I'd taken as a joke, and not because I hadn't seen this coming. I had. I just hadn't thought it would be this soon. I hadn't thought they'd realize it so quickly. I did know Zeke would've made the first move. It was the only way Griffin could be sure it was what Zeke wanted and not Zeke going along with whatever he thought Griffin wanted—following his lead, as always. And Zeke had done it apparently, seizing that free will with both hands.

Well, you know what? Good for Zeke.

"A relationship?" I repeated, my lips twitching with humor at Griffin's sudden retiring nature.

"We are," Griffin confirmed, hands cupping over his forehead to shield his eyes from Zeke's show.

"And the sex is fucking unbelievable," Zeke said, continuing with the rundown.

"Oh hell." Griffin's head thunked against the table and stayed down there. I leaned over his back to ask Zeke curiously, "How unbelievable?"

"Last night . . . ," he started with the same enthusiasm I'd seen him show for his favorite weapons—and that was considerable enthusiasm indeed.

I leaned forward further. It was all kinds of interesting what you could hear when an ex-angel who hadn't mastered his internal filter started to talk details.

I genuinely had seen this coming. I wasn't so full of it that I believed brown was this year's new magenta. It made absolute sense. Angels and demons were genderless creatures until they chose a human form (the only form they could choose, by the way . . . amateurs). In their pure crystalline form, angels were androgynous in appearance—neither male nor female. As for demons, if they had a gender in their true serpent shape, only a zoologist would have a hope of knowing for sure.

Put either creature in a freshly baked cookie dough human body and they had the hormones to work with, I guessed, unless they were like Oriphiel who didn't pack his plumbing. The others, however, angels and demons alike, I couldn't see having a strong preference either way. Created sexless, then changing into a human suit whenever they felt like it, I couldn't see them swinging hard to either end of the sexual spectrum. It wasn't as if they had a human's lifetime of social experience or gender role imprinting—although the genetics of it . . . never mind. I wasn't a biologist. I was just a trickster having the time of her life watching two guys having the time of *their* lives. Who cared how it happened? It could be like teenagers getting in a car to drive it for the very first time. Do you want a stick or an automatic? Who the hell cares? They just want to *go*.

Griffin and Zeke were different. They had had seventeen years or so of living a life they thought human.

Zeke mentioned girls. I'd seen Griffin on a date or two. They'd even flirted with me once in a while, but never seriously. None of it had seemed serious. Not the talk, not the dates. None of it.

Subconsciously I thought they always knew they were meant for each other. Two halves of a whole. Zeke needed a guide, the ultimate version of the summer camp buddy system. Griffin, the empath, needed to be needed—for the empath part of him and for the tiny molecule of his subconscious that knew he had thousands of lifetimes of inflicting pain and violence to make up for.

But despite the need on both sides, it was more than that. They just . . . fit. They may have spent seven years in a foster home together, but there was never a sense of brotherhood about them. Not the family kind. The battlefield kind, yes, but not the blood kind, not the emotional bonding of siblings. From day one they'd been partners and that could be a bonding as strong as a familial one. They'd been partners, were partners, would be partners—and now in every sense of the word. You couldn't look at them and *not* see it. They belonged to each other like the rest of us belonged to the earth under our feet.

"So?" I prompted Zeke without remorse. I wasn't too good to hear some nice juicy, mildly pornographic details. "Last night?"

Griffin sat up and cut us both off before I was able to hear anything interesting. "Zeke, I will take your Colt Anaconda and sell it on eBay. One more word about our sex lives and it's done. Got it?"

Zeke frowned. "Fine. Grump." He then turned his attention back to the rest of the bar regulars, because, after all, the two of them were regulars here as well. "So what I want to know is if anyone has a problem with this?" The Colt Anaconda Griffin had just threatened was laid on the table with a heavy thud and the steel of it wasn't any colder than the steel of Zeke's gaze.

And Zeke? Zeke did not bluff.

Most had shrugged and gone on, some never woke up to hear the announcement, but a few had opened their mouths with disgruntled, unhappy, or judgmental looks on their face. The Colt had every mouth shut and a few tequila shots bought for the happy couple. And they were happy. Zeke might not give a damn about anyone else in this world, with Leo and me as the exception proving the rule, but Griffin was everything to him. On his side, Griffin, who had not once considered Zeke a burden, for all the stolen grenades, dead robbers, beaten cab drivers, car wrecks beyond numbering, the eBay threatening and the final knocking of his head on the table in frustration, had far different emotions for Zeke behind the exasperation. He always had. You didn't need to be an empath to read them either.

I took one shot that Leo delivered and knocked it back before saying, "An ex-angel and an ex-demon getting together in a same-sex relationship. Heaven and Hell sitting in a tree, k-i-s-s-i-n-g. Congratulations." I raised another shot. "That sound you hear is the heads of moral conservatives spontaneously exploding in the distance." Leo pulled another bottle and joined us.

"Félicitations."

"Glückwünsche."

"Congratulazioni."

"Gelukwensen."

"Ho`olaule`a."

"L'chaim!"

By then the tequila was gone, but we clinked glasses anyway.

Griffin and Zeke took a cab back to their place. I had a feeling Eli would leave them alone as well as Leo and me—for a while at least. He'd seen what I did to those who hurt my brothers.

We booted out the remaining patrons, most of whom had a cab company on speed dial, and cleaned up the place. As I finished drying my hands, Leo waited and then offered me a gleaming raven feather. I remembered how Griffin had picked up the one that came from Zeke's wings when we had been in the desert. He'd studied it with curiosity, awe, and wonder. Griffin turned his back on Hell and was now a man who could feel wonder. No one could say that wasn't a miracle.

This feather was something entirely different. Well, maybe not. It had the touch of a miracle to it too. Under Leo's patient eyes, I considered it for a moment, then took it. I stroked the sheen of it.

"We're still too much alike," I said with a reluctance that tugged sharply at me.

"I know." He rested his hand on my stomach. It was warm, large, and familiar. I could actually enjoy the touch, let myself *feel* it in a way I'd never let Solomon reach me. There had been only pretense and trickery. It had been unpleasant, but I couldn't kill him without proof. I needed proof to know he was the one. Otherwise I was only killing a demon with no certainty it was the one who'd taken Kimano away from me. But I never had to feel his touch again.

"You played him." Leo who always knew what I was thinking—Leo moved until he was close enough that his breath stirred my hair and any thought of Solomon or his touch disappeared. "It was a thing of beauty."

For a trickster there was no higher turn-on than exceptionally well-done trickery.

"You did a convincing job yourself . . . of worried friend and cranky bird." His hand moved to my back.

"Worried wasn't that difficult." I narrowed my eyes and he amended wryly, "Mildly worried. I know you've set the bar more than once for tricksters, but this was different. This was personal, the majority of it, and we're all capable of being reckless when it's personal, especially when it's family."

There was no denying that, and I didn't as his hand stroked lower to the small of my back. "I knew it. You are so damn stubborn." He sighed, feeling, I knew, the still-rough texture of the healing skin through my top. It was the road rash I'd received in the alley where Zeke had been wounded. That was what Leo had meant at Jeb's wake in the desert when he'd said that I could make things easier on myself. I could've simply shifted form enough for my back to be healed. But Griffin might have picked up on the lack of pain, although it was unlikely, as concerned with his partner as he was. To be honest, that wasn't the real reason. I'd lived as Trixa for long enough that I *was* Trixa. I wanted it all, the bad with the good. When my shape-changing abilities eventually returned, I thought I would still always be Trixa, no matter what I looked like. Just as Zeke and Griffin had been remade, so had I. And I liked it.

"What's a scar or two?" I asked.

"The sign of a warrior." He turned me around and bent to press his lips gently to the area between my shoulder blades. I felt the tingle of half pain, half pleasure. In other words, I felt life, because that was what living was. Pain and pleasure. "Or a trickster too distracted by personal vengeance to keep her eye on the ball."

The enjoyable drift of anticipation that I'd fallen into disappeared instantly. "Is that a comment on my career competency?" I demanded as I turned back to face him.

"No, on the incredible depth of your ability to love." He cupped my hand in his, the feather still cradled against my palm. "You're right. We are still too much alike."

"But?"

He smiled as I said it before he did. "But we might not always be. I've changed over the years. Same spots, as you're always saying, but a different leopard underneath them. You've changed as well. You're darker. You've lost. You're not as cocky. You know now that things aren't always as you thought they'd be. That the world still holds mystery and the unpredictable, even for us. Griffin and Zeke taught you that."

He touched my jaw with callused fingers and kissed me, and it was all pleasure this time. No pain. No thought. Only the pressure of lips, the silk of tongue, the warmth of skin. Our first kiss, but it was as intimate as if we'd done it thousands of times before. It was like watching your favorite movie or reading your favorite book over and over and discovering something new. Something bright and dark, joyful and melancholy, all at once.

I was proud to be a trickster, but it was also good to be this—a silver point of light high and blazing in the apricot and violet morning sky, a moment that seemed as long as my life. Then the kiss ended; the morning star fell, as it always did. Leo carefully folded my fingers over the feather. "A token of my future esteem.

Someday, if we're ever less alike than more, give this back to me."

Waiting was hard, not knowing for certain even more so. It could be years. It could be never. It could be the best thing that happened to me, but then again, Leo already was the best thing to happen to me. No matter if we changed or if we didn't, that wouldn't. Couldn't. A book, written not that long ago from my perspective, said a wise thing. It applied to burning down demon nightclubs, to avenging brothers, and it applied now. *To every thing there is a season, and a time to every purpose under the heaven*. So elegant, so true, that even a *païen* like me could appreciate it, embrace it. *To every thing there is a season, and a time to every purpose under the heaven*. I broke a lifetime of habit to give that wise saying what it deserved.

Amen.

Amen.

Look for Rob Thurman's next
Cal Leandros novel,

ROADKILL

"Thurman continues to deliver strong tales of dark urban fantasy." —SFRevu

"A subtly warped world compellingly built by Thurman. . . . The combination of Chandleresque detective dialogue and a lyrically noir style of description are stunningly original." —The Green Man Review

Coming in March 2010 from Roc

About the Author

Rob, short for Robyn (yes, he is really a she) Thurman lives in Indiana, land of rolling hills and cows, deer, and wild turkeys. Many, many turkeys. She is also the author of the Cal Leandros series: *Nightlife*, *Moonshine*, *Madhouse*, and *Deathwish*; has a story in the anthology *Wolfsbane and Mistletoe*; and is the author of *Trick of the Light*, the first book in the Trickster series.

Besides wild, ravenous turkeys, she has a dog (if you don't have a dog, how do you live?)—one hundred pounds of Siberian husky. He looks like a wolf, has paws the size of a person's hand, ice blue eyes, teeth out of a Godzilla movie, and the ferocious habit of hiding under the kitchen table and peeing on himself when strangers come by. Fortunately, she has another dog that is a little more invested in keeping the food source alive. By the way, the dogs were adopted from shelters. They were fully grown, already housetrained, and grateful as hell. Think about it next time you're looking for a Rover or Fluffy.

For updates, teasers, deleted scenes, and various other extras, visit the author at www.robthurman.net and at her LiveJournal.